THIRD TIME'S THE CHARM

PREVIOUSLY PUBLISHED AS

BLAME IT ON THE BRONTËS

THIRD TIME'S THE CHARM

Annie Sereno

FOREVER
NEW YORK BOSTON

Forever
Hachette Book Group
1290 Avenue of the Americas, New York, NY 10104
read-forever.com
@readforeverpub

Originally published as *Blame It on the Brontës* in trade paperback and ebook by Grand Central Publishing in May 2022
First mass market edition: May 2024

ISBNs: 978-1-5387-2142-1 (mass market), 978-1-5387-2268-8 (ebook)

Printed in the United States of America

BVGM

10 9 8 7 6 5 4 3 2 1

For Bob
You transfix me quite

You know that I could as soon forget you as my existence!

—EMILY BRONTË, *WUTHERING HEIGHTS*

CHAPTER ONE

I have not broken your heart—you have broken it; and in breaking it, you have broken mine.

—EMILY BRONTË, *WUTHERING HEIGHTS*

The day Athena Murphy traipsed through Farmer Swenson's pasture pretending she was Emily Brontë, wild child of the moors, and stepped into a steaming pile of cow flop, she should have known. She should have realized at the tender age of fifteen, before it was too late, that literature would betray her. That imagination was best confined to books. That following your dreams was a load of hooey.

Athena had followed her dreams all right, straight to a Harvard PhD in English and a plum position as assistant professor at Wyatt College in San Francisco. And now here she was, scraping cow crap off her shoes again—metaphorically speaking.

"Metaphor schmetaphor," she muttered, squeezing her cherry-red Mini Cooper between two muddy trucks parked outside a store called Spin Cycle. A bike shop in Laurel, Illinois. Who'da thunk. She barely recognized her hometown anymore—strip malls and boutique shops with clever names where farms used to be, a health-food store selling vitamins in all letters of the alphabet, joggers and bicyclists competing for space on the roads. Kind of like California—without the stunning landscapes and agreeable weather.

She got out of the car, and the disagreeable humidity Saran Wrapped her in an instant. With a stomp of her ankle boots, she freed her legs of their Mini Cooper cramp and the curves of her body from a clingy rayon dress. Another thing she should have known. Traipsing through meadows was best left to wan, wispy maidens with consumption, not a Brontë wannabe who wore a size 34C bra in ninth grade and grew childbearing hips by the tenth. A figure she wouldn't trade for all the freak-of-nature model bodies in magazines—even if it hadn't fulfilled its potential yet, fertility-wise.

"If ever," Athena sighed, squinting at the clouds shaped like chubby babies.

Thankfully, the streets were deserted as she walked the four blocks to Ricki's Café. She'd been home a week, but she wasn't ready to engage in a *What are you doing here?* and *How long are you staying?* conversation with anyone.

I'm on sabbatical to research a damn book.

I'm staying until I've written the damn thing.

As for *why*... Having grown up in a farming community, Athena was accustomed to regarding death as part of the natural order of things. But *professional* death in the academic community was a different story. "Publish or perish" was the order of things. And they weren't kidding.

She pulled open the door to Ricki's Café and entered a room filled with copy machines and computers. "What the... Excuse me, miss," she said to the young woman behind the counter, "I'm looking for Ricki."

"He's delivering flyers. Can I help you?"

"No. I mean Ricki Moretti. The owner of the café." She and Athena's mother, Lydia, had been best friends since junior high.

"Oh, *that* Ricki. Sorry, the café isn't here anymore. This is DittoDocs."

"But I'm supposed to work... she..." Ricki had said,

"Come on board!" when she inquired about a job in April. If circumstances had changed, Ricki would have told her. "Do you have any idea where she is?"

"I sure don't."

A typical Midwestern turn of phrase—starting out so cheerful, not wanting to let you down, but then letting you down anyway.

"There's a card in the window with the café's new number. You can try calling," the young woman suggested.

"Thanks. I sure will."

Back outside, Athena punched the number into her phone. Ricki wouldn't *necessarily* have informed anyone if she had closed or moved. Once, after a lover had left her, she decamped to the Galápagos Islands, leaving the café open. Her regular customers made themselves sandwiches, brewed their own coffee, and dropped money into the Wonder Woman cookie jar. They didn't realize she was gone until the food ran out.

Athena was about to hang up after a half dozen rings when a male voice answered.

"As you like it," he said.

"As I like what?"

"As You Like It Café."

"What happened to Ricki's Café?"

"Sold, relocated, renamed."

"Since when?"

"Since this summer."

That voice. So calm. So deep. So . . . Thorne.

Impossible. Thorne lived in Seattle. Eight hundred eight miles from San Francisco by car. Six hundred eighty by plane.

"Hi, Thena."

A fly danced on the window behind her, buzzing its stupid tiny brain out.

"Who is this?" she demanded. "How do you know it's me?"

"Who else would you be?"

That question. So logical. So pithy. So…

She inhaled deeply, counting to ten.

Made it to four.

"Thorne."

"It took you long enough to recognize my voice."

Five. Six. Seven.

"I was expecting Ricki to answer."

"She's not here. How can I help you?"

"I'm looking for her café."

"You've reached the right place."

Eight. Nine.

"I don't get it."

"You don't have to get it."

Ten.

"Where exactly are you, Thorne?"

"Where exactly are *you*?"

"DittoDocs." And in the state of confusion.

"The address is on the card in the window," he said. "Use your phone's GPS. You'll find me."

He hung up before Athena could say she wasn't looking for *him*. Necessarily. Before she could ask what on earth he was doing in Laurel, Illinois.

As You, she typed into the phone.

…pissed me off, she thought.

…let me down.

Broke my heart.

Thanks to San Francisco's gravity-defying streets, Athena's legs were as fit as when she played intramural soccer in college. Driving the half mile to As You Like It Café was not an option. The temptation to burn rubber clear out of southern Illinois would be too hard to resist. Besides, walking didn't hurt a bit—August swelter and tight dress be damned.

But meeting Thorne Kent, the last person she ever expected to see again, much less in her hometown, hurt like a bitch.

She kept to the thin band of shade beneath the stores' awnings and slowed her pace. Forced herself to look the past dead-straight in the eye. Made herself remember.

From the hour they met in their freshman Literary Explorations class at Washington University in St. Louis, Athena and Thorne were certain they had found their soul mate. The person who embodied all their fantasies of the One True Love. She was Juliet, Beatrice, Portia, and any other Shakespearean heroine he wished as he festooned her head with garlands and wrote sonnets praising her mahogany tresses and bee-stung lips.

And though he wasn't darkly handsome, brutal, or particularly brooding, Thorne was Heathcliff from *Wuthering Heights*, the passionate lover she had been running to in the moors (or farmers' pastures), the Brontë hero who had proclaimed, "I cannot live without my life! I cannot live without my soul!" when his lover Catherine was lost to him.

Except Thorne wasn't Heathcliff. And he did—live, that is.

They planned to pursue PhDs in English at Harvard, reside in an ivy-covered cottage on a college campus with their three ethereally brilliant children and a golden retriever or two, and enlighten generations of students on the power of literature to illuminate their lives.

Except he didn't.

Her One True Love went off to law school in Seattle instead, keeping the Kent family tradition alive, if not their relationship. If the enormous geographic chasm wasn't enough to doom them, her hurt and disappointment at his betrayal of their dreams assuredly did.

Athena kicked a crushed Pepsi can halfway up the sidewalk before pitching it into a garbage can. She'd had ten years to admit Thorne had a right to resent her, too, for their breakup. A whole decade of her fricking life to wonder if she had made the right decision choosing her career over them. Refusing to compromise. But what he'd done the last time they met, the things he'd said…

She stopped at an intersection and wiped the sweat trickling down her cheek. As You Like It Café was one short block away. "You've got this, girl. You own it."

She owned it big time. There was no question, not a shred of doubt, she had full resentment rights this time around. None whatsoever.

Ricki's Café had always been a popular Laurel hangout, despite décor as austere as Ricki's tight hair bun and fierce cheekbones—medical clinic meets cafeteria. But As You Like It Café was Tudor pub meets cozy bistro, without the tackiness of most theme-styled restaurants. A dozen oak tables of various sizes were arranged around a central stone hearth and near the front bay window. Antique hutches filled with rustic crockery lined the brick walls. Pendant lamps hanging from ropes illuminated the beamed ceiling.

At ten-thirty, the empty café was in the lull between breakfast and lunch. Athena followed the aroma of baking bread to the kitchen, suddenly itchy all over, including her nose with its constellation of freckles Thorne named one night while they stargazed. A name she couldn't remember for the life of her because there he was, on the other side of the swinging door. Thorne Ainsworth Kent. The only person in the world to whom she was *Thena.*

He bent over a stainless steel counter, kneading dough. His build, broad shoulders tapering to slim hips, was as athletic as when he was on the varsity swim team. His long, big-knuckled fingers patted and prodded the dough. Squeezed it. Caressed it.

She swallowed a sigh, but it came out like a strangled cry. Thorne looked up and shook thick, wavy hair from his forehead. Its wheat-gold color was as lustrous as ever.

"It's been a long time, Thena," he said, wiping his hands on the towel tucked into his belt.

"Yeah. Long time. What are you doing here?"

"I'm fine. Thanks for asking."

"What's next? I comment on the weather?"

"If you like."

Severe storm warning. Seek shelter immediately.

"I'd like to cut the chitchat," she said, walking toward him. Away from shelter. "Why aren't you in Seattle?"

"I moved back to St. Louis about three years ago. I've been baking for cafés and restaurants in the area ever since."

From rolling in the dough at a prestigious law firm to rolling actual dough were the only dots Athena could connect as she stood drenched in flop sweat, questions buzzing around her head like the fly dancing on the window of DittoDocs.

Why hadn't her family warned her he'd returned to the Midwest?

Why *had* he returned?

Baking for a living? Seriously?

"The closer I got to thirty, the more I craved creativity in my life," he said, shaping the dough into a mound. "I quit my job and made it happen."

She used to love, love, love when Thorne read her mind—before he gave her reasons to hate, hate, hate it. She surveyed the spotless kitchen, as orderly and professional as a cooking show set. They used to binge-watch food programs, marathons that ended with him concocting delectable recipes to please his *lady fair.* And his lady was always pleased. Before he gave her reasons not to be.

"So, how've you been, Thena?"

Keep calm and carry on was Thorne Kent's personal motto.

"Fantabulous."

Keep calm and lie through your teeth worked perfectly fine for Athena Murphy.

"What brings you to Laurel?" he asked.

"I'm on professional leave for a semester to research and write a book, with a bit of waitressing on the side." *Just another chapter in my busy, full life.* She whisked her phone from her handbag. "I have to talk to the new owner of the café. What's their number?"

"You're looking at him."

Keep calm, she reminded herself as she absorbed this latest surprise. "You're kidding."

"Nope." He covered the mound with a cloth as if it were immodestly naked. "I ran into Ricki at one of the restaurants I baked for. When she told me she was selling her café, I offered to buy the equipment and supplies on the spot."

Naturally, he did. Kent family money had been leaking from his ears since birth. Thorne making an impulsive decision, though, was a new twist. Guess he had craved more spontaneity in his life too.

"If I remember correctly, this used to be Schmidt's Bakery," she said.

"It was. Gunther retired and sold me this part of the building for a reasonable price. Left me his recipes too. What do you think of the renovations?"

"If you're going for Henry VIII in the heartland, you've

pulled it off." She checked her phone as if she were expecting an important call any minute. "Where is Ricki anyway? Did she get another café? She promised me a job."

Thorne shook his head. "She's in Uruguay. No, wait. Paraguay."

"Another bad romance?"

His expression conveyed both humor and sympathy. "She was still crying when we signed the papers."

Passion and heartache at fifty-four. Maybe Catherine, exhausted by Heathcliff and all that moor-wandering, was relieved to give up the ghost in her twenties.

Thorne took another mound of dough from the refrigerator and lightly punched it in the center. "Why do you need a job? I thought professors were paid while they were on sabbatical."

"*Want*, not need." Athena rubbed her suddenly constricted throat. "I'd go stir-crazy writing all day. And a little extra money comes in handy."

"For what? Earrings?"

Her one indulgence, besides the teetering stacks of books along the walls of her apartment. He used to tease her mercilessly about it—and then buy her another pair.

"You kept them," he remarked, pointing to her coral rosebud earrings, a Valentine's Day gift from him.

Shit on a stick. She'd forgotten to take them off on the walk over. "They match a lot of my outfits."

The faintest of smiles slid across his lips. "How practical of you," he said.

How sentimental of you, his eyes said.

After she beaned him with a bowl, or better yet, a small skillet, she'd march right out of there, walk the half mile back to the absurd little car she had bought because it was both ecologically responsible and, yes, practical, and put pedal to the metal until she reached San Francisco, never to return to the Midwest, home of gooey butter cakes and gooey broken hearts, ever again.

Except she couldn't.

An assistant professor had two choices—publish or forfeit tenure. And since Athena hadn't written anything but an article or two since her dissertation, "The Enduring Legacy of Catherine and Heathcliff's Enduring Love"—subtitle forgotten—she was up the proverbial creek without the proverbial paddle.

Thorne leaned toward her as he flattened the dough with the rolling pin. "What's the subject of your research, if I may ask?"

"You may. It's the LitWit series." On best-seller lists for two years running, the series of erotic novellas deliciously described imagined sex lives of literary couples. "Have you heard of it?"

"I've seen it in bookstores. Clever marketing to include four novellas in one volume."

"I'm going to uncover the identity of the series' mysterious author, C. L. Garland," she said in her serious professorial voice. "Last year, someone in her inner circle spilled the beans and revealed she grew up in Laurel, of all places, and still lives here. Isn't that a piece of luck?"

"Unless you're C. L. Garland."

"I can't believe no one's tracked her down yet," she said, pointedly ignoring his snarky comment. "Speculation about her identity is at such a high pitch, there's a good chance *my* book will be a best seller."

Whenever Garland published a new volume of novellas, journalists released a flurry of articles full of conjecture, miscellaneous factoids, and guesstimates of the author's net worth. *People* magazine had once published an issue with a female silhouette, overlaid with *WHO IS C. L. GARLAND???* on its cover.

"Best seller. Hmm. I see," Thorne said, nodding thoughtfully.

His thought being, she was sure, that she was selling out, reducing her lofty literary ambitions to a crass commercial enterprise. As if his decision to be a lawyer wasn't a total sellout.

"I'll also explore the novellas' subtexts, metatexts, and themes of sexual repression as they relate to the role of women in a patriarchal society." She'd come up with a memorable subtitle this time.

He formed the dough into a neat rectangle. "A pretty tall order, Thena, considering the series is absolute schlock."

"Which novellas have you read?"

"None. Don't have to. Literature is literature, a potboiler is a potboiler, and never the twain shall meet."

He once stormed off the stage during a rehearsal of the university's production of *Macbeth* when the director suggested they "tweak the fussy language" to help the audience understand the play better.

"Tweak my fussy ass," he'd said, throwing his papier-mâché crown into the Three Witches' cauldron. Athena had never admired her hero so much as when he sacrificed the lead role for Shakespeare's sake.

Thorne rolled up the dough like a rug. "You have quite a task ahead of you. Are you sure you'll have time to waitress?"

"A four-hour shift three afternoons a week? Easy-peasy."

Part-time, mindless work was the perfect antidote to her career-itis. And a café in a small town where gossip was the main amusement was the ideal place to snoop. To wait for more beans about Garland to spill. Or as her department chair, Dr. Oliver Davenport, had advised, "Get the skinny."

Unless Thorne-itis interfered.

She pulled her cinch belt tighter. "Look, if you don't want me to work here, just say so."

"I wasn't implying—"

"Because, believe you me, this isn't the situation I expected when I made plans with Ricki." Not in her wildest dreams. Or nightmares.

"I have no intention of disturbing your plans, Thena."

Big of you, Thorne. Since you already disturbed them years ago.

"In fact, one of my waitresses had to go back to college," he said, "so your timing is great."

Great timing. She bit her lower lip to keep from laughing out loud.

"Besides, we'll rarely see each other," he said. "Unless it gets busy the days you're in, I'll be out of here by noon, free for the rest of the day."

"Free for what? Ambulance chasing?" Athena asked, biting every word.

A spark of anger glinted in his spring-green eyes. "Intellectual property law is my specialty."

"*Was*," she said, pointing to a tray of croissants, the most impeccably formed, enticing croissants she'd ever seen.

"Well," Thorne said, "are you reconsidering?"

A loaded question if she ever heard one.

"Why would I?"

"A café is a much different workplace than a lecture hall."

"And a legal office. What's your point?"

He shrugged. "You'll be out of your comfort zone."

"I waitressed for Ricki during college breaks, remember?" she said—rather than scream, *Comfort zone? What fricking comfort zone?* Or a personal favorite, *Take this job and shove it.*

But the only other local establishment where she could

ferret out information on Garland was Benny's Bar. Unfortunately, the combination of her curves and guys three sheets to the wind had never been a compatible one. When the news broke that the writer hailed from Laurel, she heard that a few journalists had come nosing around the bar. The double whammy of small-town boredom and Benny's killer Hurricane cocktails sent them hungover and empty-handed back to where they came from.

"I'm *not* reconsidering." Athena crossed her arms over her chest. "Let's get down to brass tacks, shall we?"

"I'm listening."

"Schedule. Does noon to four, Monday, Wednesday, and Friday work for you?"

"It does."

"Dress code. Do I have to dress like a sixteenth-century wench in keeping with your Tudor theme?"

His face lit with a smile, tightening the pale skin over his chiseled jaw and cheekbones. She shivered as his eyes slowly traveled the length of her body, from curls to curled toes. "Your own wardrobe will do. But you'll need more practical shoes."

"Noted. This is a long shot, but do *you* have a clue who C. L. Garland is?" Thorne wouldn't come right out and tell her. He'd want her to ask.

"No idea. I've only been living in Laurel since May." He dipped his hand into a bowl and let flour sift through his long fingers onto the counter. "I've got to get back to work before the lunch crowd shows up. Anything else we need to discuss?"

Another loaded question. That one weighed a ton.

"When do I start?"

"Monday at noon. But come around ten on Saturday. Kristie Prescott, the other waitress, will train you. The menu is simple and features a sandwich special every day."

"Saturday it is. Ten o'clock sharp."

"She's off until then, but I'll tell her to expect you when she arrives that morning."

"Sounds like a plan."

Interview over, short if not so sweet. Phone back in handbag. Handbag snapped shut and slung over shoulder. Clingy dress smoothed over womanly curves.

Thorne opened the refrigerator, and with his back to her, he was apparently struck by the wonder of modern refrigeration—as she was struck by the miracle she was still standing.

"Bye," she said.

"Bye," he said without turning around.

Athena walked the half mile back to her car in a daze. Safe in the air-conditioned enclosure of the Mini Cooper, her body cooled, her toes unclenched, and her heart ceased its reckless pounding. She checked her face in the rearview mirror to make sure she was still there, calculating how far Laurel was from Paraguay. Or Uruguay. Remembering, as if it were yesterday, Thorne naming the constellation of freckles on her nose:

"Stellathena. Because you shine so brightly."

All in all, it could have gone a lot worse than a baking error. Thorne carefully unrolled the sticky bun dough and spread the forgotten brown sugar and cinnamon filling across it. Ever since Ricki had left him a voicemail last week saying, "Sorry for not calling sooner but I'm a total wreck," and "Oh, by the way, I promised your old flame a job at the café"—ever since then, he'd been waiting for Athena.

Now she'd come and gone, and he was still waiting. But he wasn't sure for what. He'd had the advantage of surprise. He'd kept his cool. They'd established their terms. And yet…

After rolling the dough up again, Thorne sliced it into twelve buns, his mouth watering. Tasty, wholesome, satisfying—like a certain saucy damsel whose chocolate-brown eyes would satisfy any man's sweet tooth.

Or a particular man. Whoever *he* was.

Athena wasn't wearing a ring, diamond or otherwise, so there probably wasn't a fiancé or husband in the picture. Just the same nameless, faceless lover he'd imagined all these years. And hated. And wished for, for her sake. And hated again.

"Dammit, Thena," he growled, picturing the sway of her body in the silken dress as she had walked toward him. It hadn't seemed likely their paths would cross when he returned to St. Louis. Since he moved to Laurel though, he had expected to run into her sooner or later when she visited her family. But a semester-long visit? Working in his café? Good thing Ricki had given him a heads-up. A few years of playacting experience helped too.

With his thumbs, Thorne molded each pastry, recalling the two dimples below Athena's small waist and the mounds of her full bottom. He wasn't ashamed of desiring her warm flesh beneath his hands again. Not in the slightest. Wanting to relive their last meeting in Seattle, though, *was* a shameful wish—and deranged.

He preheated the oven and placed each bun on the baking sheet, the click of her heels on the tile floor as she left the kitchen echoing in his head. How typical of Athena to be certain she'd discover C. L. Garland's identity. In their former life, he would have joked, *What's in a name?* If they were still best friends, he would have shared the last lesson his father taught him—nearly everyone has a secret life. And that uncovering a secret life brings sorrows of its own.

But the chance of them confiding in each other again was

gone forever. Every curl twitching with irritation on her head had sent that message loud and clear. She still wore the earrings he'd given her, but that had more to do with her love of earrings than anything else.

He put the baking sheet in the oven, set the timer, and went out to the dining room to replenish the napkin holders and salt and pepper shakers. He chuckled in spite of his sour mood. With Athena on the hunt, no one in Laurel would be safe.

But *he* would be. No question about it. Thorne Kent, LLD, was more than capable of protecting himself from Athena Murphy, PhD.

He wrote the day's sandwich special on the chalkboard at the entrance. Cured salmon with capers, red onions, horseradish cream, and slices of cucumber to cool the tongue. Below the word *Thursday* he wrote the name of the sandwich.

The Taming of the Shrew.

CHAPTER TWO

But he that dares not grasp the thorn /
Should never crave the rose.

—ANNE BRONTË, "THE NARROW WAY"

Athena woke the next morning to a grinding noise coming from the kitchen, directly below her bedroom. She squinted at the clock on the nightstand. It was 7:21 a.m. Which translated to 5:21 California time. No one willingly got up at such an ungodly hour unless they knew it was to be their last day on earth. And even then…

She put the pillow over her pounding head. Thanks to the dusty bottle of vodka she'd found in the back of the pantry, she wished it *was* her last day on earth. "No. More. Alcohol," she vowed as lights pulsed behind her closed eyelids. Not another drop until she returned to San Francisco. "And I mean it."

A screech followed by a groan penetrated the floor. She pulled herself to a sitting position. Quite a feat, considering her head weighed about a hundred pounds, burdened by vodka and the memory of her conversation with Thorne. *Fantabulous.* Did that word actually come out of her mouth? And *metatexts*? Really?

Athena put one foot, then the other, on the floor, holding the bedpost until the room stopped spinning. Right before she fell asleep, she had had the most fantabulous inspiration.

Unfortunately, it had vanished from her brain like the states' capitals. And the multiplication tables. Alcohol times remorse equals...

Focus. She had to focus.

She tousled her unruly curls and adjusted her panties. Ah, there it was. Montpelier, the capital of Vermont. And her brilliant idea.

Thorne, the thorn in her side, had his uses.

As a former intellectual property lawyer, he was a valuable resource. Not only could he guide her research on C. L. Garland, he'd make sure she didn't overstep any legal boundaries. What the hell, he owed her one. Between waitressing—and spying—at the café and his professional guidance, she'd wrap up the project lickety-split. Heck, she'd even mention him on her book's acknowledgments page. And then she'd be on her way.

"My merry, merry way," she mumbled.

Easing into her bathrobe, she peed last night's excesses away and descended the stairs as if balancing a full glass of water on her head. The staircases, bookcases, pocket doors, and floors were constructed of maple or walnut. An abundance of wood had either a charming or a depressing effect, depending on one's level of sobriety.

Athena felt along the worn chair rail on her way to the kitchen. Her father sat at the table, brushing crumbs from his green plaid bathrobe, while their dog, Branwell, licked them off the floor. Named by her after Emily, Charlotte, and Anne Brontë's ne'er-do-well brother, he was a ne'er-do-anything-but-eat pug. She knelt to scratch behind his ears, cringing at the clicking noise in her knees when she stood up.

Bedhead tufts of gray hair semicircled her father's bald spot. "Top of the morning to you, Dad," she said, kissing his pink scalp.

"Carpe diem, my goddess," he said, completing their usual morning salutation.

Her mother had named her in honor of her own beloved grandmother in Greece, her father in homage to Athena, the goddess of wisdom in Greek mythology. What a joke. She was smart all right. Smart enough to realize that her low EQ, the social scientists' term for emotional intelligence, canceled out her high IQ.

Eggshells, spilled sugar, and globs of jam littered the kitchen counter. The coffee grinder, whose noise had woken her, lay on its side, faking death. She poured coffee into a mug with a faded *Beam Me Up, Scotty* printed on it. With any luck, caffeine would beam her back *down* to earth from the planet Vodka.

"Why are you up so early?" she asked her father. "You're retired. You can sleep in as late as you want."

"Force of habit. And the older I get, the less sleep I need."

After teaching high school English for thirty years, Charles Murphy had said a reluctant goodbye to the classroom in May. He was popular among the students for his good-natured tolerance. Because of school policy, Athena had never been assigned to his classes—nor benefitted from his generous grading scale.

He raised his bushy eyebrows and peered at her over his reading glasses. "How come you haven't gone back to San Francisco? Don't you have fall semester classes?"

"I'm on sabbatical." Personal leave, strictly speaking. *Without* pay. But the gory details were *her* business, not Thorne's or anyone else's.

"Oh, yes, you're here to... to... *Why* are you here?"

"I'm writing a book, Dad," she gently reminded him.

If he ever became senile, Athena wasn't sure she'd be able to tell. He had been in a state of befuddlement ever since she could remember, retreating regularly to a happy place in his mind the way Mr. Bennet retreated to his library in *Pride and Prejudice*.

"A book about what?" he asked.

"I told you already. C. L. Garland and the LitWit series. She's from Laurel and still lives here."

"That's nice." As if their small town routinely produced famous, bestselling authors.

"I'll be working in a café too." She blew on the hot coffee before sipping it. "You remember Thorne, don't you?"

"Always such a nice young man." He spread strawberry jam on a slice of toast. "Whatever happened between you two anyway?"

"It's a long story." No doubt he'd forgotten the CliffsNotes version of their breakup she'd given him years ago. "Were you aware he was back?"

"Back where?" He chucked a morsel of toast to Branwell, who scarfed it down with a snuffling noise.

"Here. In the Midwest."

Charles looked off into the distance. "I seem to recall he lived in Seattle."

"He did. He moved to Laurel after he bought Ricki's Café. Where I'll be working as a waitress." Athena dropped into a chair. This was entirely too much reality this early in the day.

"Well, how about that," he said.

"Yeah, how about that."

He examined the crossword puzzle. "What's a seven-letter word for 'try to grab'?"

"*Grapple.*" She spooned scrambled eggs from the bowl in front of him onto a dish. "Any plans for today?" *Besides shuffling around the house in a ratty bathrobe that I want to grapple and throw in the washing machine?*

"The Blakes are meeting me for lunch. We thought we'd take a gander at the new buffet restaurant in town." Fellow retirees, Wayne had taught physics and Dolores chemistry, two classes Athena had daydreamed through. Regrettable, since bodies in motion and chemical attraction turned out to be her favorite subjects in life.

The dishwasher shook as it switched to the rinse cycle. Branwell heaved himself off the floor with a fart and waddled out of the kitchen. She pushed the dish of eggs aside. "When's the last time you took Branwell for a walk?"

"Last Tuesday, was it? Wednesday?"

"You ought to go out every day. Fresh air and exercise will do you both good."

Charles retied the bathrobe belt over the small hill of his belly. "Branwell and I get enough exercise rambling around this big empty house."

He had been referring to their home as *big* and *empty* ever since he and her mother divorced twelve years ago. Athena had been a sophomore at Washington University at the time, happily in love with Thorne, eager to mend her parents' marriage with her newfound insight into relationships. But they weren't interested. *Thank you very much but we're getting a divorce. We'll always love you and Finn.*

Luckily, the campus was a twenty-minute drive from home, so she was available to her brother whenever he needed her. Sweet Finn. Three years younger, but the same age as her emotionally—which they had calculated was about eleven. Or twelve, on a good day.

She wiped a dot of jam off her father's cheek with a napkin. "It's your turn to clean the kitchen today. Don't forget."

"Humph."

"Fair is fair, Dad. You can't expect me to do all the housework." It had taken her an entire day when she arrived last week to organize and scour what had turned into the frat house from hell.

"Your mother used to manage everything," he said, his light-blue eyes filmy with tears. Whatever certainty he'd possessed in the decision to divorce had wavered to hesitancy with each passing year. Regret—the Murphy family curse.

Athena squeezed his freckled hand. "I'll do the laundry when I get back from my run. Why don't you trot along beside me?"

"I've got a puzzle to finish," he said, waving the *New York Times* in the air.

"And a tummy to flatten."

"I'll take a walk later."

"What about carpe diem?"

"The day is young, my dear." Charles got up and headed to the living room with every intention, she was sure, of staying in what Thorne had called the "comfort zone." Huh. As if he were the first person to come up with the concept. She'd always admired his intelligence, his spot-on grasp of social trends and human psychology—when he wasn't being stuffy and superior. Or turning them in her direction.

In the shower, Athena lathered soap, along with indignation, all over her body. Better get her anger out now. Because the next time she was in Mr. Keep Calm's company, she would outcalm *him*. Demonstrate, unequivocally, that he had no effect on her whatsoever. She was a more mature Thena, in control of her feelings, meting rationality and emotionality in precisely the right amount as a situation demanded.

The bar of soap slipped from her hands and circled in the eddy at her feet. Well, not *every* situation. Faculty meetings, for example, were pressure cookers. Like the one in April that had sent her halfway across the country and back home again. Not the direction she had in mind when she chose career over compromise, refusing to accept any life together other than the one she and Thorne had planned.

"*Discomfort* zone is more like it," she grumbled, putting on black running shorts, a faded hunter-green Washington University T-shirt, and her well-worn Nike sneakers.

By the time she had stripped the sheets from the beds, cleaned the bathrooms, and tidied the den and living room, the sharpest edges of her hangover had dulled. Pounding the pavement back and forth to her mother's house should pummel last night and yesterday—and the past few months for good measure—into oblivion. And if Lydia Murphy, Laurel Realty's star real estate agent four years in a row, was still in *her* bathrobe like her ex-husband, Athena would die from shock.

Though the heat would probably do Athena in first. Nine-thirty a.m. and already it was killer, baking the uneven bricks of the sidewalk. The Murphy residence was at the edge of the neighborhood described on the town's website as "hearkening back to days of yore." The Queen Anne and Victorian dwellings, framed by mature oaks and sycamores, reminded her of Dame Maggie Smith—a bit the worse for wear, but dignified.

She mentally recited the name of each family as she jogged by their house—Marino, Turner, Baker, McFadden. Like her and Finn, their childhood playmates had left Laurel for college and big-city careers. Their parents remained though, waiting for the holidays when vans filled with grandchildren arrived. Or perhaps they planned trips to Bermuda to avoid the visitations. Kids weren't *that* wonderful. Most of the ones she'd met had sticky fingers, runny noses, and smelly diapers.

The leafy avenues gradually gave way to the treeless concrete streets of the newer subdivisions. She checked the overcast sky when thunder rumbled in the distance. "Shall I compare thee to a Midwestern day?" Thorne used to tease her. Sunny one minute, stormy the next. Capricious. Exciting. Incomparable, if she didn't say so herself.

"I was too much woman for you, Thorne," she said, startling a cardinal from its perch on a mailbox. "And that's all there is to it."

She quickened her pace past a row of cookie-cutter houses when the sky darkened and the first pellets of rain fell. Suburban sprawl had overtaken the pastures of her childhood, replacing bucolic beauty with sterile sameness. The landscaping was pincushion neat and the lawns uniformly green, as if they'd been spray-painted. No cow had pooped on this grass in ages.

Athena ran faster when the skies opened all at once, soaking her to the skin. Her bun loosened and her socks squished in soggy sneakers. She laughed between curses, hoping the driver in the black BMW going the opposite direction hadn't seen her flip the bird at the jagged streaks of lightning. One zap and there went Athena Murphy, deep fried for all eternity. If the lightning didn't kill her, the incongruity would. Jogging for health and a long life and then—lights out. An example she'd use the next time she taught the concept of irony.

If she ever taught again.

"Find Garland, write the book," she repeated like a mantra with every strike of a foot against pavement. "Save your job."

She turned at the beep of a horn—from the car that had been within range of her illustrious middle finger. Great. Just great. First a deluge, then near-death by lightning, and now a road-raged driver.

She sped up.

The car accelerated.

She slackened her pace.

The car slowed.

If she called for help, who would come? The houses looked as empty as architectural models.

The side window of the car lowered, and she heard a male voice through the pouring rain. "Need a ride?"

Another bolt of lightning lit the sky above her head. Athena had two choices.

Die.

Or get into the BMW with Thorne.

No sooner did Athena strap herself in with the seat belt than the door window fogged with her hot breath. So much for playing it cool. Her entire body exuded heat.

"Headed anywhere in particular?" Thorne asked.

"My mother's house."

"Didn't you check the forecast first?"

"Of course," she lied. "I was looking forward to a classic Midwestern downpour. I didn't expect thunderbolts from Zeus."

"They do generally go together," he said, easing the car away from the curb.

"If you bother to think about it. Generally."

He frowned. "Nothing wrong with planning and taking precautions."

She would have mentioned the merits of flying by the seat of one's pants, but hers were stuck to the leather seat and weren't going anywhere. "Growing up with this changeable weather was good practice for life. A great lesson in how to deal with uncertainty, if you ask me."

Who asked her? And why was she sermonizing like a stodgy old fart?

"How do you figure?" he asked.

"Unpredictability keeps you on your toes. Teaches you

how important it is to be adaptable." Adapt or die. Publish or perish.

"Sink or swim," he said with a sidelong smile. On his glowing-with-health face.

Thorne Kent had obviously adapted quite nicely to life's storms.

Athena hadn't decided how she felt about that yet.

"Do much lap swimming these days?" She used to get hoarse cheering him on at college swim meets.

"Not since my YMCA membership expired." He glanced at her legs. "*You're* staying fit."

Before she could say *How about them apples,* a soprano voice erupted from the radio. "Whoa," she said. "It's a little early in the day for opera, don't you think?"

"I can listen to it twenty-four seven."

"That's right. I forgot. You're a fanatic."

"I prefer *aficionado.* Are you still a Groban groupie?"

"Josh brings it home every time. What is this aria from?"

"*La Bohème.* We went to see it once, remember?"

"Vividly."

Three hours of her life she'd never get back, along with all the other evenings she'd dozed in concert halls, wishing the singers would all just shut up so she and Thorne could go back home and bonk each other's lights out.

And they'd done a lot of that in their heyday. Bonked each other's lights out. And on and out again.

Speaking of vivid memories.

Thorne lowered the radio volume and turned left with a smooth rotation of the steering wheel. "Will you be staying with your dad the entire time you're here?"

She nodded. "I prefer the neighborhood. And all my stuff's there."

Every keepsake of her life was stored in her bedroom

closet, including mementos of Thena and Thorne. Programs from the college plays they'd attended and acted in, movie ticket stubs, photographs, the sonnets he'd written for her—and their love letters tied in a red satin ribbon. They couldn't imagine a better way to chronicle their emotions than with pen and paper.

"Lydia expected you to live with her," Thorne said, interrupting her memory of the Christmas she gave him a Montblanc fountain pen. "But she told me she's glad you're looking after Charles."

Athena swirled to face him. "Lydia... what? Since when do you and she...? *What?*"

"We just met, in fact. I shut the café to talk business with her."

"You... My mother..." she sputtered. "*Business?*"

"Don't blow a fuse, Thena. I'm in the market for a house in Laurel, and Lydia is my realtor." He waved a black folder with *Laurel Realty* in gold on the cover. "She printed out more listings for me."

She checked the third finger of his left hand for the first time. No ring. But that didn't mean he wasn't engaged, soon to be a man of property and husband to a snooty wife, a father, eventually, to three children, spaced exactly two years apart. The coffee she'd drunk at breakfast rose to her throat with a sickening, burning sensation. "What's the story, Thorne? Need to find a home for your fiancée and future heirs?"

Her name was probably Dagmar. They'd call their Kentettes Skip, Chip, and Scooter.

"There isn't any fiancée. And certainly no..." He winced. "No children."

"How about dogs?" They'd named their theoretical golden retrievers Atticus and Ulysses after pulling an all-nighter during finals week sophomore year.

"No pets either. My situation is, I'm renting a crappy

apartment above the café month to month. I want a house and some land to put down roots. Nothing more."

She turned to face the window, leaving a circle of fog from her exhalation. "And your family's mansion in St. Louis wasn't a deep enough root?"

"My mother and I sold it after my father died."

"Your dad. Right. Sorry," she murmured.

"Even after a year, she still wasn't coping well with her grief. I left Seattle to help her handle... well, just about everything."

When Athena heard Graham Kent had succumbed to pancreatic cancer, she and Thorne had been broken up for six years. Their *civilized contact* agreement limited them to birthday and Christmas greetings and the occasional email. To do anything more than offer her condolences and send flowers would have been awkward. The haughty Kents' disapproval of "that Murphy girl" had nothing to do with her not attending the funeral. As for Thorne putting down roots in her hometown...

"Why Laurel?" she asked. "Why not buy property in St. Louis?"

"For the convenience of living near my café. It's turned into a very fulfilling enterprise."

"I should hope so, since you've given up your law career." The words tumbled out of her mouth before she could stop them. "The career you gave *us* up for."

"Like you didn't give us up too," he admonished in his deepest, Thorne-est voice.

Athena shivered, chilled by the cold air blowing from the vent. He reached behind and grabbed a blazer from the backseat, laying it across her lap, his arm grazing her bare leg. She shivered again but not from cold.

"Listen, Thena. About what happened in Seattle."

She gripped the armrest as he made a sharp right turn onto her mother's street. Okey dokey. They were going to get this right out in the open. Clear the air. Acknowledge the elephant in the car. Hash over...

Shit. She'd run out of clichés.

"What about Seattle?" she asked, looking straight into eyes the word *soulful* did absolutely no justice to.

"If you're going to work at the café—"

"No *if.* I am."

"What I want to say is... I'd like to put it behind us."

It. That terrible weekend in Seattle.

"It's been three years, Thorne. I'm over it. Totally."

"Good, because—"

"I certainly hope *you're* over it."

"I am."

"Totally?"

"Yes."

"Good."

They were both over the terrible weekend in Seattle.

Totally.

Good.

Thorne pulled up to the curb of her mother's house on the corner. "You can keep the blazer to cover your head and bring it to the café tomorrow."

"No, thank you." Athena slipped the jacket from her legs and, opening the door, slid off the seat, her wet skin against the leather producing a resonance alarmingly close to one of Branwell's gaseous emissions. Cursing with every step, she ran up the walkway through sheets of what felt like Seattle rain, what felt like still caring.

Totally.

Lydia's ranch house, a no-frills rectangle with brand-new gray vinyl siding, was a study in contrasts to Charles's gabled three-story house with faded green shingles and crooked shutters. Athena looked around her mother's living room, considering which of the stainless steel chairs would be the least uncomfortable. She preferred the shabby furniture of her childhood home to this stark décor.

"Let's go in the kitchen," her mother said with an impatient wave of her hand. "You're dripping all over my new bamboo floor."

The ink had barely dried on the divorce decree when Charles brought Branwell home, the first pet to ever cross the Murphy threshold. The pug's occasional violations of Lydia's once-spotless floors still filled him with wicked glee.

"How are you, Mom?" Athena asked, kissing her cheek.

"Same as when you saw me five days ago. How come you're here again?"

"Geesh. Do I need a reason?" Though dropping by for cozy chats or girl talk had never been their thing.

"You usually have one."

Like finding out everything her mother knew about Thorne living in Laurel. And while she was at it, if a potential Mrs. Kent ever accompanied him on his house-hunting trips.

"A storm hit while I was jogging," Athena said. "I thought I'd drop in until the rain stopped."

"I can spare a blouse if you want to get out of your wet T-shirt."

"Don't bother. It'll dry out soon."

"Coffee?" Lydia offered, holding a blue-and-white willowware cup in the air. The complete dish set, a wedding gift from Ricki, was one of the few household items Lydia had taken when she moved out.

"No more caffeine for me, thanks." Athena had had enough jolts for one day.

She sat across from an empty cup and a plate with a cookie

on it. There was no imprint of her mother's burgundy lipstick on the cup and the cookie had a bite taken out of it.

Thorne's lips had been on that cup and cookie.

She stuffed the Thin Mint in her mouth. Mmm. Minty fresh, like he used to taste.

"Another one?" Lydia asked, shaking the box.

Athena shook her head, concentrating on this one, very delicious cookie.

"I don't care for them myself," Lydia said. "I buy them from the Girl Scouts to maintain good community relations."

"Feel free to throw them out. The Girl Scouts will be none the wiser."

Lydia grinned, and with one tap of her high heel, the trash can lid opened, and she dropped the box into it.

Not only was her mother not dressed in a bathrobe, she wore a beautifully tailored royal blue suit that hugged every curve of her body. Athena had Lydia to thank for her tall, voluptuous figure and mass of shiny dark curls—and high-maintenance eyebrows. The silver strands in her mother's hair and the fine lines around her eyes and mouth weren't the worst things to look forward to in the coming years. Years that were galloping toward Athena faster than she liked.

She got up and retrieved the box of Thin Mints from the trash can. "On second thought, it would be a shame to waste these."

"A moment on the lips, forever on the hips," Lydia said in a warning voice.

"Not the way I work out." Athena dug into the box and bit into another cookie. "I ran into Thorne while I was jogging. He gave me a lift so I wouldn't get incinerated by lightning."

"I don't understand why you don't exercise in a fitness center."

That's what she didn't understand? Not her daughter's

casual mention of the boyfriend she once expected to marry? But didn't? And hadn't seen in years? Not to mention her close brush with death?

"I enjoy being outdoors," Athena said.

"The sun will age your skin terribly. And your nose freckles something awful."

Athena shoved the rest of the cookie into her mouth rather than protest that Thorne had loved her freckles enough to name them.

"About Thorne," she said. "What's the deal with you being his realtor?"

"Don't talk with your mouth full." Lydia ran a damp cloth along the gleaming empty counter. "I'm the top real estate agent in town. Why wouldn't he consult me?"

"I get *that*. But he moved to Laurel and you didn't think to tell me?"

"I had no idea until he called my office a month ago to ask about properties."

"I've been home a week. It didn't cross your mind—"

"Obviously not." She fixed Athena with a stern look beneath her flawlessly arched eyebrows. "Why you two broke up in the first place is beyond me."

"Don't think about it too hard. It was ages ago."

"You were perfect together, despite his dreadful parents. Your relationship with him was one of the few things your dad and I agreed on."

Perfect together. Maybe. At the time. Though Athena and Thorne had agreed that perfection was the kiss of death to romance. *Dreadful*, however, described his parents to a tee. A fresh zit erupted on her face whenever she had to attend a Kent family dinner. The enormous banquet table covered with mysterious silverware intimidated her. She needed a special spoon to eat grapefruit? Another one for soup? And scratching a body part was out of the question—they'd assume she had a hideous disease. But it was the conversations about "Muffy's newest Rothko" and "the Van Holtens' place in the Hamptons" that tempted Athena to fake a coronary on the spot.

"You're Sagittarius, and Thorne's Gemini," Lydia said. "Fire and air are a fabulous combination."

"Not astrology again," Athena complained.

"If the stars were a good enough guide for the ancient Greeks, they're good enough for me. Do you remember Jeanne? The girl Finn broke up with before he went off to college?" Lydia had stayed in touch with most of her son's ex-girlfriends. The ones who had come crying to her, trying to figure out what had gone wrong, who needed an explanation for why the kindest, smartest, cutest guy in the world just wanted to be their friend.

"Is Jeanne the one who used to knit stuff for him all the time?" Athena asked.

"She's the sweetest girl." Lydia sighed. "He left all those beautiful sweaters and scarves behind."

"What about her?"

"We're meeting for lunch next week. She's Aquarius, a perfect match for his Libra. I can't imagine why he wasn't interested in her."

Athena rolled her eyes. "Really, Mom? You can't think of a single reason?"

Lydia arranged the cloth she'd used to clean the counter over the sink faucet. "As for you and Thorne, your stars must be in alignment again. He told me you'll be working in his café."

"Which brings up another question," Athena said, eager to steer the conversation away from the celestial-level failure of the Thena and Thorne relationship. "I was completely blindsided yesterday. Ricki's upset and preoccupied, so she's excused. But why didn't *you* tell me she had sold her café?"

"For the love of Pete, my job requires all my time and attention. You can't expect me to be on top of every little thing."

"But she's your best friend. She didn't mention Thorne bought the café and moved to Laurel?"

Lydia examined her nails, manicured to perfection. "Ricki and I aren't on speaking terms at the moment."

"You're kidding. You guys never fight."

"There's a first time for everything," Lydia said, sniffling. "And I prefer to call it a dustup."

"Sounds like a word Dad would use."

"I agree. The word *fight* is too masculine for him."

"What'd you argue with Ricki about?"

"About how she's so demanding. Wanting what I simply cannot give. There are limits to friendship, you know." The glass spice jars, arranged in strict alphabetical order, clicked loudly as Lydia straightened them. "Frankly, I'm relieved she went off to *reinvent* herself. Or whatever the hell she's doing in Uruguay."

Athena knew better than to correct her geography when her mother was this ticked off.

"This waitressing job," Lydia said, finally sitting down. "It doesn't sound like the best use of your time, Athena. Aren't you supposed to be writing the Gardiner book?"

"*Garland*, not Gardiner." Explaining that her project actually depended on her café job was a waste of time. Her mother was as unfazed by the idea of a famous writer in their midst as her father. "It'll be good for me to get out of the house. And out of Dad's hair."

"What little is left of it. How is he these days?"

Adult Athena would have replied he was as happy as a

clam, enjoying his retirement—and the Branwell-soiled floors. But the Athena who had held Finn crying in her arms, assuring her brother they would always be a family… "Dad misses you, Mom."

"He misses a house that isn't a pigsty." Lydia reached over and tucked a dangling curl behind Athena's ear. "Passionate Aries should never marry wishy-washy Pisces. Fire and water in our case did *not* make steam."

Gentle, bewildered Charles, reduced to an astrological miscalculation. "What exactly does that mean?" Athena asked, unable to keep the sharp pitch of exasperation from her voice.

"It means I was too much woman for him. And that's all there is to it."

CHAPTER THREE

As different as a moonbeam from lightning, or frost from fire.

—EMILY BRONTË, *WUTHERING HEIGHTS*

One of the worst things about being home again was coming face-to-face with the dread of heredity. Athena had no problem with her physical resemblance to her mother—was thankful for it, truth be told. But Lydia's verbatim recitation of her own words—*I was too much woman for him*—hung like another cloud over her as she jogged home. At least the rain had stopped, making it easier to munch on a few more Thin Mints. By the time she got back to the house, she'd eaten half the box, trashing the calorie burn of her run.

She tripped over Branwell snoring on the frayed throw rug in the foyer.

"I forgot to warn you," Charles said as he walked down the stairs. "He likes to snooze near the front door these days."

Her father was dressed in a pale-blue shirt and khaki trousers, both freshly pressed. Since her last visit at Christmas, a minor miracle had occurred. He had exchanged his dull, rumpled outfits for a snappy, color-coordinated wardrobe—a sartorial shift no amount of nagging from Lydia had ever accomplished.

"I think Branwell's trying to tell you he wants to go for walks," Athena said.

"You could have taken him with you."

"Not on a run. He'd pass out after two blocks. I stopped by Mom's place, by the way. She says hi."

"Nice try, Athena."

"She did ask how you were."

"To check if I'm ready to kick the bucket. She's always wanted to sell this house."

"Don't worry. Finn and I won't let her." She checked her watch. "Aren't you a little early for lunch?"

"I'm not meeting the Blakes yet." He patted his hair, tamed with styling gel.

Since when did her father use styling gel? And was that cologne she smelled?

"Where are you going then?" she asked.

"Oh, here and there."

"Did you clean the kitchen?"

"No time, my dear," he said, stepping over Branwell. "I have places to go and people to see."

"What places, Dad? Who?"

Charles hurried out the door and down the walkway as if he hadn't heard her. For an out-of-shape middle-aged man, he moved at a good clip. But then he'd had years of experience dodging Lydia's angry missiles, including, after one memorable argument, his beloved plaster bust of Lord Byron.

Athena cleared the kitchen table, whisked eggshells into the garbage can, and wiped the counter clean. Her father had kept his side of the chore bargain only once since she'd been home. She pushed down the teensiest bit of Lydia-like resentment as she unloaded the dishwasher. His mugs and plates were as miscellaneous as her mother's dishes were matched, proof opposites attracted—and then drove each other batshit crazy.

That was *one* invaluable relationship lesson she'd learned.

The other was that dating a guy with expectations that he'd fulfill your idea of a romantic hero was, well, *double* batshit crazy. Because, really, who could come close to the magnetism of the passionate, troubled Heathcliff in *Wuthering Heights*, or the stern, troubled Edward Rochester in *Jane Eyre*? To be loved as completely and devotedly as *they* loved. To be the only woman to save them from their darkest selves. Why should Athena settle for anything less?

She'd dated versions of Mr. Rochester, academia supplying its fair share of moody, conflicted men. Though, inevitably, their stern demeanor was due to an unhealthy obsession with the life cycle of the snail. Or a gastrointestinal disorder. As for emotional wounds that only she could heal—her would-be heroes weren't *troubled*, just too much trouble.

Her chores finished, Athena plopped onto the gold-and-maroon paisley armchair by the front window, and a cloud of dust puffed out.

"Time to talk?" Finn texted. The emoticon of a crying face was not a good sign.

"Uh-oh, what's wrong?" she asked when he answered her call. "Another fight with Mario?"

Finn and his boyfriend of two years, Mario Spinelli, rehabbed homes in the Bay Area. Though their business was successful, Finn insisted he was doing it "on the side" until one of his creative ideas panned out.

"Uh-huh. He keeps calling me 'Fuckleberry Finn.' And last night, he ate my leftover takeout."

"From our favorite Vietnamese restaurant?"

"He ate all my pho, Athena. And left the empty carton in the fridge."

"My poor Finnster."

"I may have to bunk at your place for a few days again. Or a week. Or two."

"Go ahead. You have the keys." They lived a mile away from each other in San Francisco. "Sounds like Mario's in one of his moods."

"The *silent treatment* mood. He built a cabinet yesterday without saying a single word to me."

"Were you nagging him?" Finn had inherited Lydia's fastidiousness, if not her looks or personality.

"He's such a slob. Leaves his crap all over the place. And he complains that I'm a stick-in-the-mud. Me! Who comes up with all these innovative business plans?"

"I've been meaning to tell you," Athena said, "the T-shirt I ordered from you never arrived."

"I'm having a major problem with the manufacturer. They didn't print the words backward on about twenty shirts. Can you believe it?" His voice wobbled from tenor to soprano whenever he was upset. *Believe* came out in so high a pitch that she held the phone away from her ear. "I mean, the whole concept behind my Self EsTEEm T-shirts is you can only read what's on them in a mirror."

The reverse *Ambulance* on ambulance trucks had inspired Finn's latest venture—design your own T-shirt with a word to boost your confidence when you looked in a mirror. Athena had no intention of wearing her shirt in public. People staring at her chest, trying to figure out what *cainiarB* meant, was not a welcome prospect. Besides, being a brainiac hadn't done her any favors lately, confidence-wise.

"Mom and Dad are right," Finn said. "I should get a job in electrical engineering again."

"Don't you dare. You were miserable." On the other hand, savings from his six-figure salary had sustained him the past two years. "What does Mario think?"

"Mario doesn't think. He broods and breaks things. And then puts them back together."

"Sounds like my kind of guy."

"Until you live with him day after day. I'll take calm and steady instead."

Athena unwound a long curl and examined the split ends. "News flash, kiddo. Thorne quit law, moved back to the Midwest, and bought Ricki's Café."

"*Your* Thorne?"

She flinched at the word *your*. "Mr. Calm and Steady is now the proprietor of As You Like It Café. Midlife crisis is my guess."

"At thirty-two?"

"Thirty-three, as of June first."

"Ricki must have had a midlife crisis if she sold her café," Finn reasoned.

"Who can tell? She's in a constant state of emergency. Get this. Mom told me they're mad at each other. Something about Ricki demanding more than she could give."

"Sounds like me and Mario," he mumbled.

"Anyway, here's the real kicker. Not only will I be waitressing in Thorne's café, but he's been living in Laurel, wants to buy a house here, and Mom's his realtor. Talk about my worlds colliding."

"Dude! That's cosmic. I think it's a sign."

"A sign the universe is conspiring against me."

"It means you two are supposed to get back together."

"No way, no how."

Finn and Thorne had gotten along like brothers, sharing the same taste in preppy clothes and sitcoms, especially *Seinfeld*. But loyal Finn had followed her lead and rarely contacted him except for occasional emails and Festivus greetings. He had no idea she had met Thorne in Seattle.

"I wouldn't stay here a minute longer if I weren't investigating C. L. Garland," Athena said.

"Oh, yeah, your café spy caper. Any progress on your book?"

"I read all the novellas in the LitWit series this summer, in between teaching, and worked up a rough outline. Soon as I start waitressing, I'll hit the ground running on my...Did you just call it a *caper*?"

"Makes it more fun. Hey, I've got another Garland theory."

"Hit me with it." Speculating which longtime Laurel resident wrote erotic novellas was her brother's latest "Finn Spin," as Lydia called his out-of-the-box notions.

"Try this one on for size," he said. "Maybe Garland is a man."

"No way. All the jacket blurbs and press reports refer to *she*. And pardon my bias, but I don't think a male writer can hit a woman's sweet spot the way she does."

"If Mr. Brower wrote, he could."

Jacob Brower was the hot-to-trot history teacher they both had had a crush on in high school. "He's married with, like, six kids," Athena said. "He wouldn't have time to write."

"Okay. How about this—The Charles is Garland. *Charles* L. Garland, get it?"

"What's the *L* stand for?" she asked.

"Lydia, who else?"

Athena laughed so loudly that Branwell dragged himself from the rug at her feet to the one in front of the fireplace. "Good one. Except if Dad had that much insight into what women want, Mom wouldn't have left him."

"Sure, she would. Those two were doomed from the start."

"Like my book is doomed if the café regulars don't lead me to Garland. Best case scenario, she comes to the café to write."

"I've always wanted to be a regular," Finn said wistfully.

"If you were, I'd disown you. Then where would I be without my Finn?"

"You wouldn't be lonely for long. Sergei Gudonov is waiting in the wings."

"Don't even."

"Aren't you curious to sleep with him at least once? I am." He laughed. "I call him 'Sir Gay Goodenough.' "

"Nope. We're strictly friends *without* benefits." Except for a few drunken make-out sessions. Or more than a few.

Athena had met Sergei in the produce section of Whole Foods on a dismal day in March. He'd held a beet in the air and expounded on it like Hamlet on Yorick's skull—in Russian and broken English. She'd doubled over in laughter, forgetting the gray skies and incessant rain. Most guys bored her silly by the third date. Sergei was someone who might hold her interest for a while. Thanks to Thorne's imitation of Sean Connery as James Bond—"Kent. Thorne Kent."—and asking her, "Shrimp on the barbie, mate?" in his hottest Aussie voice, she had a weakness for accents the way some people had one for blue eyes or hairy chests. Passionate, with a wild mane of dark hair and a tall, rugged physique, Sergei was—dared she think it?—Heathcliffean.

She didn't dare think it for long. The charm of his accent soon wore off—if not his charming descriptions of her "fire of spirit." His on-the-sly smoking was a childish subterfuge, since his hair and clothes smelled of tobacco. And she had no idea what, if anything, he did for a living. After about six weeks, she said, "*Dasvidaniya*, Sergei." "*Nyet*, Atheeena," he replied, shaking his shaggy head like a wet Newfoundland. An exchange they'd been repeating ever since, followed by him reading Chekhov to her and making her bowls of borscht. So, she had a weakness for Russian literature and beet soup too. Who knew?

"I'm in deep doo-doo, Finn. I'm living with The Charles. Thorne is my boss and Mom's client. And I'm looking for someone who doesn't want to be found." And in deeper doo-doo than she'd admit with Sergei.

"On the upside, you haven't gone out of your mind."

"Not yet. But stay tuned for future developments."

"Say the word, and I'll come home in a minute, Athena." Finn's voice always dropped to a bass when he assured her that she had his support.

"Just one of the many reasons why I love you, Finnster."

"At least someone does," he said petulantly.

"Do you need me out there?"

"Nah. I can deal with Moody Mario. But come back soon, okay?"

"I've got one foot out the door already."

Athena paced the living room after they hung up, debating whether she should take another shower or get cracking on her book. Or *read* a book—the best excuse to procrastinate she knew of.

Bookcases spanned an entire wall, filled with volumes on topics from Christmas traditions around the world to chess. She ran her fingers lightly across the literature section, duplicates of which were in her personal library in San Francisco. Or in some cases, triplicates, like Charlotte Brontë's *Jane Eyre* and Emily Brontë's *Wuthering Heights*. Make that *four* copies of Emily's masterpiece, each in varying degrees of disintegration. Each a memento of who she had been when she read that particular edition.

She plucked the Penguin paperback edition off the shelf. It was her very first copy, the one she had used in the Literary Explorations class where she met Thorne. The cover, a photograph of a lonely Yorkshire moor, was cracked, the pleated spine crumbling. Who was the Athena who had written *Thena Kent* over and over on the flyleaf? She was a version of Catherine Earnshaw, Heathcliff's lover, carving her name as *Catherine Heathcliff* on the windowsill of her bedroom. She was Catherine's ghost outside the window of Wuthering Heights, begging Lockwood, a lodger there, to let her inside. In love with Heathcliff beyond the grave, as Athena had believed she'd love Thorne.

She gazed out at the darkening sky. Either it had rained again or her eyes were filmed with tears. No, she was wrong. The Athena who had begged in Seattle like Catherine was not in this edition but in the hardcover volume on her bookcase shelf in San Francisco. She'd since buried that version of herself, with no chance of loving beyond the grave.

Sitting in the armchair again, she opened *Wuthering Heights* and began to read. One more time. Looking for the Athena she was now.

Thorne pulled the last of the loaves of bread he'd baked for the day from the oven and checked the time. As You Like It Café opened at eight o'clock. He had one hour to decide on Saturday's sandwich special, brew the coffee, and set the tables up—and get his head around the fact that Athena would be entirely too close for comfort for three days a week.

Sitting next to her in the car yesterday, the scent of her wet skin flooding him with memories, had been a sweet torment. The urge to bring her face close to his and kiss those pouting lips fled, though, the instant she reminded him he'd given them up for a law career.

He slammed the oven door and tossed the mitts across the counter. Damned if he'd take full blame—as he'd reminded *her*. Imagination had caught up with real life, and they'd *both* made their choices. Careers over love.

Booting up his laptop, he scrolled through sandwich recipes. He had more pressing matters to attend to than stewing over the past. It was over and done with. Regret was a waste of time. As Graham Kent's only child and heir, he'd made a reasonable, honorable decision to follow him into the legal profession. Not one to second-guess, however much Athena disagreed.

The prudence of his choice had eased some of the pain during the years they were apart, as had the expectation that they'd get another chance at happiness. That Thena and Thorne would find their way back to each other by hook or by crook. His father's deathbed confession, admitting that he'd led a secret life of passion, risk, and freedom, had turned possibility to certainty.

A conviction turned to *impossibility* within the year by yet another secret.

No, there could be no second act for Thena and Thorne. Not while the consequences of his father's deceptions were his to bear. Their drama was over. No compromises on either side, no fresh starts. Athena was better off without him.

Grabbing a blueberry muffin from a serving tray, Thorne bit into it savagely. *Better off.* The last time they had met, they'd played out a wrenching emotional drama worthy of its own opera, thanks to those two words.

A knock on the back door dropped the curtain on the scene in Seattle. Thorne waited for the memory of rain against hotel windows and tears streaming down Athena's face to fade before opening the door to admit Kristie Prescott, the café's waitress.

"Good morning and howdy-do," she chirped.

"Thanks for coming in early. Sorry I haven't set the tables up yet."

"No problem." She sniffed the air. "Rye bread with caraway seeds?"

"Right on the money again."

"Ever since Zoe was born, I have a supersensitive nose. I can smell a diaper that needs changing a mile away."

"Is Ian on dad duty today?"

"Yep. And it's a wonderful thing."

"Good news. A new waitress is coming in at ten. She'll cover the afternoon shifts on Monday, Wednesday, and Friday."

"Great! You'll have backup again."

"Would you mind training her? It won't be hard. She's waitressed before."

"Sure." She kicked off her sandals and slipped into the pair of clogs she kept by the pantry. "What's her name?"

"Athena Murphy. She's an English professor on leave of absence. If she doesn't show up and it gets busy, I'll help out." Deciding not to work in his café was the most logical, rational choice for Athena to make. The best solution all around. But as Thorne knew from long experience, she rarely changed her mind once she'd made it up.

"Um...you okay?" Kristie asked, her forehead puckered with concern as she tied an apron over her green jumper.

"Just thinking of all the things I have to do today." Like trying to stay logical and rational.

"Don't worry. I've got everything covered out there." She piled the menus on her arms and followed Thorne to the dining room.

He brewed the first urn of coffee at the beverage station for the regular early-morning customers. Widowed or divorced, most of them, loath to begin the day alone. Kind of like himself—one of the reasons he bought the café in the first place.

"Is there a pastry special today?" Kristie asked, arranging silverware on one of the tables.

"I'll make pear tarts," he said, thinking of Athena and her tart tongue and her juicy...

For the next two hours, Thorne tried very hard not to think at all as he baked the tarts, planned the week's menu, and gathered ingredients for the day's sandwiches, including the special—cheddar cheese melted over slices of apple and spiced apple butter. Everything was organized for Kristie to construct the sandwiches according to the customers' requests. Streamlined and simple, the philosophy of As You Like It Café. The way life should be.

From the dining room, he heard peals of warm laughter. He'd recognize that laugh anywhere. Athena, who was anything but streamlined or simple, had arrived.

The haphazard arrangement of barrettes in Kristie's tangled brown hair and the stain of dried apricot on her shoulder were dead giveaways she was a mom. When she told one patron "the potty" was to the left of the beverage station and another one to please use her "indoor voice," Athena couldn't help laughing.

"You think toddler talk is bad," Kristie said, crinkling her button nose, "I've gained three pounds eating Zoe's finger foods."

"Every occupation has its hazards, including motherhood, I suppose." Athena knew exactly what they were on *this* job.

"I don't dare go near Thorne's pastries. They're to die for."

"Thanks for the warning." Though if anyone should be sounding alarms, it was Athena, having hazarded death by dessert with every delectable pastry he'd ever baked for her.

The pear tarts disappeared within the first hour of her training shift. Thorne had vanished as well after introducing her to Kristie—an interaction in which he managed to avoid eye contact. "Do you usually work your shift alone?" she asked Kristie.

"Unless it's crazy busy, then Thorne pitches in. He lives in the apartment upstairs. He told me you're an English professor?"

"Uh-huh."

"So's my husband, Ian. What's your specialty?"

"The nineteenth-century novel."

"Ian's is poetry. How come you're on leave?"

"To write a book for tenure."

Now was as good a time as any to execute her plan—and practice broaching the topic of Garland without revealing her project.

"Have you ever noticed anyone writing in the café, Kristie? Stories or screenplays, I mean. Not grocery lists."

"Like in Starbucks? People tapping away like crazy on their laptops?"

"Don't forget the anxious, haunted expressions."

Kristie laughed. "No, I haven't. But that describes Ian struggling with his dissertation. He hated every minute of it."

"Do you overhear customers talk about the books they're reading?"

"Gosh, I zip around so fast, I never pay attention. Why?"

"Just wondering if there's much interest in literary pursuits around here."

Athena filled a tray with mugs of coffee and muffins for the table of four women in lively conversation by the bay window. She'd take her sweet time setting them down, the better to eavesdrop.

"Good luck with your book," Kristie said. "Ian breaks into a cold sweat whenever he thinks about having to publish for tenure."

"Writing is lonely, solitary work. Coming here will keep me sane."

"I hear you. If I didn't have a reason to get out of the house, I'd be in sweatpants all day, watching kiddie cartoons. It's only eight to twelve, Tuesday to Saturday, but I love it. And Thorne is flexible if I have an emergency."

Thorne, flexible?

Once Athena found her way around the kitchen and got the knack of timing orders, everything she remembered about waitressing fell into place. She quickly hit her stride, joshing with customers, suggesting sandwich combinations—and dropping the occasional question about what someone was reading, if they followed the best-seller lists, and if they'd heard of the LitWit series. So far, she had found little evidence of literary pursuits, though the four women's discussion about ballet had been engaging.

Kristie squeezed between two tables filled with ravenous-looking men and women in bicycle shorts and shirts emblazoned with the Spin Cycle logo. "Competitive racers," she whispered. "They plowed their way through the sandwich specials and are ready for dessert."

"Should we ask Thorne to bake more pear tarts?" Where *was* he anyway?

"No. There are some cream puffs in the fridge."

"Okay, I'll get them."

Athena shoved open the swinging door to the kitchen—right smack into Thorne. He stepped back with a moan. "Jeez, Thena."

"Sorry. I didn't realize you were here."

"How come you're still working?" he asked, rubbing his forehead.

"Training day's been hectic."

"It's noon. I thought you'd be gone by now."

Wished she'd be gone, in Thorne-speak.

"But I'm having so much gosh darn fun," she said. In Thena-speak.

He threw back his broad shoulders and slid his hands into

the pockets of his jeans. He was the only man she knew who made a pelvic thrust look nonchalant. "Truth is, I wasn't sure you'd show up at all."

"Part-time temporary jobs aren't exactly falling off the trees around here."

"Does this mean you're staying?"

She couldn't tell if the catch in his voice meant he wished she would—or dreaded she would.

"I'll be good to go solo Monday afternoon," she said. "If that's all right with you."

"It is. I'm on duty now, though, so you can leave if you want. Or not. Whatever."

"I'll go as soon as I get the cream puffs to Kristie." She brushed by him and, removing her soiled apron, tossed it into the laundry basket. It missed its target—but if Thorne's wide-eyed look was any indication, her outfit hadn't.

Not that she'd worn a blouse that draped her breasts like melting ice cream on purpose. Or her favorite Liz Claiborne jeans that were a gift of the gods to any woman with a little junk in the trunk. As for the gold hoop earrings, her choice was inspired by the chapter in *Wuthering Heights* she'd just finished reading in which Heathcliff, saved from the slums of Liverpool and adopted by Catherine's father, was assumed by everyone to be a gypsy.

Athena pulled the tray of cream puffs from the refrigerator and placed it on the counter. "We need to set a few things straight, Thorne." Now that she had his undivided attention.

"Fine with me."

"First of all, there's no reason we can't behave with civility while I'm working here."

"None whatsoever."

"We're both professionals, and this situation has nothing to do with our personal lives."

"I couldn't agree more."

"And another thing. You told Kristie I'm a professor. I prefer nobody knows anything else."

"What else is there?"

She folded her hand around a cream puff. There were ten of them, one for each year of the *else* when they weren't Thena and Thorne. "If anyone asks, say we were friends in college."

"Why would anyone ask?"

"I don't know why. They might. It's possible. You never know."

She'd have better aim with a croissant. On the other hand, a cream puff made more of an impact.

"Come to think of it," Thorne said, "we *did* hang out in Ricki's Café and other places in Laurel when we visited your family. Somebody's bound to remember we were a couple. Ricki did."

"Because she's my mother's friend. The specifics of our relationship will be fuzzy to everyone else after all this time."

"And if they're not?"

"We say we dated briefly but remained friends. And one more thing."

"Should I be writing all this down?"

"The *last* thing. Don't mention I'm researching C. L. Garland to anyone." The café patrons might not talk as freely if they thought she was gathering information.

"I won't say a word," he assured her.

Cooperative. Polite. Calm. Infuriatingly Thorne.

She picked up the cream puff, just for the hell of it, and—

"Hey, Thorne?" Kristie peeked around the kitchen door. "Ian's here, and I'm getting ready to go home."

His face lit with a smile. "Is the cutest little girl in the world with him?"

The proud mother beamed. "Come say hi to Zoe."

Athena followed them out of the kitchen, leaving the tray of weaponized pastries on the counter. This she had to see.

Kristie linked her arm in her husband's. "I'd like you to meet Athena Murphy," she said to him. "She's an English professor too."

"Ian Prescott," he said in a voice as mellow as his wife's was lively. Tall and pale, with dark, curly hair pulled back in a ponytail, he looked as sensitive as poetry required. The kind of person who still mourned John Keats's death at the tragic age of twenty-five.

"Nice to meet you, Ian," Athena said, shaking his hand. "Where do you teach?"

"At Southern Illinois College in Rosewood, next town over. And you?"

"Wyatt College in San Francisco."

"Never been there. Is it as beautiful as it looks in photographs?"

For a split second, Athena's mind blanked, unable to picture anything at all about the city she'd lived in for years. As if the move west had never happened, the job and the overpriced apartment didn't exist.

"Uh, yeah, the buildings and streetcars are…um…picturesque," she mumbled. "Lots of great restaurants."

"And you're in Laurel because…" Ian prompted.

"I'm on sabbatical to write a book. Waitress on the side."

Her present life didn't sound real to her either.

"Well, if you need any help settling in town," he said, "give us a holler."

"I'm fine, I have family here. Thanks so much for the training session today, Kristie."

"You're welcome. And now I'm going back to mommy mode," Kristie said with a laugh. "Where *is* my baby girl anyway?"

A shriek of toddler glee pierced the air. Standing in the middle of the room, surrounded by a half dozen oohing and aahing patrons, Thorne cradled Zoe in his arms. Her hazel eyes, identical to her mother's, opened wide with every silly face he made. Her head, covered in her dad's curls, shook with laughter as Thorne Kent, LLD, did the world's most adorable imitation of a monkey eating a banana.

"Zoe's just crazy about Thorne," Kristie said.

A spasm hit Athena in the gut. And it wasn't from the cheese sandwich she'd wolfed down between orders. Zoe looked like the baby she'd always imagined she and Thorne would have. Thorne, who, during that terrible weekend in Seattle, had made it absolutely clear he had no intention of having children. Ever.

Athena stretched out on her bed Saturday night, Branwell-the-pug-on-a-rug tired. The black hole that was the Internet had drained hours of her life away. She'd searched every possible term related to C. L. Garland, hoping beyond hope for a clue, however obscure, that might unravel the mystery of the writer's identity. Or, at the very least, snag a thread or two. No such luck, though the combination of *erotica* and *garland* did yield some humorous, if icky, results.

She stared at the half-empty bottle of chardonnay on the nightstand. *How to drink yourself into a stupor* would probably lead to all sorts of gruesome articles. Screw abstinence though. Drinking alone might suck, but it sucked less than hearing her father change television channels like he was desperately seeking the meaning of life. At high volume. He must have settled on a program because the babel of dialogues and soundtracks had finally stopped.

"You're never going to make it, girl," Athena moaned.

"Admit you *don't* own this situation and go back to Cal-i-for-niy-ay."

If the pathetic Charles Murphy evening routine didn't finish her off, the faded striped wallpaper and dingy furniture of her childhood bedroom certainly would. And then there was As You Like It Café to nail her coffin shut. Kristie would be a buffer between her and Thorne most days as they switched shifts. But Mondays it would be just the two of them, busting their asses to prove they were professionals with no personal issues. Two mature adults irritating the crap out of each other.

"As I *don't* like it," she muttered. "As I have no choice."

Even Finn didn't know the ugly truth. Sabbatical schmatical. Not only was she on personal leave without pay, she was also in the academic doghouse, thanks to Corinne Carew. Speaking of dogs. The bitch.

She poured another glass of wine, picturing every tidy strand of straight blond hair on Corinne's head, the impossible perfection of her teeth, and her compact body in its Chanel knockoff suits. She was Reese Witherspoon's evil twin—and Athena's worst nightmare. Following some canine instinct—territorial? predatory?—Corinne had launched a relentless campaign against Athena, criticizing everything, from her teaching style and lack of writing credentials to her appearance:

"Let your students *imagine* Miss Havisham's madness, Athena. Acting it out dramatically must be exhausting. No wonder you look so tired all the time."

"How's your book coming along? Oh, I forgot. You haven't written one yet. Need any ideas? We assistant professors have to stick together."

"Do you want the number of my stylist? I'd be happy to share her. She does eyebrows too."

Just a few of the malicious barbs Corinne had dug into

Athena during faculty meetings in the conference room where signed copies of her latest book, *Emily Dickinson: Her Spirit Lives*, were stacked beneath an oversize glossy print of her publicity headshot.

Corinne Carew was the kind of person who secured a Post-it with tape and disguised nasty remarks with offers to help.

Athena Murphy was the kind of person who wanted to slap people like Corinne into next week. An almost irresistible urge she curbed, settling for *undisguised* nasty remarks at faculty meetings like, "Instead of deconstructing Dickinson, how about deconstructing your personality?" Or reciting a stanza of Dickinson's poetry—her own version.

Because I could not stop for Corinne—
She kindly stopped for me—
The Carriage held but just Herself—
And Imbecility.

She put the wineglass on the nightstand with a shaking hand. Six plain words. As it turned out, six words, neither witty nor poetic, were all it took to derail her career.

This page is left intentionally blank.

Corinne had included a blank page, with those words typed on it, in a brochure she distributed during the April faculty meeting to announce her next Dickinson book.

Athena lost it.

Standing up—yes, dramatically—she waved the blank sheet of paper and declared this was patently absurd, a waste of paper and mental energy, and furthermore, the last thing the world needed was another book on Emily Dickinson, whose spirit was as dead as a doornail. Her huff gathered heat with every glance at Corinne's smug, satisfied expression—and with every wiggle of the bat wings under her arms.

After this meltdown, Dr. Davenport, the department chair, offered Athena two options: take personal leave and *dazzle* him with a rough draft of a book by the end of December, or *consider other avenues of employment.* So, she'd rashly promised, on the spot, to uncover the identity of C. L. Garland—*She's from my hometown! Imagine that!*—and to subject the LitWit series to its first serious academic treatment. Her monograph, dedicated to him, would assuredly bring renown to the English Department of Wyatt College. Frankly, the school could use recognition beyond its stuffy, self-satisfied circle of rich donors and alumnae. A comment she wisely suppressed.

When the chair told her that the dedication wouldn't be necessary and that her latest outburst was "the last straw," she realized he meant *she* was unnecessary. His demand for a draft of a book in eight short months was akin to a task assigned by the spiteful gods in Greek mythology—impossible. After ten tense minutes of negotiation, during which she resisted tightening his bolo tie until his face turned purple, she squeezed a *very rough draft* concession from him. Which Athena interpreted as *damn near raw.*

"Dazzle, dazzle, dazzle," she grumbled, checking under her arms. "Other avenues, my ass." Lifting five-pound dumbbells had done wonders for her bat wings. As did punching the air as she cursed Corinne during the long drive home after the end of the summer semester. And cursing Davenport too, the twit. Why would someone born, bred, and educated in Connecticut wear bolo ties? And he had to be the only department chair in academia who did not permit anyone below associate professor to call him by his first name.

She was about to send Finn a funny photo of herself flexing a muscle when her phone lit with an unknown number.

"Hello?"

"Hello, *moi umminky*. How are you?" Sergei growled.

Shit a brick. So much for hoping he'd fascinate another woman with his beet soliloquy while she was gone.

"*Umminky* doesn't mean *dumpling*, does it?" Athena said. "I hate when you call me food names." Especially pale, pasty foods.

"No, no, *nyet*. It means *my smart one*. But so what if you have body with dumplings? No skinny woman on diet for me."

"Whose phone are you using?" Anything to get him off the subject of her dumplings.

"A friend's," he said vaguely.

Sergei didn't own a phone or computer. He navigated modern life by a mysterious network of favors from *friends* she'd never met. An enviable skill, like his economical use of the English language. "Too wordy! Get to the point!" she frequently commented on student essays. Sergei *always* got right to the point.

"How long you away?" he asked.

"I'm not sure. I've run into a few glitches."

"You hurt yourself when you run?" he asked after a long pause.

"My *project*. I'm having a few problems with it," she translated.

"Forget project. Come back, and we get license."

Shit a double brick. A marriage license.

Sergei couldn't remember his address half the time, but he was never, ever going to forget her reply to his marriage proposal—"It wouldn't be the worst thing."

Six plain words. Again.

Athena scowled at the bottle of chardonnay. She damn well better rethink her *screw abstinence* policy. Thanks to one glass of wine too many, she'd screwed up royally.

"You promise we marry, Atheeena," Sergei reminded her. "I get green card. You get baby."

"I was drunk. It doesn't count."

"We have deal."

"I wasn't serious."

"You were."

"I was inebriated. Liquored up. Sloshed. Tanked."

An even longer pause followed as he tried to interpret her string of synonyms. "Tanked?" he repeated. "Like a tank roll over you?"

A few tanks. Dr. Oliver Davenport. Corinne Carew. Her runaway mouth.

"You're darn pootin'," she said, unleashing his usual diatribe against Vladimir Putin and a volley of Russian expletives.

"Okay, okay, Sergei, calm down."

"There should never have been a revolution!" he shouted. "They ruined my country!"

"The Bolsheviks?" She was never entirely sure which revolution he was raging about.

"I do not acknowledge the U.S.S.R.!"

"Nobody says you have to."

He mumbled something, followed by wounded grunts and familiar words of seduction—which intriguingly included the name Dostoevsky. For one mad moment, Athena pictured herself driving nonstop back to San Francisco, marrying Sergei, and letting him burrow his bearish body into her until she had a row of baby Gudonovs like matryoshka dolls.

Suddenly exhausted by his exertions, he wished her good night. "*Spokushki*, Atheeena. When I go to sleep, I'll dream of you and the tsars," he promised before hanging up.

As if he could choose what to dream.

Could she?

Athena pulled the covers up to her chin, remembering the

moment in As You Like It Café when Thorne bent to pick Zoe's stuffed giraffe off the floor. Every lean muscle, from strong shoulders to bodacious butt to long thighs, was molded by his shirt and jeans. Her own legs had ached to wrap themselves around his body until she had to sit in the nearest chair.

The Garland books she'd brought were piled on the nightstand. Her colleagues called the series "the NitWit series," jealous of the author's success and fortune. Every last professor wished they could tell their students to fuck off and retire to their villas and yachts. Privately, Athena referred to it as "the LitClit series," and leafing through "Prude and Prurience," she let herself surrender as Mr. Darcy put it to Elizabeth Bennet but good.

CHAPTER FOUR

She's hard to guide any way but her own.

—EMILY BRONTË, *WUTHERING HEIGHTS*

Thorne closed the laptop and shut his burning eyelids as words and numbers darted across them. His back was numb from sitting on the hard chair for hours. The thought of dragging his sorry ass to the shower exhausted him. He opened one eye to look at the clock. Nearly seven a.m. He had an hour to caffeinate and get ready before As You Like It Café's first customers arrived. The Labor Day holiday promised a busy day ahead. He'd finished most of the prep work yesterday during the Sunday closure and had caught up on bills and paperwork. Now for the next challenge of the day—Athena working her first full shift.

Getting up abruptly, he pushed back the chair and stretched his long arms to the ceiling. A few more inches and he could touch it. From a town house in Seattle with spectacular views of the harbor to a small, one-bedroom apartment sparsely furnished with secondhand décor. Contrary to Athena's assumption, he couldn't afford a mansion even if he wanted to buy one. Purchasing and renovating the café had absorbed a good chunk of his savings and proceeds from the sale of the town house.

The bedroom closet door fell off its hinges again when he opened it after his shower. The landlord kept promising to replace it. And to fix the leaky toilet. He propped the door against the wall. There was no point getting upset over temporary circumstances.

Like Athena working in his café. A twist of fate that might very well unhinge *him.*

It must have taken him longer to dress than he realized because, when Thorne looked at the clock again, the time was 7:50. He hurried downstairs and appraised the dining room. There was nothing temporary about his café. His restoration of what was once a wheelwright's workshop, a dry goods store, and then a bakery was a testimony to permanence. Every inch of refurbished brick wall and wooden floor, every decision about cutlery and furniture and lighting, had been a labor of love. He'd worked like a demon with contractors and carpenters, determined that the loyal patrons of Ricki's Café wouldn't drift away during the transition. Sure enough, they'd made their way the half mile up the street and, so far, kept returning.

And, so far, his decision to quit law was the best one he'd ever made. Without being aware of it, five years of dry-as-dirt legal work had gradually dulled his spirit like a worn brass knob. Most days had started with a pep talk. *Dad. Task significance. Potential for advancement,* he'd repeat to himself in the mirror. *A good living.* And most days had ended with one beer too many.

Thorne removed the muffin tins filled with batter from the refrigerator and preheated the oven. Today's menu would highlight classic end-of-summer fare. Corn muffins, pulled-pork sandwiches, potato salad, and coleslaw. Hearty, stick-to-your-ribs food. As he scribbled *yeast, onions,* and *mayonnaise* on the shopping list, the chime on his phone dinged.

Can't wait for dinner tonight.

Pamela Morgan, his girlfriend of the moment. A saleswoman at Macy's, she'd talked him into a purchase of Tommy Hilfiger shirts and trousers when he was shopping two months ago for a jacket. And a hand-tooled leather belt to "complete the ensemble."

He texted back:

You're up early.

Store's open already for Labor Day sale. I'll be on my feet for hours!

Raincheck on our date tonight?

No! I've been dying to go to Momou all week!!

The new fusion restaurant in St. Louis?

Cuisine's not all we're going to fuse. 😜

The best feature of texting—no one can hear you groan.

Meet you there at seven.

👍👍👍 CU then!

He slid the phone across the counter and, setting out mugs and glasses at the beverage station in the dining room, practiced imaginary texts.

This isn't working, Pamela.

You're a nice woman but something is missing.

And the old standby,

It's not you, it's me.

Most of the women he'd dated and slept with post-Athena were conveniently—expressly—antidrama. Calm, sensible women who agreed right from the beginning they had no future together. Dissuading a persistent saleswoman like Pamela was going to be more of a challenge. When he had hinted marriage was not in his plans, she emailed him links to articles statistically proving bachelors suffered higher rates of illness and premature death.

At a rap on the window, Thorne turned and saw the usual breakfast crowd, plus a couple of faces he didn't recognize. "Grub's on. Grab your favorite seats," he said, letting them in.

Eugene Farragut, one of the regulars, dropped his gaunt body into a seat at the best table near the bay window. His sour disposition and all-around cussedness had recently sent his wife, Tildy, back to her hometown of Cleveland.

"Forty-three years of wedlock," he grumbled to the elderly couple sitting at the adjacent table, as if they'd been part of his mental conversation.

"Never heard of anyone going *back* to Cleveland, Eugene," the man said with a wink at his wife.

"You have now," Eugene snapped.

"Coffee?" Thorne asked him.

"Why the hell not? And one of those horn-shaped things if you've got 'em."

"I do." Thorne pointed to the chalkboard where he'd written the day's menu. "You may want to come back for lunch and try our Labor Day special." Holidays stretched longer and emptier when you were alone. He knew that as well as any lonely soul.

Eugene's narrow face puckered into prune folds as he squinted to read the menu. "Pulled pork? What do you take me for?"

"One cup of coffee and a croissant coming right up."

Joe Richter and Dan Kroger, best friends since they lost their wives to cancer two years ago, sat at the small table next to the stone hearth. Thorne handed them menus, though their breakfast never varied—coffee and orange juice, toasted whole wheat bagels with cream cheese, and whatever berry or fruit was in season.

"My Irene believed in a good breakfast," Dan said. With his pouchy eyes and cheeks and short, stout body, he resembled a basset hound.

"Most important meal of the day," Joe agreed. "Gentleman Joe," as everyone around town called him, carried his tall, big-boned body with a grace he attributed to years of ballroom dancing with his beloved Anna. Soft-spoken with a ready smile that lit his pensive face, he was Thorne's favorite customer.

"I opened a jar of homemade blueberry preserves," Thorne said, filling their mugs with coffee. "Can I interest you fellows with a dollop on the side of your bagels?"

"*Dollop!*" Dan said with a loud hoot. "You lived in a big city too long, young man."

"I reckon the ladies don't mind fancy words." Joe nodded toward the two young women at the table nearest the beverage station. Tall and as lithe as greyhounds in skintight workout clothes, they wore their hair in matching long ponytails. "They'd probably welcome a chance to date our athletic proprietor."

"You could have your pick hereabouts, Thorne," Dan said. "The law degree doesn't hurt either."

"I'm already dating someone."

"From around here?" Joe asked.

"No, she lives in St. Louis."

The city across the Mississippi River, twenty miles away,

was as local as he cared to get. The constant teasing about his love life as one of Laurel's few eligible males was harmless if occasionally annoying. Details of dates with him as the subject of town gossip would be intolerable though.

He scribbled the orders from a table of five husky thirty-something guys in John Deere caps and denim overalls, who were glancing surreptitiously at the two women. Ricki had called them her "bachelor farmers," advising Thorne to treat them especially well, their wallets being as generous as their appetites.

"Any news from Ricki?" one of them asked him.

"Not lately."

"South America this time," another one remarked, shaking his head. "Glad no one ever broke *my* heart."

The farmer sitting next to him poked his burly chest. "Like a woman can get to it."

"Or any other body part," another one joked.

"Hey, there's nothing wrong with my man parts."

"To a hog, maybe. Or a cow."

"Now hold on just a dang min—"

"What say we put him out to stud, fellas?"

The beleaguered farmer grinned. "Out to stud. Yesiree, *now* you're talking my language."

When they all laughed loudly, the two women looked over. As quick as a gasp, they hid their red faces behind their menus. Suppressing a smile, Thorne filled bowls with blackberries for Joe and Dan and brought a loaf of pumpernickel bread with a crock of butter to the table of senior-citizen mall walkers.

By the time he had put a third batch of corn muffins in the oven and served a complete turnover of customers, his morning fatigue had lifted. He was *in the zone*, working in a steady rhythm of greeting, preparing, and serving that beat the hell out of writing briefs any day. Replenishing the coffee at the beverage station, he scooped grounds from the Starbucks bag, measured precisely sixteen cups of water, and poured it slowly into the machine, careful not to spill one drop.

"Ah, the mad scientist in his laboratory."

Thorne whirled around, splashing water across the front of his shirt.

"Oops, sorry," Athena said, grinning.

"I didn't notice you come in."

"Preoccupied with serious matters?"

"The opposite. My mind's usually a blank by this time in the shift."

"Lucky you. I don't have the luxury of emptying my brain. Not for minimum wage anyway."

"You're forgetting tips." As he recalled from her time waitressing for Ricki, they were as bounteous as her figure. Or because of it.

"Still not enough. Until I write the book, I'm hostage to my gray matter."

"You always have been."

"Once a nerd, always a nerd—is that what you're trying to say? Huh?"

"Now wait... I didn't..."

She flashed another grin. "Chill, Thorne. I'm joking. Civil and professional, remember?"

"Yeah. I remember."

He snapped shut the lid of the coffee machine. Her pink blouse and brown skirt were made of the same silky material she had worn the day she inquired about the job. The dress that had swayed with every movement of her body. Every swing and sway and swoosh. He slammed the coffee machine lid again to be sure it was closed.

She gestured to the crowded dining room behind her. "Quite a fan club you've got here. I'm impressed."

"I'm proud to say I haven't lost any of Ricki's loyal customers. Not yet anyway."

"Don't worry," she said, making a zipper motion across her lips. "I won't scare anyone away."

"This I have to see. Thena holding her tongue."

A chastened look crossed her face. "People change," she mumbled.

"Apparently. You've never shown up anywhere an hour ahead of time."

She tucked an errant curl behind her ear. "My dad was rolling a ball back and forth to Branwell, and I couldn't watch anymore. Mostly because he dragged his belly across the floor to get it. The dog, I mean. Not my dad."

Memories of playing chess with Charles and laughing at *Seinfeld* with Finn tugged at Thorne's dormant affection for her family. Even Branwell would welcome him with a lick of his hand. A home-cooked meal was always waiting for him and Athena on their visits to Lydia after the Murphy divorce.

"How *is* your father?" he asked, following Athena to the kitchen. "I heard he retired, but I haven't seen him since I got here."

"Talk about change. He ditched his shlumpy clothes and dresses like an executive. Well, a junior executive. If he had smartened himself up sooner, he might have had a shot at an administrative position."

"But he loved teaching."

"His answer to my mother whenever she nagged him to 'aim higher.' "

Athena walked briskly behind the counter and grabbed an apron from the hook on the wall. The lily-of-the-valley scent of her perfume sent another pang of nostalgia—or some other pang—through him. He picked up a knife and started slicing the tomato on the cutting board. The rotten one he meant to throw away. "What's Finn up to these days?"

"Busy marketing another creative idea. Need a T-shirt affirming how gorgeous and brilliant you are? Not that I think you're... what I mean is..." she stammered.

Blushes rarely disturbed the warm olive tone of her skin, but her face bloomed suddenly. He pretended not to notice, chopping the tomato to within an inch of its departed life. "Finn's in business?"

And you think I'm gorgeous and brilliant?

"He prints shirts with the adjective you want to describe the ideal you," she explained, ripping open a box of five hundred–count paper napkins. "The word is backward so you can read it in the mirror and feel good about yourself. My brother, engineer-turned-psychologist."

"One academic discipline can lead to an altogether different one. I learned a lot about botany researching the master's thesis I had planned to write."

"'Shakespeare and the Language of Flowers,'" she murmured, citing its proposed title. "Too bad you never did."

He tossed the tomato into the garbage and sopped up its juice from the cutting board. "I did something better—protected intellectual property."

She pursed her mouth. That full, pouty mouth that no doubt wanted to protest, yet again, his career choice—if she hadn't promised to zip her lips. And he'd zip *his* and not compare her to her mother, Lydia, Charles's perpetually disappointed wife.

"That's not to say practicing law is nobler than teaching," he said.

"Of course, it isn't. It just pays better."

One of the practical reasons he'd offered to justify his decision to go to law school. But Athena didn't make an impassioned speech this time about money not buying happiness. Expressed no recriminations about his "slavish devotion to the Kent way."

"I better get out there," was all she said.

Thorne split open the other box of napkins on the counter. "The pork and salads will be ready in half an hour."

"All right." She lifted the apron over her head and tied it around her waist. "Look at us. Slinging hash instead of invectives."

"Look at us. Being calm and sensible."

"Like I told you," she said with a sharp glint in her eye, "people change."

He tried not to look at the contour of her breasts beneath the snug apron. Because some things never change.

"The breakfast crowd is winding down," he said. "You might want to ask whoever's lingering if they want more coffee."

"Will do." And Athena sashayed out of the kitchen, leaving her sweet lily scent behind.

"Not. Bad. At. All," Thorne said to the rhythm of his knife chopping an onion. He stirred mayonnaise into the potato salad, added celery seed to the coleslaw, and heated the pork. "This. Just. Might. Work."

Athena had kept her cool.

He had kept *his* cool.

She had nipped a difficult subject in the bud.

He had followed her cue.

She needed a job.

He needed a waitress.

They both, apparently, needed napkins.

And it didn't mean a damn thing that the lily of the valley, in the language of flowers, meant *the return of happiness.*

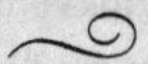

By noon, the dining room was filled to capacity. Athena was a blur, rushing into the kitchen to unload a tray of dirty dishes and weaving in and out of tables, a coffeepot in one hand, a notepad in the other. Kristie was competent and well-liked, but Thorne detected a different energy in the air today. Conversations were livelier, for one thing, thanks to Athena asking patrons their opinion of books and movies. And as their tongues loosened so did their belts, sparing today's special the indignity of becoming leftovers.

When he heard the booming voice of Bernie Benson, he looked out the kitchen door. The new mayor's ambitions for small-town Laurel were as oversize as his tall, portly body. He laughed at something Athena said while the city councilman, whose name Thorne never remembered, peered at her behind wire-rimmed glasses.

Thorne approached their table, his hand extended. A little ass-kissing with the powers that be was in order. Distasteful but, he reminded himself, all for a good cause. "Enjoying your day off, Mr. Benson?" he asked as they shook hands.

"I certainly am," the mayor said with an appreciative glance at Athena, who left to serve a table of teenagers. "Nothing like a little sass to go with a sandwich, eh, Childers?"

"I'd say we got a *lot* of sass," Childers replied.

Thorne made a mental note to memorize the councilman's last name. And to ask Athena if she'd mind cutting down on the wisecracks.

"We need more of her age demographic in this town," Childers said, shifting his bony frame in the chair. "The thirty-somethings simply don't stay."

Mayor Benson pushed his plate aside. His round, shiny

face struggled to replace joviality with gravity. "Right on the money, Childers. We have to find ways to attract young people to Laurel and keep them here."

"Creating jobs is one solution," Thorne said. "Health care facilities, for instance, are excellent sources of employment."

"Berryman Memorial Hospital is two counties over. Don't need another one here," the mayor groused.

"But there isn't an assisted living facility, mental health clinic, or urgent care center to serve the community's needs."

"The good citizens of Laurel have done just fine with Berryman."

"The good citizens of Laurel deserve better."

"Costs money."

"Creates jobs."

They'd batted this topic like a Ping-Pong ball ever since Thorne first presented his proposal at the Breakfast with the Mayor event last month. *Patience and persistence*, he told himself. *Diplomacy.*

Athena stopped at their table again. "More corn muffins, gentlemen? Baked fresh by the innkeeper himself."

"Put Miss Sass on a billboard," Mayor Benson said with a wink. "We won't have any trouble attracting people to our town. No matter *what* their age."

Screw diplomacy. The hell with kissing ass.

"I would ask you to treat Miss Murphy with respect," Thorne said sternly.

The mayor's grin faded, and he made a quick survey of the room. Thorne had spoken in too low a voice to be overheard by anyone but Childers—and Athena. Her eyebrows were arched in amazement as she stared at him.

Childers's pale face turned even paler. "The mayor didn't mean—"

"No. Kent is right," the mayor said gruffly. "I was out of

line." He rose and bowed slightly toward Athena. "My apologies, Miss Murphy."

"Apology accepted."

Slapping a few bills on the table, he beckoned to Childers and, with a brusque "Good day, Kent," walked away.

Damn. If the mayor was on the defensive, he'd avoid the café altogether. Steer clear of Thorne and his good cause.

Athena nudged his arm. "Gee, I didn't think you cared."

"I don't tolerate disrespectful behavior in my café."

"You realize you may never see them in here again. And possibly their cronies."

"Good riddance." He watched as the two men stopped to shake hands and chat with the other patrons on their way out. All wasn't lost. The mayor needed As You Like It Café for his politicking purposes as much as Thorne needed him for *his* purpose. Benson would be back.

"And you were worried *I* would alienate customers," she said, grinning.

"Strictly speaking, it *is* your fault, Miss Sass."

"Nice try, Mr. Kent. Just so you know, I've mastered the art of spilling drinks on laps. Accidentally, of course."

"Guess I came to the mayor's rescue in the nick of time."

"And mine."

Civilized, professional, with a touch of friendly banter. They were a lot better at this than he expected.

Athena pointed to the table of teenagers. "Nice group of kids. They've put a rock and roll band together and asked if they could have a gig here."

"Tell them I appreciate it, but no thanks. Between you and me, I don't want my customers popping antacids. Or the senior citizens turning off their hearing aids."

"Renaissance music would be more appropriate to your Tudor theme. If you can find someone who plays it."

"Light entertainment a few days a week isn't a bad idea. I'll advertise at the college." He turned to walk away but she stopped him. The hairs on his arm rose at her light touch.

"Thanks, Thorne, for... um..." She made what she used to call her "dorkorama face"—crossed eyes, scrunched nose, puckered lips. "For defending my honor."

He mumbled something in reply; he had no idea what. Because that face was still incredibly adorable.

One of the teenagers waved his empty glass in the air. "Miss? Can I get more orange juice?"

"Coming right up," she called out.

"Yoo-hoo! Athena!" a woman in a Laurel Garden Club T-shirt called out.

"Be right there, hon."

The door opened, and three women carrying shopping bags from Suzie's Seconds, a consignment store across the street, entered.

"I can stick around if you need help, Thena," Thorne offered.

"No, it's okay. I've got this."

"I'll come back down later and show you how to close."

"Okey dokey, artichokey."

He should go upstairs and resume work on his laptop. Or treat himself to a long shower. A long, cold one. He should do anything but stand there watching Athena sprinkle her special combination of sugar and spice all over his café.

The crash of the laptop hitting the floor woke Thorne with a jolt. The angle of sunlight slashing the living room wall meant it was late afternoon. He shot up from the sofa, rubbing his bleary eyes. He had to get back down to the café and clean the coffee machine, start a dishwasher load, wash aprons and towels, and refrigerate the perishables. As he tucked his shirt into his pants, trying to decide which pastry to bake tomorrow, the door buzzer sounded.

"It's me," Athena said on the intercom.

"Okay," he replied, pressing the button to let her in. He watched from the landing as she climbed the stairs from the building's back entrance to the second floor. "Sorry if you waited for me to close. I'll be right down."

"Don't bother. Everything's cleaned and refrigerated. I closed for Ricki lots of times."

"Did you refill the salt and pepper shakers? Kristie always forgets."

"Uh-huh."

"And bolt the top lock on the front door?"

"Yep. All you have to do is the laundry." She looked over his shoulder into his apartment. "Is this a bad time?"

"Not at all." At the thought of his date with Pamela later, his head began to throb.

"Can I come in for a sec?"

"Be it ever so humble." Thorne stepped aside with a flourish. "Laurel's version of a penthouse."

Her eyes registered surprise as she looked around. The apartments he'd rented as a student were luxurious in comparison. "Boy, *this* is a switch," Athena said.

"It's cheap, the café's downstairs, and I don't have to worry about noise from an apartment above."

"Did any of the new property listings interest you?"

"Nope. Not a one."

"I hope my mother isn't losing her touch."

"No, she's great. I have special requirements, though, which make the search a challenge."

"Like?"

"Like an affordable lot to build on or a house with separate living quarters. In case... uh... if my mother ever has to live with me. She's been dividing her time between condos in St. Louis and Jacksonville, Florida, since last winter. My aunt and uncle are down there. But a time may come when she can't manage on her own."

"You might need to expand your radius beyond Laurel."

"Lydia said the same thing. But I'm not ready to..." He was going to say *compromise* but caught himself in time. "I'm not in a hurry."

"Can't rush major decisions," she said agreeably.

Quite a few curls had come loose from Athena's bun, and a blouse button, right above her waist, was missing. He pictured her slowly unbuttoning the rest, letting the blouse fall off her shoulders, and lifting one long leg, and then another, out of her skirt. Those sexy ankle boots could stay on. Until he eased them off her feet, inch by inch. He wouldn't be in a hurry.

He cleared his throat—and his mind of its striptease. "Did you have a question?"

"A favor to ask." She reached up to smooth the hair on the left side of his head. "You've got a serious bedhead thing going on."

"I took a nap." Complete with sex dreams he apparently hadn't woken from.

"I'm ready to hit the hay myself." She raised her arm to cover a yawn, revealing a bit of pink skin at the gaping buttonhole. Blood rushed to his face—and another place—at the image of her falling, falling, falling into his bed.

Thorne braced himself against the back of the sofa. "What favor did you have in mind?"

"I want to pick your brain about intellectual property law. Specifically, how far I can legally pursue and reveal Garland's identity."

"How far do you intend to go?"

"No rock unturned. No possibility unexplored."

A strategy that included coming up to his apartment smelling of lilies, touching his hair, and gazing at him with those big brown eyes.

He was wide awake now.

He mentally slipped her skirt and shoes back on and buttoned her blouse.

"Some rocks can't be budged," he said.

"I figured. Which is why I'm asking for your legal advice. And to keep your ear to the ground."

"I don't follow."

"If you hear people talk about Garland in the café, let me know what they say."

"I've never heard her mentioned."

"You go to meetings for local businesses, like my mother, don't you? Rotary Club, Chamber of Commerce, that sort of thing?"

"Occasionally."

"The subject of a bestselling author living here doesn't come up?"

"If it does, I haven't gotten wind of it."

She tapped her chin, frowning in concentration. "Garland has loads of money. Money always leaves a trail. The manager of the Laurel Bank may know who she is."

"She doesn't necessarily use a local bank."

"It's worth checking out though."

"Client confidentiality."

"She's got to have a lawyer. Somewhere. You can help me find him or her."

"I don't practice law anymore. I'm done with it all."

"Yeah, but it's not as if you've erased years of legal connections from your life."

"No. But I believe writers' privacy and property should be respected. Their protection is what I dedicated my career to."

Athena stepped back with a puzzled look on her face. "You don't want to help me, do you?"

"Isn't it obvious?"

"Why the hell not?"

"You're in way over your head. And, frankly, I think writing about an author who bastardizes literature is beneath you."

"I forgot. You're the elitist who thinks literature is spelled with a capital *L*."

He'd once penned an impassioned letter to the university newspaper decrying the "dumbing down" of American culture. A letter she'd proofread for him.

"You used to agree with me, Thena."

"I can't afford to be a purist. The LitWit series is a gold mine, and I'm tapping into it."

"Fool's gold," he countered.

"I didn't come here to debate." She shifted her handbag to her other shoulder with a weary sigh. "All I'm asking is for you to point me in the right direction and keep your eyes and ears open."

"No can do."

"Why not?"

"It doesn't sit right with me."

Her eyes narrowed. "If you removed the poker from your butt, it would sit just fine."

"If you had thought this through before you took on the project, you wouldn't be in this predicament."

Her face darkened. Any minute another button might pop from her blouse. "You can't begin to comprehend what's at stake here," she said in a near-whisper.

"Not my concern."

"The hell it isn't." Her lower lip quivered. "You owe me one, Thorne. After Seattle."

A car's brakes screeched from the street below. A collision averted. But *he* wouldn't be as lucky. He drove straight on. "The way I see it, you owed *me* one, Thena. I simply evened the score."

Athena tilted her head and regarded him with a mixture of hurt and surprise. "Wow. I didn't see *that* coming."

He would have preferred that she slam the door instead of pulling it gently closed behind her. Opening the refrigerator, he grabbed a can of beer and gulped six mouthfuls without stopping. Sure, one reason he refused her request in Seattle was because she'd turned down his marriage proposal seven years before. What guy wouldn't want to get even? She had shoved the diamond engagement ring back in his hand and told him to "stick it where the moon don't shine." All because he "copped out"—her other memorable words—and went to law school.

They could have made it work. They could have met each other halfway emotionally *and* geographically. But Athena never did anything halfway. And dammit to hell if her uncompromising spirit wasn't one of the things he loved about her.

Used to love about her.

Thorne threw back his head and guzzled the rest of the beer. The photograph of him and his dad on the end table caught his eye. It was taken years ago on a sailing trip when he was in college. Years before he knew the truth about his father, the truth that gave him no choice but to refuse Athena in Seattle. To let their relationship sizzle and burn and die the second time around.

He examined the photograph. The sun shone on their faces. The ocean gust barely stirred the thick, wavy hair that had been passed down through generations of Kents. Thorne's face was open and innocent, his body strong and athletic. As strong as it would need to be. For his father's arm, draped casually over his shoulder, had turned out to be a heavy burden indeed.

CHAPTER FIVE

Youth is gone—gone—-and will never come back: can't help it.

—CHARLOTTE BRONTË, LETTER TO ELLEN NUSSEY, APRIL 22, 1848

Athena groaned as she bent to touch her toes for her pre-run warm-up Thursday morning. "No pain, no gain, eh, bud?"

Branwell shifted in the armchair with a frown until he was turned completely away from her, settling in for a nap. Considering her achy muscles, she was tempted to do the same. Her feet weren't doing much better. Two waitress shifts in ankle boots and she was ready to sacrifice style for comfort. And give in to Thorne's advice to wear practical shoes.

She cocked her head to better hear her father singing in the shower. It was the same song he had whistled as he'd buttered his toast at breakfast. A Broadway show tune from his vintage album collection, most likely.

"Whaddya think?" she asked Branwell. "*The King and I* or *Carousel*?"

He replied with a grunt from a questionable part of his body.

Stretching on the porch, she breathed deeply of the crisp fresh air and waved to the elderly Marino couple next door, chatting in their rocking chairs. Two days of rain had lifted the dome of oppressive heat. Typically, cooler weather would appear in fits and starts until late September. Winter was too far off to worry if she'd brought enough warm clothes. In any case, she'd be out of here well before December thirty-first, Dr. Davenport's deadline.

Wouldn't she? Sure, she would. Even if conversations about the LitWit series she had initiated in the café yesterday had meandered in the direction of gossip. Like the steamy affair between Miss Nugent, the high school guidance counselor, and Mr. Stine, the married history teacher. And the expanding waistline of Ursula Moore, the unmarried city clerk.

Even if Thorne had flat out refused to help her.

"Thanks for nothing," she muttered, jogging down the street.

Nothing but negativity wrapped up in a sniffy attitude. Like she gave a shit that he thought the Garland project was beneath her. Which, maybe it was. A little. But she didn't have the luxury to be high-minded. Not when her career was at stake.

Athena broke into a brisk run, thankful for the thunder- and lightning-free sky and for the early-morning quiet with only birdsong to intrude on her thoughts. She needed a clear head to strategize and think the project through—as Thorne had pointed out she'd failed to do.

"Come out, Garland," she said between panting breaths. "Come out from wherever you are."

Dollars to doughnuts, somewhere in Laurel, at this very hour, the author was writing. She featured morning settings in many of her books, describing "the dew of morn" and "the sun-kissed dawn." Sex before breakfast was a signature Garland scene too, the country squire asking the milkmaid, "Got milk, fair maiden?" And she replying, "Got wood, kind sir?"

Slim clues at best. C. L. Garland was a needle in Laurel's

haystack, someone who had disguised her wit and literary daring so effectively that, when Athena finally uncovered her identity, she wasn't sure if she'd hug her or hit her upside the head.

She'd longed to befriend another kindred spirit besides Finn when she was growing up. As close as she and her brother were, she had craved the special bond of a sister. Someone to share the experience of the first period, first date, first kiss. Doing her homework in the kitchen, she would sometimes imagine she was sitting around a lamplit table in the Haworth Parsonage with Emily, Charlotte, and Anne Brontë. They'd read to each other and spin tales of their imaginary worlds, Glass Town and Gondal. Athena wouldn't have the patience to write in minuscule script in miniature books like they did, but that would be okay. She'd make them laugh with her wicked imitations of the curate. They'd bemoan Branwell's dissolute life, take their dog Keeper for walks, and brush each other's hair before bed.

In her fantasies, Athena would leave out the part where Emily yells at her to leave her alone already. Doesn't she know by now she'd rather wander the moors by herself? And Emily and Anne dying tragically young of consumption and Charlotte from complications of pregnancy.

The Brontë sisters aren't really dead anyway, Athena thought as she passed houses as silent as tombs. *They live forever in their books.*

"If it isn't Thena Murphy."

Athena stumbled and nearly pitched forward, startled by Thorne jogging next to her. "Where the hell did *you* come from?"

"Is that an existential question?"

"If you want it to be."

"I don't. Wondering where I'm *going* keeps me up nights."

"I'm too busy to worry either way."

"Life's an everlasting quest, Thena."

"Life's a pain in the kahoonies, Thorne."

The lively gleam he used to get when they verbally sparred shone in his eyes. He was breathing heavily, his sweaty T-shirt clinging to his muscular chest, smelling so...so Thorne. Ivory soap–clean with a hint of fresh rain in a forest. A scent that aroused anything but clean thoughts.

And a few resentful ones.

"You're pretty far from your apartment," she said. Instead of, *One stinking favor. Was that too much to ask?*

"First cool weather in ages, thought I'd put the mileage in. And Lydia told me to check out a house for sale on this block. The couple is divorcing, and I might be able to negotiate a reasonable price."

"She must mean the O'Neal place." Athena pointed to the rundown Victorian directly ahead with a *Laurel Realty* sign on the lawn.

"I'd rather not buy a fixer-upper," he said, "but Lydia encouraged me to keep an open mind."

Her mother? An open mind?

"I'm not surprised the O'Neals are calling it quits," she said. "They used to throw food at each other whenever they fought. I think my mother took a few pointers."

Pete and Geraldine O'Neal's arguments were legendary in Laurel. They'd last for days, often spilling out into the street, to the entertainment of the neighbors. Though their fury never escalated beyond hurling bread rolls or slabs of raw steak at each other, everyone agreed it was a mercy they were childless.

"Food throwing, huh?" A smile came and went across Thorne's lips. "Good thing I stayed away from the café yesterday."

"I never threw anything at you. Why would I start now?"

"I assumed you'd be hopping mad about what happened in my apartment Monday."

"I should be. You didn't consider my request for one lousy minute."

"Sure, I did. And I decided not to give you what you wanted."

"S'okay. You gave me something else."

"Another reason to piss you off?"

"A reason for why you were such a jerk in Seattle. Your candor is much appreciated."

He fixed her with a piercing look. "We always *were* honest with each other, Thena. We had that much going for us at least."

"Honest enough to admit you won't help me because you're still hurt I wouldn't marry you?"

"Something like that."

Seven years they'd maintained *civilized contact*, and all the while his heart, apparently, had been as bruised as ever. The kind of smoldering, eternal passion worthy of a literary hero.

"I'll put this out there," Athena said. "Any chance you'd reconsider advising me?"

A lock of hair fell over his forehead when he shook his head. The shoelace on one of his sneakers was loose, reminding her of the nineteen-year-old boy she'd fallen in love with.

"No problem," she said airily. "I have other irons in the fire." And the sublime satisfaction that he wasn't completely over her.

"Are you coming to the café tomorrow?" Thorne asked.

"I made a bucketload of tips Wednesday. What do you think?"

"And no hard feelings?"

"Are you kidding? Hard feelings are what we do best."

As they walked past the O'Neal house, a window in the room to the left of the door creaked open. A woman sat in front of a computer eating an apple, her patrician face with its long nose, high cheekbones, and hooded eyes illuminated in its glow. Athena recognized the cloud of hair in an instant—Geraldine. Her hair had turned white in her early thirties, a horror for most women. But she carried it off with the elegant aloofness she did everything, except her marital spats, and Athena admired her for it. And for the fact that, no matter how public her marriage, the rest of her life was utterly private.

"Is she Mrs. O'Neal?" Thorne whispered as if afraid to provoke an airborne apple.

"Yes. That's Geraldine."

"Lydia told me she wants to make a quick deal. The house holds too many memories."

"As if you can move away from memories."

Open mouth. Insert foot. What else was new?

"The property does have charm," he said. "I'll make an appointment to see it. Till tomorrow then?"

"Yeah. Tomorrow. And tie your shoe."

Thorne bent to tie his shoelace and then waved goodbye with what may or may not have been a wistful look in his spring-green eyes. Athena watched his loping stride until he disappeared around the corner. When she had told him about Finn's T-shirts and blurted out he was "gorgeous and brilliant," he'd pretended he hadn't heard. Just now he'd glossed over her comment about moving away from memories—in both instances to spare her embarrassment. When it came to EQ, he put her to shame.

You make it awfully hard to hate you, Thorne. And why do you look as young as the day I met you?

And then it hit her. "Younger Than Springtime" from *South Pacific* was the song her father had been singing in the shower.

"Older than dirt, am I," she sang, jogging in the opposite direction from Thorne—literally *and* figuratively. She didn't need his help at all. If anything, he'd be too much of a distraction. Their old friend Quentin Scott would do. She could always count on Quentin in a pinch.

After her run, Athena settled into an armchair by the front window, scrolling her phone contact list for Quentin's number. With a selection of comfortable sofas and armchairs to park her fanny and books tumbling from every available surface, the living room was her favorite room in the house. The visual clutter reminded her of the Where's Waldo books. If her father were in there, he'd be hard to spot amidst the paisley upholstery, flowered wallpaper, and area rug splashed with a brightly colored geometric pattern. Lydia would introduce a new interior design style without discarding the previous one until she was sure she was satisfied. Thanks to her perpetual state of dissatisfaction, she'd left them in a William Morris–meets–Piet Mondrian limbo.

Charles appeared in the foyer dressed in a navy-blue tracksuit.

"Top of the morning, Dad."

"Carpe diem, my goddess."

"What are your plans for *seizing the day*?"

"A walk with the dog, for starters." The leash stretched behind him, taut from Branwell's refusal to budge. "Come on, boy. Let's get moving."

Branwell got up to snatch the dog biscuit from his hand and then plopped on the floor again.

"Where'd you get your outfit? You look great," Athena said. The Charles in workout clothes—Finn would never believe this. She snapped a photo without her father noticing.

"A sporting goods store," he said. "I'd never been in one before. Why are there so many varieties of sneakers?"

"A different style for each sport. The tracksuit makes you look buff, by the way."

"Good. I'm trying to drop a few pounds. Or thirty."

"New duds and exercise. Are you getting spiffed up to attract a girlfriend?"

His face flushed every color of red as he lined up a row of biscuits to the front door. "The romance ship has sailed for me, Athena. Unlike your mother, whose sails still billow in the wind."

Dating most of the eligible men within a fifty-mile radius of Laurel since her divorce was, like buying Girl Scout cookies, Lydia's contribution to "community relations."

When her father finally lured Branwell out the door, Athena texted the photo of him to Finn with the caption *The Charles 2.0.* Her brother's Charles L. Garland theory might not be as far-fetched as it sounded. Their father's odd comings and goings were certainly open to suspicion. And the attention to his appearance might be due to his self-assurance as a publishing success. Finn's idea was a rock she couldn't leave unturned. But first things first.

Quentin answered her call after seven rings. "Uh . . . hullo?"

"Rise and shine, camper."

"Oh, hi, Murph."

"Did I wake you?"

"I think so," he said groggily.

"Aren't you supposed to be at work?" It was eight a.m. in Seattle, a time most lawyers were already at their desks.

She heard a thud and "Crap," and then heavy breathing.

"Sorry. Dropped the phone," he mumbled. "Shit. I'm supposed to be in court by eleven. Good thing you woke me up."

"I can call back Saturday."

"Hell, no. It's great to hear from ya, Murph. I miss you."

"I miss you too, you big lug."

Athena, Thorne, and Quentin had been best friends since they met in a Shakespeare seminar sophomore year. Quentin was Falstaff to Thorne's Prince Hal, both on stage for the student production of *Henry IV* and off. Burly, boisterous, and big-hearted, Quentin was fond of saying he was "in my cups," and he usually was. It didn't hinder him from acing the LSATs and going to law school with Thorne. While he may have been ungainly physically, he maintained a graceful balance, staying friends with them both after their breakup.

"Has Thorne filled you in since the last time we talked?" Athena asked.

"You and him in the café. Your book. His house search. Hey, sorry I didn't tell you he moved back to the Midwest. It was one of those *in the vault* things. And you were bound to run into each other eventually."

"I totally get the vault." It worked both ways. Thorne must have kept their awful weekend in Seattle a secret because she never detected a hint of it in her conversations with Quentin.

"You calling about Robin?" he asked.

Her heart skipped a beat. Robin, the girl Thorne left behind in Seattle? Or the girl he returned to the Midwest for? Most likely a wealthy one-percenter like him, with a brother named Chad and a trust fund. "Is she Thorne's latest inamorata?"

"Uh...He didn't mention...? Whoa, wait a minute. Coffee. Must have coffee."

"Take your time."

"I'd rather not...uh...I don't want to talk about...um..."

"Robin."

"The thing is, Murph, it's...complicated. I'm talking all kinds of serious shit."

"Like what?"

"Like...uh. Shit. I ran out of coffee filters."

"Use a paper towel."

"Can you hold? Gotta see if I...uh...have any."

"Are you there?" Athena asked after a few minutes. Just how long did it take to look for paper towels?

"Yeah, I'm back. What were we talking about?"

"Never mind. Forget it." She'd get the details out of him one of these days. If Quentin got deep enough in his cups, he didn't just spill the beans, he cooked and served them.

That is, if she even wanted to know about this complicated Robin person Thorne was in all kinds of serious shit with.

"I won't keep you," she said. "I called to ask a favor. You're a criminal defense lawyer, and—"

"A fucking brilliant criminal defense lawyer," he said over the sound of running water.

"The best. So, if you could—"

"Jeez, Murph. You haven't killed anyone, have you?"

"Not yet. I need to consult an intellectual property lawyer about the book I'm writing. If you connected me to a good one, I'd owe you big time. I asked Thorne, but he doesn't want anything to do with the legal profession anymore."

"Thank you, Graham Kent," he mumbled.

He really *was* suffering from caffeine deprivation. Thorne's father was why he became a lawyer in the first place.

"Can you recommend anyone?" she asked. "If they don't charge exorbitant rates, all the better."

Another long silence followed, filled only with the tinkle of a spoon stirring in a cup.

"Quentin?"

"Yeah. Got it. Lawyer recommendation. I'll see what I can do."

"Intellectual property, not murder."

"Hey, I was joking."

"So was I. I think. You ought to come out here. We can go to the WashU campus and revisit our old haunts."

He whistled. "Murph and Thorne reunited in the same latitude and longitude. I never thought I'd see the day."

"We haven't reunited. We're just..." She searched for a term as noncommittal as Gwyneth Paltrow's "conscious uncoupling." Like "unconscious coupling." But that only covered *her* side of the story. Unless she disturbed Thorne's sleep too. "We're employer and employee."

Quentin convulsed into one of his heartiest Falstaffian laughs. "Thorne, your boss! That'll be the day!"

Friday morning, Athena drove to work with as much cheer as the overcast, muggy day allowed. Singing "You Raise Me Up" with Josh Groban helped, as did wearing comfortable footwear. She'd found an old pair of her mother's librarian shoes in the basement, soft-soled oxfords like the kind Miss Marple wore. Perfect for sleuthing. Lydia had quit her job as a reference librarian the same year she quit her marriage, jettisoning a career and husband without a backward glance.

Though she was in college at the time, Athena felt as though she'd lost her special status as the daughter of a librarian. The day she got her first Laurel Public Library card, Lydia let her sit at the reference desk and help her assist patrons. She was allowed to wander the stacks, any time and for as long as she wanted, without adult supervision.

Checking out more books than the permitted limit was her and Lydia's little secret. Her mother didn't just walk away from her job. She'd walked away from Athena's best mother-daughter memories.

Belting out the fervent song lyrics with Groban about being strong, she turned onto the road that followed the perimeter of the expansive public park. Mist hung between the trees like cobwebs, and the crows and mourning doves seemed to float from branch to branch. Young women clustered around the jungle gym and swing set, watching toddlers play. Mothers, not babysitters, she guessed, observing how they leaned into each other like fellow soldiers in the trenches, exchanging tactics.

On the far side of the park, the eerily slow movements of a group of people caught her attention. Lifting her foot off the accelerator, she opened the window to get a better view. Tai chi in Laurel, Illinois. Would wonders never cease.

Athena rubbed her eyes at the sight of a familiar bald head. Her father, dressed in a black tracksuit with matching headband, had to be a hallucination. He would no more weave his heavyset body, chanting to himself, "I am a reed, I am a willow"—or whatever the heck—than she would.

At the loud beep of a car horn behind her, she pressed the gas pedal and drove away. Tai chi, impatient drivers, and the latest surprise—a huge aluminum abstract sculpture of what appeared to be a female nude where the Civil War cannon used to be. Laurel was certainly living up to the promise on its Main Street banners, proclaiming *Past, Present, Progress* in bold red letters. Thorne might have been onto something settling here.

"Boy, am I glad you came in early," Kristie exclaimed when Athena entered As You Like It Café. "I've been swamped all morning. And nearly everybody wanted sandwiches for breakfast. I think somebody posted pictures of Thorne's latest creation on Facebook."

Athena checked the chalkboard for the day's special. Lamb carpaccio, roasted red peppers, Kalamata olives, and baby arugula paninis he'd named The Grecian. An amusing homage to her or a lopsided apology? Either one would do.

Hurrying into her apron, she replenished the coffee machine. "Is Thorne here?" she asked Kristie. Her first order of business at every shift—get a bead on his whereabouts. Her second was to survey the room for anyone remotely resembling a writer. Nope. Not a laptop or haunted expression in sight.

"Thorne had errands to run," Kristie said. "Hey, he mentioned you've been friends since college. Us too. Ian and I met at the University of Illinois."

Lucky for them. They made it to *us*.

"My brother graduated from U of I," Athena said, organizing the tea selections. "I'm curious. How'd the subject of me and Thorne come up?"

"I overheard him talking about Washington University to Joe and Dan, and I remembered you saying you went there. So, I asked if you two knew each other then."

"Yep. Thorne and I go way back. Ancient history."

But not so long ago, she'd forgotten how inseparable they had been, from the day they met to the day they broke up. Like Catherine and Heathcliff, even after her brother, Hindley, banished Heathcliff from the house when their father died. Emily Brontë's depiction of their youthful attachment was as affecting as ever. This reading though, the English professor in her was a little impatient with Emily's overuse of names beginning with the letter *H*.

She wiped the beverage counter clean as Kristie described how lucky she was to have moved to the Midwest for college.

"People are so nice here. And I'd never have met Ian, who is the world's kindest guy," she said. "I do miss my family in Denver though."

"Is Ian's job keeping you here?"

"Uh-huh. When I resume my career in hospital administration, I'll be able to find work anywhere. But I'm sure you know how hard it is to get a faculty position, especially in English."

"I sure do." To get one—and keep one.

Athena took orders, prepared sandwiches, and refilled mugs of coffee, her shoulders slumped with a vague sense of defeat. *Find Garland, write the book, save your job*, she repeated to herself.

Her pep talk was soon rewarded by the sight of the two super-fit women who always came to the café in workout clothes, leafing through a book. She'd recognize the cover anywhere—a volume number in the upper-right-hand corner, and the words *The LitWit Series* superimposed on a purple velvet curtain, lifted to reveal the soft-focus image of a naked embracing couple.

She drew closer to their table, waiting for the opportune moment to discuss Garland and the novellas and get her project rolling.

If only they weren't laughing so hard that their long ponytails swayed behind their heads.

"Would you believe this crap gets published?" one of them said. "Three books a year, no less."

"Rubbish. Absolute rubbish," the other one said. Her British accent had the unfortunate effect on Athena of conveying authority.

" 'And then the Scarlet Pimpernel plucked his lady's petals, one by one.' "

"Bloody hell. That's bloody awful."

If only they'd shut up.

Athena slunk away, her vague sense of defeat having blossomed into humiliation at their assessment of the LitWit series.

"Athena Murphy, as I live and breathe," a woman called out as she passed her table.

Athena waved meekly while Nora Johnson examined her from behind reading glasses.

"Look at you, all grown up," Nora said. "How long's it been?"

"Years."

Twelve, to be exact, since Nora's husband, Vic, and Athena's mother, Lydia, had an affair and combusted their marriages.

"Feels like yesterday," Nora said.

Her red, spiky hair was streaked with silver, her skin lined, but the glare of her amber eyes could still burn the clothes right off her opponent's body—a glare seared into Athena's brain ever since Nora marched up to the Murphy house and gave Lydia a piece of her mind—and her right hook.

"How have you been, Mrs. Johnson?"

"I can't complain. The way I see it, most people are worse off than me."

Athena didn't want to ask but there was no way around it. "And how's your son?"

"Happily married to a young woman who appreciates him, thank you very much." Nora glanced at Athena's left hand. "No wedding ring, I see. Never got hitched, huh?"

"No," she replied glumly.

"Jimmy won't be surprised."

Worn down by his begging, Athena reluctantly went to the high school senior prom with Jimmy. He was the star of the football team, as he reminded her all evening. After constant chatter about "interception" and "the end zone," she couldn't take it anymore. Faking menstrual cramps, complete with moans and abdomen clutching, she called her father to pick her up.

Her excuse didn't fool Nora one bit. And while she was spared more dates with Jimmy, Athena had to endure his mother's frequent references to "Aunt Flo" and "women's trouble."

"You resemble Lydia to a tee," Nora remarked. *Floozy* and *hussy* were written in the cartoon cloud above her head.

"Everyone says so," Athena said.

"I haven't seen you in my store since the shit hit the fan."

"No, I guess not."

Another casualty of the Lydia-Vic affair was having to boycott Go Figure, Nora's bra specialty shop. A curious occupation for a woman whose own chest was ballerina flat. But as Nora liked to say, "Somebody's got to fit all these busty gals in the Midwest."

She eyed Athena's breasts. "You're looking a little droopy. Come by anytime. I've got a shipment of underwire bras just in. And sensible panties for those days when Aunt Flo visits."

Considering the state of her sex life—as dead as Dickinson—Athena might as well wear granny panties.

Kristie placed a dish in front of Nora. "One Grecian without olives as you requested," she said, hurrying away like she had to catch a bus.

Athena pulled a pen and notepad from her apron pocket. "It was nice to see you, Mrs. Johnson, but I have to get to work."

Nora peeked inside the panini as if she expected a frog to leap out. "I'm not done talking."

"Um... sorry. I—"

"Your mother dodged a bullet when she dumped Vic. The

divorce was a blessing to me too. The simpleton travels the country in an RV, impersonating Elvis at music festivals. What are you up to these days?"

I'm impersonating a professor with a secure future.

I'm impersonating an author of a best seller I haven't written a word of yet.

I'm impersonating someone who wants to hear what you have to say.

Hearing more laughter from the bloody awful critics—wouldn't she just love to yank their ponytails till they yelped?—Athena lifted her chin and squared her shoulders. Not *everyone* thought the LitWit series was rubbish. Hello? Best-seller lists? And why should she skulk around as if she were ashamed of her project? It's not as if being discreet had gotten her anywhere. It was time to ditch the spy caper—*no fun at all, Finn*—and ask people straight up about C. L. Garland. Starting with Nora, since she wasn't done talking.

"Wouldn't know the woman if I fell over her," Nora said after Athena briefly described her book.

"Is it possible any of your Go Figure clients do?"

"Wouldn't tell you if they did. If Garland wants her life to stay private, more power to her," said the woman whose husband's affair had publicly embarrassed everyone involved.

Nora dove into the panini with a gusto belied by her slender, petite build. "This is damn good. Better than anything Ricki ever made." Her visits to Ricki's Café had come to a screeching halt, since Ricki was best friends with the woman who had slept with her husband. The economics of a small town were as tangled as those of a small nation.

"Glad you like it, Mrs. Johnson," Athena said.

"Call me Nora. You don't have to address me like I'm a schoolmarm. You're no spring chicken yourself."

"It was nice to see you again, Nora." *You old biddy hen.*

Nora chuckled. "Aren't we a pair. Polite as can be. Like whenever I run into Lydia around town. The woman should get an Academy Award."

"Twelve years is a long time."

"Don't kid yourself, hon. It's a blink of an eye where love is concerned."

After Kristie left, Athena served a steady stream of customers. They ate, they lingered, and they ate some more, easing their way into the weekend. Forget jogging. Waitressing would keep her fit, provided she resisted Thorne's drool-worthy scones enticing her beneath the domed serving platter.

The door opened, and she braced herself for yet another patron, but the drool-worthy man himself entered. As she cleared a recently vacated table, she watched Thorne stroll around the room, greeting everyone with a warm smile. His loose-limbed, athletic movements were confident and unassuming at the same time. He flicked wavy hair from his forehead. He always did go too long between haircuts, relying on her to set up an appointment with a stylist. She'd recommend Venus de Stylo in Troy, a nearby town, if they weren't, as she'd told Kristie, ancient history.

Besides, she had more important things to do than think about how inseparable they used to be. Or remember the feel of Thorne's thick hair through her fingers. Like arranging the mugs and bowls on the hutch and filling the napkin dispenser. Adjusting her bra straps so she didn't droop.

She pushed the kitchen door open, letting it swing in a wide arc behind her. Placing a stack of glasses on the counter, she looked around with a sigh. The dishwasher had to be loaded, the towels folded, the knives...

"Hello, Thena."

...sharpened.

She turned to face Thorne, blowing a loose curl off her cheek. “Hey.”

“Kristie texted how busy it’s been. I have paperwork to do before I go out tonight, but I can close for you.”

So that Robin person was why he was dressed in a Ralph Lauren polo shirt and God-knows-who pants.

“Don’t bother. I can manage.” She pointed one foot toward his tasseled loafers. “I’m wearing practical shoes. And I wouldn’t want you to get your nice clothes dirty.”

“You sure?”

“Positive.”

“By the way, I saw the O’Neal property today. Unfortunately, the house needs too much work, and the lot isn’t big enough.”

His opinion, or the woman’s he’d taken to see the house? Robin Whoever.

“Did you meet Geraldine?” she asked.

“No. But Lydia says hi.” He tore a wad of paper towels from the roll and wiped a puddle of lemonade off the counter. “Let me at least load the dishwasher. You look dog-tired.”

Athena squinted at her reflection in the metal cabinet. Her hair was going every which way, and her face was sweaty, as if she’d run a marathon. Meanwhile, Robin Whoever was primped and preened and pretty as a picture, ready for her date. “Gee, just what every woman wants to hear. *You look like a dog.*”

“That’s not what I said.”

“But it’s what you meant.”

“Don’t twist my words around, Thena.”

She was hot, exhausted, and his loafers really pissed her off. For Pete’s sake—tassels? “I know what I heard.”

He threw the paper towels into the trash can. “It boggles the mind how you can turn an offer to help into an argument.”

"Guess I haven't lost my touch."

Thorne never did like to fight. But there was such a thing as being *too* reasonable. *Keep calm and drive your girlfriend crazy.*

"Is it your book?" he asked. "Is that what's bothering you? Or your job in California?"

She'd die before sharing the particulars of her career and its current status—in the toilet—with him. For whom she'd given up said career.

"My job's awesome, and my book's coming along fine and dandy. When I'm on task, I'm unstoppable."

And apparently annoying, according to the reaction of a few patrons to her questions. Admitting to their waitress that they'd heard of Garland or read erotic novellas was clearly not what they had in mind when they dropped into the café. Another detail she hadn't "thought through," to quote the man who planned everything.

Athena retrieved a jar of Dijon mustard from the refrigerator. "I called Quentin yesterday. We had a nice chat."

"Oh, yeah? What about?"

"Legal advice, for one thing. Since you didn't…cooperate." She twisted the lid of the jar but it wouldn't open. "Who's Robin?"

Thorne clenched his jaw, a flinty look in his eye. "What did that big mouth tell you?"

"Ooh, the plot thickens. First Quentin is all hush-hush about your mystery woman. And here *you* are getting all hot under the collar."

Patches of red colored his chiseled cheekbones. He tightened his lips into a firm line. "I most certainly am *not* getting hot under the collar. And there's no *plot*."

"Now I *am* intrigued. Thorne losing his cool. Who is she? How long have you been together?"

"What's with the third degree?"

"I figured she's your date tonight. Or the lover you left behind. Which is it?"

"What's it to you?" He shoved an open drawer closed. "Who'd *you* leave behind?"

So, Sergei did have his uses.

"As a matter of fact, my boyfriend—"

"How long have *you* been together?"

"Long enough."

"Are you in love?"

In love. Shit. He loved this Robin person. Quentin had hemmed and hawed because Thorne's bruised heart had healed and he *was* completely over her.

"My personal life is none of your business," she said.

"And mine is none of yours."

Athena hit the jar of mustard against the counter to loosen the lid, and it cracked.

"Losing your cool, Thena?"

"Now wait a minute. I'm the one who—"

But Thorne strode through the kitchen, to the dining room, and out the front door before she could figure out who should be mad at whom this time.

CHAPTER SIX

Thoughts are tyrants that return again
and again to torment us.

—EMILY BRONTË, *WUTHERING HEIGHTS*

Among life's pleasures, the purr of a BMW's engine was right up there with sex, Shakespeare, and freshly baked bread. Thorne maneuvered his sleek machine through highway traffic on the way to Pamela's apartment. In the distance, the Gateway Arch gleamed in the setting sun. The sky's vivid splashes of orange, red, and purple would change soon to dark blue and then to black.

He shifted gears, hearing his father say, "Everything fades in time, son. Beauty, passion, memory."

The hell it did.

Pamela never seemed to notice Thorne was distracted by memories of passion. Or by Athena's very real, very present beauty. She was satisfied, evidently, with their shared enthusiasm for food and his deference to her fashion sense. Tonight, like every other Saturday night, they would check out the latest new restaurant in the city, she'd rate it on a scale of one to ten, and they'd go back to her apartment and have sex. Which he rated a five, or if he'd bought another shirt or belt from Macy's, a six.

He muted the tenor's voice blasting from the car's speakers to answer his phone.

"Still pissed off at me, dude?" Quentin asked without any preliminaries. "It's been a week."

"Yep. Still pissed. Thanks to your big piehole, Athena knows about Robin."

"Sorry. She caught me post-beer and pre-coffee."

"You could have given me a heads-up after you talked to her. I was caught completely off guard."

"How do you think *I* felt? I had to play the bumbling idiot and say stupid shit like, 'It's complicated.' "

"Bumbling idiot isn't much of a stretch. Lucky for you, she thinks Robin is my girlfriend and I want her to keep thinking that. Got it?"

"Yeah. Got it. How are my two favorite people getting along anyway?"

"With witty banter and the occasional tiff."

Quentin chuckled. "That's foreplay for you guys."

"Not a chance. You're way off the mark." Especially while a boyfriend was waiting for Athena in San Francisco. Whoever the hell *he* was. "I'm driving. Was there anything else?"

"Going to see your mom?"

"No, she went to Florida for the winter a couple of weeks ago."

"Here's a heads-up for you," Quentin said. "Murph called twice this week to find out if I had any info on lawyers yet. I've been stalling, but I can't put her off much longer."

"You'll think of something. Bullshit is your middle name."

"Oh, man. I hate lying to a friend."

"Look at it this way. You're saving her from a wild-goose chase."

"You know what? Sometimes I'm tempted to tell her everything," Quentin grumbled.

Thorne gripped the steering wheel, switching lanes as a Mack truck loomed in the rearview window. "You wouldn't."

"Nah. I wouldn't. But why don't you? I mean, you see her all the time now, and—"

"Because it *is* complicated." He didn't dare admit to Quentin how much he wanted to tell Athena everything too.

"It sucks being caught in the middle. And if you had walked away from the Robin situation like I told you to... Forget it. I'm being an a-hole. How's he doing?"

"Okay. He'll turn twenty-one soon. I'm waiting on his decision to leave the group home in Albuquerque and come live with me."

Medication, psychosocial intervention, a supportive and loving environment—as Robin's legal guardian, Thorne had done a crash course on all the necessary treatments for an acute paranoid schizophrenic. A house with separate living quarters, in a community with a mental health clinic, would hopefully attract Robin and convince him to relocate. In any case, wherever he lived, Thorne would be forever deeply involved in his care.

"Weird how life works," Quentin said.

"Is that a general or specific observation?"

"Specific. Like, you wouldn't have even known Robin existed if Jessica hadn't died in a car accident. What was it? A year after your dad died?"

"Almost to the day."

"She and Robin would be out there right now, living their lives, and you—"

"Yeah. Right. Got it. Life's weird."

And it demanded tough choices. If it weren't for Robin, he and Athena would...

Thorne steered the car—and his uneasy thoughts—in a different direction. "How's life in Seattle?" he asked Quentin.

"The health nuts and fitness freaks drive me crazy. I saw some guy in a suit rollerblading to work."

"*I'm* a health nut and fitness freak."

"Yeah, but you're also my drinking buddy. Don't get any ideas about dumping me."

"I can't. You know too much."

Joking aside, Quentin was irreplaceable. Thorne might grab a beer or work out with other guys, beef about world affairs with them, but different life priorities and a lack of shared history kept them at the level of acquaintance. True friendship was as rare as true love.

"Ever think about moving back here?" Quentin asked. "You know, now that your mom's with relatives in Florida?"

"I considered it, the first winter she went down there. But these *are* my old stomping grounds. And then I ran into Ricki and... you know the rest."

Quentin chuckled. "The rest being you get to live in Murph's hometown."

"What's that supposed to mean?"

"Nothin'. Hey, gotta run. I have a hot date in an hour. Are we cool about the Murph thing?"

"Yeah, we're cool."

On impulse, Thorne took the exit leading to the former Kent family home, and soon entered a wooded neighborhood of imposing mansions and lush manicured lawns. In the dusk, the porches and windows twinkled with lights. With a few exceptions, stable, privileged lives had unfolded here for generations. He cruised past the Monroes' Italianate manor, recalling the scandal they'd endured when their son was arrested for insider trading. The substance abuse problems of the Petersons were public knowledge. And then there were Graham, Beryl, and Thorne Kent.

When they first got together, Athena would joke she was "taking a bite out of the upper crust." Later, secure in her love, he admitted he was the namesake of a distant, corrupt ancestor. That the Kent family wealth had been derived, in no small part, from fraud and crooked deals. "Aha! So, you were born with a *tarnished* silver spoon in your mouth." She had laughed. At the time, he had no idea just how tarnished.

Thorne parked at the end of the long driveway of the dignified Georgian he'd called home. The new owners, a professional couple and their young son, were as healthy, prosperous, and happy as his own family had been. Resting his head against the seat, he watched the graceful dogwoods outside the library window sway in the breeze. His father had planted the trees at his wife's urging that he spend more time outdoors, away from the office. He'd reluctantly gone on an African safari because she wanted to broaden their horizons. Then there were the diamond jewelry pieces and fur coats she never asked for. Gifts to Thorne's kind, loving, trusting mother from...

From his duplicitous cheating father.

Every gesture, every concession, every gift from him was to expiate his guilt. If his death had a silver lining, it was that Beryl had been spared the ugly truth. Had the seams of Graham's double life split, his duplicity would have torn her apart.

"Take care of her," he had whispered to Thorne on his deathbed. "She is my passion. My true love and soul mate."

But he wasn't referring to his wife. His "true love and soul mate" was Jessica, an artist in Albuquerque with whom he'd had an affair for twenty years. Their love story unfolded between gasps of pain, always reaching the same conclusion—Thorne must promise to provide for her and make sure no one ever found out. The community's censure and pity would devastate his mother. Beryl's injured heart would never recover from the betrayal.

Twenty years. To this day, Thorne barely grasped the enormity of the deception. He tried to remember if there had been any uncharacteristic behavior or stray remarks, anything his father might have done to alert him to his secret life. But no. Nothing. The man he most trusted and admired in the world had duped him too.

Nevertheless, Thorne kept his promise, turning over half his share of the Kent mansion sale to Jessica. She'd refused the money until he persuaded her it was the best way to honor Graham's memory and wishes. He made one stipulation—she must desist from all communication with the Kent family and anyone associated with them. And she complied.

Until her final communication a year later that turned his life upside down—a letter revealing he had a seventeen-year-old half brother and Jessica had designated Thorne his legal guardian in her will.

When Thorne met Robin at the facility Graham had financed in Albuquerque, he couldn't bring himself to ask if he and their father had been close. If they shared a love for sailing or laughed at the same jokes. Whatever the terms of their relationship, Graham clearly had not shirked from his responsibility to his son, a responsibility Thorne had since assumed.

Once Thorne accepted that his life would never be the same, he gave up his law career, sold his town house, and followed *his* passion. Which curiously, fatefully, led him to the hometown of the woman he'd given up to follow in the footsteps of his father. The twisted circle of life.

"Weird how life works," he said softly.

He was about to pull away and drive to Pamela's apartment, to lose himself in another night of mindless eating and sex, when a light on the front porch came on. The new family, the heirs to his happiness, spilled out of the house, laughing, their arms around each other—innocent, by all appearances, of deception and betrayal.

As Athena parked her Mini Cooper behind Kristie's Odyssey minivan outside As You Like It Café, a text message appeared on her phone.

Quentin wrote:

Sorry, Murph. No lawyer wants to get involved.

Why not?

Garland's mystique generates sales.

Don't follow.

Potential lawsuit from agent or publisher if you blow her cover.

I'll risk it.

What for?

Filthy lucre. My book might be a blockbuster.

The truth was that she had nothing to lose. No book meant no career. And what could they sue her for? Her anemic checking account? As she waited for Quentin's response, she stared at the *Baby on Board* placard stuck to the minivan's rear window. As if people would suddenly drive more cautiously when they saw it. And the silly thing was practically upside down. Someone could rear-end the van trying to read it, another example of irony she'd cite for her students if—no, *when*—she taught again.

Quentin text:

LOL. You'll need the filthy lucre for legal fees.

Shakespeare was right. We should kill all the lawyers.

Aw, Murph.

Not you, doofus.

He signed off with a GIF of a caveman drinking a mug of beer. It was funny, but she couldn't shake the feeling that Quentin was laying the blockhead act on a little thick.

Athena unfolded her body from the cramped car and pulled open the door to the café. The hell with playing it safe. She'd forge ahead without legal advice. Bring on the lawsuit. Someone was bound to uncover Garland's identity, so it might as well be her. And bring on the ill-gotten gains. She'd buy a bigger car. Big enough to live in after the lawyers sucked her dry.

She typed *Working Title: Hiding in Plain Sight* into the Notes app on her phone. Four words down, another hundred thousand or so to go.

Rushing up to her, Kristie thrust a pen and order pad into her hand as if they were in a relay. "I'm outta here. Zoe spiked a fever. Which usually means an ear infection and a visit to the doctor."

"I'll cover your shift tomorrow if you need me to. Thorne?"

Kristie pointed to the ceiling. "In his apartment. He's in a weird mood, like his brain's in a galaxy far, far away. He blanked on a name for today's sandwich for the first time ever."

He'd seemed distracted to Athena as well when they'd worked their Monday shifts. Her joke about Laurel being a witness protection community fell as flat as a prairie road. Either his dry wit had dried up or he was still irritated by her questions about that Robin person.

Or he was hiding a deep, dark secret.

Putting on her apron, she tapped her head a few times to

knock that dumb idea from her brain. Thorne was incapable of hiding a secret—deep, dark, or otherwise. His clenched jaw and furrowed brow gave him away every time. He once planned a secret Valentine's Day getaway for them to St. Barts. During the weeks leading up to it, he jumped at noises and frowned until he got headaches. When Athena said she knew what he was up to—an outright lie to pry the truth out of him—he was so relieved that he confessed every detail.

And yet... something about his reaction to her questions was suspicious.

She read the day's special on the chalkboard. Fig relish, prosciutto, fontina cheese, and fresh herbs on sourdough bread.

Suspicious? Thorne?

Figment of Your Imagination, she wrote on the board, giving the sandwich—and her conjectures—a name.

Taking a deep breath, she looked around the half-filled room. Not a would-be writer in sight. Time to get cracking.

"Good afternoon," she said, pouring water for the two women seated by the bay window. While their gray hair suggested "women of a certain age," their peasant blouses, wraparound skirts, and espadrilles suggested "forever young." And their open countenances suggested open minds. They might welcome a discussion of the LitWit series.

"You must be Lydia Murphy's daughter," one of them said after she'd taken their orders. "You're her spitting image."

"Yes, I'm Athena. How do you know my mother?"

"We used to see her in Ricki's Café. Plus, she's our realtor. This is our first time here. Is the food as good as Ricki's?"

"Better."

The woman extended her hand. "I'm Phyllis Staunton, and this is my partner, Theresa Becker."

"Nice to meet you. Have either of you heard from Ricki?"

Athena asked. According to Lydia, she and her best friend were still "good and mad" at each other.

"Not a word. We made the pots she ordered but put them in storage till she gets in touch." Phyllis pointed to the shop across the street next to Suzie's Seconds. *Lotsa Pots*, the sign in the window said. The *s* after *Pot* was a lot smaller, as if it were an afterthought. Or someone had an offbeat sense of humor. "Your mother looked high and low for a suitable building for us. Finding a place big enough for our wheels and kilns was hard as heck, but she came through."

"She's the best in the business," Athena said.

"Are you a real estate agent as well as a waitress?" Theresa asked. "A lot of folks have to juggle multiple jobs these days."

Gee, Mom. Thanks for bragging about my PhD and career.

"I'm an English professor on leave to write a book."

Theresa clapped her hands, making all the gemstone rings on her fingers shimmer. "Wonderful! What's it about?"

"The LitWit series. Have you heard of it?"

Theresa's face reddened, and Phyllis looked around furtively as if she hoped no one had overheard. "Those books are fantastic," she whispered.

Athena dropped into a chair, ignoring the waving hand of a woman at the next table. "I'm also investigating the identity of C. L. Garland. Wouldn't you love to find out who she is, especially since she's a lifelong resident of Laurel?"

They exchanged glances, and Phyllis shook her head so vigorously that the tiny bells on her earrings chimed.

Holy crap—Phyllis was C. L. Garland! Or she knew her personally. Or maybe Theresa was Garland. Athena had finally hit the jackpot.

And she mentally added *earrings with tiny bells* to her shopping wish list.

"You can trust me," she assured them. "I'll only reveal what is absolutely necessary in my book."

Both women sat up like meerkats. "What do you mean?" Phyllis asked.

The group of guys Thorne referred to as "bachelor farmers" walked by on their way out the door. "Wednesday is called 'hump day,'" one of them said. "My favorite day of the week, if you catch my drift."

"Like anyone would hump you," another one jeered.

"And if anyone did, it wouldn't be your *drift* they'd catch," another one said, red-faced with laughter.

"Go on, Athena," Theresa urged.

"I mean we can collaborate," Athena said. "Find a balance between privacy and disclosure."

Phyllis leaned toward Athena. The irises in her pale-blue eyes were pinpoints. "Let me get this straight. You think one of us is C. L. Garland?"

"I thought...maybe..."

"Oh, that's a good one!" Phyllis said, laughing.

Theresa tittered. "I *wish* I'd gotten rich writing erotica."

"Don't we all," Phyllis said.

"So, you're not...neither one of you is..." Athena's voice—and hopes—faded.

"We don't really care who Garland is," Phyllis said. "Don't want to know, to tell you the truth."

"Why not?" Athena tried not to sound too incredulous.

"It's more fun imagining the actual writers wrote the novellas," Theresa said.

"The writers themselves? Really?" This was a twist Athena could not have anticipated.

"Take Jane Austen, for instance," Phyllis said. "I like to think there was more going on beneath her prim bonnet than she let on. And under her knickers."

Athena laughed so hard that even the customers she was neglecting smiled. She leaned forward, her pen poised above the order pad. "Please. Tell me everything you like about the LitWit series." She'd incorporate their opinions in the preface of her book, ballast against any reviews that called the series "rubbish." And the next time a certain pompous former English major/former boyfriend made a snide remark about "bastardizing" literature, she'd have a rebuttal ready.

Phyllis smoothed a stray hair. "For one thing, as much as I love Austen, everybody's done her to death. Garland adapts other writers, too, like Dickens and Tolstoy, which is refreshing."

"She always includes synopses of the original texts," Athena said, jotting down her comments. "Do you find them helpful?"

"Very. And not only do I read the original book after I've finished the novella, I read other books by the author."

"You do this because of the series?"

"Certainly. It was a lot more fun reading *Anna Karenina* when I pictured Vronsky wearing nothing but his epaulets," Phyllis said. "And a you-know-what to beat the band."

Athena bit her lip to keep from laughing again. "I'm curious. You said you were partners. Why does Vronsky turn you on and not Anna?"

Phyllis grabbed Athena's hand, making the row of silver bracelets on her wrist jingle. "We're not lesbians, my dear. We're *business* partners, not *partner* partners."

"Sorry," Athena mumbled.

"And divorcées," Theresa said with a sigh.

"I'm a double divorcée," Phyllis said. "I refer to my former husbands as 'Numbskull' and 'Dumbbell.' I ditched Dumbbell at menopause because that's when the fun really starts."

"Phyllis!" Theresa remonstrated.

"They don't call them hot flashes for nothing," Phyllis said.

"I think her blood sugar is low," Theresa said to Athena. "Can you bring our orders soon?"

"Two green teas and two specials coming right up," Athena said between hiccupping laughs.

"And a couple of eligible males if you got 'em," Phyllis added.

As if on cue, two men walked in. Athena recognized the taller one immediately. She remembered him helping Mrs. Richter, her high school art teacher, set up easels and mix paints. "Nice to see you, Mr. Richter," she said. "I was sorry to hear about your wife. She was one of my favorite teachers."

"Thank you. And who would you be?"

"Athena Murphy. My father knew her too. He recently retired from teaching English at the school."

"Ah, yes, Charles. He came to Anna's funeral with the Blakes. Nice to meet you, Athena. Call me Joe." He pointed to his companion. "I'm stuck going out with this fellow these days. The widowers' club."

His friend smiled, brightening his hangdog face. "Dan Kroger. We usually come for breakfast but thought we'd try lunch for a change."

"You won't be disappointed. I recommend today's special sandwich." Athena nodded toward the two women. "Want to share a pot of tea and lively conversation with Phyllis and Theresa?"

"Don't mind if we do," Joe said, tipping an imaginary hat at them. "If it's fine with the ladies."

"The ladies are perfectly fine with it," Phyllis said, pulling out a chair. "As long as we can brag about our kids and grandkids."

Joe patted the pocket of his trousers. "I've got a wallet and phone full of pictures."

"Look out. Here comes Gloomy Gus," Dan said when a thin, hunched man pushed the front door open.

"Who is he?" Athena asked, watching him settle his angular body into a chair by the hearth.

"Eugene Farragut, another breakfast regular. Whatever you do, don't mention Cleveland," Joe warned her.

"A city on the tip of everyone's tongue," Phyllis quipped.

"Serve him first, Athena, so he doesn't complain," Theresa said. "If no one else minds."

"Not at all," Joe said. "More time to enjoy your company."

"Be careful. He'll find *something* to chew you out about," Dan told Athena. "His temper drove his wife back to her hometown."

"Poor Tildy," Theresa said. "Married to a sourpuss all those years."

"Poor Eugene too," Joe said. "He'll never admit it, but he's hurting. He and Tildy never had children, so he must be pretty lonely."

Athena approached Gloomy Gus's table. "What can I get for you this beautiful September afternoon?" she asked, clicking her ballpoint pen.

"What's beautiful about it?" he grumbled, twisting his wedding ring. Dark stubble shadowed the folds of his lean face. The cuffs of his wrinkled blue shirt were frayed.

"Can I interest you in our sandwich special?"

He snorted. "Fig relish? Not on your life. What's wrong with a plain cheese sandwich, that's what I'd like to know."

"One plain cheese sandwich," she said as she wrote on the notepad.

"And a slice of onion."

"Cut thin or thick?"

"Thick. Want to taste the dang onion. And a dab of horseradish if you got it."

"We got it."

"And make it quick. I missed breakfast."

"Coffee?"

"Hell no. Who wants to get all hyped up on caffeine in the middle of the day?"

"Only people without the sense God gave geese. I'm Athena, by the way. What's your name?"

"Eugene Farragut."

"Nice to meet you, Eugene. Can I ask a personal question?"

"You can ask. Doesn't mean I'll answer."

"Has anyone ever told you that you look like Humphrey Bogart?"

His mouth opened wide enough for more cranky remarks to escape. But none did. Only a hoarse guffaw, rusty from disuse. Everyone in As You Like It Café turned and looked—and opened *their* mouths in shock.

"How'd you get him to laugh?" Theresa asked, wide-eyed, when Athena passed their table.

"Haven't you heard? I'm also a card-carrying member of the Hurtin' Hearts Club."

They all smiled, assuming she was joking, having no idea she was *president* of the club.

Athena never spent Saturday night alone if she could help it, even if it meant eating borscht with Sergei. But as she'd recently discovered, it was the perfect time to file her nails, organize her earrings—Dear God in heaven, what was she doing with twelve pairs? Not counting the other twenty in San Francisco. Or the bell earrings she'd just ordered online—and catch up on email.

Miss you, Dr. M! one of her students wrote.

This place sucks without you ☹ another one told her.

She missed her students too, more than she'd expected. If she'd ever had any doubts, she was now certain teaching was as natural and necessary to her as breathing.

Come back soon!!! the last email said.

Their warm messages took the sting out of her professional exile. She may not have published, but she was popular. Damn popular. And while her situation had a special Corinne Carew twist, she wasn't the only assistant professor whose job was on the line. Stan Harris in the Poli Sci Department, whom she occasionally ran into at the campus bar happy hour, had developed an eye tic, worrying he would get the heave-ho for, well, spending too much time at the campus bar. Without reading it, she deleted Stan's email with the subject line *Freaking out here!!* and turned on the small TV in her bedroom. Lying in bed, she flipped through the channels until she found an old black-and-white PBS special.

No wonder her father kept the television volume loud and worked the appliances until they groaned for mercy. Noise filled the lonely hours. The sound of Julia Child whacking a chicken into another dimension did the trick—until she remembered Thorne's hilarious imitation of Julia's high-pitched voice. His sublime renditions of her recipes. The way he'd fill a fork with *poulet* or *boeuf* and bring it to her mouth, coaxing her to eat. She, opening her mouth, he—

Her phone rang before she tasted Thorne's tongue. "Hey, Finn. What's happening?"

"Everything. Nothing. Tell me what you think of this guy's profile: 'Playful architect seeks playmate for this, that, and the other.' " He had been exploring dating apps and websites since his last argument with Mario over whether *Chippendale* was spelled with one *p* or two.

"What did Mario do this time?"

"He put a dish of fried flounder in front of me and said, 'Surf's up, big kahuna.' "

Athena held the phone away from her face to muffle her laughter. "What's the insult? The flounder or the kahuna?"

"He's pissed I won't surf with him, and he's rubbing my face in it. Can you see me in a wet suit? He's built for it, but I'm not."

Obviously proud of his fit musculature, Mario wore clothes that looked like they'd been spray-painted on his body.

"My skin sunburns, and I have a paunch like The Charles," Finn griped. "On top of it all, Mario sabotages me with his cooking."

"Don't be silly. He's not the slightest bit devious."

"Fried fish? What's that about? And forget surfing. It's on my fuck-it list. And so is he. I'm checking out this architect guy."

"What do *playful* and *playmate* even mean? Someone so flaky would never commit."

"Who cares about commitment?" Finn asked in his highest soprano voice. "I don't want to get married anyway."

"You're afraid to, as a child of divorce," Athena said, channeling Dr. Phil.

"You sound like Mar... Forget it. I want to be free."

"Mario's the most serious relationship you've ever had. Don't walk away from it."

"*You're* doing great single. *You're* free to meet interesting men like Sir Gay."

"Freedom's not all it's cracked up to be. And Sergei stopped being interesting a dozen *dasvidaniyas* ago."

"At least you have an awesome career," Finn said. "Unlike me."

On the television, Julia put the mutilated chicken into the oven with a flourish, confident it would emerge as the most delectable poultry to ever grace a table. Now *that* was an awesome career.

"My job's hanging by a thread, Finn. Bitch-face Corinne finally got to me, and I let her have it right in the middle of a faculty meeting." She never could hide anything from her brother for long.

"Where does she live? I'll... I'll short-circuit her electricity. Or hack her computer," he said in his deepest voice.

"Don't you dare do anything illegal. It's bad enough I'm stuck here trying to salvage my career."

"*Salvage*? Shit. How bad are we talking?"

"Let me put it this way. My book on Garland is my get-out-of-jail-free card."

"You should have told me sooner," he chided her.

"You have your own problems. And I'm beyond embarrassed. I'm talking abject humiliation here. Promise me you won't tell a soul."

"Cross my heart."

"Not even Mario."

"As if," he said with a sniff.

"I mean it, Finnster. You tell anyone, and I'll personally make a T-shirt for you with the word *Snitch* on it. And it won't be printed backward."

"Oh, all right," he grumbled.

They'd been sharing secrets since they could talk. Athena would take Finn's to the grave. She couldn't rely on his promises to do the same, especially if he was tipsy. She didn't speak to him for two weeks when, after he'd been drinking champagne with their parents on New Year's Eve, he told them she was at a party in St. Louis instead of at a sleepover with her high school friends, her alibi.

"Any luck with the Garland search?" Finn asked.

"I need more than luck. I need a miracle."

"Let me put my engineer brain to work. I'll come up with a plan."

"As long as your plan doesn't involve T-shirts."

"Any other words of advice about surfer boy before I get off?"

"Make it work with Mario. It's a lonely world out there."

"Why are you all *stay together blah blah blah* all of a sudden?"

"Because you two truly love each other."

"Like you and Thorne did?" he asked quietly after a long pause. "Is that how you know?"

Beyond the curtained window, Athena pictured the stars sparkling brilliantly in the night sky. "Stellathena, because you shine so brightly," Thorne had said the night he named the constellation of freckles on her nose. "Like my love."

"You love me?" she'd asked.

"I love you. And you love me."

"How do you know?"

He'd taken his hand and placed it over her bounding, joyous heart. "This is how I know."

CHAPTER SEVEN

Silence is of different kinds, and breathes different meanings.

—CHARLOTTE BRONTË, *VILLETTE*

Growing up, Athena could always count on one thing—whatever drama had unfolded in the Murphy household during the week, all would be forgotten, if not forgiven, during Sunday dinner. Her father uncorked a bottle of wine, her mother presented her latest culinary creation, and peace was temporarily restored. Baba ghanoush and souvlaki were as commonplace to Athena and Finn as macaroni and cheese was to their friends.

Laurel was eerily quiet, the streets empty, as she drove to Lydia's house for dinner. The peculiar sensation the world was asleep belonged to Sundays. Naturally, her mother hadn't invited Charles. Except in the morning, Athena rarely saw him. Where he went after his recently reformed breakfast of oatmeal and fruit smoothie was anybody's guess. His new juicer was another deafening appliance to fill the lonely silence.

Pulling into the driveway, she snapped the visor down against the blinding setting sun. The days were getting short and cold and the trail of C. L. Garland even colder. A description of the scope and challenges of the project—excluding pointless gossip, annoyed café patrons, and uncooperative former boyfriends—had become Chapter One. Chapter Two comprised an elegant essay on "David Copafeel." By letting David Copperfield and his saintly Agnes go at it like rabbits, Athena asserted, Garland had done nothing less than turn the Victorian notion of woman as "the angel in the house" on its head.

Two chapters down. Not bad, considering the novellas' eroticism was a pesky distraction from scholarly analysis. Wet panties—another challenge she should add as a footnote.

Athena walked up to the house with one of the bottles of merlot she'd brought. Depending on her mother's mood, she might or might not need the second.

"Your hair needs a trim," Lydia said as soon as she entered. "And for pity's sake, your pants are ripped."

"The distressed look is all the rage. And speaking of distress and rage, I've been meaning to tell you that Nora Johnson eats lunch at the café occasionally."

At the mention of the woman she'd wronged, Lydia's hand flew to the cheek Nora had hit. Athena had a delicious vision of dispatching Nora to San Francisco to deliver her trademark punch to an unsuspecting Corinne.

"She always invites me to stop in at Go Figure," Athena said as they walked to the kitchen. "I think I'll take her up on it."

"Don't let me stop you." Lydia examined the zit on Athena's forehead. "There's no reason in the world a woman your age should be getting pimples."

"Stress," Athena said.

"Sweets," Lydia countered.

Thorne's pastries, to be precise.

"And it's *one* pimple. Singular." Athena looked more closely at her mother. "Something's different with you."

"Everything's the same with me."

"No . . . wait. You're not wearing any makeup." Lydia kept fully equipped makeup bags in every possible location—home, car, office. "And I didn't know you even *owned* a pair of jeans."

"I'm trying out a new look."

"So's Dad. He's been working out and bought nicer clothes."

"Took him long enough." Lydia pulled on a loose string of wool dangling from Athena's favorite sweater. "You could use a wardrobe makeover yourself."

Lydia, 2. Athena, 0. And only five minutes had elapsed. Athena debated running back to the car for the other bottle of wine. She grabbed a corkscrew and plunged it into the bottle. "Nora told me her ex-husband travels all over the country in an RV."

Lydia hummed as she stirred a bowl of olive tapenade as if the mention of her former lover didn't disturb her in the least.

Athena poured them each a glass of merlot. "He impersonates Elvis at music festivals."

Lydia snorted. "The man had a few screws loose, no question about it. Whoever heard of a vice principal playing in a garage band?"

Vice Vic, as he insisted the students call him, performed every year in the high school talent show. He wore his dark hair like Elvis, forelock and all, and his full, sensuous mouth had incited many a crush. The night he serenaded Lydia with "Blue Hawaii" at a faculty party marked the beginning of the end of the Murphy and Johnson marriages.

Athena sipped her wine. "So how come you . . . you know . . ."

"If he hadn't been such a great kisser, I wouldn't have gone from here to the corner with him. And don't get me started on Vic Johnson's johnson." Lydia held a plate of spinach balls aloft. "Eat up."

Athena stuffed two of them into her mouth, desperately trying not to think of her former vice principal's balls. Or penis. Or the size thereof.

Her mother set out a bowl of quinoa salad, another of brussels sprouts, and a plate of tofu.

"What's the main course?" Athena asked.

"You're looking at it. I'm going vegetarian for a while. Ricki told me I..." Lydia sat down and spread a napkin across her lap. "Never mind. I don't want to discuss her."

Athena piled a mound of quinoa salad onto her plate. "I can't believe you two haven't made up yet."

"We talked. Briefly. She had the nerve to say I was 'stuck in my ways.'" She speared a cube of tofu and wiggled it in Athena's direction. "Does this look like someone incapable of change? Someone who hasn't worn makeup for six days?"

Personally, Athena thought her mother's fresh-faced look was an improvement over her mask of mascara, blush, and lipstick. "You know Ricki," she said. "Change is her middle name."

"Selling her café. Going to Paraguay." Lydia emptied her glass of wine in a few mouthfuls. "*Crazy* is her middle name."

"She called from Paraguay?"

"Sandusky, Ohio. Her brother Tim lives there."

The wine nearly shot out of Athena's nostrils as she suppressed a laugh at Ricki's scattershot itinerary. "Give it time, Mom. You'll work it out."

Lydia poured herself another glass of wine. "Thorne's looked at more houses recently, but nothing suits him."

"The person he's house searching with might be the persnickety one," Athena said, returning her mother's sidelong glance with a sidelong comment.

"He's always alone. I thought the O'Neal property would ring his bell, but no go."

"What's Geraldine like these days?"

An indulgent smile slid across Lydia's lips. "Sharp-tongued as ever. She gives as good as she gets, that one."

"You like her, don't you?"

"Always did. She's original and witty. I wish we'd known each other better. She's lived here all her life, but she and Pete kept to themselves."

"When they weren't arguing in public."

"They might have killed each other if they'd stayed indoors."

A hazard that didn't seem to have concerned her mother in her fights with Charles.

"Where will she move when she sells the house?" Athena asked.

"All she said was she was going to live 'high on the hog from here on out.' Though God knows with what money. She can't have saved much after working temp clerical jobs. And Pete wasn't the world's most successful car salesman."

"She must expect a profit on the sale of the property."

Lydia sighed. "The market's been in a slump lately. I'm keeping my fingers crossed Thorne doesn't change his mind about buying."

"Don't worry. His apartment is a dump. He can't wait to get out of there."

Crap.

Her mother's eyebrows arched in surprise. "You've been in Thorne's apartment?"

"Just once. To discuss the café. It's doing marvelously." Athena tried to spear a brussels sprout but it rolled off her plate. "Tell Ricki next time you talk to her."

"*If* I talk to her. And don't change the subject." Lydia poured more wine into Athena's glass. "A man who's looking for a house is usually ready to settle down."

"It is a truth universally acknowledged."

"Any chance you two will pick up where you left off?" Lydia asked, giving no indication she'd caught Athena's reference to Jane Austen.

Where she and Thorne had left off was Seattle. Her bawling her eyes out, a weeping, wailing mess. Him making it clear in his calm, dry-eyed way he would never get married.

Athena chewed a tofu cube, wishing she had something sharper between her teeth. Like a steak bone. "No chance whatsoever. For one thing, he's rarely in the café during my shift. And for another, we're both dating other people."

The past week, Thorne had been as elusive as Charles. The few times she'd seen him, his countenance was as bland as her father's oatmeal. That Robin person, whoever she was, couldn't be very exciting.

"I worry about you, Athena," Lydia said with a gentle pat on her arm. Two glasses of wine always smoothed her mother hen feathers. "You're not getting any younger."

"I'm doing fine. Remember Sergei?"

"Which one is he?" As if her daughter had so many boyfriends that she couldn't keep track of them all.

"The Russian guy." *The decoy.* "He definitely has potential." *To drive me nuts.* "We're taking it slow, seeing where it goes." *Nowhere.*

"We should FaceTime or Zoom so I can meet him. Does he have a good job?"

"Uh-huh." Athena scrambled to invent one in case her mother pursued Sergei's nonexistent career. Interpreter? Travel tour guide? "And his family has money. Lots of it." Smuggled out of St. Petersburg in the hem of his great-grandmother's sable coat. Or so he claimed.

"Worthless rubles," Lydia said with a dismissive wave. "Just don't take it *too* slow. Time catches up with you before you know it."

As if the loud gong of Athena's biological clock didn't deafen her every time Kristie talked about Zoe. Which was constantly. She'd brought her to work Friday, since neither Ian nor his parents were available to babysit. "See what I mean about Thorne being flexible?" she'd gushed. The café patrons took turns holding and entertaining the toddler, claiming she smelled good enough to eat and was so very squeezable.

When Athena Velcroed her little sneakers—was there anything more adorable than baby shoes?—she sniffed and squeezed to find out for herself. And she was quite sure she made Zoe laugh harder than Thorne this time.

"Thanks for the advice, Mom," she said between gulps of wine.

"At least you listen to me. But not Ricki. No siree, Bob." Lydia scraped stray grains of quinoa off the tablecloth with a butter knife. "I've always told her she's too needy. No wonder Janice broke up with her. I saw disaster coming a mile away."

"Her last girlfriend? How long were they together?"

"Nearly a year. Janice is a saint. And one smart cookie. If *I* were her partner, I'd have cleaned up my act real fast. Ricki is entirely too demanding."

Talk about the pot calling the kettle black. But Athena didn't have the heart to lob another nasty ball into her mother's court. Not while Lydia's lips were trembling, trying to hold back tears. "Don't give up on your friendship, Mom. Ricki needs you more than ever."

Lydia blew her nose on a napkin. "She has a funny way of showing it."

Finn, and now her mother. Since when had Athena turned into the relationship advisor of the Murphy family? Her track record for staying the course was laughable. And while she'd had school and work friends, she'd never been particularly close to them or had a *bestie*.

The shadows in the kitchen had deepened as evening fell and Athena's wine buzz darkened to the blues. Seeing her mother bereft of her best friend brought her loss of Thorne's friendship front and center, reminding her of the times she had needed his reassurance that getting the car's transmission replaced was no big deal and those pants did *not* make her butt look big. He would have told her that the nasty politics of academia were not the end of the world—and she would have believed him.

"It gets dark too soon these days." Lydia rose and looked out the window above the kitchen sink. "I'm going to a realtors' conference in two weeks, and I can't wait. A change of scenery will do me good."

"Where to?"

"Atlanta. Tony, the regional manager of Laurel Realty, will be traveling with me." She snapped the blinds shut, knocking a small cactus off the windowsill. "The planets must be off their alignment or something. Everything feels kerflooey."

Athena looked down at her ripped jeans. Whatever possessed her to buy them? "I think you're onto something with your planet theory. Finn and Mario are having problems too."

"I told him not to get a roommate. Putting up with someone else's habits is a pain in the neck."

"Mario's not his roommate. He's—"

"Finn could afford his own apartment if he'd get a real job," Lydia said, turning the kitchen light on.

"Their rehab business is doing great."

"All that money for an engineering degree down the drain."

Finn's Self EsTEEm T-shirt business would only irritate Lydia if she mentioned it. Athena should order one with *Never Satisfied* printed backward on it and send it to her mother anonymously.

"There's nothing wrong with manual labor," Athena said. "Besides, he enjoys building things."

"I saw Karen the other day. The girl he went to the junior prom with. I promised I'd give him her phone number."

"Don't bother. Seriously. Don't."

Lydia shoved three plates into the dishwasher rack and slammed it shut. "All right. I won't."

The tense quiet that followed was punctuated by the snap of plastic lids as Lydia put the remains of their barely eaten meal into Tupperware containers. Athena drained the last drop of merlot from her glass, trying to think of a subject besides lost friends and a son's romantic choices. "My book on C. L. Garland is going well. I wrote a couple of chapters already. I could use your help though."

Lydia neatly folded a dish towel, put it in a drawer, and sat down again. "I'm listening."

"Can you get me all the listings of house sales in the area for the past two years, not just Laurel Realty's sales? I'm especially interested in buyers of the McMansions in the new developments."

"You think one of them might be Garland?"

"Listed under her real name. But yeah, possibly."

"I know nearly everyone in town, especially how much they can afford for a house."

"So, someone suddenly investing in an expensive home would catch your attention?"

"It certainly would."

Something Lydia had said about Geraldine living "high on the hog" tugged at her brain. And Geraldine's privacy, her wit. But Athena was too wine soused to focus.

"I'll be glad to look into the sales for you," Lydia said. "Detective work will be fun."

"Thanks. To be honest, I didn't think you'd help. You

didn't seem that interested when I told you a famous writer lived here."

Lydia's lips curled in a sly smile. "She's not the only author in Laurel. Your father used to write too."

"Dad? When? What did he write?"

"Love poems. For me. They weren't bad either. Some were published in tiny literary journals."

Athena let out a low whistle. "Boy, learn something new every day."

"I don't remember why he stopped writing them."

Angrily hurled missiles might be one *reason.*

Lydia plucked a tissue from her pocket and dabbed her eyes. "You never come to me for heart-to-heart talks. You and Finn always preferred your father. That hurt sometimes."

"Sorry," Athena mumbled.

But Lydia's reaction when Finn, a high school freshman, announced he was gay had hurt too. Charles had hugged and kissed him, assuring him of his complete support—while she went upstairs to pack for a librarian's conference, never to mention the topic again. Until he went off to college, Finn dated girls and took them to proms to spare her feelings.

Lydia blew her nose and dried her eyes. "How does a medium-rare hamburger with blue cheese and onion sound?"

"I thought you'd never ask."

Polishing off the second bottle of merlot with Lydia was worth waking up hungover. It wasn't often Athena got to see her mother's vulnerable side, the side that missed her best friend and reminisced about love poems. "Please. Stop. Now," she moaned to the rhythm of the knocking in her head. She had sobered up before the drive home but had fallen asleep without hydrating.

She opened her eyes as the noise continued. It wasn't in her head. Someone was pounding on the front door.

"Dad?" she called feebly, squinting at the clock. He hadn't been home past ten a.m. for weeks. She'd either have to answer the door herself or wait for the visitor to give up.

Athena checked the time again: 10:20. In just one hour and forty minutes, she had to be at As You Like It Café for her Monday shift.

She sat bolt upright, waited for the walls to stop moving, and put her feet on the cold floor. The temperature must have dropped significantly in the night. Shivering in her bathrobe, she stumbled down the stairs. "All right, all right, I'm coming," she called out as the knocking persisted.

This was no ordinary person waiting on the other side of the door. This was six-feet-plus of male Neanderthal with sulky eyes and a prominent jaw covered in stubble. His denim jacket, T-shirt, and jeans were one size too small to contain the proverbial shithouse that was his body. His longish blond hair was unkempt, like he'd just rolled out of his cave bed and was ready to hunt fresh meat.

Athena closed her eyes halfway to block part of him out of her field of vision. "Can I help you?"

His glance over her body was like a rough hand rubbing her skin. "I'm Karl Guterson. From Hoglund Construction. Mr. Murphy said to come by today. Are you the lady of the house?"

How fricking old did she look? She flipped her hair over her shoulders, causing a minor breast oscillation beneath the bathrobe. "I'm his daughter, Athena."

He focused on her forehead, trying manfully, she supposed, not to look past her neck. But he did anyway, all the way down to her bare feet. "Your father wants me to check out the greenhouse. See what needs fixing."

Greenhouse was a flattering name for the ramshackle structure the former owners had built in the backyard. Since the Murphys had moved in, mice and spiders were its sole life-forms, setting up residence in the broken clay pots beneath the rickety potting table.

"Did he say why he wants it repaired?" she asked.

"To grow stuff. Herbs, vegetables."

The Charles? His one demonstrable household skill was hanging picture frames, most of them askew. She'd never once seen a trowel or spade in his hands.

"He's not here," she said. "Can you come by another time?"

He pointed to the fence door. "The latch is unlocked. Since I'm here, what say I go back and have a look?"

"Sure. Go ahead."

As the coffee brewed in the kitchen, Athena watched Karl examine the door and windows of the greenhouse. He was a Garland novella come to life, one based on *Lady Chatterley's Lover* perhaps. She yelped at the sensation of wetness on her ankle. Branwell snuffled as he licked a glob of dried egg yolk off the floor. "Too slobbery, dude."

Right back at ya, his bulging eyes said.

"Wrong-o. He's not my type."

Though she might have been better off if she *had* dated guys like Karl. Or what Karl seemed to be—straight up, uncomplicated, not a whiff of a Brontë hero about him.

She knelt to scratch behind Branwell's ears. "You remember Thorne, don't you?"

He grinned.

"Yeah, so do I. All too well."

Karl was as raw as Thorne was refined. One primitive man, the other an old soul of limber mind and body, pale as a brooding hero, with eyes that expressed every emotion from mirth to melancholy.

And the sooner she tracked down the mysterious writer and wrote her book and put miles between herself and those eyes, the better off she'd be. Meanwhile, she'd turn over a rock or two and test Finn's theory that their father might be Garland.

"What do you say, boy?" she asked Branwell. "Want to do some snooping? See if The Charles has any other surprises in store for us?"

He grunted and waddled away, his nails scratching the floor. He'd always shown disapproval when she and Finn called his master "The Charles."

By the time Athena had showered and dressed, Karl was gone. With a half hour to spare before going to the café, she made a quick inventory of all the rooms and closets, including the attic. No expensive art, decorative objects, or first edition volumes in sight. Her father's new clothes and juicer hardly counted as extravagances. He drove the same Honda Civic he'd taught her and Finn to drive in. Furthermore, the only time she observed him write was when he worked a crossword puzzle. If Charles Murphy, author of love poems, was the wealthy, prolific C. L. Garland, then Corinne Carew was Athena's bestie instead of her beastie.

Eager to exercise, Athena parked six blocks from As You Like It Café. The autumn air, sharp as a radish, snipped the last throbbing thread of her hangover. By the time she put on her apron and took note of the day's special, she was raring to go. Thorne, though, looked as if he needed a week of sleep. His shirt and pants were as rumpled as his hair, his eyes red rimmed in his haggard face.

She walked up to him, a pot of coffee in one hand, a plate of banana muffins in the other. "Hi, there."

"Morning," he grumbled, pouring lemonade from one pitcher to another.

"Uh...you mean *afternoon*."

One of the bachelor farmers winked at her. "Mondays are tough after a bachelor weekend, aren't they, Thorne?"

"I was up working late last night."

"Ooh," the farmers said. "*Working*."

"Working *hard*," one of them said, nodding like a bobblehead.

"Can I get you gentlemen today's special?" Thorne asked.

The heftiest guy in the group nodded to the greyhound-slim women sharing a sandwich at the opposite table. "I'll have half of one like them. I wanna see how long it takes me to get hungry again."

"Us too!" three of the farmers called out.

"Four half-sandwich specials coming right up," Thorne said, yawning.

"On second thought," one of them said, "make mine a double."

"And mine."

"I'll have a triple."

The farmer who wanted to test his hunger limit grinned. "Never mind half. I'm going for a triple too."

"That's five whole sandwiches all together. Got it?" Athena asked Thorne.

"Five. Got it. Excuse me, I'm a little...groggy."

Worn out from sex with that Robin person, asleep in his apartment upstairs. "Horny Thorny in the morny," Athena used to call him. Morning was, hands down—and clothes off—their lustiest time of day. They'd tug and pull and grind and lick and come, and then go off to their respective classes, lit with a postcoital glow.

"You've got the *hot-off-the-press* look, if you don't mind my saying so," she said in a low voice.

His eyes shot open as if he'd been injected with caffeine. "Press…hot…what?"

"Remember? You used to say everybody on campus could tell we'd had sex. It was written all over us like freshly printed news."

If she had to look clear-eyed and unsentimentally at who they used to be, *he* damn well had to. And if that used-up Robin person, snoring in his bed, did not compare favorably to her, well, tough toenails.

"I wasn't…I didn't…" Thorne ran a hand roughly through his hair, mussing it even more. "I'm tired because I've been paying bills and catching up on business paperwork. Nothing else."

Okay. Nobody was in his bed upstairs. Good to know. It was absolutely none of her business. But still, good to know.

"Maybe you should open the café later," Athena said blithely. Because that's how she felt. Blithe. "Skip breakfast, serve lunch and dinner instead."

"I have considered changing the hours, but it would require a more complex menu. And more staff. And as I told you, I like my afternoons free."

For *what* exactly, she'd love to find out. Since the day she'd encountered Thorne jogging, she never saw him around town or her neighborhood.

"Want me to take care of the bachelor farmers' order?" she asked.

"No thanks. I got it."

"How's my favorite curmudgeon?" Athena called out when Eugene shuffled in.

He gave her a thumbs-up and sat at the table closest to the beverage station.

"I haven't seen him at breakfast in weeks," Thorne remarked. "I thought he moved. Or hated the food the way he hates everything."

"He's one of the lunch regulars now, like Joe and Theresa, Phyllis and Dan. They've invited him to join them, but he prefers eating alone." The foursome, to her delight, was on a tour of the Botanical Garden in St. Louis for the day. She waved to Eugene. "I'll be right with you."

"No rush, missy. Take your time," he said.

"They all come for your shift. And the grouchiest man in Laurel is being nice." Thorne's eyes crinkled with a smile. "Can you tell me how you pulled off this magic trick?"

She shrugged. "Guess I make them feel special."

"Special," he repeated.

"A little extra attention goes a long way."

"A long way," he said, gazing intently at her.

His eyes deepened to moss green and pulled her in, closer, closer, down to the heath, where they were lying together, arms and legs entwined, the sun warming their bodies, his lips melting her—

"Uh, Thena? Did *you* get enough sleep last night?"

Athena closed her mouth and wiped what she guessed was a dopey look off her face. "Sorry. My mind wandered." Across the misty moors, through the sweet heather...

Wait. Why was she picturing a scene from *Brigadoon* instead of *Wuthering Heights*?

She looked around the room to shift mental gears while Thorne went to the kitchen. The bachelor farmers were staring at the two women comparing data on their Fitbit smart watches. A young guy in a suit thumbed away at his phone between sips of coffee. Suzie, the owner of Suzie's Seconds, was sharing with her lunch companions the latest reports of so-and-so's stint in rehab and who'd been seen kissing whom and where and when. The clothes she sold were secondhand, but her news, gathered between the clothes racks, was firsthand.

Thanks to a chat with Suzie last week, Athena knew all about the DUI offenses of the alderman Jonas Thacker and the shopping habits of the postman Mike Harrison. Suzie was intrigued by his purchases of women's clothing when the sole female in his life was his beagle, Ruby.

What Athena did not know was anything at all about C. L. Garland, whom Suzie was *not* intrigued by in the least.

After swabbing a table clean, she texted Lydia, reminding her to check house sale listings. And reminded herself not to get discouraged.

"Athena? Sweetie?"

She spun around. Her father and Wayne and Dolores Blake, her former teachers, stood behind her. The Blakes were dressed alike as usual—sweater-vests over plaid shirts buttoned to the neck and tucked into the elastic waistbands of their denim slacks. Students had joked they looked like hobbits. While their faces were still childlike and cheerful, their brown bobs had morphed into gray pixie cuts.

"You didn't tell me you were coming, Dad." Athena hoped he'd remember his promise to stay mum about her former relationship with Thorne.

"We decided at the last minute to eat here," he said. "We're tired of buffets and fast-food restaurants."

"This table's ready just for you." She gave each Blake a brief hug. "Nice to see you again."

"Welcome back to our little corner of the world, Athena," Dolores said.

Thorne came up to them, carrying a tray of sandwiches, and put it down to shake all their hands. "Welcome to As You Like It Café. Wonderful to see you, Charles."

"Your café gets great reviews on Facebook," Charles said. "We wanted to see what all the fuss was about."

Her father on Facebook? What was the world coming to?

"I hope it meets your expectations," Thorne said. "Please, make yourselves at home."

"Thank you," Charles said. "And when you get a free moment, stop by our table for a chin wag."

"Will do," Thorne said.

Athena pulled out the chairs for them while Thorne brought the sandwiches to the bachelor farmers. "Coffee for everyone?" she asked.

"We prefer herbal tea if you have it," her father said.

Of course. The Charles 2.0 drank herbal tea.

Wayne slapped Charles on the back. "He's looking great, isn't he? We've got him exercising and eating better."

"We can't take all the credit," Dolores said. "A certain lady by the name of Vivienne may have something to do with it."

"Who's she?" Athena asked.

"The woman who leads our tai chi class. She's as graceful as a swan," Dolores said.

"That *was* you in the park, Dad. I thought I was seeing things."

Mischief lit his blue eyes. "There are a lot of things about me that would surprise you."

"But tai chi? You were never into physical stuff."

"I wouldn't say never. Your mother and I took dance lessons for a year."

"You did? When? Where was I?"

"Before the Johnson business." His euphemism for his wife's affair—the calm neutrality of which infuriated Lydia. "The lessons were my idea. I thought they'd get her interested in sex again."

Athena waited for the floor beneath her feet to open wide and swallow her. The Blakes sat down and busied themselves unfolding their napkins and arranging silverware.

"Your mother simply couldn't keep up with me," Charles said.

"What? The rhumba? The tango?" Athena asked, her voice cracking.

He leaned over and whispered in her ear, his bushy eyebrow tickling her cheek. "I'm referring to the horizontal mambo, my dear."

CHAPTER EIGHT

Time brought resignation, and a melancholy sweeter than common joy.

—EMILY BRONTË, *WUTHERING HEIGHTS*

There was nothing like the crunch of dried leaves beneath her feet and the bracing chill of an October day to make Athena nearly swoon from nostalgia. Countless happy memories floated on the smoky air. Jumping into leaf piles with Finn when they were kids. Hayrides with high school friends. Hiking in farmers' fields, imagining the bales of hay were the Penistone Crags where Catherine and Heathcliff would meet.

Discovering her One True Love in a freshman literature classroom ablaze with autumn sunshine.

Athena buttoned her jacket as she walked among the groups of students changing classes on Washington University's campus. Thanks to her alumna library privileges, she'd spent a very productive morning researching and reacquainting herself with Elizabeth Gaskell's *North and South*, a novel she hadn't read in years. Garland hadn't altered the title in the LitWit series, a tongue-in-cheek reference, no doubt, to the sixty-nine position favored by the lovers, Margaret Hale and John Thornton.

Hurrying off the walkway as a bicyclist sped by, she twisted her ankle in a small ditch. "Shit," she muttered, hobbling to the nearest bench. But the pain shooting up her leg was quickly replaced by another affliction—Thorne walking toward her across the green, across the years. Nostalgia in the flesh.

His black blazer accentuated the athletic triangle of his broad shoulders and narrow waist. Gray serge trousers and cordovan shoes were reminders the barista and baker had been a lawyer in the not-too-distant past. A style of dress she'd always been quick to label as snobbish.

Too quick. After all, her anti-snob attitude was a form of snobbery too. An uncomfortable conclusion she'd drawn recently while reading the chapters in *Wuthering Heights* in which Catherine lived with the wealthy Linton family for five weeks. Heathcliff scorned her when she returned for taking on their refined airs and conventional manners. In the past, Athena would nod in agreement with him as she read. Now she wasn't so sure. Would it have killed Heathcliff to... what? Wash his hair? Put on a clean shirt?

Would it have killed her to learn which spoon went with which food at the Kent table?

"What brings you here?" Thorne asked, sitting beside her on the bench.

Athena patted the satchel holding her laptop and notebook. "Library research. And you?"

"On my way to a lunch date. I had time to spare, so I've been walking around campus."

A date he was so eager for that he showed up early.

"This is the first time I've been here since I got back," she said.

"I come often for lectures and exhibits."

"And poetry readings?" They had never missed a single one.

"There aren't as many these days. Sign of the times, I guess."

"You've spruced up pretty nicely for Robin," she said. His jaw was clean-shaven and not a stray wheat-gold strand poked out from his impeccably trimmed hair.

"I'm not meeting Robin."

"Who then?" The question slid off her tongue before she could swallow it.

He flicked a speck of lint off his pants. "Pamela."

"Playing the field. Good for you." Athena crossed her leg and jiggled her foot, ignoring the throbbing sensation in her injured ankle. Which didn't hurt as much as Girlfriend Number Two. "One boyfriend is more than enough for me. He's pretty high-maintenance."

And a challenge. In a single conversation, Sergei might flit from a discussion of Russian architecture, waving an onion, to blini, to Rasputin. But on the subject of their green-card marriage, with a baby as bait, he was persistent and focused.

"Where is apartment spare key? I will set up nursery while you're gone, Atheeena," he said the last time they'd talked.

"You'll do no such thing."

"The room with little light. So baby Boris sleep."

"Boris?"

"Or Anastasia."

She ended the call, claiming she had to go to work. And resolved to let future unknown caller numbers go directly to voicemail. And name a baby girl Anastasia someday.

"What's your boyfriend's name?" Thorne asked.

"Sergei. Sergei 'Loony' Gudonov."

"Pretty insensitive language, Thena," he said, frowning.

"Well, pardon me. Did you leave your sense of humor in the state of Washington?"

"Mental illness isn't a laughing matter."

"All I meant was, he's a little . . . eccentric. Like no one I've ever known." Let Thorne interpret that any way he wanted.

He pulled the cuffs from his jacket. "Sorry. I just got off the phone with Mayor Benson. I've been advocating for a mental health clinic in the community, but he's so damn resistant."

"A clinic for military vets with post-traumatic stress?"

"Vets are one group that would benefit. I've been in touch with personnel at the nearby Air Force base. They're definitely interested."

She had always admired Thorne's commitment to causes. The inner-city literacy program he'd initiated junior year had been a resounding success.

"I haven't seen the mayor or his sidekick since you defended my honor," she said. "Guess they're boycotting the café."

"The councilman completely ignored me at the last Chamber of Commerce meeting. I did get a chance to put out some feelers about Garland though."

"And?" Athena asked eagerly.

"Came up empty. I have an appointment with the manager of the Laurel Bank soon. I'll ask her if she knows anything."

She uncrossed her legs and turned to face him. "I thought you said you weren't going to help me."

"Change of—"

Athena filled in the blank. It was either a very good thing or a not-good-at-all thing that Thorne couldn't bring himself to say *heart*.

"My opinion of the project is neither here nor there," he went on. "It would be petty not to do what I can."

"How about legal advice?"

"Sorry, Thena. I'm drawing the line there. I'm finished with that life."

"Fair enough. And thanks."

A couple walked by, sharing the earbuds of an iPod. Two

mourning doves protested mildly when they crossed their path and then resumed nuzzling beaks. On the north end of campus stood the hawthorn tree on which *TK* had carved his initials inside a heart with *AM*. Coupling, harmony, and memories of happier days, all around her.

"They chopped our tree down," Thorne said in a low voice as if he'd read her mind.

Our tree. The lovely, graceful hawthorn with their carved initials, under which he'd asked her to marry him while placing a wreath of its flowered branches on her head. The garland was in one of Lydia's hatboxes in Athena's bedroom closet, disintegrating into a circle of decayed twigs. As for the diamond engagement ring she'd instructed him to stick in his keester, he'd sold it and donated the money to charity.

Athena let out a pained sigh that had nothing to do with her ankle. But for the sake of spoons and snobbery and wounded pride, she might not have rejected his proposal. "Nelly, I *am* Heathcliff," Catherine had cried. "Nelly, *I* am Heathcliff," Athena murmured.

Thorne lowered his head to hers. "Did you say something?"

"I was thinking how the chopped hawthorn tree is a metaphor for us."

"Once an English major..."

"And daughter of an English teacher. I found out recently my dad used to write love poems for my mother."

"Are you serious? Charles?"

"Yep. And he took dance classes with her to save their marriage."

"A poet and a dancer. Incredible."

"He does tai chi in the park too. He's been brimming with vitality and passion beneath his quiet exterior all this time, and I didn't see it."

She'd dismissed her father as C. L. Garland too quickly.

Writing erotica might be one of those *things* about himself he said would *surprise* her.

Thorne turned and locked his eyes on hers as leaves fell to their feet like technicolored rain. Athena waited for him to say something, anything, to match the eloquence of his face. Beseech the angels to fling him from the heavens onto the heath like Catherine did in *Wuthering Heights*, for instance. Or implore Athena to haunt him beyond the grave as Heathcliff entreated Catherine.

A jet screamed through the sky, startling the mourning doves to flight. Thorne looked away and waved a fly from his face, breaking Athena's flight of fancy. Wouldn't she ever learn?

"What was with the laser-beam eyes, Thorne?"

"I was holding on to a thought."

"What about?"

"You."

"A good one for a change?"

"So many people have hidden lives. Or are deceitful. But not you, Thena."

"What you see is what you get," she agreed.

"You've always been straight up. Authentic."

"Saves time," she quipped. "Besides, I'm too lazy to keep track of more than one life."

Her heart thumped like a sixteen-year-old girl who'd been told by the boy she's crushing on that she's wonderful.

Get a grip. You are *wonderful. And you don't need Thorne Kent to tell you so.*

"I hope your boyfriend appreciates what he has in you," Thorne said solemnly.

"He certainly does." A fast track to citizenship.

The bells in the university chapel rang the time. "I better get going," Athena said. "I'm relieving Kristie at noon."

She rose, forgetting her sore ankle, and sank back down again.

"Are you hurt?" he asked.

"My ankle. I turned it in a ditch."

"Let me have a look."

Thorne leaned over and untied her shoe, sliding it off her foot. As his long, bony fingers kneaded her flesh like dough, caressed her arch, and massaged her ankle, heat radiated through her body. Flames might shoot from her hair. Or from a more private place. How could a man who smelled Ivory soap–clean make her feel so dirty?

Nostalgia, that's all this was. Remembering how he used to nibble on what he called her "edible toes" and then make his leisurely way up her leg, around her navel, across her nipples, along her lips, and down, down, down again until she forgot every preposition she'd ever learned.

"It's a sprain," he said. "If your ankle was broken, you'd be in a lot more pain when I pressed on it."

And if you remembered how we used to screw the sheets right off our bed, you'd be in a lot more pain now too.

When he sat up again, his flushed cheeks and, if she wasn't mistaken, the impressive bulge in the crotch of his attorney pants suggested he remembered perfectly well.

She eased her foot back into her shoe and retied it. Suppressed a satisfied smile.

He cleared his throat. "Do you need help getting to your car?" As if he could walk any better than her with that boner.

"No. It's parked nearby."

"Breakfast was slow. Want Kristie to cover for you?"

"Nah. I'm okay."

"Wrap your ankle as soon as you get to the café. The first-aid kit is in the pantry."

"Sure thing."

He helped her get up from the bench, holding her hands longer than was necessary.

"Is there something else?" she asked as he stood there without saying another word. Waiting for the blood to return to his brain probably. And yes, she was loving this.

"Looks like we'll be working together Friday," Thorne said. "Kristie's mom is coming in from Denver for the weekend, and she's taking time off. Any chance you can work Saturday afternoon?"

"Sorry. I have to pick Finn up at the airport. He's coming home to stay for a while." One argument too many with Mario over purloined pho, she supposed. "And then I've got to head to the public library."

"Hope I get to see Finn while he's here. See you Friday, then."

"See you."

"Thena?" Thorne called out as she walked away.

"Yeah?"

"Thanks for the great job you're doing. I appreciate you being so personable with the customers. And professional."

Professional enough to endure the memory of their hawthorn tree, his disastrous proposal, and one very erotic ankle probe.

"Thanks for the employee evaluation." And slinging the satchel over her shoulder with what she hoped was fetching insouciance, Athena hobbled to her car.

Thorne whistled as he filled the café dishwasher for the third time Friday afternoon. He'd been on his feet since six a.m. The chilly rain hadn't kept hungry patrons from running him ragged all morning. To make matters worse, two of his stove burners had died. But none of it dampened his whistle-happy mood.

Pamela had broken up with him over lunch Wednesday, sparing him the trouble. He was "emotionally unavailable." His mind was "always on something else." Or *someone else.* Guess she was more perceptive than he gave her credit for.

Waves of laughter rippled across the dining room, signaling Athena had arrived for her shift. He tucked his shirt into his pants and wiped mustard off his wrist. A few minutes later, she burst through the kitchen door, bringing on her rain-damp skin the fragrance of lilies of the valley.

"It's as crowded as O'Hare Airport out there," Athena exclaimed.

"Business hasn't let up since I opened. How's your ankle?"

"Much better. Unlike my hair, which is frizzing like I put my finger in an electrical socket."

He'd love to bury his face in that chaos of curls. Smell her sweet neck. Kiss her full lips. Cravings he'd been fighting since the day she first walked into his kitchen and he'd steadied himself against the counter to keep his knees from buckling.

Athena wound her hair into a bun. "You okay?" she asked through the two barrettes clenched between her teeth. "You have a weird look on your face."

"Pamela and I broke up." Good save.

She snapped both barrettes closed over the bun. "With Robin for backup, you'll recover nicely."

"Do you have backups for... what's his name?"

She grinned, crinkling her adorable nose with its sprinkle of freckles. "Sergei comes with his own internal backups."

And Thorne hated every single one of them.

Because he had read between the lines. When Athena had described her boyfriend as "high-maintenance" and "eccentric," it wasn't an insult. What she really meant was that he was unpredictable, exciting. Passionate. Like no one she'd ever known.

"How'd it feel, being back on campus?" he asked. Instead of so many other questions.

"I felt old—like, fossil old. Remembering how young I was when we were students there."

"But you work at a college. You're used to being around callow youth."

"Campus life is different as a professor. And I don't have memories of being young and stupid at Wyatt College." She frowned and bit her lip, looking blankly at the stack of dishes on the counter. "Okay. Stupid. Definitely. But not young."

Her downcast expression while describing her professional life was a switch from her usual enthusiasm. "Thena, is there something... Do you want to talk—"

"Nope." She reached for an apron on the hook, quickly put it over her head, and tied it around her waist. "We good to go on sandwich ingredients?"

Talk to him? Share her troubled thoughts? Why would she when she had Sergei to turn to? Thena and Thorne didn't confide in each other anymore. End of story.

"The ingredients are ready," he said.

Thorne followed her out of the kitchen, and as if a light had been suddenly switched on, the dining room came alive with chatter and motion. Forget his freshly baked bread and creative sandwiches. Athena's earthy warmth was what the customers came for. She maneuvered between the crowded tables, dispensing coffee, tea, and witticisms. His parents had pronounced her sense of humor "unseemly" and "lacking couth." They were so busy trying to fix him up with debutantes and daughters of their friends, any other woman besides "that Murphy girl," that they never gave her a chance.

Deep inside, he didn't entirely blame Athena for resenting his decision to honor the Kent tradition instead of their commitment. When they were "old and grey," as Yeats wrote in his poem "When You Are Old," or when she was married to someone who saw "the pilgrim soul" in her, as he did, he'd reveal the whole sad, sorry story. But hell, what a long time to wait. When Athena had admitted she'd underestimated her father's passion, the temptation to tell her everything, as if she were still his dearest friend in the world, had been excruciating.

"Thorne!"

He forced himself to look away from Athena cutting Eugene's sandwich into squares. The crabby old fart was actually smiling.

"Oh, hi, Joe."

"I called your name a half dozen times," Joe said. "Head in the clouds?"

"Thereabouts. How've you been?"

"Wonderful. We just got back from the Science Center with our ladies." He pointed to Theresa and Phyllis sitting at a table with Dan. "Thanks to Athena, we've been enjoying the pleasure of their company."

"What did Athena have to do with it?"

Joe looked fondly at her across the room. "She saw the possibilities."

Thorne would have liked to hear more about these *possibilities*, but the entrance of Mayor Benson and the councilman caught his attention. They stood in the doorway, knocking rain from their umbrellas. "Sorry, Joe. I have to—"

"Mend fences?"

"How do you know about that?"

"Small town, big mouths," Joe said with a wink. "Go to it, young fellow."

Thorne walked toward them with as big a smile as he could fake. "Mayor Benson, where would you and..." Shit. He'd forgotten the other man's name again. "...and your assistant—"

"*Councilman*," the mayor said, ignoring his outstretched hand.

"And the name is Ned Childers," Childers said through pinched lips.

"Where would you like to sit?" Thorne asked.

"Close to the hearth, if possible," Childers said. "Glad the fire's lit."

"Beastly weather," Mayor Benson complained. "We're soaked through."

Thorne dragged an empty table by the wall to the hearth. When he had brought the menus to them, he extended his hand again. The mayor had no choice but to shake it.

"No shoptalk today, Kent," he grumbled.

"But we never get a chance to discuss—"

The mayor raised his big paw of a hand to silence him and read the menu, his glasses perched at the end of his bulbous nose. "I'll have the tuna melt and iced tea."

"The same," Childers said.

"I have an appointment in an hour, if you can step to it," Mayor Benson said, handing Thorne the menus.

"Coming right up."

He was on his way to make the tuna melts but stopped as a muscled young stud sauntered over to Athena. He recognized him as one of the café's renovation crew. Kevin? Kyle? Thorne pulled the cloth from his belt and proceeded to wipe a table next to them. Karl, that was his name.

"Mr. Murphy gave me the go-ahead," Karl was saying to Athena. "If you see my truck in front of your house, you'll know I'm working on the greenhouse."

Great. God's gift to women, down to his low-slung belt and very capable hands, would be swinging his badass bod around Athena on a regular basis.

She said something too low for Thorne to make out, but

whatever it was, it made Karl laugh. And stick his caveman chest out. Try as he might, he heard only snatches of their conversation—two-by-fours, roof flashing—but *all* of Karl's parting words, tossed over his shoulder with a grin as he ambled to the door.

"Don't forget, Athena. That's Karl with a *k*. As in *kiss*."

He would have loved to hear her reply—ideally, something along the lines of "Get lost, sleazeball"—but she had crossed the room to take more orders.

And he had wiped a table clean to within an inch of its life.

Thorne was headed to the kitchen to make the tuna melts—and punch a mound of dough—when Athena beckoned him to the large round table where the Garden Club members were gathered.

"They've been asking why you called today's special Love's Labour's Lost," she said.

The fried green tomato and grilled portobello mushroom with goat cheese on sourdough bread was one of his more inspired sandwich creations. But then he'd been feeling inspired lately. Something to do with autumn. Or a stroll through campus. Or recovering nicely from a breakup.

"It's the title of a Shakespeare play, isn't it?" one of the women asked.

"Most of his sandwich specials are, Yolanda," another one chided her.

"The farmer who brought the tomatoes said they were grown down south," Thorne said. "He gave them to me in exchange for listening to his sad story."

"I *told* you the tomatoes came from somewhere else," one of the men said. "You can't get green tomatoes here this time of year."

"Who cares?" Yolanda said. "I want to hear the sad story."

"So do I," the other women chimed in.

"Go on, Thorne," Athena said.

"The farmer had been working on his family's farm for years, promising his fiancée they'd marry once the business was passed to him," he told his captive audience. "He came back to the house one evening to find her engagement ring on the table. And discovered an email later saying she'd had enough of tractors and promises and was moving to Wyoming with a ski instructor. Love's labor was lost."

The women at the table exchanged appalled glances. "How can anyone be so cruel?" one of them asked.

"Apparently, the ski instructor swept her off her feet," Thorne said.

"I hope they get swept away by an avalanche," Yolanda said.

"Breaking up by email," one of the men said, shaking his head. "Never heard of such a thing."

"They split up by text messages these days too," another man remarked.

Thorne could feel Athena watching him. *She* knew the story behind Shakespeare's play. How the King of Navarre and his companions tried desperately, and failed, to renounce the company of women.

Yes, Thena. The name of the sandwich is also about how hard it is to fight desire.

"Tell me," she said, "was the farmer headed to Wyoming to win her back?"

"I'm not sure. I doubt it," Thorne said.

"He'd be a damn fool if he was," Yolanda said.

"Hell if I would," one of the men grumbled.

"When you truly love someone, pride doesn't matter," Athena said.

Like her crying her heart out for him in Seattle.

Oh, Thena. If you only knew.

"The fiancée sounds heartless, but maybe she had a good reason," she said, deftly filling her tray with glasses, mugs, and plates. "And it wasn't some Adonis on skis."

"What reason, Athena?" Yolanda asked eagerly.

"There are two sides to every story. My guess is, the farmer lost sight of them as a couple. He let the family business take priority over their relationship."

The Garden Club members nodded, shrugged, and chewed their Love's Labour's Lost sandwiches while that Murphy girl walked away, the tray balanced on her arm, hips swaying.

"Kent! We're waiting on our tuna melts over here," Mayor Benson barked.

Thorne took his good-ass time constructing the sandwiches, slowly adding the mayonnaise to the tuna, cutting an onion to transparent slices, and melting cheese, along with regret and a curse or two, over the whole damn thing.

Athena drove to St. Louis Lambert International Airport Saturday afternoon with Branwell in the front passenger seat. He sat at attention as he always did when he went for a drive, drooling, like her, to Josh Groban singing in Italian. She didn't understand the lyrics any better than a dog—a crying shame, since she'd suffered through so many operas.

She turned onto the county road leading to the highway, and Branwell whimpered. "I know. I can't wait to see Finn either."

He turned to her with a look of anxiety on his pug mug and moaned.

"Don't even think about upchucking in my clean car."

He slid off the seat and curled up in the footwell with a doleful look. And whimpered some more. She soon saw why. Up ahead, the sign for Moran and Ruckman Veterinary

Clinic appeared. *Children are for people who can't have pets* was their clever slogan for the month.

"And flatulent dogs are for people who can't have children," she muttered.

Branwell covered his face with his paws.

"Sorry, bud. And relax. I'm not taking you to the vet."

He clambered back into the seat with a grin.

Finn was already waiting at the passenger pickup area, a backpack straining his shoulders, both hands gripping suitcases. His curly mop of strawberry-blond hair, large hazel eyes, and ruddy complexion combined the best features of their parents. He was as tall as Thorne, but his University of Illinois sweatshirt couldn't disguise a Charles tendency for pudge.

"Welcome home, Finnster," Athena said, helping him load his luggage into the trunk.

"Home. Yeah. Thanks." He leaned into the car window, and Branwell licked his cheek. "At least *somebody* loves me," he said plaintively.

"*Everybody* loves you, me most of all. And if they don't, I'll box their ears." She got back in the driver's seat, kissed his other cheek after he strapped himself in with the seat belt, and adjusted the rearview mirror. "Tell me why this latest fight with Mario has sent you packing."

"It's over," he said, cuddling Branwell on his lap. "We called it quits."

"Oh, no, Finn. For good?"

"For better. But not *for better or for worse*."

"I'll help you sort things out." Athena Murphy, rescuer of broken relationships. Except her own.

"They're already sorted. We're done," he said, sniffling.

"You said the same thing last year when you moved in with me for two weeks," she said, making a left turn out of the airport parking area.

"Your apartment isn't far enough this time."

"Home will be more fun with you here, that's for sure."

"I can hardly wait to fight with The Charles over the TV remote."

"It's all yours. He's hardly ever around. Remember the text I sent of him in workout clothes?"

"Is *The Charles 2.0* for real?"

"For *surreal.* He does tai chi at the park, walks Branwell, and eats healthy food. Something's up with him but I haven't figured out what yet."

"Tai chi. Wow." He shifted in his seat to face her. "You look great. I think the break from teaching has been good for you."

"The break from Davenport and Corinne, not teaching," she said, merging onto the highway.

"How's it going with Thorne? You never mention him."

"It's going. Thorne is Thorne." *Authentic*, he'd called her. Like himself.

"And your book?"

"Moving along at a glacial pace. Before global warming."

Finn reached across to lower the volume of Groban's voice. "Remember when I said I'd come up with a plan to help you find Garland?"

"Yeah?"

"I've drawn up an algorithm of all the variables. If I cross-check them with what I know about everyone in town—"

"Whoa. What language dost thou speak, Sir Finn?"

"Math and engineering. I mapped out Laurel like an electrical grid, and I'm going to mark which people to investigate. You know, test the circuits."

"I don't know from circuits. And go back a bit. You don't know *everyone* in Laurel."

Finn grinned, looking as mischievous as Tom Sawyer.

"Pretty much. Stevie DiMarco and I cruised town on our bikes one summer and made a list of everybody's names from checking their mailboxes. We spied on them too."

"Uh... isn't that a federal offense or something?"

"We were twelve. And bored. We wrote notes addressed to people we didn't like, saying, *I saw what you did*, or, *Get the money soon or else*."

"You didn't," she said.

Even Branwell looked shocked.

"We did."

"Where's Stevie now? State prison?"

"In Chicago, married to a woman about ten years older than him. They have three kids."

It was Athena's turn to grin. "Older woman, huh? I'm not surprised. Stevie and I made out under the bleachers in the park once. During a Little League baseball game."

Finn turned to her, a look of mock horror on his face. "You bitch. He was my first crush."

"He tasted like Skittles."

"Maybe I *won't* help you."

"Actually, your plan's not bad. Hardly anyone but the young and enterprising move from Laurel, so your list is probably still good to go. If you've kept the evidence of your criminal activity."

"It's buried in one of the boxes in my closet. I'll dig it out when I get home."

Athena switched to the middle lane as a motorcyclist roared up behind them. "I'm hearing a lot of interesting gossip at the café. Unfortunately, none of it's about Garland."

"Gossip, huh? Fill me in."

One of their favorite activities as kids was to come home from Sunday Mass and share whispered conversations they'd overheard and signs of forbidden intimacies they'd witnessed.

No one but Athena and Finn were aware the choir master and organ player were in love, having watched the progress of their affair on the church balcony—until the lovers drove away in a Winnebago, waving goodbye to their spouses.

"Okay, here goes," she said. "Mrs. Jensen, the secretary of the Lutheran church, absconded with the steeple repair funds."

"My fourth-grade teacher? Who let me be the hall monitor all the time? No way."

"Way. And she stole a pair of very valuable silver candlesticks. *Antiques Roadshow*–worthy."

"She used to tell us to 'straighten up and fly right.' "

"This isn't gossip but guess what Dad told me? He and Mom took dance lessons to spice up their sex life."

"They *had* a sex life?"

"Latin dances, no less."

"The Charles, whose only bold act was cutting the Under Penalty of Law tags off our pillows?"

"The very same. Apparently, *his* sex drive was on overdrive, not hers."

"Get out!" Finn said in his highest soprano, inducing a frightened fart out of Branwell.

Athena opened the windows, letting in a welcome blast of fresh air. Finn covered Branwell's eyes, squinting in the brilliant sunshine. "I just had another inspiration," he said. "My next business will be making sunglasses for dogs. A different style for every breed."

She glanced at Branwell's snout. "Unless the breed doesn't have an actual nose to prop them on."

"You sound like Mario. He made fun of my latest T-shirt idea, and it was the last straw."

She waited for him to continue, carefully navigating the steep curve of the exit.

"There are tons of famous quotes, so I figured why not print *them*," he said. "*I'd* wear a shirt saying *It takes a village*, wouldn't you?"

"Sure. What did Mario say that was such a deal breaker?"

"*It takes a village idiot.* And then he laughed his stupid laugh, standing there in his wet suit, dripping all over our hardwood floor."

Luckily, her ringing phone diverted her own urge to laugh.

"If that's him, I don't want to talk," Finn said.

"Hi, Mom," Athena said. "I just picked Finn up from the airport. We're on speakerphone."

"Hello, Finn. How's my baby?" Lydia said.

"Terrible," he said, pouting.

"How come you're home?"

"I broke up with Mario."

"Roommates are a pain in the ass. Move out and get your own apartment."

He looked at Athena and rolled his eyes.

"I'm not staying on long," Lydia said. "I'm headed *to* the airport with Tony for the conference in Atlanta."

"Have fun," Athena said.

"I called to tell you I emailed the real estate listings you wanted. None of them raise a red flag though. The McMansions were bought by people who've always been rich."

"Shit," Athena muttered.

"Don't curse. And listen, I need a favor. Tony and I plan to travel for a while after the conference. Business is slow, and I haven't had a break in ages."

"Are you two . . . um . . ."

"No. Nothing like that," Lydia snapped. "Can you house-sit till I get back, Athena? One of my assistants was supposed to, but she had to cancel at the last minute."

"Sure. I'll be glad to." With only two and a half months

left to write her damn-near-raw draft, retreating to a quiet house, away from Charles's noisy appliances, Branwell's intestinal tract, and Finn's voice modulations as he dealt with his breakup, was a boon. "How long will you be gone?"

"I'm not sure. My neighbor on the right has the key and instructions. Don't forget to bring the mail in every day and put the trash out Tuesday nights."

"I'll help too. I've got nothing else to do," Finn said forlornly.

"If you're that unhappy, then consider making up with Mario," Lydia said. "Good friends are hard to find. And keep."

Athena and Finn swiveled to face each other, mouths open wide. Mario had graduated from *roommate* to *friend* in a few short minutes.

"Toodle-oo," Lydia said breathlessly. "Gotta go. Bye."

"Do you ever get the feeling our parents are total strangers?" Athena asked as she turned onto the county road.

"And fourth-grade teachers who *abscond*," Finn said. "What a weird word."

"I thought you'd like it."

He hit his head against the seat and sighed. "Ultimately, no one knows anybody, do they?"

Including the sister of a brother who had had a brief career as a juvenile delinquent.

"No, they don't," Athena said. "But don't make a T-shirt saying so. It's too depressing."

"Mario," he mumbled. "Shit."

The sun shone brightly as they drove up to the Murphy house, but their dark mood shadowed them. She didn't mind sharing her brother's pain. It came with the territory. It always had. He was her Finn. Sweet, sensitive, loyal, true.

And at the moment, gobsmacked at the sight of Karl

attaching a ladder to the side of his truck. Finn got out of the car, holding on to Branwell for dear life. "I'm either attracted or scared to death," he whispered to Athena standing beside him. "Or both."

"You're barking up the wrong tree. He already gave me the once-over check and a come-on."

Karl lumbered over, and his eyes practically grunted as he took in every inch of Athena's body beneath her tight sweater and leggings. He pointed to the house's drooping gutters and crooked shingles. "Mr. Murphy told me I might as well repair the house too while I'm at it."

"Will you be coming by often?" Finn asked in his deepest bass.

"I reckon I will," Karl drawled.

Branwell, dangling over Finn's arm, yelped a question mark.

"No such luck," Finn murmured. "But a guy can dream, can't he?"

CHAPTER NINE

I'll walk where my own nature would be leading.

—EMILY BRONTË, "STANZAS"

Athena lay in bed late Sunday morning, trying to think of a good reason to get up. She'd dumped her laptop into the trash can last night—thanks to a trail of dead ends in her project and drinking scotch with Finn and Charles. The sun streaming through the window hurt her eyes, already irritated from reading tedious county records at the public library yesterday.

Perusing back issues of the local newspaper, the *Laurel Chronicle*, though, wasn't the least bit boring. The Police Blotter section had particularly riveted her. Hazel Forster, the church lady to beat all church ladies, had been discovered asleep in a pew of the Methodist church, clutching an empty bottle of Gordon's gin. And Geraldine O'Neal had been captured on camera leaving *High-Fructose Corn Syrup Will Kill You!* signs above the snack shelves in Huck's convenience store.

Well, Lydia did mention her wit and originality. If *Geraldine* were C. L. Garland, Athena's task would be a blast instead of a slog. But no such luck. Weaving seamlessly, anonymously into Laurel's social fabric suited Garland's purposes perfectly. Drawing attention to herself at a convenience store was the last thing she'd do. Athena's dutiful, if fruitless, library research would become a mere mention in the first chapter about her book's challenges, now titled "No Rock Unturned."

She grabbed the pen and notebook on the nightstand and scrawled *weave, seam, fabric* beneath her puny attempt—two brief paragraphs—to write her own novella based on Anne Brontë's novel *The Tenant of Wildfell Hall.* She couldn't come up with an erotic Helen Graham and Gilbert Markham scenario to save her life, mostly because Gilbert gave her the creeps. And forget a witty title. Academic papers were one thing. It took a genius like Garland to turn literature on its head.

A witty, literate genius like... like Thorne.

Athena threw off the covers—and her fleeting crazy idea. This was what desperation and a scotch-sour stomach did to a person. No way in hell would Thorne *bastardize literature.* Besides, he was male, a *recent* resident of Laurel, and living *below* his usual economic standards. Furthermore, if he had Garland's money, he wouldn't have to toady up to Mayor Benson for funds to build a mental health clinic.

"And he's working his business connections to help you, you ninny," she muttered, retrieving the laptop from the trash can.

She showered until the water turned lukewarm and, putting her bathrobe back on because, what the hell, it was Sunday, went down to the kitchen. Finn sat at the table, frowning at his laptop.

"Fresh joe?" she asked, pointing to the coffeemaker.

"Uh-huh." He glanced up. "You should get dressed. Karl's dropping off supplies for the gutters."

She tugged at the collar of his pressed shirt. "You spiffed up for him, I see."

His face reddened in an instant. "I'm 99.9 percent positive he's not gay."

"And the other .1 percent?"

"Wishful thinking." He bent his head and pointed to the center of his scalp. "He wouldn't be attracted to me anyway. I'm losing my hair."

Athena peered at the world's smallest bald spot. "You're crazy. Your hair's as thick as ever."

"Have you taken a good look at Dad? How long do I have till *I'm* as bald as a cue ball?"

She filled the coffee mug to the brim and sat across from him. The dull pain in her abdomen reminded her she was ovulating—and that perimenopause was looming, her eggs were dwindling, and her fertility was fading. "You're not the only one worried about time. Do you hear that?"

"Hear what?" Finn asked.

"My biological clock, tick-tick-ticking away."

His eyes widened like they used to when she read him scary bedtime stories. "Since when do you want a baby?"

"Since I turned thirty. It's my dirty secret."

He grinned. "You'd make a great mom. Like, the best."

"And you'd make the best Uncle Finn. Can I sign you up for babysitting duties now?"

"You bet. Does this mean you're going for it? It would be a good reason to hook up with Sir Gay."

"Hell no. I'm broody, not nuts." And a little disappointed he hadn't considered Thorne. "While we're on the subject of Sergei, I told Mom he was my boyfriend so she wouldn't bug me to get one. Back me up if she grills you about him."

"What'd you tell her?"

"He's rich and has potential."

"For what?"

"I kept it vague. Let her fill in the blanks."

Athena drank her coffee, listening to the tap of Finn's fingers across his laptop keyboard. A pair of chirping sparrows darted past the window, arguing about something. Probably their kids. "Where's Dad?" she asked.

"Dunno. He left early, bright-eyed and bushy-tailed."

"I thought if the scotch didn't wear him out, belting out songs from *Hello, Dolly!* all night would."

"I think you're right. He's got *something* going on. Any theories?"

"Nope. But I'm 99.9 percent positive he's not C. L. Garland," Athena said. "I've looked everywhere for new or expensive stuff around here and didn't find a thing."

"The royalties may be in a bank or investment account."

"I think he'd spend *some* of the money though, don't you? He'd kill for first editions of his favorite books."

And yet.

So many people have hidden lives, Thorne had said. Who's to say her sweet, befuddled dad wasn't one of them? Despite what she'd told Finn, she hadn't completely dismissed the possibility their father was the mysterious author. One explanation for his daily disappearances might be that he went somewhere to write.

Finn slid a sheet of paper across the table to her. "Here. I finished the Garland algorithm and narrowed the list down to five suspects. They all grew up in Laurel, still live here, and have jobs or personality traits that suggest they may be writers."

"*Suspects*. I like your style, kiddo." She read the names, none of which she recognized. "Where do we go from here?"

He pulled an index card from his pocket and handed it to her. He'd printed *Feng Shui Your Way* above a drawing of a movie camera. Below the camera was *Murphy Media Enterprises*.

"I'll have this mock-up made into business cards," he said.

"We'll show up at the suspects' front doors, introduce ourselves as executive producers, and announce they've been chosen as possible contestants in a home makeover show. While I *audition* them, you'll measure rooms and take notes."

"Nose around, in other words." She tapped the card against the edge of the table, mulling over Finn's latest oddball scheme. "Why would anyone take the bait?"

"Who wouldn't want a free house renovation? And no one can resist being on TV."

"Except someone hiding her identity."

He clapped his hands. "Exactly! If one of them refuses, it'll be a clue they may be her."

"There's so much wrong with this, it just might work."

"So, we're on?"

"I'll think about it."

Branwell shuffled in, sniffed his bowl of low-calorie dog food, and stomped out with a look of disgust. "Don't feed His Highness more than two small meals a day," Athena said. "And no snacks whatsoever."

Finn looked puzzled.

"I'm going to Mom's place to house-sit," she reminded him. "You're taking over here."

"Whew. Dad asked if I'd work on the house instead of Karl. I'll use cleaning and cooking as an excuse not to."

"He's trying to save money by not hiring Karl. See, I told you he couldn't be rich like Garland."

"And I'm not as good a carpenter as Mar... as you know who."

Athena got up to refill her mug. "Any day now you'll be back in San Francisco making up with Mario. You'll see."

"No. I won't. Not going to happen."

She sat back down again, struck by his mournful tone. "What's going on, Finnster?"

He sucked in a deep breath as if he'd nearly drowned. "Mario asked me to marry him. I said no."

A proposal from hunky, handy Mario, and he'd refused? What was *wrong* with this family?

"It's why he's been so mean and calling me names," Finn said, wiping his eyes.

"Okay. So, it's a more serious argument than usual. But you guys will—"

"There's no turning back from the things we said to each other, Athena. No turning back." His voice was in as low a register as she'd ever heard it.

She reached across to hug him and patted his shaking back. "Give it time, my Finnster," she murmured. "Give it time. Everything will work out just fine. You'll see."

Athena knew her words were total twaddle when, opening her bedroom closet later to pack, she pulled down the hatbox containing the hawthorn garland Thorne had made for her. She placed it on the bed and opened it. He had lovingly removed every thorn and created a perfect circle. And while the blossoms were dried and the twigs brown and misshapen, the wreath was no less beautiful than the day he had crowned her and asked her to marry him.

She was about to take it out of the hatbox when her phone rang.

"Dr. M? It's me. Do you have a minute?" a low, breathy voice inquired.

Elise Waters, Dr. Davenport's administrative assistant. Athena rarely heard her actual voice, since she mostly spoke in conspiratorial whispers. Her anxious expression and penchant for caftans made her look more matronly than a millennial should.

"Nice to hear from you, Elise. How's every little thing?"

Morale has deep-sixed since you left.

The English Department is batting zero.

Students are signing petitions to eighty-six Corinne Carew. Or so Athena fantasized.

But instead, Elise whispered, "Awful. I have to type an article on Alexander Pope for Dr. Davenport, and Misty is sick again."

"Antibiotics didn't work?" There was no remedy for the tedium of Pope.

"No. And Puddles has a hairball. She's been puking all over my apartment."

"Sorry about that. Are Daisy, Jasper, and Ralph okay?"

"They're super!"

Athena pictured Elise's pleased smile. She guessed there were few people in her life who knew the names and medical conditions of her cats.

"You want to hear Dr. Carew's latest insult?" Elise said. "She left a brochure on my desk for a YMCA membership. Professor Perfect says spin class will 'strengthen my core.'"

"Like riding a broom did for her."

Elise giggled. "You're such a scream!"

"Stand-up comedian is my backup job."

"Oh, Dr. M! Your job is what I'm calling about! But you can't say a word about it to anyone."

"I won't. I swear."

"Dr. Davenport had me place an ad in academic journals and websites for an assistant professor."

Athena's heart thudded. Her chest tightened as if it were squeezed in a vise. *Her* core wasn't strong enough for this sucker punch. "Are you sure it's to replace me?"

"I overheard him tell the dean you'll never get your book done on time. He wants to get a head start on the search," Elise reported breathlessly.

Athena stared out the window, clutching the phone. The

sky had turned pearly gray, and a drop fell here and there, as if the clouds couldn't make up their mind to rain or not.

"I feel like quitting," Elise was saying. "I feel like telling Dr. Davenport he can type his own boring article on Alexander Pope."

Her threat snapped Athena out of her funk. "Don't you dare quit your job. You need money for cat food and vet bills." And a YMCA membership. Which wasn't the worst suggestion.

"Then I'll let Mrs. Davenport's calls go through," Elise grumbled. "And I won't warn him when she's on her way to his office."

Screening calls was a routine responsibility for an administrative assistant. A busy department chair couldn't always stop what he was doing to talk to his wife. A view of the parking lot from her office window, though, had doomed Elise to a more questionable task.

"Don't do anything that jeopardizes your position," Athena said. "Promise me."

"Okay. Promise. Um...did you...uh...did you write the book yet?"

"It's coming along."

"Will it be finished by the deadline?"

"Yes. It will. Definitely."

"Any way I can help?"

"You already have, Elise. I don't know what I'd do without you."

"Aw, Dr. M."

"Keep your ear to the ground for me, okay?"

"Anything for you, Dr. M. Bye."

Athena flung off the bathrobe and hurriedly dressed in a sweatshirt and jeans. What had she ever done to Dr. Oliver Davenport and the English Department of Wyatt College but give them every ounce of her dedication and enthusiasm? Sure, her immersion-in-the-text teaching style occasionally produced unfortunate results. Like setting a desk on fire while portraying the madwoman in Mr. Rochester's attic, who burned Thornfield Hall to the ground in *Jane Eyre*—and compelling her spellbound students to flee for the exit. Her blowups at Corinne *were* over the top, her publishing credentials meager. But her classes always had waiting lists, her students went on to enroll in more English courses than the required ones, and their evaluations of her positively glowed.

Athena pulled on socks and tightened the shoelaces of her sneakers until she winced. Corinne was behind this; she was sure of it. She had wheedled Dr. Davenport to replace Athena with a fresh-out-of-grad-school candidate, one who wouldn't dare tell Dr. Carew to kiss his or her sweet ass. Come to think of it, just about everything Corinne asked for from the chair, she got. A leave of absence in the middle of winter to visit her ailing grandmother. In Barbados. A brand-new computer, printer, and scanner. A newly carpeted office with a window.

It was ludicrous to suspect Corinne and Dr. Davenport of having an affair. Not only did he live in mortal fear of his domineering wife, but the stray hairs poking out of his ears, his nose, the back of his neck—and the *mole* on the back of his neck—were too gross, even for ambitious, manipulative Corinne.

The simple truth was, Athena had given her all to the English Department, and they didn't want her anymore.

She dropped onto the bed, listening to the rain drum the window, remembering the weekend in Seattle when it poured incessantly. The weekend Thorne told her he didn't want her anymore.

Elise's call had put her off balance, but it wasn't the first time Athena had questioned what the hell she was doing with her life. Doubts had nagged her from the beginning of her career. Intellectual pursuits didn't fulfill *all* her needs. And dating would-be Brontë heroes didn't even come close. When the opportunity arose, three years ago, to present a paper on the influence of the late eighteenth-century German literary movement Sturm und Drang on Romanticism at a conference in Seattle—where Thorne lived and worked—she had seized it.

Let's get together for drinks, she'd emailed him. They were, after all, safely ensconced in their "civilized contact" phase. Quentin, fortuitously, was out of town for the weekend.

Drinks on the Friday night of Athena's arrival led to a tour of the city the next afternoon after she'd presented her paper. They huddled beneath his umbrella, exploring Pike Place Market, the aquarium, and the Space Needle. At first, Thorne was as polite and formal as the lawyer he had become. But as they brought each other up-to-date on their lives—Athena giving hers as comical a spin as possible—his reserve melted to warmth and good humor.

Hours later, both drenched to the skin, he accompanied her to her hotel room so she could change into dry clothes for dinner. But once the door closed behind them and his rangy body stood electric with sexual energy before her, he was the Thorne she had fallen in love with, down to his boyish smile and the unruly lock of hair she ached to brush off his forehead.

When they woke up Sunday morning, entangled in the sheets, their bodies feverish from a night of lovemaking, the rain still fell. But Athena didn't care. One night of scorching, mind-blowing, blissful sex nearly made up for all the years they'd been apart. She and Thorne were older, wiser, certain, finally, of what really mattered—a life together.

Or so she had assumed from their pillow talk. Until the love of her life slipped back into his clothes as quickly as he'd slipped out of them and apologized—apologized!—for not showing more *restraint*. They should never have let themselves get *carried away*. He wished her well and hoped they'd always be *good friends*.

Getting up to pluck a tissue from the box, Athena caught her tearful reflection in the mirror above the dresser. That morning in the hotel room, her face was similarly smeared and blurry from kissing—and from weeping miserably, without *restraint*, without pride, as she begged Thorne to give their relationship another chance. She wanted to get married, have his babies, and live anywhere he wanted. They'd make it all work. Career *and* love *and* family.

And Thorne had turned to her, his hand on the doorknob, pity in those spring-green eyes, and said he had no intention of getting married, ever, he would never have children, absolutely not, and—the real kicker—"You're better off without me, Thena."

The translation of Sturm und Drang was *storm and stress*. Now whenever Athena came across the term, she cringed at the memory of her weekend of passion and shame, cursed the city of Seattle, cursed herself, and, most of all, cursed the man who broke her heart—twice.

She carefully lifted the hawthorn garland from the hatbox and placed it on her head. "The hawthorn lives a long life," Thorne had said. "Its wood burns hotter than most trees."

As their love was meant to burn. And last.

A dead flower fell to her shoulder, and then another, falling, falling.

Athena pocketed the bachelor farmers' generous tip and checked the time again. Nearly one o'clock and she hadn't seen Thorne yet. By this time on Mondays, they'd already crossed paths as their shifts overlapped. Could it be a foot rub and the memory of a hawthorn tree had disturbed his *keep calm* philosophy?

She sighed. She should talk. Remembering Seattle hadn't exactly been a walk in the park for her. And choosing which earrings to wear every day was a walk through an emotional minefield. The ones he'd given her invariably recalled a special occasion. What they said on the occasion. What they did. Where they did it.

She removed the silver snowflake earrings, his gift for her twentieth birthday, and stuffed them in the pocket with the tip money. Just so he wouldn't think she was sentimental. Because she wasn't. The hawthorn garland was safely back in the hatbox, in the bedroom closet, in the house she was moving out of, where it would stay until it crumbled to dust.

Heading to the kitchen with a tray of dishes, Athena stopped in her tracks when she saw Thorne get out of the passenger side of a red sports car. A tall woman in a tight pink skirt and black leather jacket emerged from the driver side. Probably that Robin person. Long auburn hair and large sunglasses covered part of her face, the rest of which resembled—shit—Nicole Kidman.

Wasn't there a rule, redheads should never wear pink?

And since when did Thorne go for glamour-pusses?

Athena put the tray down on an empty table and went to the bay window, pretending to arrange the chrysanthemums in the vase on the sill. His oh-so-casual hand-on-hip, her twirling-keys-on-one-finger said it all. They were making plans for another session between the sheets, his apartment next time. As Athena pictured that Robin person lolling around his bed, wearing nothing but the sunglasses—and a big wart on her behind—he glanced at the window and waved.

She lurched back. "Sonofabitch."

"What'd you say, dearie?" an elderly woman at a nearby table asked, her hand to her ear.

"I asked if you wanted another sandwich," she said in a loud voice.

"No, but another cup of tea would be nice."

By the time Athena returned to serve her, the sports car was gone, and Thorne had entered the café. His relaxed saunter toward Athena wasn't as annoying as his post-sex smile.

"Sorry I left before you got here today," he said. "I had an appointment to see a house with an agent Lydia shares the listing with. It's out of my price range but has the separate living quarters I need."

So, the beautiful, statuesque redhead wasn't his girlfriend. Not that she cared.

He shrugged. "Oh, well. Either they accept my bid or they don't."

So, his *keep calm* philosophy was firmly in place. He wasn't disturbed by memories of Thena and Thorne at all. Not that she cared.

"You feeling all right?" he asked, waving a hand in front of her face. "You haven't said a word."

She forced a smile. "Uh... yeah. I'm just a little... preoccupied."

"Did Finn arrive safely?"

"Right on time."

"And is your book going okay?"

"Hunky dory. It'll go even better when I move into my mother's house, where there are fewer distractions. I'm staying there while she takes a mini-vacay."

"With Ricki?"

"Didn't I tell you? Those two are going through a rough patch."

A smile slid across his lips. "Lover's quarrel?"

"Yeah. Right. Very funny."

"Quite a crowd today," he remarked, looking around the room.

"A lot of people are off work for Columbus Day."

"I have invoices to catch up on, but if you need help, let me know."

She handed him a stack of glasses. "Just drop these off in the kitchen. I'll handle the rest."

The rest meaning more probing and questioning and investigating. Elise's news was *not* going to get her down. She was forging ahead, doing what she came to do, and by golly, nothing was going to stop her.

"Find Garland, write the fricking book, save your damn job," she muttered.

"We only read about dirt, not smut," the Garden Club members replied, laughing, when she brought up the topic of the LitWit series.

Dan joked about the Midwest being a hotbed of corn and porn, but he blushed to his ball cap when she asked if he read the novellas with Phyllis. "We're too darn old for that nonsense."

She suspected quite a bit of *nonsense* had transpired between them by now, but Phyllis wasn't there to contradict him.

"Check with the Blakes," Joe suggested.

"Good idea." Though as her former teachers and her father's best friends, Wayne and Dolores were dead last on the list of people with whom she'd discuss a writer of erotica.

"I do wonder, though, if it might shame Garland to be found out," Joe said. "Or her husband and family."

His tone was gentle, but Athena had detected mild disapproval of her project since she first told him about it. She wanted to protest that Garland wasn't entitled to fame, fortune, *and* privacy, but she would sound small and mean-spirited. "Good point, Joe," she mumbled.

She had considered asking Geraldine O'Neal if she had any clue about Garland. But whenever she jogged by her house, Geraldine was in the same position at the computer and, at the sight of Athena, sent shards of icicle-eyes her way.

After a couple more hours of shrugs, blank stares, and useless information—Did she look like she cared that the Post Office was getting a fresh coat of paint?—Athena was tempted to stand in the middle of the dining room and yell, "Does anybody here have a flippin' idea who the hell Garland is?"

She'd love to think there was a conspiracy among the writer's *inner circle* to protect her. What a compelling chapter that would make. But as she brewed a third urn of coffee, she concluded there was no such circle, and that an elusive author of erotica held as much interest to the residents of Laurel as dryer lint.

Halfway through Athena's shift, Kristie came through the door, followed by Ian pushing Zoe in a stroller. "What a packed house," she said. "I'm glad I have the day off."

Athena patted her pocket. "Tips are great though. Everybody's in a good mood."

"The weather helps," Ian said, removing Zoe's bonnet. "It's as warm as summer."

"Is Thorne here?" Kristie asked. "We came by to get my paycheck."

"He's upstairs."

Ian tousled Zoe's mop of dark curls as Kristie texted Thorne. "You're probably not interested, Athena," he said, "but a tenure-track position has opened at Southern Illinois

College. Our English Department is hurting for a dynamic teacher."

She laughed. "Who says I'm dynamic?"

"Thorne. I mentioned the vacancy to him last time we talked."

Thorne, who had never observed her teach—nor dramatically burn a desk in the service of literature.

"Keep it in mind," Ian said, "in case your circumstances change."

Like Dr. Davenport advertising her job. Like her enthusiasm for the Garland hunt waning like the moon. Like—

"Here comes Thorne," Kristie said.

But no announcement of his appearance was necessary. Zoe's excited bouncing, accompanied by the squeak of her carrot toy, was proof enough. He knelt in front of the stroller. "And how is the lovely Miss Zoe today?"

The lovely Miss Zoe flashed all eight of her teeth and offered him her toy. Thorne pretended to eat the carrot, sending her into paroxysms of laughter.

Athena was torn between bonking the head of the man who would never have children with the darn carrot—or planting a kiss on his smacker for telling Ian she was a dynamic teacher. For believing in Professor Murphy.

For maybe—admittedly a gigantic maybe—hoping she'd apply for the position.

Thorne got up and handed Kristie her paycheck. "Another bonus this week. Buying supplies from the warehouse store you recommended has saved me a small fortune."

"We're experts on buying in bulk," Ian said. "Especially diapers."

Kristie sniffed and wrinkled her cute button nose. "Speaking of diapers..." Scooping her daughter in her arms, she carried her to the restroom.

"Any progress on your book, Athena?" Ian asked. The second time today someone had inquired about her writing.

"Leaps and bounds." The second time today she had bullshitted someone blind.

"As an English professor, what do *you* think of Garland's novellas?" Thorne asked him.

"My professional opinion is they're mind candy."

"Amen," Thorne said with a sharp glance at Athena.

"But my personal opinion is that Garland's laughing all the way to the bank," Ian said, grinning. "And I'm jealous and pissed off I didn't think of the series myself."

"Amen," Athena said—with a sharper glance at Thorne.

When Thorne crossed the room to chat with Joe and Dan, she discussed with Ian the courses she had taught at Wyatt College. He listened intently, asked pointed questions about her syllabi, and bemoaned the difficult family-work balance. Athena had never changed a diaper in her life—not counting Wetty Betty, the doll she and Finn used to feed bottles of water to watch her pee—but she had other balance issues to bemoan. Like life-life. Work-work. Love-love.

A young woman came into the café as Ian discussed the book he was writing on Walt Whitman. Athena reflexively checked Thorne's location in the room, but he hadn't noticed her entrance. She was Christmas-tree-angel beautiful. Long blond curls framed the perfect oval of her face. Her enviable combination of full bosom and slim hips was enhanced by her bohemian ensemble—violet suede jacket over a lavender blouse and long floral skirt. It swished around her ankles as she walked toward Ian, smiling. With her full lips and perfect teeth.

"Amazing timing," Ian said. "Amy, this is Athena Murphy, the professor I was telling you about. Athena, this is Amy Marsden, chair of the English Department."

Amy's large blue-gray eyes widened, and she extended her

hand. "Oh, yes, Athena. So glad to meet you. You must come visit the campus."

"I gave her my pitch," Ian told her. "Now if you can convince her to join our faculty..."

Athena didn't need convincing. Athena was experiencing her first girl crush. And not just because Dr. Marsden's engaging manner was light-years from Dr. Davenport's arrogant one as she described the available position. But because she had run into the café, having recognized the Prescotts' minivan, to tell them the floppy ear of Zoe's bunny was hanging out of its door. And because she had a small patch of blue paint on her chin. And admitted to Athena she didn't always know what she was doing in her job. One of those people who were perfect because they didn't think they were perfect and you wanted to be as imperfectly perfect as they were.

Amy left in a flurry of flowing hair and skirt without catching Thorne's attention. Athena was thankful, too, the bachelor farmers had already left. Her CPR skills were rusty.

Kristie returned with Zoe, and Athena permitted herself one kiss on her chubby cheek goodbye. Whoever packaged the sweet scent of toddler would deserve every penny of the fortune they'd make. She texted Finn as soon as the Prescotts were gone.

Business idea: baby-scented air fresheners, car fresheners, etc.

Forget tick-tick. Your biological clock is a time bomb.

So's my career. Your harebrained feng shui scheme is on.

"Thena." Thorne's pronunciation of her name was as severe as his expression.

"What is it?"

He pushed a stray lock from his forehead, revealing a deep frown. "I've had complaints from customers today."

She waved her phone. "First time I've had it out this afternoon. I texted Finn."

"It's not about your phone. They said you've been interrogating them about Garland."

"Interrogating? They used that word?"

"A few did. They said you're a nice waitress but too nosy."

She tapped one foot, trying to think who might have complained. The rude thirty-something couple who'd bitched that their grilled cheese sandwiches were runny? The weird piano tuner guy from Sharps & Flats who always pointed to the menu instead of speaking?

"I realize your book is important to you, Thena, but please keep your research out of my café. Do we understand each other?"

Admonished. By the Boss Man. A side to Thorne Kent she'd rarely seen. And it was kind of hot.

"Am I being clear?" he said with a stern look and a flint in his eyes to spark another kind of heat.

Athena was about to say "crystal" as icily as she could when Mayor Benson barreled into the café, announcing his arrival with a loud greeting to everyone.

"He's without his sidekick for a change," she observed. "It would be a good time to butter him up."

"I'd rather get a root canal," Thorne said with a grimace.

"I can help."

"With the root canal?"

"That too."

His serious expression morphed into a smile. "What do you suggest?"

"Humor works wonders."

"Benson wouldn't recognize a joke if a pie hit him in the face."

"Pie throwing can definitely be arranged."

"Careful. I might have to come to your rescue again."

"I can take care of myself. *And* get you in good with the mayor."

"As long as no accidents are involved."

"How about a *mishap*? Involving ice cubes?"

"I mean it, Thena."

"Watch and learn, Thorne."

As they approached his table, Mayor Benson waggled his head. "No business today, Kent. It's a holiday."

"Just checking if you got my email yesterday."

"Which one? I get hundreds."

"The one with a link to an impact study of community mental health clinics."

"I'll check with Childers. He does my emails." He rubbed his stomach with a grin at Athena. "I could eat a horse. How about you pick a sandwich for me, young lady?"

"Sorry. No equines on the menu."

The mayor chuckled. "You make me bust a gut every time."

"My specialty. The *café's* specialty today is toasted mozzarella cheese and grilled tomatoes with basil. In honor of Christopher Columbus."

"You add lettuce and a few strips of bacon, and we're good to go."

"One Italian BLT coming right up."

"With extra B. Going to the Oktoberfest Saturday?" he asked her.

"I haven't decided yet."

"It's as much fun as the community Halloween party. I never miss it."

"Glad to hear you'll be there," Thorne said to him. "I've rented a booth. I'll match every pastry I sell with my own money. The proceeds will go to post-traumatic stress research."

My hero, Athena scribbled on the notepad.

"I think Miss Murphy should have her own booth." The mayor wiped his mouth, though he hadn't eaten anything yet. "Raffle off a night on the town with her. Bet we'll raise enough money for all our causes."

"Wait a minute—" Thorne began.

Placing one hand strategically on her hip, Athena flashed her lusty serving-wench smile. "Sounds like a fabulous idea to me."

Thorne turned to her with an incredulous look. "What about Sven? Your boyfriend?"

Right. Like he forgot his name.

"Sergei doesn't have to know."

"It's a little...exploitative, don't you think?" he asked her in a low voice. "If not downright misogynist?"

Was there anything sexier than a feminist man?

"All for a good cause," Athena said breezily.

"That's the spirit!" the mayor exclaimed. "I'm buying the first ticket."

"And Mrs. Benson?" Thorne asked.

The mayor winked at Athena. "Mrs. B and I are on the same page when it comes to good causes."

Not on your life, Athena wrote beneath *My hero*, summarizing her two main categories of possible romantic partners. Tearing the paper from the notepad, she shoved it in her pocket, dislodging the snowflake earrings.

"You dropped these," Thorne said, picking them up from the floor.

"They...uh...they kept getting tangled in my hair."

He placed the earrings in the palm of her hand, gazing at her with not-so-calm eyes, tangled in the memory, probably, of making love the morning, afternoon, and evening of her twentieth birthday when he gave them to her.

Not that she cared...

But she did.

Athena's biggest challenge on her Wednesday and Friday shifts wasn't being less *nosy* but trying to stay awake. Since she'd moved into her mother's house, she'd barely slept a wink. There was such a thing as *too* quiet. The creaks and groans of the walls and floors of her childhood home, a kind of white noise, had lulled her to sleep every night. Lydia's state-of-the-art house sealed out the world like a Tupperware container. Closing a window or door, she imagined she heard the snap of an airtight lid. Not until the wee hours of Saturday morning did she finally fall into a deep, satisfying slumber, enhanced by dreams of Thorne rolling dough, baking pastries, and rolling some more. Thanks to his Oktoberfest preparations all week, nearly every refrigerator and shelf in As You Like It Café was stuffed with jelly rolls, hot cross buns, and other sexually suggestive treats.

The Oktoberfest festivities in Laurel's public park were in full swing by the time Athena arrived at four o'clock. The achingly blue sky was cloudless, the shade beneath the vibrantly colored oaks and maples deep and cool. The grass was trampled with stroller wheels and the feet of hundreds of people. Ever since she could remember, the promise of lively band music and beer, lots and lots of beer, had attracted the most reclusive citizens to the event. C. L. Garland might very well be among them.

Passing the bandstand where the high school color guard

was going through its routine, she waved to Eugene, sitting on a lawn chair. "Glad you came," she said. "It's a beautiful day to be outdoors, isn't it?"

"You're not whistling Dixie." He opened the lid of his cooler. "Want a beer?"

"You brought your own?"

"Can't trust the stuff they sell here. For all I know, it's watered down or they added crap to it. Like pumpkin. Who the hell wants to drink beer that tastes like pie?"

"*I* sure as hell don't."

His thin cheeks creased in a smile. "You look darn pretty all gussied up."

"What, this old thing?" Athena smoothed her rose-colored blouse, its bodice embroidered with bluebells, and swirled her denim skirt. She'd welcomed an excuse to get dressed up for a change. To wear clothes she *would* mind getting stained with café food. After weeks of wearing Lydia's comfortable oxfords though, the ankle boots pinched her toes. But sacrifices had to be made occasionally to the gods of style. Her turquoise post earrings were *not* courtesy of Thorne, for a change.

"Yo, Eugene," one of the bachelor farmers called out. "Going to join in the fun?"

"When I'm darn good and ready," he groused.

"When will that be?" another one asked.

"None of your beeswax."

"I can bring you something to eat," Athena offered, pointing to the smoking barbecue pit where people were lined up for bratwurst, sausage, and sauerkraut.

He waved her away. "Get on out of here, missy. You're not on duty today."

"All right, Eugene. You have a good time, you hear?"

A red-faced man wearing lederhosen, with an accordion

strapped to his chest, rushed by as she strolled across the grass. The instrument emitted pitiful bleats as it bounced against his body. A stick-thin teenage couple, faces in their phones, collided with a guy carrying a paper plate in each hand, one filled with sandwiches, the other with grapes. He tripped over his own feet, the grapes tumbled to the ground, and the T-shirts of the suddenly alert teenagers were smeared with mustard and relish. The guy stumbled away mumbling, "Well, shit," while the teenagers frantically texted. One of the elderly mall walkers who frequented the café stomped blindly through the grapes and sandwiches, leaving colorful streaks on his immaculate white sneakers. A few moments of silly mayhem to remind her of the innocent pleasures of small-town life.

And some not-so-pleasurable moments. But it was too late for Athena to duck away. Mayor Benson had already spotted her and was walking toward her, wearing his widest campaign grin. He was accompanied by an attractive middle-aged woman who, judging by her tolerant expression, had to be his wife.

"You look thirsty," he said, shoving a plastic cup filled with flat beer in Athena's hand.

"You might have asked her first, Bernie." The woman turned to her. "How do you do? I'm Sharon Benson."

"Nice to meet you. I'm Athena Murphy."

"I heard you're back in town for a while. Please let me know if there is anything I can do to make your visit more enjoyable. Or if there are any concerns you'd like to air."

Another kind, reasonable, lovely person married to someone who was . . . not.

"Thanks, Sharon. Be sure to come by As You Like It Café. We'd love to see you there."

The mayor hitched up his pants. "I had Childers put a

banner on Thorne's booth advertising the raffle for a night on the town with you. Have you seen it yet?"

Athena's throat tightened as badly as the ankle boots squeezing her toes. "You can't be serious."

"Last I checked, quite a few raffle tickets had already sold." He nudged his wife's shoulder. "Isn't that right, Mrs. B?"

"There is no way I could possibly know," Sharon replied. "Mr. B."

"I . . . I thought you were joking," Athena said.

"I wouldn't joke about a serious issue like post-traumatic stress," he said, assuming a solemn expression. "Thorne promised to match the ticket sales with his own funds the way he's matching his bake-sale proceeds."

Pre-traumatic stress built rapidly inside her. In his defense, Thorne *had* objected to the idea—until she put her foot in it and agreed with the mayor that it was for a good cause. She gulped half a cup of the gross beer, scanning the park for the best- and worst-case date scenarios.

Best case—Karl, who leaned against a flagpole, devouring a bratwurst. If she had a burning interest in anthropological fieldwork. And a need to find out if she'd made a mistake all these years dismissing men who didn't meet her Brontëan standards.

Worst case—Mayor Benson. She wouldn't go anywhere with him unless Sharon came along—and they ditched him after fifteen minutes. She had a feeling Sharon wouldn't mind.

And then there was Thorne, who would be both the best *and* worst date.

The mayor turned to talk to a group of middle-aged men wearing Kiwanis Club hats. Sharon leaned toward her. "If you want to get out of this *night on the town* baloney, come down with a headache. A migraine is my ailment of choice when I don't want to fake a smile for hours."

"Thanks for the tip, but I think I'll hightail it out of here instead."

With a wave goodbye, Athena walked toward the Garden Club stand displaying yellow and orange chrysanthemums.

"Want to buy a gourd, Athena?" Yolanda asked. "Or some colorful mums?"

"Another time," she promised.

She ditched the beer in the garbage can near the Lotsa Pots booth, where Phyllis and Theresa sat beneath a huge umbrella. Every conceivable size and shape of terra-cotta vessel was spread out on the table. A young couple was examining the garden gnomes lined up on the grass, a few of which bore a passing resemblance to Joe or Dan.

"Every lawn should have one," Phyllis told them. "It's not a home without a gnome."

"Where are Joe and Dan?" Athena asked.

"They helped out for a few hours, then took off for a beer break," Theresa said.

Phyllis pointed to the man with the accordion playing a polka on the bandstand stage. "The darn oompah music got on their nerves. It sure as heck gets on mine. Like Numbskull, husband number one."

"I thought you said Dumbbell was more annoying," Theresa said.

"Not once I started wearing earplugs. Shoulda brought them today."

Athena spotted the Blakes among the crowd gathered around the stage, and after saying goodbye to Phyllis and Theresa, she joined them. They wore matching shirts and sweater-vests and were bouncing in place to the rhythm. "Have you seen my dad?" she asked them.

"Out gallivanting with Vivienne is our guess," Wayne said.

The verb *gallivant* and Charles did not belong in the same sentence. "Are they dating?"

"Who the heck knows," he said with an indignant sniff. "We're in the dark about him these days."

"Don't feel bad. He never tells me or Finn where he's going either."

"Charles, the man with a secret," he said, twirling Dolores away.

Sergei, the man with too many secrets, had left a long voicemail on her phone last night, enumerating all the reasons she must "follow up through" on her promise. "You don't want them to take Sergei away, do you, Atheeena?"

Uh, yeah, actually, she did.

She looked across the lawn as the sun sent a single strong ray through the stand of evergreens. Pulling her sweater from her handbag, she draped it across her shoulders. Most of the park was in shadow, but it wasn't hard to spot the As You Like It Café booth. Festooned between two supporting poles was a white sign screaming *A Night on the Town with Athena Murphy* in bright purple letters.

"You can stuff your banner up your oompah," she muttered, turning to leave.

Weird thing about ankle boots though. They had a mind of their own. Hers didn't budge an inch as Boss Man himself emerged from behind the booth, dressed in a tailored white shirt and jeans, her favorite guy outfit. He strolled toward her, as casual as could be, and still her feet didn't move.

"Shouldn't you be manning your booth?" she asked him.

"All the pastries are sold."

"And the stupid raffle tickets?"

"Every last one."

"Have you no shame," she said, "reducing me to mere chattel?"

"Shame?" His megawatt smile could have lit the entire park, if not Laurel itself. "Not a drop. And if I recall, you encouraged the raffle."

"I was breaking Bernie's balls."

"Somehow I think your sarcasm was lost on him."

"Out of curiosity, which made more money? Me or the pastries?"

"You. It seems a tart tongue is preferable to a tart."

She couldn't help smiling. "Sounds like one of my witticisms."

"I learned from the best."

They looked over to the bandstand as the crashing chords of the accordion died down to a few mournful notes. The applause subsided and then quickly resumed when Mayor Benson climbed the stairs to the podium.

"Everybody having a good time?" he bellowed into the microphone.

Two squirrels scampered between Athena and Thorne's feet as *time* echoed loudly.

"Yes!" the audience shouted, sending the squirrels up the nearest tree.

"Oktoberfest isn't just about beer, brats, and band music," he went on. "It's about community. It's about being there for each other."

"You betcha," a man yelled, holding up a hot dog and empty beer cup.

"We've raised a lot of money today for community needs. I'd like to thank all of you who contributed to our fundraising efforts." The mayor waved a piece of paper in the air. "Including the lucky man who bought the winning raffle ticket for a night on the town with our very own Athena Murphy."

Between the hoots and hollers and her own thundering heartbeat, Athena was reeling. Back in her hometown for two months and she'd already been sucked into its vortex like a mobile home in a tornado. She grabbed Thorne's hand to keep from flying away—and as quickly released it when his name resounded over the microphone.

"Thorne Kent, you lucky son of a gun," Mayor Benson said over loud clapping. "Get up here with your lady."

"You didn't," she said between clenched teeth. "You didn't buy a ticket."

Thorne shrugged, one of his infuriating, big-shouldered shrugs. "It was worth a shot."

Before she could retort she'd like a shot at him, literally, he reached for her hand and pulled her to the stage, her sweater falling off as she walked up the steps.

"Kiss! Kiss! Kiss!" the crowd chanted as they stood in the spotlight.

Thorne's hair shone like gold, his eyes glittered, his face glowed with robust health, and once again they were on the campus stage. She was Katherine to his Hal in Shakespeare's *Henry V*, poised to assume the throne as Queen and King of England. "Kiss me, Kate," he'd commanded. And she did.

His lips met hers, those warm, hungry lips she remembered so well, sending her heart to her knees, melting the ankle boots right off her feet.

He wasn't Hal. He didn't even have to be Heathcliff. He was just Thorne.

And Thorne was good enough.

CHAPTER TEN

I am paving hell with energy.

—CHARLOTTE BRONTË, *JANE EYRE*

Funny thing about kissing. Athena didn't remember leaving Thorne's arms, walking from the stage, retrieving her sweater, or driving back to her mother's house. What she *did* recall was getting into bed, taking care of business, and sleeping like a baby. Her mind cleared and spirits lifted, she'd cleaned the house from top to bottom Sunday morning.

I expect you to keep everything shipshape, Lydia had emailed yesterday—yet another reminder since beginning her travels with Tony. She wouldn't put it past her mother to return without warning and, before unpacking, run her fingers along every surface to check for dust.

With energy and ambition to burn, Athena had also written the third chapter of her book, a humorous, insightful discussion of Garland's "Scarlet Fetters," exploring the many kinky uses of Hester Prynne's puritan bonnet strings. Imagining ingenious uses of Dr. Davenport's bolo tie strings for more malevolent purposes kept her writing into the night.

Still turbocharged, she zipped around As You Like It Café Monday afternoon, pursuing her *keep investigating in Boss Man's café* strategy. She was subtle, not *nosy*. She inquired, didn't *interrogate*. A tactic she planned to use on Thorne to get him to talk about what had happened at Oktoberfest, lip-wise.

His lips had been tightly sealed all day. Unfortunately, no one else's were. Nearly everyone in the café ribbed her about their stage kiss. She laughed it off as "for a good cause" and "we were only playacting"—in between trips to the restroom to scream into her apron.

Her arms loaded with a tray of dirty dishes, Athena pushed open the swinging door to the kitchen with her hip. Thorne pulled pumpkin muffins from the oven, flipped a sandwich on the grill, and stacked plates in the dishwasher. Multitasking—an effective avoidance strategy.

"It's busier than stink out there," she said. "Thanks for sticking around."

"Uh-huh."

Mumbling worked well too.

"I didn't expect it to be this crowded," she said, clearing the tray. "I thought everyone would be recovering from Oktoberfest."

"Mmm," he said, examining a fork for...microbes? The chemical properties of stainless steel?

"Have *you* recovered?"

He shook his head. "Too much beer."

Hollows shadowed his pale cheeks, and he looked as if he'd been up a couple of nights, tossing and turning instead of taking care of business.

Forget subtle inquiry. When it came to that kiss, she was going full-bore Athena.

"Your kiss made *me* a little drunk," she said.

He pried the muffins from the pan, looking at each one as if it were a priceless jewel. Apparently, one cannot speak when one is absorbed in the size and shape of a pumpkin muffin.

"Everyone's been teasing me about it," she said. "Guess we looked pretty convincing."

"Guess so," he said.

"Hard to tell what was acting and what was real."

Oh, yeah. Full-bore.

"About the night on the town you won," Athena went on, getting a serving platter from the cabinet. "Are you going to take a rain check or cancel altogether?"

"Haven't decided yet."

"Need Girlfriend Number Whatever's permission?"

He looked her in the eye for the first time that day. "An advantage of multiple girlfriends is not having to ask permission."

"An advantage of being an ex-girlfriend is not having to grant it," Athena said, piling the muffins onto the platter.

Thorne leaned against the counter, his mouth on the verge of a smile. "Would you deprive me of an evening of your company and scintillating wit?"

"I'll pay you back for the ticket."

"I never thought I'd see it. Thena losing her nerve."

"I haven't lost a damn thing. In case you hadn't noticed."

He licked a dot of icing from his finger. "Are you referring to our kiss?"

"Duh" was all she got out, thanks to the icing, his finger, his tongue. *Our kiss.*

"It wasn't a big deal," he said.

"Who said it was a big deal?"

"We gave the crowd what they asked for," he said with an annoying shrug.

"And, as usual, you delivered a stellar performance." She turned on her heel to leave the kitchen.

Shit. She should have said *we* delivered.

Shit, shit, shit.

"Thena?"

She spun around. "What?"

Thorne fixed her with the brooding look he had perfected for the stage—dark, smoldering, swoon-worthy. "About that kiss."

"Yeah?"

"You've still got it."

One Mississippi. Two Mississippi.

"And you still can't have it."

This time she nailed it.

Thorne stretched his weary body on the worn cushions of the sofa Tuesday night, nursing a mug of tea. Kristie had been called away on a Zoe emergency, and he'd found it harder than usual to keep up with a full day of kitchen tasks and waiting tables. He scrolled mindlessly through the television channels. The commercials seemed even more absurd when the volume was muted, especially the advertisements for drugs. The actors' faces once they'd been happily medicated conveyed a chilling vacancy. Nobody should ever feel *that* good. Pain might be a reminder of mortality, but it was also a sign you were still alive.

Alive—and living in the crappiest apartment in Laurel, if not all of southern Illinois.

He watched as the cheap venetian blind gradually broke loose from its bracket and dangled across the window. His bid on the house had been rejected, the real estate agent had texted earlier. Her face and figure were attractive enough, but he'd yet to see her eyes. So, while she'd thrown him every hint in the book she'd welcome a night out—"Want to meet for drinks?" she'd added to the text—he couldn't bite. Maybe the emoticon of a face wearing sunglasses that he'd sent with his "No thanks" text would clue her in.

At least the bad news about the house had been offset

by good news. A music major at Southern Illinois College had replied to his ad for a performer of Renaissance music. Within fifteen minutes of listening to Ivy Hagstrom play her mandolin this morning, he'd hired her to work Wednesday and Saturday afternoons, starting next week. With her long ash-blond hair, translucent skin, and diaphanous dress, she was as ethereal as Ophelia in *Hamlet*.

"Women, women, women," Thorne said softly, thinking of all he'd encountered in his lifetime. Each alluring in her own way. But only one who embodied womanhood for him.

Everything Athena saw and felt and knew was shining in her warm brown eyes for the world to see. She was open and honest and affectionate and smart and aggravating and delightful...

" 'She is spherical, like a globe. I could find out countries in her,' " he recited, remembering a favorite line from Shakespeare's *The Comedy of Errors*.

And that kiss at Oktoberfest. Hot damn. His only "stellar performance" had been pretending it hadn't knocked his socks off. Three years since they'd kissed and her full lips were as fresh as ever, her body in his arms warm and responsive.

His phone rang, pulling him off the stage at Oktoberfest, away from Athena's mouth, her fluttering eyelashes, and the sweet *oh!* she had uttered between breaths. He cleared his throat and drank a mouthful of tea before answering. "Hi, Mom. How are you? Are you enjoying the fruit basket I sent?"

"Yes, very much," Beryl said. "But it's too hot here for October."

"Did the super fix the air conditioner yet?"

"Finally. But there was an awful cockroach in the kitchen this morning. I never have this problem with insects in St. Louis."

"That's Florida for you."

His mother's wavery voice touched him to the quick. Nearly every conversation began with a complaint about her living situation. Last spring, he replaced the windows of her St. Louis condo because she claimed they leaked during heavy rains. Thorne was all too glad to help, but the support of her sister and brother-in-law in Jacksonville was a welcome relief. Aunt Evelyn and Uncle Orson had been close to Thorne's parents, traveling with them and spending holidays together.

"Are you having a beautiful autumn there?" she asked.

"Pretty nice." Describing the crisp air, stunning blue skies, and extravaganza of colorful leaves would make her miss the Midwest even more.

"I do wish you'd come down to visit."

"I'll try. The café keeps me busy." She had raised only mild objections to his career change, being preoccupied with grief.

"Don't work so hard. I always told your father, 'Take a break, we have everything we need already.'" Her voice caught in a sob. "Oh, I still miss him so much."

The faithful heart. Thorne knew it well.

"Christmas. I'll come down for the holiday," he promised. "Unless you've made other plans."

"No. I'll be here with Evelyn and Orson."

He heard what sounded like pearls rattling.

"Thorne?" she said faintly. "Any good news for me? Are you seeing anyone special?"

"No. No one special."

"It's an awful thing to be alone in this world. I do wish you'd settle down. That Murphy girl...do you ever hear from her?"

As a matter of fact, he almost said. But why bother

admitting he saw Athena nearly every day? There was no relationship between them but employer and employee. She had a career, a boyfriend, and she was going back to San Francisco. More to the point, his parents had found her hearty laugh, her dismissal of decorum, and her unguarded comments intolerable.

He smiled, remembering Athena's honest if blunt appraisal of his mother's hairstyle as "Bride of Frankenstein meets Betty Crocker." Within earshot, unfortunately, of the mortified Beryl Kent.

"Sometimes I think we made a mistake, your father and I," his mother said.

His heartbeat quickened. Had she known about Jessica in Albuquerque all along? "Are you saying...you think your marriage was a mistake?"

"Oh, dear me, no. Your father was a prince. I'm talking about that Murph—about Athena. If I had to do it over again, I would be more welcoming to her."

He looked at the suspended window blind, swallowing the lump in his throat. "It means a lot to hear you say that, Mom."

"Find someone to love and spend your life with, Thorne. It's never too late."

They talked a little longer about her golf game, the Netflix programs she liked, and Evelyn's arthritis. His promise to his father was a cloud over every conversation with his mother, obscuring his way. Like Hamlet, he wrestled with his dilemma. Tell her the truth? Protect her from the truth?

Long after they hung up, he looked out into the dark street, relieved by a few streetlamps and the lights behind the curtained windows of Sharps & Flats. The tuner preferred working on the instruments at night. Occasionally, Thorne heard the discordant notes of piano keys, minor chords that were the soundtrack of his life.

"You still can't have it," Athena had said.

And I still can't risk it, he might have answered.

Risk falling in love with her all over again.

Risk believing he didn't have to be alone.

Risk confessing that everything he'd said in Seattle had been a damn lie.

"Have I recovered yet?" Thorne asked, repeating Athena's question about Oktoberfest.

As if in answer, the venetian blind fell off its other hinge and clattered to the floor.

No, he never would. Not from all they had lost.

As for that kiss... he wouldn't recover from it either. And he didn't want to.

Athena's resolve on Monday to keep investigating had weakened as the café patrons continued to joke about her and Thorne. On Wednesday, she took stock of the situation—three measly chapters completed, two short months to write the rest, and one dubious plan she'd devised while constructing sandwiches. A community book club, established as of today, might yield clues about Garland and maybe, just maybe, get people more curious about the writer in their midst.

And less curious about the former Thena and Thorne duo in their midst.

Joe waved her to his table, where he and Theresa lingered over mugs of coffee. "You look like you lost your puppy, Athena."

"I'm discouraged. My Garland project is going nowhere fast."

"Anything we can do?"

"As a matter of fact, there is." She dropped into a chair. "Laurel doesn't have a book club, does it?"

"No, but it should. I keep promising myself to read more, but I never do," Joe admitted.

Theresa pecked his cheek. "You're not the only one, dear."

"I'd like to start a reading group. I won't be here much longer, and I want to leave something positive behind for the community." Which, Athena didn't realize until this minute, was the God's honest truth.

"You already have, hon." Theresa held out her hand. Her rings were gone except for one—a garnet stone surrounded by pearls. "It's a friendship ring. Joe gave it to me at Oktoberfest."

"At our age, we can't waste any time," he said with a chuckle.

Phyllis and Dan entered, arm in arm.

"Athena wants to get a book club going. You two in?" Joe asked when they joined them.

Dan lifted his cap and scratched his forehead. "What kind of books are we talking about?"

"How about revisiting the classics?" Athena asked.

"As long as we don't have to revisit the writer who takes a year to finish a sentence," Phyllis said. "James Somebody."

"Henry James," Athena said.

"All those commas. Geesh."

"Actually, I meant the classic titles Garland adapts for the LitWit series. You said yourself, Phyllis, you read the original books after the novellas."

"Ever since 'War and a Piece of Ass,' I've been hooked on Tolstoy," Phyllis said.

"Who?" Dan asked.

"And Vronsky in *Anna Karenina*," she said with a rapturous sigh.

"Who?" he repeated.

"How would the book club help your research?" Joe asked Athena.

She looked at each of them in turn. "I was hoping you'd all play detective. As you're reading the classic texts, compare them to Garland's novellas, paying close attention to her minor characters and settings. Notice how they differ from the originals. They may be based on people or places you recognize, and you'll spot clues to Garland's identity."

"Serious literature *and* sleuthing. Count us in," Theresa said.

"I'm up for it. How about you?" Phyllis asked Dan.

"Sounds like an excuse to read dirty books, if you ask me," he said.

"Don't worry, lambkin, I'll explain all of them to you."

"Will I have homework?" he asked, grinning.

"And pop quizzes. And detention if you're a naughty boy."

"Okay with me, teacher."

"Has anyone told you about Laurel's Halloween party, Athena?" Phyllis asked.

"Mayor Benson mentioned it. The town didn't have one when I lived here."

"Be sure to come. It's a lot of fun. While we're there, we can rustle up more people to join the book club."

"That's a great idea," Athena said. "What should we call it?"

"How about This Time Around Book Club?" Joe suggested, squeezing Theresa's hand.

"Sounds good to me," Dan said.

"Maybe this time around I'll like *David Copperfield*," Phyllis said.

Joe pointed to the entrance as Wayne, Dolores, and Charles, accompanied by a tall woman with a mane of flowing silver hair, entered and hung their jackets on the coatrack. Athena hadn't bothered asking the Blakes about Garland. Since her father had told them about her project, she figured they would have contacted her by now if they knew anything.

"They would be a great addition to the club," Joe said. "Though it might bore the pants off Charles and Vivienne. They've read everything already."

"I'd say their pants are already off," Phyllis said.

"Phyllis!" Theresa admonished her.

"How do you know her? Do you do tai chi too?" Athena asked, curious about Vivienne—if not her father's pants.

Phyllis hooted. "That'll be the day!"

"We ran into all four of them at the Saint Louis Art Museum," Joe explained.

"She knew the names of all the artists," Theresa said. "And quoted from books she and Charles had read."

"Good match," Joe said, nodding. "Good match."

In all the years since her parents' divorce, Athena had never considered her father in a romantic relationship. Why the heck not? Had she absorbed Lydia's criticisms so thoroughly that she couldn't imagine another woman falling for him?

When the foursome approached, Joe and Dan brought a spare table and chairs from across the room and arranged them next to theirs. "Come and sit a spell," Joe said.

"Don't mind if we do," Wayne said, settling into a chair next to Dolores.

Charles kissed Athena's cheek. "I was hoping you'd be working today. We miss you at the house."

"Good day to drop in. It's not too busy. How are you and Finn getting along?"

"We do all right. When he's not mooning over Mario." He turned to Vivienne. "You've met my son. Now, I'd like you to meet my daughter, Athena."

"Vivienne Vanderfelder," she said in a low, throaty voice. The haughty beauty of her ice-blue eyes and fine-boned face was arresting. A simple gray tunic and flowing black pants floated gracefully over her whippet-thin body.

"Nice to meet you," Athena murmured.

"And you. Charles has told me all about you." Vivienne pronounced his name as if she held a bubble in her mouth.

His face glowing, Charles held out a chair, and she folded herself into it like a handheld fan. Athena noticed everyone at the table primp their hair and straighten their collars. In a flash, she was in the Kent dining room, worrying she had BO, suppressing coughs for fear they'd assume she had TB, and wanting to leave PDQ.

"Vivienne moved back here from Boston this year," Charles told Athena.

"Back? You're from Laurel?" Athena asked, trying to disguise her amazement. Certainly other Laurel locals knew the names of artists and read voraciously and carried themselves as if they wore crowns on their heads. None that she knew, but...

"I moved away when I went off to Radcliffe many, many years ago," Vivienne said. "I haven't been in Illinois for ages."

"I have a PhD from Harvard myself," Athena said.

"Ah, yes. Charles told me."

At least *one* parent bragged about her accomplishments.

"May I inquire why you returned?" Athena asked.

May I inquire. Why didn't she get down on bended knee while she was at it?

"My dear husband passed away." Vivienne extended her slender hand to Charles, who enfolded it in his. "Since I inherited the family property here, it was a good time to take possession. And to give some thought to my future."

"The Mortenson place," Charles explained to everyone.

"Oh, the Mortenson place," they all repeated.

The Mortenson place, as it was generally known, was a stately Queen Anne mansion on the edge of the city limits. It had been rented for years, usually by college professors and their families. "Shabby genteel" was a generous description of its tumbledown condition, though its ornamental spindles and round towers showed traces of former glory.

"Charles has been enormously helpful, organizing my library," Vivienne said. "I've brought hundreds of books and have been in quite a state getting them in order. I don't know how I would have managed without him."

Charles looked like he was about to bust his buttons with pride. "Beautiful library," he said. "Magnificent room."

Everyone else looked like they were in quite a state hearing Vivienne say "quite a state."

"Uh... is anyone ready to order?" Athena asked, pen poised over the notepad.

"The Vidalia onion sandwich looks divine," Vivienne said, looking over the menu. "Want to share one, Charles?"

Phyllis mouthed the word *divine*, and Theresa concealed her smile with one hand.

"Leave room for dessert," Athena said after taking all their orders. "We have a fresh batch of chocolate chip cookies."

The mention of cookies didn't even register with Vivienne, who looked as if she'd never eaten dessert in her life. The rest shook their heads, mumbled no, blamed diets, and described the pain of sugar withdrawal.

As Athena prepared sandwiches, she couldn't help laughing, remembering Sergei's voicemail last night. She had been in the middle of a particularly juicy passage in "Scarlet Fetters"—Arthur Dimmesdale ripping off Hester Prynne's apron and tying her to the bed with it—but interrupted her reading to listen to Sergei announce he had given up smoking. His hyper, barely intelligible speech had nicotine withdrawal all over it. "I'm dying, Atheeena! But I do this for baby Boris! For strong sperm!"

Charles rubbed his stomach when she brought the Vidalia

onion sandwich he was sharing with Vivienne. "I've worked up a dickens of an appetite, thanks to tai chi," he said.

"Funny you should mention Dickens," Phyllis said.

As she told Charles, Vivienne, and the Blakes about the This Time Around Book Club, Athena cleaned tables and poured coffee for the few remaining lunch customers. She nearly dropped a stack of saucers when someone grabbed her shoulder from behind. "Nora! You startled me."

"Tough beans." Nora pointed to Charles and Vivienne. "Mark my words, Charles has his hands full with that one. Came into my shop the other day with her nose in the air and walked out again, like it wasn't good enough for Her Highness. I don't carry many A-cup bras anyway."

"I hardly know her," Athena mumbled, feeling guilty that she had no reason to dislike Vivienne—but disliked her nevertheless.

"*No one* knows her. She's a good seven or eight years older than your father if she's a day."

And on her way to Radcliffe before the young Charles would have been aware of her existence.

"Vivienne Vander-something," Nora sniffed. "Damn highfalutin name, in my book."

A name fully loaded with matching consonants, like *Corinne Carew*—if Athena needed an excuse for not liking her father's friend.

"Would you like a table near the window?" she asked Nora.

"Never mind. I've lost my appetite." Her amber eyes twinkled. "You know what *revenge sex* is, don't you?"

"Sure." When it came right down to it, the few guys Athena had slept with after Thorne were out of revenge. One nearly made it to serious boyfriend status—until she overheard him making fun of Finn.

"Well, Charles and I had a hootenanny of a time after we got cheated on," Nora said.

"You... my dad?" Athena sputtered.

"I never tell lies, not even white ones," Nora said as if she were wearing starched underpants. "Unlike some people." She was never, ever going to let Athena forget she had ditched her precious son at the prom.

"Hootenanny," Athena repeated in a daze.

"And a half. Though you'd never know it to look at him."

Too stunned to move, she watched Nora bustle out of the café.

Nobody knew *anyone* just looking at them. Secret currents ran deeply in everyone, and mild-mannered Charles Murphy was no exception. Apparently, Garland wasn't the only one hiding in plain sight. Athena might have figured this out sooner if she hadn't spent so much time with her nose in books.

A regretful thought, followed by Mr. Regret himself, entering the café. Athena noticed Thorne before he saw her. And in those few unguarded minutes, his face revealed a touching melancholy that washed a wave of sadness over her. Once again, he was her dear friend, needing sympathy and an understanding ear. She knew the look. She'd comforted it many times before.

"Thorne?"

He blinked and rubbed his eyes as if the last thing he expected was to see her standing in front of him. "Thena. Everything all right?"

"Yeah. Easy shift. You didn't have to come in."

"I wanted to get prep work done for tomorrow."

"Everything all right with *you*?"

"Could be better."

"Want to talk about it?"

He opened his mouth, and she waited for the words to spill out like they used to. *I'm worried about my*... or *Do you think you can help*... But he merely nodded toward the kitchen. "Rolling up my sleeves and chopping food will help me sort things out."

She got it. He was holding himself in and keeping her out. Banter, spar, joke—that was their thing now. No sharing of feelings, no consoling words or gestures. Just bittersweet memories of what they once were to each other.

She'd had a similar sobering realization while reading the chapters in *Wuthering Heights* in which Heathcliff had returned from a three-year absence. Catherine's joy in being with him again, though married to Edgar Linton, turned to despair when he eloped with her sister-in-law, Isabella. Revenge sex, Emily Brontë style. It had been too late for Catherine and Heathcliff—and it was too late for Thena and Thorne. The three years since Seattle had splintered them once and for all.

"Hello there, Thorne."

Athena turned to see her father and Vivienne walking toward them. Thorne extended his hand, and they shook heartily. "Always a pleasure to see you, Charles."

"Likewise. I came over to introduce you to Vivienne. My dear, this is Thorne Kent, the owner of this café."

Thorne and Vivienne made small talk that Athena strained to hear through her father's comments to her about Finn. Something about him rooting around in the attic? A wig? And did Vivienne just mention the Hamptons? It made sense. Exchange her Jane Goodall look for the ladies-who-lunch look, and she'd be Beryl Kent. Minus a thousand appointments with a stylist. Plus a thousand books read.

"Meeting Vivienne brings you up-to-date on the latest Murphy family news," Athena said to Thorne once the couple had returned to their table. In another life, she'd have told him about the hootenanny and a half with Nora.

"I've got another news item," he said. "I just met with the manager of Laurel Bank."

"Great! What happened?"

"I started out asking her discreet questions, hinting at Garland, but she beat me to the punch."

"Please tell me she's her client."

"She spent a full five minutes bemoaning the fact Garland *wasn't*. Another dead end, I'm afraid."

"Thanks anyway," Athena said glumly. "On a more positive note, I've started a book club. Already got a few people interested in reading the classics Garland adapts."

"Good for you."

"Wanna join us?"

He ran a hand through his hair. "If I had more time, but—"

"Yeah. Besides, we don't want them ribbing us about that kiss."

"Listen, Thena, can we…" He trailed his finger along the side of her face, a gesture so gentle and fleeting that she wasn't sure he'd touched her. "Never mind."

"What is it, Thorne? Tell me."

"Nothing," he murmured. "Just wanted to say I was glad to help."

And so much more, she was sure. But he took off his jacket, rolled up his sleeves—literally—and headed to the kitchen. Sorting things out, whatever they were, on his own.

If she were Catherine Earnshaw Linton—never Catherine Heathcliff, after all—she'd go into a rage, throw a fit, or starve herself for a day or two. But post-Seattle Athena was beyond such histrionics. And present-day Athena had come to the conclusion that Catherine had spent a good part of her brief, passionate life off her rocker.

Thursday morning, Athena and Finn sat in her Mini Cooper, parked in front of the house of their first Garland *suspect*. She was having second thoughts about his *Feng Shui Your Way* plan. And third thoughts. And fourth.

"This isn't going to work, Finn. Nearly everybody knows I'm a professor and you're an engineer, not executive producers. And if they don't, they'll find out when they ask around."

"I *was* an engineer. And we both live in California."

"What's that have to do with anything?"

"People associate California with TV and movie producers. As far as anybody knows, I've become one of them. And you're my silent partner."

"Do you even know what a silent partner is?"

"Don't have to."

A yellow button-down collar peeked out of the neck of his ivory cable-knit sweater. His khaki trousers were crisply ironed, his baby face clean-shaven. "You look like a preppy, not somebody who makes million-dollar deals," Athena said. "And who polishes their Docksides?"

"I do. And you look like a scaredy-cat."

"Them's fightin' words."

"Ready when you are."

"Just this one house," she said in a warning voice. "If we mess up, we're stopping."

He tucked a clipboard under his arm as he opened the car door. "Don't forget your prop."

"I have a prop?"

"Pretend you're measuring rooms while you look for forensic evidence," he said, tossing her a tape measure.

"Uh, just to be clear. This isn't a *murderer* we're looking for."

"You never know, Athena. You never know."

"Actually, I do. Looking for Garland is killing *me*."

The doorbell rang like a melodious wind chime. A tall, bone-thin woman in yoga pants and ballerina flats opened the door.

"Are you Willa Faulk?" Finn asked.

"In this life and the next."

Athena and Finn exchanged hopeful glances. Such an offbeat response was promising, as was her intelligent, keen gaze.

"We hope we aren't interrupting," he said. "We have an offer for you to—"

"I was meditating. A feather floating across the room is an interruption when you're meditating." She closed her eyes, rippled her hands above her head, and then shot them open again. "*You* are the feathers. Who are your spirit birds?"

There was a fine line between offbeat and out to lunch, and Athena had the distinct impression Willa Faulk had crossed it.

"Sorry to have disturbed you," she said, tugging Finn's elbow. "We can come back another time."

"You'll do no such thing. My mantra has already disappeared into the miasma." She waved a hand across their faces, nearly slapping them both. Two spirit birds, down for the count. "Follow me," she commanded.

"Feels like we're back in California," Finn whispered to Athena as they entered the living room.

"We're not in Kansas anymore, Toto. That's for sure."

The room was as stark as a cell—a solitary confinement cell. The only objects in it were a mat on the floor and a lamp shaped like a lotus flower. Through the doorway, Athena could see what must have been the dining room—it had a TV tray and a folding chair. And nothing else. If there were any books in the house, a writer's necessity, they most likely disappeared into the miasma.

Finn held out his business card, and Willa snatched it with

a small yelp. "Uh...we wondered if you would be willing to...uh," he stuttered.

Her eyebrows shot up as she read the card. "You want me to be in a movie?"

"Not you. Per se. And it's television not—"

She patted her bony chest. "I need a *large* screen to capture my *large* spirit. I am an eagle, you see."

"Uh...um..."

"We do home makeovers," Athena said. "It's your house we're interested in." *And not your imitation of Gloria Swanson in* Sunset Boulevard.

"You intruded on my meditations for..." Willa glanced at the card. "For what exactly?"

"We didn't mean to," Finn said. "You see...uh..."

"It's not an intrusion. Fate brought us here," Athena said. "Your home abundantly demonstrates the principles of feng shui. No makeover is necessary."

"Feng what?" Willa asked.

"We were destined to be witnesses to the finest example of our design philosophy." Athena pretended to shoot photos of the empty room with her phone. "Now it is our mission to send your message out into the world."

"My message! Yes!"

Willa bowed deeply, nearly touching her head to her knees. And stayed in that position as Athena and Finn slowly inched away from her.

"Feng shui, we're on our way," Athena whispered as she grabbed his hand and hurried out the door.

"Shouldn't we have said goodbye or something?" Finn looked back at the house as they walked to the car. "You barely let me talk, Athena. It's like *I* was the silent partner."

"You sounded as much like a producer as she sounded like a sane person. Why did you pick her for the list?"

"Stevie and I thought she was cool. We'd watch her stand on her head on her porch. And other weird positions."

"A prerequisite for writing erotica. And, apparently, for going batty."

"How'd you come up with that bullshit about *design philosophy* and *our mission*?"

"From reading bullshit student essays, Mr. *Per se*."

He grinned. "Willa reminds me a little of Dad's girlfriend, Vivienne. But a bizarro-world version."

"I've been meaning to ask what you think of her."

"I like her a lot."

"Really? Why?"

"Because he's not *The* Charles when he's with her. He's The *Charles*."

"Whatever, spirit bird." Athena started the car and glanced at his list. "Who's next?"

"Gail Mueller. Remember her?"

"Nope."

"I do because Mom was always sending her library overdue notices."

"An avid reader, huh? You might be onto something this time."

A sixty-something woman with a child's round features and a plump figure, Gail readily welcomed them. She was so happy that Lydia's children had become successful in the television industry and invited them to measure her rooms after they explained their purpose.

If Athena could get into the rooms. Nearly every one was packed floor-to-ceiling with newspapers, magazines, empty pizza cartons, and other mysterious treasures of hoarders—including a significant portion of the Laurel Public Library collection. None of which were classic titles. Willa would have had a heart attack on the spot. And Lydia too.

After ten minutes, Athena couldn't take it anymore. A house that cluttered could never produce uncluttered prose, Iris Murdoch and her messy house and brilliant novels be damned.

She signaled *no* to Finn, and they slowly made their way out, detained by Gail pleading with them to share a meat-lover's pizza with her.

Finn hit his head against the car seat and exhaled from deep inside his chest. "I couldn't *breathe* in there. Did you smell that smell? Like dead cats."

"I think there were a few buried under all the crap."

"Is it me or is everyone in Laurel out of their fricking minds?"

"I can't tell anymore." She laughed. "I dated Sergei Gudonov."

She could always depend on *one* person to be sane and rational. Even if he sometimes drove *her* crazy. Thorne Kent.

"I think I'll brush up on my French," she said. "That way, if I run into a guy in Whole Foods extolling the virtues of *aubergines*, I'll be ready."

"Can I visit you if you move to Paris?"

"*Oui*. Me and all my French lovers."

Who the hell was she kidding? Athena Murphy was a one-man woman, and that's all there was to it.

"Karl wants to date you," Finn said. "In case you weren't aware of it."

"I am. Whenever he comes into the café, he goes into full flirting mode. But how do *you* know?" she asked, checking the next address.

"He told me when I interviewed him last time he was at the house."

"Say what?" she said, making a sharp right turn at the next intersection.

"To find out if he had any poop on Garland. But I didn't use *that* word." He pulled his shirt cuffs from his sweater sleeves. "God, he's like this gigantic, spectacular Nordic god."

"He's straight," she reminded him.

"He's hot."

"Stick to the subject. Why on earth would you ask the guy who's fixing our roof about Garland?"

"Think about it. He's probably been in everybody's house in Laurel, right? He'd know if someone was a writer."

"Hmm. Not bad. Any luck?"

"No. But it was worth every minute trying."

"There is a method to your madness." Athena reached across to hold his chin and shake his head. "Who's my genius baby brother? Who's my genius baby brother?"

"I am, I am," he said, panting like a puppy.

They didn't bother giving their spiel to Finn's next suspect, Naomi DeSantos, because she introduced herself as an author of science fiction as soon as she opened the door. "I can only talk for a few minutes. I'm on deadline," she said breathlessly, looking both exhilarated and stricken. An announcement the secretive Garland would never make. Nor was it likely Naomi would foray into the bedroom of literary characters. Unless she wanted to give them antennae and green skin.

"Good pick though, Finn," Athena said as they drove to the next house. "An actual writer."

"Stevie had a crush on her. He said she looked like Joan Baez. Whoever she is."

"A beautiful folk singer with the voice of an angel. And much older than him."

"Like Vivienne and Dad?"

"Like Vivienne's *grandmother* and Dad."

By the time they had spoken with Donna Jamison, retired

editor of the *Laurel Chronicle*, who couldn't remember where she'd put her keys, what the keys were for, or if she had keys, Finn was ready to pack it in. He rifled through the business cards. "We're as nuts as everybody else, Athena."

"Speak for yourself. And we've got one more to check. We have to see it through."

"You sound like Mario with his commitment speeches," he grumbled.

"We survived the twilight zone all day. I'm not giving up now."

Though when Bridget Carver, suspect number five, recognized Finn as one of the "brats" who had put nasty notes in her mailbox, and they had to run to the car to escape her fury and shovel, Athena admitted defeat. She was laughing too hard to have energy for anything else.

"I can't believe she remembered me," Finn wailed as they sped away.

"Please tell me Stevie didn't have a crush on her too," she said between gasps of laughter.

He checked his notes. "She's on my list because she was a pole dancer. Plus, she taught at the college. I figured the combination of brains and lack of sexual inhibition made her a candidate."

"It's still possible. But I don't want to risk death to find out."

"Nah. Her house is a shack. She wouldn't live there if she were rich."

"Your algorithm leaves a lot to be desired, Finnster. I think I'll trust my gut from now on."

"Murphy's law at work," he said with a sigh. "Anything that can go wrong will go wrong. At least we didn't have to deal with boyfriends or husbands."

"I have a feeling they've all run for the hills." She squeezed the back of his neck affectionately. "This was fun. For a couple of Murphys, we did all right. I had no idea you had such a sense of adventure."

"Huh. Try telling that to Mario."

"I mean it. Thanks for helping me."

"I told you I have your back."

"I wish I'd known what a rascal you were."

"I'm still a rascal. Some people just don't appreciate it."

"What was in the note you and Stevie put in Bridget's mailbox?"

He grinned. "I'll never tell."

CHAPTER ELEVEN

I have to remind myself to breathe—
almost to remind my heart to beat!

—EMILY BRONTË, *WUTHERING HEIGHTS*

Athena was surprised Thorne didn't leave As You Like It Café during her shift Wednesday afternoon as he usually did. Days of chilly rain had discouraged people from venturing outside, and business had come to a standstill. She'd served only six customers since noon.

The mystery of his presence was soon explained, however, when a young woman entered, carrying a mandolin. She was slender with the delicate features of a fairy and skin the color of skim milk. Without a word to anyone, she arranged herself on a stool by the bay window and strummed "Greensleeves."

" 'Alas, my love, you do me wrong to cast me off discourteously,' " she sang in a lilting voice.

Athena's former discourteous lover relieved her of the tray she was carrying and placed it on a table. "Thanks for the Renaissance music suggestion," Thorne said. "Her audition went very well. Now I want to see how the patrons respond."

" 'And I have loved you, oh so long, delighting in your company.' "

"What's her name?" Athena asked.

"Ivy Hagstrom, a music major at the college. She'll be performing on Wednesday and Saturday afternoons."

"She's lovely," she said, searching his face for signs of attraction—the lingering gaze, dilated pupils, drool. Nope.

"She plays the lute and harp too. More bang for the buck," saith the practical innkeeper.

"Finn used to listen to Renaissance music. Until Lydia asked him, for the sake of her nerves, not to."

"How is your brother?"

"Fair to middling. He said he'll drop by for lunch one of these days." She'd made Finn promise, like Charles, that he wouldn't breathe a word about her history with Thorne to anyone at the café.

"Tell him I said hi and hope to see him," he said.

" 'Greensleeves was my delight, Greensleeves my heart of gold,' " Ivy trilled.

"Remember this song, Thena?"

"Doesn't everybody?"

Thorne regarded her with a bemused smile as the memory came into focus. An actor sang "Greensleeves" in the first campus theatrical production they attended together, a drama about Henry VIII written by an English Department faculty member.

"This song was in that awful play," Athena said. "The one with Henry VIII's wives beheading *him*, one after the other. Even the queens he didn't execute."

"Including Catherine Parr, who outlived him. Talk about rewriting history."

"The woman seated behind us started crying when Anne of Cleves held Henry's head in the air."

"She was the wife of the professor who wrote it."

"Weeping from embarrassment," she said, laughing. "You gave her your handkerchief, remember?" One of many kind gestures that wound Thorne around her heart.

"Oh, right. And she made a face, opening it to check if I'd already used it."

"How was she to know Kents always carry a spare?"

Thorne had never devised oddball schemes like Finn. And his idea of fun had always been more cerebral than madcap. Yet everything they'd done together had been in a spirit of discovery and delight. If there was a vein of humor, they'd mine it—though Athena never got the joke in opera.

The café patrons applauded Ivy when she finished singing, and Thorne gave her a thumbs-up. Her face aglow, she flitted her fingers at him. Infatuation, plain as day. Athena knew the signs, having seen them on every smitten female who encountered Thorne on campus. It had been no small pleasure to be the object of their jealousy. It had been, in fact, wickedly satisfying.

"The gang showed up," he said, nodding toward the large table next to one of the hutches where Joe and Theresa, Phyllis and Dan, and the Blakes settled into their chairs.

"Makes an even dozen for the day," she said.

"I'm glad it's been slow. Too many people might have made Ivy nervous on her first day."

Athena glanced at the timid maiden whose maxi dress, split to the thigh, displayed one long, lean leg and who sang the Elizabethan song "Come, You Pretty False-Eyed Wanton" like a wanton. If she was nervous, then Henry VIII was every woman's dream guy.

"Ivy is very attractive, isn't she?" she asked. To be absolutely sure.

Thorne shrugged. "I guess so."

"She's as slim as a model and has such pretty pale skin."

"She looks anemic to me. But you know students. They never eat right." Thorne examined a mug on the tray. "Did Ian tell you the college has an opening for an English professor?"

"Yes. And I met the department chair when she came to the café. She encouraged me to apply."

"Oh, yeah?"

"Yeah."

Athena waited for him to ask if she was even remotely interested in the position. To look remotely interested in whether she was remotely interested.

"Second one chipped this week," he said, putting the mug back on the tray. "I should get unbreakable dinnerware. What do you think?"

I think you shouldn't bring up a subject unless you want to discuss the subject.

"They didn't have melamine in Tudor times," she said.

"True," he said, grinning. "Just mad kings and headless wives."

"Or the reverse," she said over her shoulder as she walked away to serve the newcomers.

She was getting really good at nailing exits.

"Just us chickens today," Phyllis said when Athena approached their table. "We're the only ones dumb enough to come out in this weather."

"Will this be a late lunch or early dinner?"

"Doesn't matter what you call it, hon. We closed shop early. We might sit here all afternoon."

"Lovely music," Joe remarked.

"It was my idea to hire a musician to create atmosphere," Athena said.

"As good as your idea to start a book club," he said.

The This Time Around Book Club—composed of these six and Athena, Charles, and Vivienne—had held its introductory session at the Murphy house Monday evening. They'd created a Facebook page and chosen seven p.m. every Tuesday as their regular meeting time. It would change to monthly once she returned to San Francisco and they'd done what they could to support her Garland project.

She'd found it comical to watch them watch Vivienne out of the corners of their eyes or behind their hands holding wineglasses. But not at all amusing to find herself, along with the rest of them, leaning forward to listen whenever Vivienne Vander-something spoke in that throaty voice of hers.

"Are you coming to the Halloween party Friday night, Athena?" Phyllis asked.

"I haven't decided yet. Where's it held?"

"At the VFW Lodge, right around the corner. The theme this year is to dress up as a character opposite yourself."

Corinne Carew. All Athena would need was a blond wig, a knockoff Chanel suit, and the phoniest smile this side of a hemorrhoid commercial.

"Last year, the theme was a character *like* yourself," Phyllis said. "Mayor Benson came as Superman. We all had a good laugh."

"Including Sharon, I imagine," Athena said.

"She wasn't there. Had a headache or something."

"Where's the best place to get costumes?"

"The Theater Department at Southern Illinois College," Phyllis said. "They lend them for free until Friday afternoon, but you're responsible for any damage."

"Just how wild do these Halloween parties get?"

They all became suddenly fascinated by their menus, leaving her question unanswered. Others soon crowded her mind.

Would Thorne be at the party?

If so, who would he come dressed as?

Who would he come with?

An hour later, as the six friends debated dessert, Athena caught up on kitchen duties. Ditching her yellow work gloves after she had scoured pans and scrubbed the sink, she noticed Thorne's laptop on the bottom shelf of the counter. A few of the Garden Club members had requested watercress sandwiches. No time like the present to look for recipes.

As soon as she figured out the laptop password.

Thorne would use *Sonnet* and the Roman numeral of whichever Shakespearean sonnet reflected the progress of their love. If he still did this, it wasn't likely he'd kept the eighteenth sonnet, comparing her to a summer's day. Or number 109, which began "O, never say that I was false of heart."

Athena tapped her chin, considering which sonnet *she* would find meaningful now. She typed *Sonnet XXX*, the thirtieth, whose opening lines were, "When to the sessions of sweet silent thought / I summon up remembrance of things past."

Bingo.

As she jotted down ingredients, summoning a few sweet, silent thoughts, the door swung open. "What the hell are you doing?" Thorne demanded.

Boss Man was back with a bristling stance and scowl, looking decidedly less appealing than the man who had remembered their first date.

"Research," she stammered.

"I told you to keep your Garland business out of my café."

"I'm looking for recipes. Which *is* café business," she retorted, pissed off that she had stammered.

He crossed the room in a few long strides. "My laptop is my private property. I expect you to respect it."

"Excuse me for taking initiative." She spun it around to show him the screen. "Some of your customers wondered if we could add watercress sandwiches to the menu."

He frowned as he read and, snapping the laptop shut, put it back on the shelf. "You should have told me. *I* would have searched for the recipes."

"I didn't think borrowing your laptop was a big deal. Can we at least discuss the sandwiches?"

"Go ahead."

"They're easy to construct, make a nice presentation, and they're packed with nutrients."

"Watercress isn't always available."

"The Garden Club has started growing it hydroponically. They'd provide it."

"Add it to the menu then. But don't forget, my laptop is off-limits." Thorne turned to leave but then swiveled around. "How did you figure out my password?"

"Oh, a little bard told me."

But Boss Man was not amused. As Athena watched those shoulders, that butt, and those long, sinewy legs walk away, she remembered a line from *Much Ado about Nothing*: "I never can see him but I am heart-burned an hour after."

The hell with it. Business was slow and the barometric pressure low, giving her a killer sinus headache. She should be researching Garland and the novellas, not recipes. Penning, not punning. Wadding her apron into a ball, she lobbed it into the laundry basket.

"Do you mind if I leave early?" she asked Thorne, who was filling salt and pepper shakers at the beverage station.

"No. Not at all." He fumbled with the base of a shaker, spilling pepper all over the counter. "Sorry for overreacting. I was rude and out of line."

"Been there. Done that." It wasn't often Athena was on the receiving end of a rant. She'd remember how bad it felt the next time she was about to lose her shit in a faculty meeting.

If she ever attended another faculty meeting.

She had set her phone ringer to mute, dreading another call from Elise. One breathlessly informing her an applicant for her job had wowed the faculty during an interview. And what did Dr. M want to do with the posters of the windswept Yorkshire moors hanging in her office?

"Uh... Thena?" Thorne said.

"Yeah?"

"We okay?"

Thorne might *keep calm*, but his eyes registered every shifting emotion like a stormy sky. She never could resist them, especially when they expressed sensitivity and contrition.

Nor could she resist mentally reciting the last two lines of Sonnet XXX: *"But if the while I think on thee, dear friend, / All losses are restor'd, and sorrows end."*

"We're okay, Thorne. Be sure to check if the gang wants dessert." Athena slipped into her coat, and with a wave to everyone, including Ivy, left the café.

She'd parked on a side street of gentrified brick buildings with *For Rent* signs in the windows. As she turned the ignition key, the door to one of them opened, and Geraldine O'Neal emerged. Her hair was tucked beneath a cloche, and she wore a duster coat over her rail-thin body, looking for all the world like Virginia Woolf. Darting her eyes up and down the street, she got into her Volvo and sped away.

What was she doing in this neighborhood? More importantly, why was she so furtive?

"Sonofabitch," Athena whispered.

Geraldine, a lifelong resident of Laurel, was private, clever, and, as Lydia had said, *original and witty*. She tapped her fingers on the steering wheel as the pieces of the puzzle fell into place.

Geraldine was renting *a room of her own*, as Woolf described, to write in solitude, editing on the computer at home. As bestselling author C. L. Garland, she had written herself out of her bad marriage. She had drawn unwanted attention, putting the signs up in Huck's convenience store, but everyone was entitled to a brief episode of madness, especially when high-fructose corn syrup was involved.

Athena gunned the engine and drove to the O'Neal house, forming a game plan. Since Geraldine was too impatient for subtlety, she'd ask her straight off the bat if she was Garland. Or address her by that name and gauge her reaction. At best, she'd confirm her suspicions. At worst, Geraldine would bean her with a sandwich or whatever food she had handy.

She parked in her driveway next to the Volvo and checked the window. For once, Geraldine wasn't at the computer. Climbing the porch steps, Athena shivered, partly from cold, partly from cold feet, devising a reason to be invited inside. Besides a feng shui home makeover.

The door swung open at her knock. Holding the dreaded sandwich, Geraldine looked down at her through hooded eyes. Her billowy white hair, freed of the cloche, haloed her head. "I'm not buying anything," she said. "And if you're one of those wackadoodle preachers, you can take your hokum elsewhere."

She was original all right. No one had ever mistaken Athena for a preacher.

"I'm Athena, Lydia Murphy's daughter."

"I'm not showing the house today," she said, taking a ferocious bite of the sandwich.

"I'm not here about the house sale." Athena looked past her into the living room. Whaddya know. A wall of bookcases stuffed with hardcovers and paperbacks. "Mind if I come in?"

"I certainly do mind." Geraldine tilted her head upward, revealing the long line of her nostrils. "Oh, it's you. I see you jogging by all the time. You're too top-heavy to be bouncing up and down on the pavement."

Athena thrust out her top-heavy chest. "I've stopped by

to invite you to join the This Time Around Book Club. I've started a group in town—"

"Don't like groups. Never have."

"It's just a few people who enjoy reading the classics."

"I do my own reading."

"And writing?"

She frowned. "What do you take me for? An imbecile who can't read or write on her own?"

Athena glanced at the sandwich. Would barbecue sauce leave a permanent stain? "About the book club. Membership is—"

Geraldine smiled triumphantly. "I knew you were selling something."

"But I'm not. There's no fee to join."

"Don't you know by now, child? Everything has a price."

With those words of wisdom, she slammed the door, leaving Athena feeling foolish—the more so for being flattered Geraldine had referred to her as *child*.

To their credit—or maybe not—the citizens of Laurel refused to let pocked plaster walls, scuffed linoleum floors, and the pungent odor of disinfectant in the VFW Lodge get in the way of their bacchanalia. By the time Athena arrived at the Halloween party Friday night, they were already drunk as skunks—thanks to the enormous bowl of red punch—and halfway through the roast meats and casseroles filling the long banquet table. The light was mercifully dim, discouraging incriminating photos, selfie or otherwise, as they whooped it up on the dance floor.

She smoothed the folds of the brown muslin gown she'd found in the college's Theater Department storeroom under the category "miscellaneous." The plain, unadorned dress with its simple white lace collar—that she couldn't squeeze into without the accompanying corset—would suit a pilgrim, nun, or governess. To Athena, it screamed *Jane Eyre* the minute she saw it. Charlotte Brontë's fictional governess, who mastered the heart of her employer, Mr. Rochester, was as opposite to Athena as the party theme required. Passionate yet stoical in the face of hardship and a broken heart, Jane never lost her dignity. And her triumphant declaration at the end of the novel, "Reader, I married him," was the reverse of Athena's defeated admission, *Reader, he dumped me.*

Standing next to a plastic skeleton that was missing an arm, she scanned the room for Geraldine in vain. A pointed question or two, and an apology for disturbing her *while she was writing*, might make up for her disastrous visit Wednesday. There was no sign of Thorne either, but most of the café regulars had shown up.

Dressing as punk rockers must initially have seemed like a great idea to the Garden Club members, but they were clearly having misgivings. They tugged on their tight sequined pants and struggled to keep their mohawk wigs on straight. Mayor Benson, wearing a long-haired black wig, bandanna, and bell-bottom pants, waved to her with more enthusiasm than she was in the mood for.

"The missus couldn't make it," he said, coming up to her.

"A migraine?" Athena said.

"How'd you know?"

"Lucky guess."

He tugged on the peace sign medallion around his neck. "Who are you dressed as?"

"A Victorian governess."

"It doesn't suit you. Not enough... something."

"Less is more, if you have imagination," she said sweetly.

"Darn if you don't keep me on my toes," the mayor said

with a chuckle. "Kent is one lucky man, winning the raffle. Have you two had your night on the town?"

"Not yet."

"After that kiss, what are you waiting for?"

"We're both too busy."

Busy forgetting. Busy remembering.

He raised his empty glass. "Time for a refill. Can I get you some?"

"No thanks."

"Come on, it's a party," he said, nudging her with his elbow.

"Governesses didn't drink."

"Not even in the twenty-first century?" he asked with a wink.

"Not even."

She turned away, nearly colliding with the five bachelor farmers dressed as either hobbits or dwarfs. "Tolkien or Disney?" she asked them.

"Disney's seven dwarfs, minus Doc and Dopey," one of them answered.

"Hey, wait, we thought *you* were Dopey," another farmer said.

"Very funny, Grumpy."

"Who are *you* supposed to be, Athena?" another one asked.

"Guess."

They scratched their bearded chins, tugged on their peaked caps, and hooked their fingers in their wide belts.

"Dunno."

"A nun?"

"A Thanksgiving pilgrim?"

"A pioneer lady?"

"Jeez, Athena. Who?"

"Jane Eyre," a male voice answered.

Thorne flung a cape over the shoulders of his broad-lapeled

black frock coat and strode over to them. From his cravat to his knee-high leather boots, he was a nineteenth-century gentleman come alive. One who'd left his horse, flanks steaming from the rough ride, still gasping for breath. And his lover too.

"Edward Rochester, I presume," Athena said as coolly as her pounding heart allowed. And she presumed he'd come alone, without Girlfriend Number Whatever or that Robin person. Because no sane woman would let him out of her sight for a second when he was dressed like this.

"Mr. Rochester of Thornfield Hall," he said with a deep bow. "You *are* Jane, governess to Adèle, are you not?"

"Yes, sir. I am."

The bachelor farmers looked at each other. "Who are they talking about?" one of them asked.

"Book characters, I think," another one said. "Come on. Let's get beers at Benny's Bar."

"You drank half the punch bowl already."

"Didn't touch me."

"Neither did any of the women."

"Very funny, Dopey."

"I'm Bashful, remember?"

"G'night, Athena. G'night, Thorne," they said as they filed out the door.

"I didn't think you'd show up, Thorne," Athena said. "You never liked parties."

"I came to track Mayor Benson down. He's been ignoring my calls and emails."

"Your outfit should get his attention."

"I considered carrying a riding crop."

"He's dressed as a hippie. Appeal to his liberal tendencies."

"Benson doesn't have any." He opened his coat to reveal a burgundy satin vest. "What do you think of this costume?"

"Are you really supposed to be Mr. Rochester?"

"He'll do, since you're Jane Eyre. But I was aiming for Heathcliff, your favorite character."

"How sweet. You remembered," she said drily.

"You always said I was nothing like him. And the theme of this party *is* opposites."

"Add a surly expression and saturnine disposition and you could pull it off."

"If you can do demure, I can do surly," he said, trying to curl his lips into a sneer.

"No kidding. When I borrowed your laptop, you were halfway to any of the Brontë bad boys."

"You mean there's hope for me yet?"

"If you try extra hard."

He adjusted his cravat. His sneer melted into a smile. "Happy to oblige, Thena."

"Too little, too late, Thorne."

It was his turn to parry her thrust. But he didn't. Head bowed, he twisted a silver button on the vest. "Is it?" he asked hoarsely. "Is it too late?"

This was her cue to swoon, to fall helplessly into the arms of her hero. To go along with the game and pretend they still had a chance for happiness. And she might have if Phyllis and Theresa, in black turtleneck sweaters and shag hairstyle wigs, hadn't come up to them. Athena had the almost irresistible urge to cross the room, dunk her head in the punch bowl, and drink herself into next month.

"None of us know a lick about music so we came as The Beatles," Phyllis said. "I'm Ringo, and Dan's George."

"And I'm John, and Joe's Paul," Theresa added.

Phyllis stepped back to look over Athena and Thorne. "And you two are . . . ?"

"Jane Eyre and Edward Rochester. But it was a complete coincidence. We didn't plan it," Thorne assured her.

"Yeah. Complete coincidence," Athena said.

Curiously, Garland hadn't included any of the Brontë sisters' novels in the LitWit series. A regrettable omission since there were infinite possibilities for sex-capades in the dark corridors of Thornfield Hall, Wuthering Heights, and Wildfell Hall.

"Ladies," Thorne said with another bow, "I espy our esteemed mayor near the bowl of grog. Pardon me while I converse with him."

Don't go. Ask me again if it's too late, Athena wanted to say. But she was demure Jane Eyre, so she had to suck it up and let him walk away. Stay put and watch his mile-long legs sweep across the room in those boots.

"Are you uncomfortable in your dress?" Phyllis asked her. "You look like you're having a tooth pulled."

No. Just my heartstrings.

"The corset digging into my ribs is torture," Athena said.

"Dolores came as Scarlett O'Hara but left early," Theresa said. "She kept tripping over her hoop skirt."

"Between you and me and the gatepost, Wayne made a ridiculous Rhett Butler," Phyllis said. "Too short and stocky."

"But that's the point of opposite characters," Theresa said.

"Did my dad come with the Blakes?" Athena asked.

"I haven't seen him," Phyllis said. "Or Vivienne. Talk about masquerade."

"What do you mean?"

"Miss Hoity-Toity in plain-Jane clothes? I'm not buying it." Phyllis nodded toward Thorne, who was staring at the floor as Mayor Benson talked, index finger poking the air. "I don't know, maybe it's his costume. But something tells me there's more to Thorne than meets the eye too."

No. There wasn't. If there was anything Athena was absolutely certain of in this life, it was that Thorne was Thorne, through and through.

And she'd never meet another man like him again. He'd set the bar, once and for all.

Suddenly dizzy and faintly nauseous, Athena excused herself, nodding dumbly to Theresa's anxious question if she was all right. Why had she come to the silly party anyway? Nearly everyone was crocked, so recruiting new members to the book club was a long shot. And the chance that Geraldine, or Garland herself, would show up was an even longer shot. She should be home, writing her book. This very minute, someone was reading Dr. Davenport's ad for her job, polishing their résumé, sending it through cyberspace, and nailing the coffin of her career shut with one click of the computer mouse.

She pushed open the door of the VFW Lodge and gulped deep breaths of the bracing night air. Her hand felt clammy on her hot forehead. Sweat trickled down her face, though she shivered with chills. Taking a few steps, she tried to focus on the bright streetlamps piercing the darkness. Smaller, smaller, the lights became, until they were mere pinpricks. Until utter, infinite blackness descended like a shroud.

"Thena. Thena, wake up."

Athena's eyes fluttered open. Thorne's voice came from far away, but his face was inches from hers, his breath warm on her cheek. The night sky had become the ceiling of his apartment, the hard ground transformed into his cape on the sofa, cushioning her boneless, weightless body. "What happened?" she whispered.

He held a glass of water to her lips. "Drink first."

"I'm a little woozy."

"Drink," he ordered.

"Yes, sir."

He cradled her head as the cool water slipped down her throat. "When I saw you go pale all of a sudden, I followed you outside," he said. "You fainted a few feet from the door, so I brought you here."

"How?"

"I carried you." An exertion that had clearly forced him out of his frock coat and vest.

"Sorry I missed those heroics."

"Getting you out of your costume was a lot harder."

"Getting into it was no picnic either." Athena looked down at her body, freed of its governess gown. The Victorians had it right. A hint of nudity was much more enticing than nudity itself. Her thin cotton slip, the final layer of too many undergarments, hugged the contours of her hips and thighs. Her full breasts, bound by the corset, heaved like every heaving bosom ever described in romance novels.

"It's a miracle that women breathed in these things," Thorne said, twirling one of the corset ribbons. "No wonder you passed out."

"What they call a good old-fashioned fainting spell. Bring on the smelling salts," she joked. "And in the middle of our date, no less."

"Date?"

"You're the lucky guy who won the raffle, remember? Let's count this as our night on the town."

"Luck had nothing to do with it." His spring-green eyes glistened. "I bought all the tickets."

Before she could think of a devil-may-care remark, anything to make him move away so she no longer smelled his clean skin or admired the Saxon beauty of his chiseled face or was tantalized by his lower lip, the lip she used to bite when he made her come, come, come—before all that, he teased her breasts with feathery kisses, his hand traveling slowly up her neck, tarrying to caress the curves of her face, lingering at her mouth, which she opened to let him dip his finger in. Which she sucked. Because the devil may care but she didn't.

Thorne reached behind her head and unsnapped the barrettes. Her curls tumbled to her shoulders. As their lips met and tongues entwined, she felt for the buttons on his shirt. One, two...she made it to four but, delirious from kissing, tore off the rest, heard them roll onto the floor. She tugged and pulled at his cravat, tossing it into the air as he released her from the corset, held her breasts in his hands, and partook of his delight without asking permission. Though she'd already given it.

Keep calm and tear my clothes off.

The brawn of his chest, the silkiness of his skin, drew a groan from a place so deep inside she had to stop, gasping for air. "We shouldn't," she whispered. "This is madness."

"Let's blame it on the Brontës," he whispered back.

And he lifted her like the hero he was and carried her to his bedroom, leading the way with his triumphant penis, swelling like every throbbing member in every bodice ripper ever written.

CHAPTER TWELVE

I often cry when I am happy, and smile when I am sad.

—ANNE BRONTË, *THE TENANT OF WILDFELL HALL*

So, they went and done it, and done it good.

Athena sat on the edge of Thorne's bed, hurriedly hooking her corset. Dawn was inching its way across the sky, and the last thing she wanted was to be seen walking to her car parked outside the VFW Lodge still dressed as Charlotte Brontë's heroine. Not a repressed Jane Eyre either, but an unbridled Jane, freed after a night of passion with Mr. Rochester—a night worthy of a Garland novella.

Correction. The last thing she wanted was to regret one minute of the hours she and Thorne had just spent together. There would be no apologies and no embarrassment, no shedding of tears. Thena and Thorne were above petty feelings and grudges and Sturm und Drang this time around.

Putting on the dress she'd retrieved from the living room floor, she paused to watch him sleep as she'd done so many mornings before. Sex always supercharged her. Every nerve in her body had sizzled as 1:16 a.m., 3:22 a.m., 4:36 a.m., slowly ticked by. Not Thorne. He gave himself over to deep slumber like a child, one arm flung over his head, his lips slightly parted.

She tiptoed to the window and peeked through the venetian blinds. Bands of red and violet streaked the eastern sky and unseen birds chirped their way down the deserted street. "Red sky at morning, sailors' warning," the saying went.

Nonsense. The skies could no more portend good fortune or disaster than Lydia's silly horoscopes. Any more than making love could predict they...

More nonsense. What she and Thorne had done was raw, slippery, grunting sex. Nothing more.

"And we done it good," she mumbled.

"Hey, you," Thorne said sleepily. He lay on his side, his head propped on one arm. His ruffled hair and drowsy eyes made her want to get back under the covers and do it good some more.

"Hey, you too." She straightened the lace collar and secured her bun with the barrettes she'd found in the sofa cushions. "That was some night on the town."

"It certainly was."

"Worth buying all the raffle tickets for?"

"And then some."

"Jane thanks you for a lovely evening, but she has to leave by daybreak."

"Remaining in character. I approve."

"Acting always did stoke the embers of our passion." After they played the title roles in the campus production of *Romeo and Juliet*, they'd stayed in bed nearly two days straight.

He patted the mattress with a grin. "And the embers are still smoking."

She bent over to put her shoes on. "Sorry. There won't be an Act Two."

"Jane can't leave until I dismiss her. Don't forget, I am master here."

With one cocked eyebrow, Athena looked around the

sparsely furnished room. "Your set design leaves a lot to be desired."

"Anything else left to be desired?"

"Not a thing. Though I noticed you haven't picked up any new moves since our last romp in the hay." She had no problem bringing up Seattle. Last night had canceled their dreadful encounter. It wasn't raining, for one thing. And for another, she had positively no urge to weep or beg. None whatsoever.

Throwing off the covers, Thorne bounded out of bed and put on the shirt she'd practically denuded of its buttons. It wasn't long enough to hide his penis, which, though spent, was at half-mast. *Horny Thorny in the morny* indeed. "And Sven? Does he have all the right moves?" he asked, pulling on his briefs and pants.

Sven? Who the hell was Sven?

"Your eccentric boyfriend," he said.

"Sergei? What can I say? He makes love with a Russian accent."

It wasn't her imagination. He winced at the words *makes love*.

He started buttoning his shirt, and then stopped because there were only three of them. "Is it serious between you and him?"

She wanted to laugh.

She wanted to cry.

"We're as serious, I imagine, as you, Robin, and all the rest. While we're on the subject of sexual partners, my IUD is firmly in place, but I make Sergei wear a condom anyway. And you?"

"Never leave home without one." He stood next to her at the window and opened the venetian blinds. A faint etching of lines around his eyes and mouth hinted at his age. Looking at his pale face, at the touch of sadness time had stamped upon his features, her heart throbbed for the old man he would someday be. For the old woman *she* would be...without him.

"I wish I were a girl again, half savage and hardy, and free," Catherine had lamented, knowing she and Heathcliff could never be who they once were to each other.

So do I, Athena confessed to herself.

She shook slightly to shrug off the melancholy twining its arms around her. "Well, Thorne," she said brightly.

"Well, Thena."

"We've come a long way, haven't we? We've turned a page, finished a chapter. Closed the book. I'd say we're ready to write a new story."

Dear Zeus and all the gods in heaven, she was babbling like an English professor with a brain lesion. But Thorne was much too close. If there was anything more irresistible than his clean scent, it was his postcoital scent. Sweet, doughy, like a delectable pastry.

"What are you suggesting?" he asked.

Us. Me and you together again, waking up in each other's arms every morning until we take our last breaths.

" 'Red sky at morning,' " she whispered.

"What did you say?"

Sailors' warning.

Athena stood straighter, easing the pain of the corset digging into her ribs. "All my energies are directed toward my book and career before I return to San Francisco. But I don't see what harm a little discreet sex between former lovers would do. As long as you and Robin aren't...um...serious."

He rested his forehead against the window. "We're not."

"Any of the others?"

He shook his head.

"Neither are Sergei and I. So, let's call our new story 'Friends with Benefits.'" Could she sound any more chipper?

"Discreet and *secret*."

"Not even Finn would know. I tell him everything, but he can't be relied on to keep his mouth shut."

"Like Quentin. He's got the loosest tongue in the Pacific Northwest, especially if he's been drinking." Thorne brought her hand to his lips and kissed it. "I'm game if you are."

"We are pretty terrific between the sheets."

"And good friends, despite everything." He smiled. "You're the only person I'd lend my handkerchief to these days."

"And you're the only person whose handkerchief I'd borrow." But it wouldn't be for tears. There would be no more tears.

"It doesn't get any chummier than that."

"Friends with benefits it is."

She'd heeded the sailors' warning. So, why did she feel shipwrecked?

"I can sew the buttons back on," she offered as he tucked his shirt into his pants.

"Thanks, but I learned how to sew. A necessary skill for a confirmed bachelor."

Athena blinked back a forbidden tear. Thorne's resolve to never marry depressed the hell out of her. A rainy day, got-the-blues sadness.

Forget Thena and Thorne. Forget their past, their broken promises, and their heartache. It was a lonely world, and he should have someone to walk through it with him. She loved him too much to wish him anything but love and happiness, marriage, and a family.

Yeah. She loved him as much as ever. Big, fricking surprise.

"Why did you betray your own heart, Cathy?" Heathcliff had cried.

Why indeed, Athena?

Putting one foot in front of the other, she walked to the doorway of the bedroom and turned, forming her lips into a smile. "You'll be busy at the café today, but wanna hang out at the Botanical Garden or something on Sunday?"

"I'd love to, Thena, but I can't." Thorne pointed to a stack of folders on the dresser. "I've got a pile of work to catch up on."

"What am I saying? I've got a *mountain*. See you Monday, then."

She smiled again, not entirely guiltless of the satisfaction that, unlike Seattle, *she* was the one walking out this time. Walking out, making her exit, leaving the stage after one of the best performances of her life.

Tuesday morning, Athena dragged one of the armchairs and an end table to the fireplace and set up her laptop. If Lydia's house could be compared to a macrobiotic meal, the Murphy home was comfort food. And boy oh boy, did she need comfort. Unfortunately, the house was as drafty as it was cozy. Branwell installed himself on the rug in front of the hearth in November and hardly budged until March.

His pug mug sent accusatory looks her way as she typed her latest chapter, a rather thin appraisal of Garland's novella "North and South." Four days since her night of Brontëan abandon and Branwell kept sniffing the air as if he smelled sex on her skin and in her hair. Thankfully, no one at the café had suspected a thing as she and Thorne worked the hectic Monday shift together. They'd exchanged trays and passed each other from kitchen to dining room with nary an awkward moment. Though when Dolores told everyone Wayne had to practically tear her out of her Scarlett O'Hara gown, they did share one titillating glance.

Branwell whined at the sound of Charles's careful tread down the stairs. He had changed from his tracksuit to a white shirt and black trousers and was carrying an overnight bag. As far as Athena knew, he hadn't taken a trip since visiting Finn and her in San Francisco a year ago.

"Carpe diem, my goddess," he said.

"Top of the morning to you, Dad."

"No time to walk the dog today," he said, retrieving his parka from the foyer closet. "Can you take him?"

Branwell put his paws over his face in a futile attempt to be invisible.

"Sure. I came by to cook dinner for you and Finn. And then the This Time Around Book Club will be here at seven."

He patted the tufts of hair on either side of his head. "Sorry, I can't make it. I have another...engagement. I won't be back till tomorrow."

She pointed to the overnight bag. "Spending the night with someone? Vivienne maybe?"

"I most certainly am not," he said, coloring to the dome of his bald head. "Vivienne and I are platonic friends, Athena. Strictly platonic."

"So where are you going?"

"If you must know, I will be stargazing with Sam Fisher, a retired science teacher. He wants me to observe some interesting celestial phenomena on his telescope."

"I never heard of a Mr. Fisher when I was in high school."

"Phil was before your time."

"I thought you said his name was Sam."

He zipped the parka closed. "So it is. So it is."

Athena twined a curl around her finger as all the clues

about her father clicked into place again. Forget Geraldine O'Neal. Finn had been right from the get-go, postulating Charles was Garland. The poems he'd written for Lydia, his surprising sex life, his quiet personality that preferred privacy to fame. He wasn't stargazing with Sam Phil Fisher. He was traveling to an appointment with his agent or editor.

"Dad, there's a lot riding on my book. Everything, in fact. My job's on the line. If you're C. L. Garland, you have to tell me."

He regarded her blankly for a moment and then, throwing back his head, exploded in laughter. Even Branwell looked like he was ready to split a gut. "That's rich, Athena! That's a humdinger!"

Finn hurried downstairs, wearing only one loafer. "What's going on? What did I miss?"

"Your sister thinks I'm..." Charles paused to catch his breath between laughs. "She thinks I write the LitWit series."

"It's not *that* preposterous," Athena grumbled.

He waved his hand, taking in the mishmash of furniture and worn rugs. "If I were a rich, bestselling author, would I live like this? Or not share the money with my children?"

Finn grinned. "Gee, thanks, Dad."

"What's with the sudden interest in astral bodies?" she challenged him.

He gripped the handle of the overnight bag. "One of the joys of retirement, my dear. Discovering new hobbies."

Athena indulged a long, mournful sigh. Geraldine was back to being her prime suspect. Difficult, elusive, food-throwing Geraldine.

"I am sorry to hear about your job," her father said. "On the line, eh?"

"One more inch over and..." She made a cutting gesture across her throat.

"It's a dog-eat-dog world out there." Branwell farted agreement. "Is there anything I can do, Athena?" her father asked.

Turn back the clock a few months. Or a decade. Or two.

"No, but thanks for asking."

"I'm here if you need me." He opened the front door. "But not today. Not until tomorrow. *Late* tomorrow. Or maybe the day after that. Uh... you get the general idea."

Finn plopped onto the rug next to Branwell after Charles left. "Sorry, Athena. Another theory shot to hell."

"Like my career."

"I'll take career problems over love problems any day."

It was on the tip of her tongue to confess she had both. "What should I make for dinner?"

"I don't care. My appetite's gone to shit," he said in his lowest baritone.

"Don't complain. You're looking pretty buff. No more Charles chunk."

He rubbed his flat belly. "A lot of good it's doing me."

"Patience, Finnster. Time heals all wounds." Well, not all. A truth she wouldn't admit to him, since he was hurting badly over Mario's latest offense—photos of him at a bar with another guy. On his and Finn's joint Facebook page, no less.

Finn took his phone from his pocket and held it up so she could see pictures of Karl unloading shingles from his truck. "I texted these beauties to you-know-who. Right after I answered a personals ad for..." He scrolled through the phone. " 'Caring liberal seeks sensitive lover to share his love of life and the outdoors.' "

"You hate the outdoors." The slightest sunburn or an insect bite sent him running to the nearest pharmacy.

"Yeah, but I'm sensitive. *And* a liberal. And, as a bonus, entrepreneurial."

"I'm almost afraid to ask."

He pulled Branwell onto his lap. "No, listen. This is great. I want to fix and sell stuff couples break when they fight or throw out when they split up. I'll call the shop All It's Cracked Up to Be. Or, Them's the Breaks. Whaddya think?"

What Athena thought was that her kid brother, with his missing loafer and inside-out sweatshirt, was losing his marbles. "I wish you'd come up with that idea when Mom reduced Dad's Lord Byron statue to smithereens. FYI, she called last night from South Carolina. Or maybe North Carolina, she wasn't sure. She said she's leaving the itinerary to Tony."

"Mom? Giving up control?" Finn asked, eyebrows raised. "Who is this Tony anyway?"

"Her mentor, I think she said. Oh, and she asked how 'the Mario situation' was going."

"What'd you tell her?"

"I was so surprised she asked, I said the first thing that came to mind—improving."

"*Worsening* is more like it. Love sucks," Finn griped. "I should have known if you and Thorne could break up, everybody else was doomed."

From Thena and Thorne, the gold standard of relationships, to Thena and Thorne, sex without strings. As if she weren't depressed enough.

And a part of her, a teeny tiny part, was tired of hearing Finn bitch and moan. She was on the verge of telling him to step up to the plate and go to bat for his relationship, but the baseball metaphor would go right over his head.

"How are you and Thorne doing anyway?" he asked. "Is it a hassle working together?"

"We're handling it better than I expected." Athena saved the document she'd been typing and shut down the laptop.

"Apparently, there's a tenure-track position available in the English Department at Southern Illinois College."

"So?"

"So, nothing."

Finn stopped scratching Branwell's belly. "You'd move back here?"

"Did I say that? All I did was mention a possible option. Not that I'd even consider it."

"I have options too. I've been designing websites. An old friend from college connected me to businesses in St. Louis, and I'm making decent money. Does the café need one?"

"It has a Facebook page but no website. Why don't you stop by and ask Thorne if he wants one? He'd love to see you."

"I always liked hanging out with him." Finn tugged on Branwell's ears, making the pug smile. "We used to laugh our heads off watching *Seinfeld*. The Festivus episode was our favorite."

"I loved the Airing of Grievances ritual." And boy oh boy, she had plenty of those.

"And Feats of Strength," Finn said, lifting Branwell above his head, having not a clue that Athena's feat of strength was laughing as she recalled the happy years when Thorne was a member of her family—when what she really wanted to do was bawl her eyes out.

Wednesday was as drab and dreary a day as only the month of November could deliver. Having spent an unproductive meeting with the This Time Around Book Club members last evening, Athena's mood was as glum as the weather. If any of them showed up at the café, she just might scold them for gossiping about the absent Charles and Vivienne instead of discussing *The Last of the Mohicans* and Garland's novella

"The Lust of the Mohicans." Though when she woke in the night to the beat of rain on the roof, she did wonder if her father's eyes were fixed on the stormy heavens as he had claimed they would be.

Athena brought a tray of sandwiches to the Garden Club, who'd commandeered the two largest tables, leaving the bachelor farmers squeezed around a small one. She couldn't help grinning. From a distance, they appeared to be one massive body, their movements—fork to mouth to plate, napkin to mouth to table—in perfect synchrony.

"There's the smile I've been waiting for all afternoon," Karl said when she passed his table on the way to the kitchen.

"No calls for jobs yet?" she asked.

"Not in this weather. And I'm waiting on supplies for your house."

"Too bad."

"Too good. For me. To be here. With you."

"Sounds like something you'd carve on a tree."

"Huh?"

"People used to . . . never mind."

Ever since he came in, Karl had been commenting on her various charms. Okay. So, he appreciated her *bounce*. Made note of how well her green blouse complemented her brown eyes. Bless his heart. Bless his young, clueless heart that had no idea she was too jaded for flattery. Though when he asked her to recommend books for him to read—"You being a smart professor and all"—Athena's curiosity was piqued. What books had *he* read that had formed his attraction to an older woman with unmanageable curls and quips?

Ivy arrived for her Wednesday gig and, casting a mournful look around the room, strummed dirges on her mandolin. Just one of those days, Athena figured. A day that felt like everyone in the Renaissance had up and died all over again.

While she distributed dessert orders to the Garden Club, an old, bearded man wearing a fisherman's cap, collarless white shirt, woolen brown vest, and baggy trousers entered the café. He sank slowly into a chair, tucking his head between his shoulders. Though Athena had never seen him before, something about him was vaguely familiar.

"Welcome to As You Like It Café," she said, handing him a menu.

"Thank you," he said in a raspy voice.

"Feel free to take off your cap and get comfortable."

"I'm comfortable enough." He squinted at the menu through foggy eyeglasses. "I'll have the grilled cheese and a cup of tomato soup."

"Tea or coffee?"

When he shook his head, his gray hair shifted slightly to the right, the cap to the left.

"Anything else?" she asked.

"No, thank you."

Another lonesome guy, rusty at conversation. If he started coming regularly, she'd encourage him and Eugene to sit together. Suggest to Thorne he create a curmudgeon special. Meanwhile, she'd bring him extra napkins in case food got caught in his ratty beard.

Athena refilled the coffee machine, watching Ivy walk toward her out of the corner of her eye. "Can I get you anything?" she asked her. *An alcoholic beverage? An antidepressant?* And one of each for herself while she was at it.

Ivy wound her long hair around her hand. "Will Thorne be in today?"

"He only works lunch hours if it's very busy."

"But he scheduled me for afternoons. I thought..." She tugged on the coil of hair. "He'll be here this Saturday though, right?"

"Far as I know."

"He better be."

The look of determination on the fair maiden's face was unmistakable. One week into the job and she'd already set her sights on Thorne Campus-Crush Kent. Athena had no choice, really, but to nip this clinging Ivy in the bud. Which was why, a half hour after she'd persuaded Karl to introduce himself to Ivy and they were still talking, she experienced the rare satisfaction of killing two birds with one stone.

When the elderly man had finished his lunch, she went to clear his table. His head was bent over the small notebook he was writing in. Like a child, he'd left the crusts of his sandwich uneaten.

"Care for dessert?' she asked.

He looked up, startled. Something in the flash of his large hazel eyes made her stagger back. What grown man discards bread crusts? And how could he have a wrinkle-free face *and* gray hair? And those eyes—

"Finn! What the hell are you doing?"

"Shh! You'll blow my disguise," he whispered.

"Disguise." She dropped into the chair across from him. "Seriously, do you hear yourself?"

"I'm spying for you. Eavesdropping on conversations in case someone talks about Garland. Or if they *are* her."

"And here I thought you were auditioning for a part in *Fiddler on the Roof.*" She tugged at the beard, which slid readily off his chin. "Where on earth did you find this getup?"

"From the attic, where Mom stored the Halloween costumes." He removed the glasses. "An old pair of Dad's. I was starting to get cross-eyed."

"Why didn't you warn me?"

"I wanted to see if I could fool you too." He gripped the

sides of the vest. "Pretty good, huh? Nobody recognized me at the public library either."

"Not bad. Until you left bread crusts behind. I can't believe you still don't eat them."

A shadow passed across his face. "Mario always cuts them off for me."

"You know what I think, Finnster?"

"What?"

"I think the only thing you're disguising is that you love Mario and want to be with him."

He blinked a few times. "That's one of the cheesiest things you've ever said."

"You're welcome." She riffled through the notebook filled with his illegible handwriting. "You call this evidence?"

"I wrote down more than a dozen conversations, here and at the library, without anyone noticing," he said proudly.

"And?"

"Not a word about Garland or the series."

"I could have told you that and saved you the trouble."

He wrinkled his nose as if he smelled a bad odor. "Does Garland go into excruciating detail about body ailments in her books?"

"Never."

"Then none of them were her because that's what most people talked about. What's *lumbago*?"

"*Rheumatism.*" Athena sighed. "Must be the shit weather making everyone feel like shit."

"Shit," Finn said.

"I've come to the conclusion that my brilliant theory that the café would be a hotbed of information was ludicrous and absurd. Waitressing has been a colossal waste of time."

"You should be writing instead. Without all those adjectives you just used."

"I agree, Tevye."

"You know what I think, Athena?"

"What?"

"I think you keep working here so you have an excuse to be near Thorne."

"That's one of the cheesiest things you've ever said."

"You're welcome," Finn said.

Since her call from South—or North—Carolina, Lydia had texted Athena a half dozen times, including selfies, a first. The itinerary wasn't the only thing her mother had relinquished control of. Her hair was loose and blowing in the wind, her face still free of makeup, and she wore T-shirts instead of blouses. "I've been in touch with Ricki," Lydia texted. "She likes my new look." Evidently, Tony had persuaded her to "make more of an effort" with her best friend, but "it's hard as hell, dammit."

Now whenever Athena looked in her mother's tidy drawers or saw the suits in her closet arranged from light to dark fabric, waves of tenderness for Lydia's growing pains rushed through her. She resolved to be less sarcastic and more supportive—all that good-daughter stuff—if not compulsively organized. Or spic-and-span.

She stared at her laptop on the kitchen table, trying to ignore the mess guaranteed to send old *and* new Lydia into a tizzy if she saw it. Unwashed pots crowded the sink, the garbage can overflowed, and a lump of dish towels waited to be folded on the counter. After hours on her feet as a waitress, housekeeping was rock-bottom on her list of priorities. With one exception—the bedsheets were immaculate.

Athena hit send on her email to Dr. Davenport and permitted herself a whimper. She was exhausted from emitting her battle cry, "I will not be defeated!" while revising the four chapters of *Hiding in Plain Sight*. In her letter to the chair, she had requested a deadline extension, promising to work diligently on the book while she taught next semester, assuring him she'd complete it by spring break. The identity of C. L. Garland was still a mystery, she admitted, but surely this paled against her astute deconstruction of the LitWit series.

"Diligently," she muttered. "Surely."

She checked her phone for the time and messages: 6:46 p.m. Still no text from Thorne. He would have closed the café hours ago. Barring fire or a sudden onset of illness, he should be with her now as they'd agreed, drinking wine, anticipating the sweet delights of their friends-with-benefits plan.

Unless Mr. Keep Calm had changed his mind and decided that sleeping with his ex–would-be-fiancée was too messy, too risky, and the furthest thing from calm. Or maybe he and that Robin person *were* serious, and a booty call was off the table. Or he was so satisfied from screwing Girlfriend Number Whatever's lights out that he didn't need any more sex. They hadn't discussed being exclusive in their arrangement. Did no-strings sex imply no-*limits* sex?

Athena shot out of the chair and opened the window a couple of inches. A blast of cold wind took her breath away for a moment, and then she opened it all the way and pushed the screen up too. She rushed to the living room, doing the same to every window, sucking lungfuls of fresh air, unsealing the Tupperware lids of the sterile, suffocating house.

Just breathe.

You're free. You're happy. You're totally capable of having casual sex with Thorne. Whatever the terms.

You're at one with your inner power.

If she weren't wearing a snug sweater and even snugger jeans, she'd assume a tai chi position.

"Thena?"

She gasped and jumped like a startled rabbit. Thorne leaned over the sill of one of the living room windows. "You okay?" he asked.

"Peachy keen."

"Sorry I'm late. Café business, and then Quentin called, and I couldn't get him off the phone."

They were on. She nearly jumped again—for joy this time.

Or did she actually jump? And was she smiling too much? She closed her mouth and concentrated on looking deadpan. She should ask what Quentin was up to.

"Your face is all scrunched," Thorne said. "Like you have a headache or you're holding in a sneeze."

"It's my writing-all-day look."

"What's with the weird smile?"

"I just thought of something funny."

"Funny and sad is my guess."

She put her hands on her hips and flung her hair over her shoulder. "Are you going to stand there all night analyzing my expressions? Or are you going to get in here and do what you came for?"

He threw one long leg over the sill and pulled himself through the window with a roguish grin. "What I came for."

His wheat-gold hair was irresistibly windblown, his cheeks ruddy from the autumn chill. In a russet cable-knit sweater and brown corduroy pants, he was the incarnation of her favorite season. Too bad Lydia's furniture was uncomfortable and her bamboo floor pristine. Otherwise, she'd straddle him right here, right now, front and center and every which way.

Thorne drew closer and, wrapping his arms around her, tenderly bit the lobe of each ear. He nuzzled her neck and coaxed her mouth open with the tip of his tongue until she thought she'd go mad, until she couldn't kiss him hard or deep enough. "This is more like it," he growled.

"Mmm," she agreed.

She gripped the muscles of his back as his hands roamed the curves of her waist and hips. His velvety lashes flittered, and a vein beat on his temple to the rhythm of her heartbeat. Oh yeah, Thena and Thorne still had it. The heat, the urgent need to grind and buck and plunge and sink into ecstasy. Except this time, it was simple, uncomplicated, in-the-moment. No looking back—and no looking forward.

He slipped his hand beneath her sweater, caressing his way to her aching breasts. The hell with Lydia's floor. Or maybe the ergonomic chair would do if they—

His phone's urgent horn ringtone abruptly ended her urgent gymnastic calculations.

"Sorry," he mumbled, stepping back.

The old Thorne would never have left his ringer on when sex was on the schedule. The new Athena held her tongue as he stared at the phone screen. His face blanched, and the fine line above his nose deepened. Turning his back to her, he answered the call. "Yes? What! When? Oh, no! All right. Yeah. Uh-huh. I'll get the first plane out."

He hung up and stood stock-still, his back hunched as he clutched his sides. Through the open window, Athena heard the soft *whoo* of an owl. The branches of the maple tree scraped the roof in answer to the wind. She placed her hand lightly on his shoulder. "Thorne? Is something wrong?"

"Yeah. An emergency."

"What happened? Is it your mother?"

"Yes. My mother." He rumpled his hair and looked distractedly around the room. "Sorry, Thena. I have to go."

"Can I help in any way?"

"No. I... I have to get a flight to Albuquerque tonight," he said, checking his watch. "Or at the latest, early tomorrow morning."

"New Mexico? I thought your mother was in Florida."

The color came and went on his face. "She's...uh...she's visiting a friend there."

Unblinking eyes, neck rubbing, evasive speech—he was exhibiting all the signs of a liar she'd learned about in acting class. What the hell. Thorne didn't have to hide the truth from her. Juggling girlfriends—Pamela, Robin, Girlfriends Multiple, and now this mysterious *she* in Albuquerque with her emergency—was his God-given right as an unencumbered, virile male.

And for the first time, as Athena considered his array of romantic possibilities, sadness for his essential loneliness washed over her, drowning her jealousy.

"I might be gone awhile," he said. "Can you and Kristie manage the café until I get back?"

"Of course. We'll take care of everything."

"I'll call or text when I have a better idea how long I'll be there."

"We'll hold down the fort. Don't worry about a thing."

He was so preoccupied that she wouldn't be surprised if he went out the window the way he'd come in. But he opened the front door, letting in another gust of cold air. His stricken face tugged at her heart, and at her arms that wanted to hold and comfort him.

"Guess I'll see you when I see you, Thena."

"Guess so, Thorne."

They had their own separate lives. Independent. Private. No sharing of secrets. No asking of questions. And decidedly no airing of grievances.

CHAPTER THIRTEEN

They forgot everything the minute they were together again.

—EMILY BRONTË, *WUTHERING HEIGHTS*

Athena preferred walking to jogging in the short, dismal days of November. She could better indulge her melancholy, stretching it out like her leisurely pace through the somber dawns and shadowy dusks. She devoted the brief daylight hours to hard daily shifts at the café and the long nights to harder shifts on her laptop, feverishly writing Chapter Five. Her provocative discussion of Garland's expertise on corsets, crinolines, and pantaloons would be a diversion from the sorry fact that she hadn't a clue who the writer was.

She'd been late for the This Time Around Book Club's meeting Tuesday because, while locking up As You Like It Café, she espied Geraldine hurrying down the street. Following a few yards behind, she saw her enter the same building she'd emerged from three weeks ago looking like Virginia Woolf. A light went on in a second-floor window but was extinguished after ten minutes. Athena watched like a gumshoe in an old detective movie, waiting for her to come out. But Geraldine didn't reappear and, unable to withstand the cold, Athena reluctantly left.

She hung her woolen scarf and navy-blue peacoat on the coatrack in the entrance to the café. She'd dug them out from the recesses of her closet, cursing her expectation she'd be back in San Francisco before winter. Fat chance of that happening. None of her strategies, or Finn's, had panned out, including her ambitions for the book club. If the first three meetings were any indication, the members were more interested in dissecting the sex scenes of the LitWit series than mining it for clues.

"Howdy do," Kristie chirped as she waved to her across the dining room. Athena didn't think it likely she suffered from any form of seasonal affective disorder.

"Been busy?" Athena asked. "I came in early to get an apple cobbler baked before you leave."

"Typical Saturday. Nonstop. But I've been through labor; I can handle anything."

And I've been through Corinne Carew. Without a baby to show for it.

Grabbing a bowl in the kitchen, Athena mixed the cobbler ingredients, adding the additional spice of an expletive or two. Dr. Davenport had yet to answer her email and approve her request for an extension. She'd stuffed her phone in the sofa cushion last night to stop compulsively checking it. But after a half hour, she gave in. And there it was, the number two on the mail icon.

A Canadian pharmacy wanted to sell her boner pills! At a discount!

Swinging Singles promised to find her lasting love!

To add insult to injury, the proprietor of the café she slaved away in, the man who had left abruptly mid-foreplay, had only texted four times in the nine days he'd been gone. Two were a joint message to her and Kristie checking to make sure everything was running smoothly. The other ones said, "Pretty hot for November here," and, "Albuquerque has great cafes." Big fricking whoop.

"No, everything is *not* running smoothly, Thorne," she said, peeling a Granny Smith apple so fast that it flew out of her hand. "Not. Smoothly. At. All."

The kitchen door swung open, and Kristie entered with a stack of plates. "Ian called asking why Zoe's poop is green," she said, giggling.

"Let me guess. Watercress sandwiches."

"We made too many yesterday, and I didn't want them to go to waste. She loved them!"

They had decided to forgo a daily special sandwich, relying on the simplest menu items to serve every day. And store-bought bread.

While Kristie talked about Zoe's upcoming birthday, Athena recalled Thorne's irritation when she used his laptop to search for a watercress sandwich recipe. Why hadn't she thought of it before? He'd been worried she'd discover something personal in his files. Photos of him and his girlfriends and their excursions, a visual chronicle of his busy dating life since they broke up. Gentleman that he was, he wanted to spare her feelings.

She looked up from the apple she was slicing—pulverizing—to see Kristie waving her hand in front of her face.

"Earth to Athena. Did you hear what I said?"

"About what?"

"About Ian and me having lunch with Amy Marsden, the chair of the English Department."

"Dr. Marsden. Yes. She emailed me the listing for the open position." Along with a hysterical cartoon from the *New Yorker* about the da Vinci painting *Mona Lisa*.

"Would you consider applying?" Kristie asked.

"No, I wouldn't." It would mean defeat. It would mean Corinne Carew had won. It would mean she harbored fantasies about a life in Laurel with Thorne.

"If you decide to stay in the area though..."

"I won't be staying. My life's in San Francisco."

My overpriced apartment. My beleaguered career. My pitiful social life that revolves around talking to foreign men in the produce section of Whole Foods.

On the plus side, she hadn't heard from Sergei for nearly a month. He'd given up, she hoped, at long last.

"Too bad you're leaving," Kristie said. "Everybody here adores you."

Not *everybody*. Not anymore.

"Oh, I meant to tell you, Athena. Eugene's been asking for you. Says he's got news."

"He found his sense of humor?"

"Don't I wish."

After putting the cobbler in the oven, Athena went out to the dining room, armed with an apron, notepad, and resolution to beam a pseudo smile all afternoon. She wasn't the only one who needed to fake a good mood. Ivy looked like she'd just watched three tearjerkers on the Hallmark Channel. The black cloak she wore over her flimsy dresses was in a pool beneath her stool, suggesting she was in mourning—and Athena had a pretty good idea for whom.

"When will Thorne be back?" she asked Athena forlornly.

"I'm not sure."

She strummed a few notes on her mandolin. "My music has been off-key since he left. I feed off his energy. It's like a force field."

Poor kid. She had a bad case of Thorne-itis.

"I saw you and Karl talking again Wednesday," Athena said. "Anything happening there?"

"He jokes too much. I think guys should be more serious, don't you?"

"I prefer a balance of both."

"Thorne is serious in just the right amount."

"Want some advice?" Like, *back off.* "Take charge of your conversations with Karl. Steer them in the direction *you* want them to go."

"I don't want them to go anywhere," Ivy said, swiveling on the stool and letting her hair fall across her face. Athena had the distinct impression she had been dismissed.

She crossed the room to Eugene's table near the hutch. "How's the curmudgeon business these days?" she asked him.

"Booming," he said. "You got any of those sandwiches with the fried egg and three kinds of cheeses?"

"The coronary special? Nope. One-ingredient sandwiches only."

He chuckled. "Like sass on rye?"

"With a side order of sarcasm."

"Just what the doctor ordered. I'll have one. Along with a grilled cheese sandwich."

"Coming right up." She filled his water glass. "Kristie said you had news?"

A smile creased his weathered face. "I talked with Tildy yesterday. First time since she left."

"How'd it go?"

"She didn't hang up."

"Sounds promising. Did you tell her you miss her?"

"Who said I do?"

"You can't fool me, Eugene."

"Or me." He leaned across the table. "The thing about being alone is, you watch people more. See stuff other folks don't notice."

"Oh, yeah, like what?"

"Like the way a certain handsome café owner watches a certain wisecracking waitress when she isn't looking, for instance."

She plucked a ball of fuzz off her sweater and examined it as if she'd never seen fuzz before. "Watches me? Really?"

"Like a hawk." He arranged the knife, fork, and spoon in a neat row next to his plate. "Figured I oughta tell you. One good turn deserves another."

"What good turn have I done you?"

"Gave me guff right back, knowing I don't mean it. Made me feel I wasn't so terrible. And if I wasn't so terrible, maybe I had a chance with Tildy."

Athena kissed him lightly on the forehead, partly out of affection for the old coot, partly to hide the tears welling in her eyes. "You make sure she gets a taste of your soft, gooey center, you hear? Let her remember why she fell in love with you in the first place."

"Not rightly sure why she did."

"There must have been something about you that kept her from running in the other direction."

He grinned. "She did run. But I ran after her."

"Then I suggest you run after her again. But not an ounce of guff, you hear?"

"Yes, missy. I'll save it for you."

Knowing that in two brief months she had helped a troubled marriage, brought Joe and Theresa and Phyllis and Dan together, and launched a community book club, albeit non-productive Garland-wise, was small consolation to Athena. She needed an Athena to turn *her* life in the right direction—toward San Francisco, tenure, and a meaningful relationship. And away from the irrational, crazy hope Thorne's hawk-eye on her had stirred up.

She wound the cord onto the vacuum cleaner and put it back in the broom closet, having made Lydia's house shipshape. She'd been in go-mode since the This Time Around Book Club meeting at Theresa's house earlier this evening. While they discussed which Jane Austen hero was sexier, Mr. Darcy or Mr. Knightley, the voices in her head were telling her to pack her belongings, load them into the trunk of the Mini Cooper, and get the hell out of town. Admit to Dr. Davenport her book was a dumb idea, born of desperation, dying an ignoble death. She'd beg him to keep her job and promise to write an apology and a retraction of every nasty thing she'd ever said to Corinne Carew—with a page left intentionally blank.

Humiliating. But so was imagining Thorne still loved her or wanted to pick up from where they left off ten years ago. And being dead wrong.

Chucking the last load of laundry into the washer, she rehearsed how she would say goodbye.

Sorry to leave you short-staffed, but Ivy, I'm sure, will be happy to replace me.

Best of luck with your endeavors.

Let's stay in touch.

Athena was about to go to the kitchen but stopped when she heard a rap on the front door. She turned on the porch light and peeked out the side window. The man himself, with a few days' stubble and red-rimmed eyes, waited on the other side of the door. "You look like shit, Thorne," she said, opening it. A safer salutation than *Alleluia.*

"Good thing it's dark. I wouldn't want to scare the neighbors."

"You scared *me.*"

"Sorry I didn't call first. My phone battery died."

"You didn't charge it at your apartment?"

"Drove straight here from the airport," he said, yawning. "Couldn't take going home."

"Good time in Albuquerque?"

"Shit time in Albuquerque."

"Get your scruffy butt in here."

Thorne shuffled into the living room and sank into one of the ergonomic chairs. Someone this despondent couldn't possibly have spent twelve days enjoying the pleasure of another woman's company. He hadn't lied. He *did* go to Albuquerque for a family emergency.

"Thanks, Thena. My place depresses the hell out of me."

"Depresses…oh, Thorne, is your mother all right?" She had often wondered how she would address her if they got married. Mrs. Kent? Miss Beryl? Your Highness? While she was slightly less chilly than her husband, she would never have permitted Athena to call her by her first name. Or *Mom*.

"She had some medical tests done," he said. "It was touch-and-go for a while, but it turned out to be a false alarm."

"She must have appreciated you being there, especially since she was far from home. Did she go back?"

"Back where?"

"To Florida."

"Florida. Yeah. I made the arrangements." He rubbed his temples as if he had the headache from hell. "Have any beer? Or something stronger?"

"How about a kiss first?"

Their lips had barely brushed against each other when he pulled away. "Sorry," he murmured. "I'm dead on my feet."

"A beer will revive you. Follow me."

They sat at the kitchen table, sipping Heinekens. Thorne looked around the room she'd restored to Lydia-level spotlessness. "Not exactly cozy here either."

"Antiseptic is my mother's design style. How's your house search going?"

"At a standstill. Is Lydia coming back soon?"

"Not sure. Last I heard she was headed to DC."

He reached into the pocket of his worn brown leather jacket and handed her a small white box. "Here. I got these for you in appreciation of your hard work at the café. I brought back a Navajo kachina doll for Kristie."

Inside the box was a pair of earrings shaped like leaves in the spring-green color of his eyes. "These are not helping," she said, holding them up to the light.

"Helping what?"

"My name is Athena, and I am an earring-aholic."

"Trying to get over your addiction?"

"And failing miserably."

Her Thorne addiction wasn't doing any better either. And no, she wasn't packing her car to leave. Not tomorrow anyway. Or the day after.

She looked at the earrings more closely. "They're charming. What are they?"

"Ferns. Specifically, *Astrolepis sinuata*."

"English, please."

He tapped his knuckles on his forehead. "Brain's still stuffed with botanical terms from my thesis research. They leak out once in a while. *Astrolepis sinuata* means *wavy cloak fern*. They're native to New Mexico."

"*My* brain's stuffed with writing my book and reading Garland's latest volume in the LitWit series. With the new release, the press is in a tizzy again over her identity."

"Are you enjoying it?"

As Thorne peeled the label off the beer bottle with his long fingers, she tried not to think of him peeling off her clothes.

"One of my favorite Jane Austen novels, *Sense and Sensibility*, is included," she said. "But Garland's takeoff, 'Sins and Sin's Ability,' is my least favorite novella in the series."

"Why? What's wrong with it?"

"The action feels rushed, for one thing."

"Maybe Garland's tired of writing."

"She has my sympathy. But her wit has lost its edge too."

He gulped mouthfuls of beer. "Wit is hard to sustain."

"You of all people defending Garland," she said, putting the earrings on. "My, my."

"Just saying," he mumbled.

"I didn't like 'Sins and Sin's Ability' but—"

"The *title* is clever."

"All the titles in the series are. Criticisms aside, though, it's inspired me to take my book in a new direction." Besides the trash can. Which was still a viable option.

"And what direction would that be?" he asked.

"In the novella, Elinor and Marianne Dashwood have a foursome with their lovers, Edward Ferrars and Colonel Brandon. As I was reading, it occurred to me—orgies are a *male* fantasy. Women, not so much."

He nodded thoughtfully.

"I mean, one serviceable penis does the job, thank you kindly," she said. "And being observed by one one-eyed willie isn't as intimidating as being observed by *two* one-eyed willies."

Thorne of the more-than-serviceable penis nearly choked on his beer, laughing.

"I'll discuss female writers who assumed male pseudonyms," Athena went on. "George Sand, George Eliot, and Emily, Charlotte, and Anne Brontë, who changed their names to Ellis, Currer, and Acton Bell. Since the initials C. L. aren't gender specific, I'm going to postulate Garland is a man, and he's flipping the pseudonym convention by assuming a female identity."

"But since the beginning, Garland has been referred to as *she*. Before her identity even became an issue."

"A cunning ruse."

Thorne frowned. "Are you sure it's a good idea to change direction when you're already deep into the project?"

He had no way of knowing she'd emotionally changed direction from Laurel to San Francisco and back again.

"Speculation on gender will highlight the challenges of uncovering Garland's identity."

"Maybe she wrote the orgy scene to capture male readership."

"A definite possibility. I'll write a chapter on the readers' demographics too. The information shouldn't be hard to find."

"Sounds like you have a substantial book already."

"You think?" Maybe she had been too hard on herself. It *was* a damn good academic treatment of popular literature.

He slid his empty beer bottle across the table. "I'd go so far as to say it can stand on its own without any discussion of who Garland may be."

"Gee, Thorne. If I didn't know any better..."

And then it hit her like a gush from a fire hose. Reports that Garland hailed from Laurel were no more reliable than her gender. Thorne—brilliant, witty, literate Thorne, who had spent the last five minutes defending the writer he allegedly scorned—fit the bill perfectly. His frequent burn-the-candle-at-both-ends fatigue. His reaction to her using his laptop, where his manuscripts were likely stored. And the most telling evidence of all—if any man could write panty-wet erotica, it was *Horny Thorny in the morny.*

"What's with the deer-in-the-headlights look, Thena?"

"You're Garland, aren't you?" she whispered.

"Are you out of your mind?"

"Come on, you can tell me, since I've worked it out."

He sat back and folded his arms across his chest. "I know you've got a lot on your plate and you're stressed out, but this is ridiculous. And insulting."

"You have to admit, you are a likely—"

"Do you honestly think I would waste a minute of my time on such a lowbrow pursuit?"

"The novellas aren't completely without merit."

"I agree. Which is why I defended 'Sins and Sin's Ability.'"

"You read it?"

"I browsed through a copy of the book at the airport. I get what Garland's doing, but I strongly object to our literary heritage being sacrificed to . . . to . . ."

"Filthy lucre?"

"Precisely. And may I remind you, I contacted my business connections to get information on her for you."

His voice was steady, his eyes focused. His open countenance hid neither secrets nor lies. It was impossible Thorne was Garland. Mostly because he would never be so deceptive, knowing how much the project meant to her. Not in a million years.

"You're right, Thorne. I *am* stressed. I apologize for my moment of madness."

"Forget about it," he said, rubbing his forehead wearily.

Athena reached across the table and took his hand in hers. Thorne had exerted himself on her behalf for a project he didn't believe in. Had put his life on hold for two weeks to help his mother. And, most importantly, he treated everyone with unwavering kindness and respect. The kitchen was bleak, the windows dark with night, but a flame glowed steadily between her and Thorne—the understanding of each other's true character. And it would never go out.

Just last night, she'd tossed *Wuthering Heights* across the bed in the middle of reading. Heathcliff's relentlessly cruel revenge on everyone within his orbit after Catherine's death was repulsive. And all that gnashing of his teeth!

Whatever had she been thinking, believing monstrosity was desirable?

"I miss this, Thorne," she said simply. "I miss us."

"We always could talk things over."

"To death sometimes."

He cupped her chin in his hands. "And talk about things we weren't even saying."

"Is it weird that I know exactly what you mean?"

"It's Thena-Thorne weird. Which means it's okay."

"This is a good time to tell you then. I accidently burned the café down."

"Ha ha! Likely story."

"Suzie announced she's officially run out of gossip. And the bachelor farmers stiffed me."

"That'll be the day," he said, laughing.

God, it felt good to cheer him up and make him laugh.

"I didn't fake-smile at any of Mayor Benson's jokes while you were gone. True story."

"I knew I could count on you."

"You betcha you can."

"You betcha you can too."

The harsh light of the lamps deepened the shadows beneath his cheekbones and the circles under his eyes. "When's the last time you slept?" she asked.

"Ages ago. The motel was the pits." He drew closer and rested his head on her shoulder. "Any chance I can crash here? I'd rather not be alone tonight."

Every chance in the world.

Taking his hand, she led him to the bedroom, removed his jacket, and unbuttoned his shirt—slowly and carefully this time—and helped him step out of his shoes and jeans. Thorne dropped onto the bed and held one hand out to her. "Would you lie next to me until I fall asleep, Thena?"

Athena nodded, teary-eyed, touched by his entreaty. She nestled into the curve of his body, holding on to the arm he wrapped around her. Holding on for dear life.

When Athena woke the next morning, Thorne had already left—but not before writing her a gracious thank-you note and baking her a pepper and onion frittata. A fricking frittata. In the time it took him to make it they could have been . . . But no. She got it. His depression and fatigue from the trip still lingered. And spending a friends-with-benefits morning was a luxury he couldn't afford while the café's inventory and accounts were backlogged.

Nor did they get together later that day, after a busy Wednesday shift. Dealing with a broken freezer, a coffee machine on the blink, and a busted faucet in the restroom drained Thorne's already depleted energies. Even Ivy kept her distance, seeing his harried state. When he begged off Thursday night, too, to catch up on vendors' bills, Athena had no problem with postponing welcome-back sex. She could wait another night or two. She'd been waiting for years.

That evening, Athena set up her laptop on the Murphy kitchen table, where she'd eaten dinner with Finn. Encouraged by her progress on the additional chapters of her book, she resisted sending Dr. Davenport an email nudging him for a response. Against all odds, she might meet the deadline. Though the book's working title, *Hiding in Plain Sight*, would have to be changed to one that didn't call attention to Garland's elusive identity—and her failure to uncover it.

While she debated editing the sixth chapter, a probing dissection of "Sins and Sin's Ability," or having another slice of key lime pie, she heard a shriek.

"Finn? What's wrong?"

"Come here! You've got to see this. Holy shit!"

She rushed into the den, where Finn sat on the floor, phone in hand, staring up at the flat screen television on the wall. *San Francisco Earthquake*, the headline ran beneath dramatic footage of collapsing buildings, a car on fire, and a sidewalk at a ninety-degree angle.

"Oh my God!" She dropped to the floor next to him. "How much of the city is affected?"

"Can't tell yet." He held her hand like he did as a kid, afraid of a horror movie. "I'm freaked. I can't get ahold of Mario."

"Cellular service must be down."

The newscaster announced that the northernmost section of the city was the hardest hit. "Not our neighborhood, thank goodness," she said.

Finn pointed to a tilting building on the screen. "But what if he's renovating in there and can't get out?" he asked in a panicked voice. "What if a gas line explodes?"

What if Corinne Carew had been sucked into an enormous fissure and was wondering, at this very moment, if her spirit would live like Emily Dickinson's?

"Don't jump to conclusions. Statistically speaking, it's not likely," Athena reassured him—and herself. A couple of days ago, she'd been ready to drive back to San Francisco. She might have been huddled under a table right now, frantically reviewing the condition of her underwear should she end up in a hospital.

The channel switched to a commercial, and they sat in silence as a woman contemplated her moderate-to-severe arthritis.

"I love him so much," Finn said in a near-whisper. "He makes fun of me ad nauseum. And I get sick to death hearing about surfing and body fat percentage. But Mario gets me. He's my best friend."

She squeezed his hand. "There's nothing better than a lover who's also your best friend."

A best friend to hold until he sleeps, easing his tired body into deep slumber. Listening to his every breath until it becomes your own.

"Mario told me nothing happened with that guy on Facebook," Finn said. "He was trying to make me jealous."

"Don't let him get away. Go back to San Francisco and fight for your man."

"If I can find my man." He thumbed another text into his phone. "C'mon, Mario. Answer."

Athena twirled the fern earrings as more images of the earthquake drama unfolded. Sleepy, stable Laurel looked more appealing in comparison. Affordable, friendly, with prospects for economic growth. The fear every tornado season you'd be spun into a vortex, never to be seen again, kept you on your toes, encouraged a healthy respect for nature. There was no *season* for earthquakes, just a year-round state of dread.

Thundering knocks on the front door made them both jump. "Did Dad mention anyone was coming over before he went out tonight?" she asked.

"No. Maybe Karl forgot a tool or something."

Or maybe Thorne couldn't bear another night without her. He'd gone to Lydia's house, and not finding her there, was now banging on the Murphy door with pent-up sexual desire.

"Be right there," she called out. Opening the door, she nearly fell to the floor in shock.

"Atheeena. I come for you."

All six feet four inches of Sergei Gudonov loomed in the dark entryway. The skin around his blue eyes was as wrinkled as his black pants and billowy gray shirt. His dark curly hair had grown to his shoulders, and a scruffy beard covered his pale face. He'd stepped out of the tsars' steppes into the Midwest, and apparently the journey had utterly exhausted him.

"How did you get this address?" Athena asked him. "I never told you where my father lives."

"I saw it on envelope you mail once. I write it down."

"Pretty sneaky, Sergei."

"I am man of many talents."

"Come in before you freeze."

He entered the foyer, slapping his broad chest. "Ah, I am here. In middle of America."

Beneath the ceiling lamp, silver strands shone in his hair. He'd aged in the few months she hadn't seen him—whatever his actual age was. A spasm of guilt hit her in the gut. Not once while she watched the news had she worried about him being injured in the earthquake.

"Give me big bear hug," he said, wrapping her in his embrace.

Athena patted the folds of flesh around his waist. "You've put on some weight." About fifteen pounds, if she wasn't mistaken.

"It happen when I stop smoking. For baby Boris." Sergei lifted a Krispy Kreme bag. "The car is full with these. Doughnut bags and coffee cups. I love America! And sprinkles! I love sprinkles on my doughnuts!"

She looked over his shoulder at the white Lincoln Continental parked on the street. "How did you get a rental car? You don't have a driver's license."

"It is friend's car. I drive from California to see my Atheeena. I take chance with no license."

"Why didn't you fly?"

He leaned closer and whispered in her ear with his coffee breath. "They want to deport me. I get on plane, who knows where they take me."

Uh-oh. The green card shit just got real.

She closed the front door, fighting the impulse to jump into the Lincoln Continental and drive away. Knowing Sergei, he'd left the keys in the ignition.

Finn came up behind Sergei and punched him lightly on the arm. "Sir Gay, my man! Have you come to make passionate love to my sister?"

Athena shot him an arrowhead glance, but he was too busy fist bumping Sergei to notice.

"I make so much love to her, she won't know Chekhov from Turgenev," Sergei boasted.

Finn turned to her, his face bursting with suppressed hilarity, as Sergei walked to the living room. "Somebody's getting laid," he whispered. "And it's about time."

"No, no, no, no, no!" she hissed. "I can't have sex with him!"

"Not even once? For fun?"

"Haven't you been paying attention? I'll never get rid of him."

"Or you *will* finally get rid of him. He might be one of those guys who's more excited by the pursuit than the capture."

No use beating around the bush. Finn had opened his heart to her about Mario. The least she could do was update him on... well, bush.

"There's another reason. I had sex with Thorne. And no way in hell am I sleeping with two guys at the same time."

Finn looked as shocked as if an earthquake had opened the ground beneath him. In the living room, Sergei strode back and forth, swinging the Krispy Kreme bag in a wide arc. Athena gripped her brother's arms. "Listen. Focus. This is what you have to do. Get him totally shit-faced so the last thing on his mind is sex."

His face lit with a mischievous grin. "Are you sure? He's smoking hot."

"Feel free to have a go."

"But I'm a one-man man, Athena," he said in mock indignation.

And, as she'd realized not so long ago, she was a one-man woman.

While Finn plied Sergei with Grey Goose vodka, Athena hit the pavement for a jog. Between the earthquake and the other natural disaster that was her Russian suitor, she was jumping out of her skin. Beneath the streetlamps, the small puffs of her breath in the cold air were ghostly white. This was one pickle she was in. For all her imagination, she never pictured Sergei coming clear across the country to claim her. Deportation issue aside, his visit was spontaneous, romantic—and a royal pain in the butt.

Porch lights and lamps lit most of the homes. A few had open curtains, revealing a woman reading a magazine, a man gesturing to a television screen, a couple of kids wrestling on a living room rug. Struck with a sudden idea, she headed toward the O'Neal residence. This time she wouldn't let cold or fear deter her.

Athena slowed her pace as she neared the house. It looked slightly sinister, its Victorian structure shadowed by deep nooks like an Edward Gorey illustration. She was in luck—the curtains were open. A lamp shone in the room where Geraldine usually sat at her computer. Its screen was lit.

Tiptoeing across the lawn, Athena dropped down behind the bushes. Her heart raced as she pondered her next move. If anyone saw her, how would she explain herself? She wouldn't. She'd just run. In the dark, no one would recognize her anyway. And then she'd return once the coast was clear. Because she was doing this thing—catching Geraldine in the act of working on a manuscript.

She held her breath to better hear the drumbeats and bass notes issuing from the house. The insistent, repetitive rhythms were either those of a jazz recording or... No. Geraldine couldn't possibly be watching porn.

Unless kinky videos inspired the erotic novellas of the LitWit series. This latest crazy idea just might pay off.

Athena rose from her crouched position, wincing at her creaking knees. As she started to climb the porch steps, a voice sent a chill clear down to her Nike sneakers.

"Great Land o' Goshen, child! Why are you skulking in my rhododendrons?"

And before Athena could answer—or pee her pants—Geraldine hit her upside the head with a long, hard object that was either a baguette or a very impressive sex toy.

"You've got moxie, I'll give you that," Geraldine said, drawing her blue satin robe closed around her thin frame.

"Thanks. I think."

Athena sipped the sherry she had been given, trying desperately not to look at the object-that-was-not-a-baguette on the sofa between them. Geraldine had lowered the volume on the stereo so that the jazz rhythms sounded like the heartbeat of a frightened animal. Or a chickenshit would-be spy.

"What brings you out this time of night?" Geraldine asked. "Running from a man?"

Athena didn't have enough moxie to admit she was. "I'm taking a break from writing a book. I have to clear the mental cobwebs now and then."

"A book, eh? What about?"

"Ever hear of C. L. Garland?"

Geraldine snorted. "Who hasn't?"

"I'm writing about her series and trying to—"

"What a wuss, hiding behind a pseudonym. Gutless Garland, I call her."

"The mystery of her identity generates sales," Athena said.

"Her silly books would sell without all that poppycock."

Geraldine, poppycock intolerant, didn't have a wuss bone in her body. Athena had officially run out of suspects.

She glanced at the would-be baguette. "Do you . . . uh . . . ever read the novellas?"

"Don't have to. Get all the sex stimulation I need." Geraldine's glass of sherry dinged loudly when she placed it on the coffee table. "Pete and I can't stand living together, but we can't keep our hands off each other. What you might call a conundrum."

So *that* was the word for the O'Neal marriage. A conundrum.

Athena cleared her throat. "Where *is* your husband?"

"He rents an apartment in town, and I go over there for conjugal visits."

Prisoners of love, Athena nearly quipped, but thought better of it.

"Is the apartment in one of the renovated buildings near As You Like It Café?" she asked.

"Yep. Should have thought of separate residences years ago. It dents the budget, but it would have saved us a lot of aggravation."

And money on food bills.

"I'm taking the house off the market," Geraldine said. "Haven't gotten around to telling your mother yet."

"She's out of town but you can call one of her assistants."

Geraldine lifted her head to its imperious angle. "What *are* you doing here, creeping around my bushes?"

"To see if you were writing. Would you believe me if I told you I thought *you* were Garland?"

"Huh. I can believe anything. It's the *why* I never figure out."

"You match her personality profile. And whenever I jog by, I see you at the computer."

"Emails to Pete. We Zoom too. If they'd had the Internet when we first got married…Oh, well. No use crying over spilled milk."

Athena nearly spit out the sherry, trying not to laugh. If Geraldine wasn't so formidable, she might tell her the O'Neal food fights had brought needed excitement to boring Laurel.

"When I saw a shadow moving across the lawn, I thought someone was trying to rob me," Geraldine said. "I came around from the backyard to clobber them one."

"I'm sorry," Athena said. "I shouldn't have—"

Geraldine rose abruptly, looking as majestic—and frightening—as a fairy-tale wicked queen. Athena got up too, not as majestically.

"When someone starts apologizing, it's time to end the conversation," Geraldine said. "Don't you think?"

"I suppose so."

"And there's no point in sitting around if you've got nothing else to say."

"I'll show myself out. Thank you for the sherry."

Athena made it out the door and down the steps without a further pronouncement from Geraldine and hurried past the rhododendrons to the sidewalk. She glanced back once to see her standing on the porch, shaking the object-that-was-not-a-baguette.

"Here, take this," Geraldine called out. "You look like you need it more than I do."

Pretending she didn't hear, Athena ran as fast as her body, shaking with laughter and mortification, would let her.

CHAPTER FOURTEEN

Existence, after losing her, would be hell.

—EMILY BRONTË, *WUTHERING HEIGHTS*

Thorne placed two loaves of freshly baked sourdough bread on the counter and stirred the pot of apple cider. The first snowfall of the season had brought customers in droves to As You Like It Café. Better yet, once they peeled off their layers of clothes, they settled in for a few hours of eating and drinking. After years of academic pursuits, baker, barista, and bistro boss were his most satisfying occupations.

Boss. Hardly. Athena and Kristie had managed the café like a well-oiled machine while he was gone. He glanced at the clock when he heard laughter in the dining room—Athena had arrived for her Friday shift. On Wednesday, he'd overheard Joe ask if she'd still be in Laurel at Christmas to meet his daughter and her family when they came to town. She would, she replied, but planned to return to San Francisco shortly afterward.

Five weeks and she'd be gone. A reality check that made him go to the restroom, splash water on his face, and turn off the faucet so tightly that the handle broke.

Five. Short. Weeks.

The thought of her leaving glided smoothly over his brain this time. For once, picturing her departure didn't deflate his spirits like a fallen soufflé. Practice did make perfect.

Athena gone. For good. Never to return except to visit her parents.

Forgetting the bread pans were hot, he turned one over to loosen the loaf. "Sonofabitch," he cursed, shaking his burned fingers. Who the hell was he trying to fool? Searing pain was what he was in for once she left.

Athena popped her head around the kitchen door. "It's crazy out here. Can you help out? We're low on napkins and spoons."

"I'm on it."

The door shut behind her but swung open again. "Uh, Thorne? Is everything working again? All the stuff that fell apart Wednesday?"

"Restroom faucet's fixed. I banged the coffee machine a few times, and it's been cooperating ever since. The repairman showed up late Thursday and got the freezer running."

She looked down and traced the tile square with her foot. "And you?"

Who'd fallen apart and into her arms.

"Rested and recovered. Thanks for letting me stay with you the other night."

"Hey, anything for a morning-after frittata." She hit her forehead lightly with the palm of her hand. "Not that we... It's not like there was a... I mean—"

"I always know what you mean, Thena."

She rolled her eyes. Her adorable eyes. "That makes one of us."

"That's what friends are for, right? Understanding us when we don't?"

"And backing us up when the café is mobbed," she said, waving the order notepad.

"Be right there."

As Thorne filled the napkin holders and restocked

silverware, he made a quick head count to calculate how much food to prepare. Charles and Vivienne, the Blakes, Joe and Theresa, Phyllis and Dan, three of the bachelor farmers, and a few new faces.

Kristie hurried over, untying her apron. "Shift's over. I'm bugging out." She pointed to the bay window, where Ian and Zoe were watching the snow fall. "We're taking Zoe to the park. It'll be the first time she's ever played in snow."

"You can't leave until I give her a hug," Thorne said.

If the toddler's rosy cheeks and dimpled smile weren't irresistible enough, her chubby hands reaching for him were almost more than Thorne could take. "How's my favorite little girl?" he crooned as he cuddled her.

"Go bye-bye!"

"To play in the snow?"

"Snow, snow, snow!" she squealed.

With one final squeeze, he handed her back to Ian, and the happy family headed out to enjoy their afternoon. Athena was watching him with a quizzical look, wondering, probably, why he, who'd vowed he'd never have children, was gaga over Zoe.

A mystery to her, as her relationship with her boyfriend was to him. Sergei. He was like no one she'd ever known, she'd said. An eccentric genius, probably. So smart only someone like Athena could relate to him—and he to her.

It wasn't likely they were in love though. For one thing, being away from each other for months would be intolerable. He'd once excused himself from a family trip to England because they would have been apart for two weeks. And for another reason, if Athena loved Sergei, a friends-with-benefits arrangement would be out of the question.

Unless she'd changed. Unless the years had altered her views of love and commitment. A sad thought, but one he wouldn't dwell on. Not while he benefitted from the arrangement.

As he cleaned tables, he pictured her warm, voluptuous body beneath his, felt her soft skin and the tug of her strong thighs around his back. Athena was a feast, a cornucopia for the senses. He had only five weeks to indulge in her colors, her scent, the sweetness of her skin on his tongue. Her—

"Thorne?"

Ivy was looking up at him as if she needed directions somewhere. He reddened, embarrassed she might have read remembered ecstasy on his face. "You don't perform on Fridays," he said. "How come you're here?"

"I've been eating lunch. Didn't you notice me?"

"Uh...no."

"I'm with Karl." She pointed to the strapping guy dwarfing the small table in the far corner. "We're kind of on a date. It's definitely a date."

"Hi, Ivy," Athena said, walking by. "Are you and Karl enjoying the sandwiches I recommended?"

"We are. He ate most of mine though. I eat like a bird." She thrust out her unremarkable chest. "We're on a date."

Feminists forbid him, but Thorne did like a woman with an ample bosom. Regressive maybe, but Athena's bountiful breasts had imprinted him forever.

"I had a feeling you two would hit it off," she said to Ivy. "It's why I suggested Karl introduce himself to you."

Well, well, well. So, Athena hadn't fallen for the charms of the young swain. She'd diverted them.

"I followed your advice about how to talk to him," Ivy said.

"Did you turn the conversation to music?" Athena asked.

"Uh-huh. He thinks mandolins are really cool. Do you think mandolins are cool, Thorne?"

"I think they are beautiful instruments," he said, trying to keep his eyes from straying to Athena's breasts.

"Karl and I are going to a Renaissance festival next

weekend," Ivy said in a curiously shrill voice. "What do you think about that, Thorne?"

"Those festivals are always entertaining. I think you two will have a great time."

She flung her braid over her shoulder and, turning on her heel with a sniff, marched back to her table. Hell if he knew what her snit was about—or why Athena was grinning. "What's so funny?" he asked.

"She was trying to make you jealous, ding-dong."

"Jealous? What are you talking about?"

"She's got a major crush on you. Like the entire female population in college, remember?"

"How can she even...I'm much older. If anything, Ivy's like a...like a sister to me."

"Sister, huh? Oh, dear. Make sure you let her down easy."

If only Ivy were his sibling instead of...The uncharitable thought crept in, the two weeks in Albuquerque having wearied him to the bone.

Robin had wandered from the group home, leaving his meds behind. Days of frantic phone calls to hospitals and police stations were punctuated by torturous hours in a rental car, searching for him, following any lead. Finally, a trucker reported he'd picked up the missing young man. Exhausted, confused, and in full-blown paranoia, Robin let Thorne bring him back with yet another promise to comply with his medication regimen.

When he'd returned from the ordeal, sleeping with Athena curled inside his arms had been the respite he needed. He'd woken feeling more refreshed than he had in years. A catharsis to make up for the one he badly needed—telling her everything.

Thorne straightened the chairs that a young couple had left askew. During the flight home, he'd resolved to confide in her about Robin. Emotionally drained, the conversation weighing on his mind, he couldn't even respond to her kiss. But when she discussed her work on her book, the project she was dedicated to, he decided not to. She'd be leaving soon to resume her independent, exciting life, the fulfilling career she loved. To unburden himself, to explain why he'd rejected her in Seattle, would be selfish and unfair. To ask her to pursue the position at Southern Illinois College would overstep the mark.

"But damn, Thena, I miss you. I miss my best friend," he said softly, watching her throw her head back and laugh at something Phyllis had said, the fern earrings caught in the tumble of her curls.

Feeling a tap on his shoulder as he wiped another table clean, he turned around.

" 'No soup for you!' " Finn exclaimed, quoting one of their favorite lines from *Seinfeld.*

"Ha! I haven't heard that in ages." Thorne clasped his hands in a hearty shake. "I was hoping to see you before you went back to California. Good thing you weren't there during the earthquake."

"One disaster avoided. My love life, though, is a train wreck."

"Athena mentioned you were living with a guy named Mario." And the spurned proposal—about which he refrained from making comparisons to his own.

"*Was* living with him," Finn said. "But not anymore. He's impossible. He didn't tell me for six hours he wasn't even *in* San Francisco when the earthquake hit."

"You must have been worried sick."

"Yeah. Meanwhile he's up in Portland with his brother, ignoring my calls."

"Did your apartment withstand any damage?"

"Not as much as I did. By the way, did Athena tell you I can design a website for your café?"

"Yes, she did. Let's set up a time to meet and work out the details."

"And exchange life stories."

"I'm looking forward to it, Finn."

A draft of frigid air rushed through the room. A hulking figure wearing a ratty overcoat and a five o'clock shadow—five o'clock *yesterday*—towered in the doorway. The man waved, knocking the shoulder of a woman reaching for her hat on the coatrack. "I park the car, Finn. I see Atheeena now, yes?" he bellowed.

"Come here, Sergei," Finn said. "I want you to meet someone."

Sergei. Damn. He and Athena *were* in love. Here he was in all his bulk and dishevelment because they missed each other desperately.

"Heads up, Thorne," Finn said. "He's in town to see Athena, and he's a handful. He showed up unexpectedly last night. Drove cross-country from San Francisco."

The romantic, impetuous hero. The fervent lover with the loyal heart. Thorne scanned the room, but Athena was in either the kitchen or restroom. She had gotten what she had wanted all along—a version of passionate Heathcliff. Thorne, the pale substitute, was only good for booty calls. And it sucked. It sucked big time.

Up close, Sergei's bloodshot eyes and sickly color screamed *hangover.* Pink sprinkles were caught in his long, tangled hair. Seriously? This was who Athena had fallen for? He didn't look like a genius of anything but bad grooming and questionable personal hygiene, so the attraction had to be pure animal lust. They'd probably screwed themselves silly till dawn, making up for lost time. Bringing Thorne's chances of making love to her again to a big, fat zero.

"Sergei, I'd like you to meet Thorne," Finn said. "He owns this café."

"Capitalist! Yes!" Sergei put his big paw out for a fist bump.

"Nobody does that anymore," Thorne said, putting his hands in his pockets.

Finn cocked one amused eyebrow while Sergei stared at his fist as if it didn't belong to him.

"I don't understand," Sergei said. "Is American way, yes?"

"No. How long did it take to drive from California?" *And how soon can you leave?*

"The hours go fast when I know I see my Atheeena."

"A capitalist would be more specific. Time is money, after all. But you wouldn't know that unless you were a man of business. Which I suspect you're not."

"Suspect?" Sergei threw back his shoulders. "I am man of ideas. New ideas, all the time."

"Me too," Finn piped up.

"Do any of these ideas hit pay dirt?" Thorne asked Sergei.

Sergei tilted his head "You speak English, or no?"

"Have you ever made a killing?"

"I kill nothing!"

Finn, his face red from trying not to laugh, grabbed Sergei's elbow. "My dad's at the table near the fireplace. Let's join him."

Hesitating for a moment as he regarded Thorne suspiciously, Sergei followed Finn.

Athena emerged from the kitchen with a tray filled with sandwiches. As she placed them on Joe's table, Phyllis pointed to Sergei, whose presence had practically silenced the room. Judging by what she used to call her "shit-on-a-stick face," Athena hadn't expected him to show up at the café.

"Atheeena!" Sergei called out. "*Lyubov moya!* Finn bring me to you."

She walked over to Thorne, looking flustered. "Surprise visit," she said.

"Finn filled me in."

"This was not my idea. Finn probably didn't know what else to do with him."

"You could have taken the day off to spend with your lover." Now that he thought about it, why hadn't she?

She tucked an errant curl behind her ear. "I suppose. Except I've been plotting all day how to get rid of him."

Now *he* wanted to fist bump. "Is 'love 'em and leave 'em' your new motto?"

"You should talk. But Sergei isn't my lover and never has been, though he's been pursuing me for months. I had Finn pound him with vodka shots last night. *Odin, dva, tri*, he was out like a light."

One, two, three, Thorne wanted to carry her to his apartment, to his bed, and make up for lost time. For now, he'd have to settle for being an actor in whatever scene was coming up next. The one where she sent this imitation Heathcliff back across the moors or tundra or wherever the hell he came from.

"Showtime," she said, smoothing down her apron.

As Thorne and Athena approached him, Sergei bounded out of his chair and rolled up his sleeves. At the end of each beefy arm was a clenched hand—but not for a friendly fist bump. Thorne instinctively shielded Athena, though it was obvious the darts flying from Sergei's inflamed eyes were aimed at him. The dining room was so quiet that he heard a car door slam outside.

"Finn just tell me you and my Atheeena were lovers long ago. When you were students of literature. Almost marry."

"Finn!" Athena said. "I'll kill you!"

Finn bowed his head like a scolded child. "Sorry," he mumbled.

"Is true?" Sergei asked Athena.

"Is true," she said.

Thorne observed the various reactions of the café crowd as they absorbed this nugget. The bachelor farmers grinned and nodded to each other. As frequent patrons of Ricki's Café, they would have seen Athena and Thorne together. Joe smiled his private smile, as if he'd already suspected. Phyllis and Theresa whispered to each other while Dan lifted the ball cap on and off his head. Ivy's pale face suddenly found color while Karl appraised Athena from head to toe, making Thorne want to roll up *his* sleeves.

Sergei poked the air with his thick index finger. "You tempt her to come to your rich American café. Steal her from me."

"Athena doesn't belong to anyone," Thorne said. "She's her own woman."

"You're darn tootin'," she said, coming from behind him.

"Tootin'?" Sergei scratched his head, and pink sprinkles trickled out of his hair. "Who is this Tootin'?"

"It means I'm not your girlfriend, Sergei."

He stepped forward and thumped his chest. "Is girlfriend."

"Come any closer," Thorne warned, "and I'll thump *you*."

"I'm not afraid of man who bakes," Sergei scoffed.

"Would you like a demonstration of my knife skills?"

"Okay, cool it, guys," Athena said.

Sergei turned to her. "Come to Francisco with me. I make you borscht. I read you books."

"I have to write my own book. Remember?"

"You write it there."

"I have more research to do. I'll return in December."

"I stay here then. Keep an eye on my *myshka*."

"You'll do no such thing."

"I stay."

"You go."

"*Nyet.*"

"*Da.*"

Customers' heads went back and forth as they followed this volley. Thorne couldn't help but feel sorry for the guy, fighting a losing battle with books and…since when did Athena like beet soup?

"Marry like you promise, Atheeena. Have baby Boris."

Books, Thorne got. Borscht, not so much. Marriage and baby Boris were a total mystery. "What the hell's going on?" he whispered to her.

"Green card," she muttered.

"Still confused."

"Baby as bait."

"Clear as mud."

"Go along with me, all right? I'll explain later."

"Can't wait."

Athena emitted a deep sigh, shaking her head. "I'm sorry you have to find out this way, Sergei."

Everyone in the café sat forward. Every eye was focused on the bearish figure with the mournful eyes.

"This does not sound good for Sergei," he said.

"I know we talked about getting married so you wouldn't get deported."

"Oh," the café crowd said.

"And I give you baby," Sergei boasted.

"Aha!" they exclaimed while Finn chortled loudly in the background.

A seemingly logical transaction—to everyone but Thorne. The Athena he knew would no sooner marry a man she didn't love and have his baby than she'd marry a man who'd gone to law school instead of graduate school.

"There's one problem, Sergei," she said. "I should have mentioned it before."

"What, my Atheeena?" he bleated.

She looked down at the floor with a contrite expression. "I have a criminal record. Oh, nothing like murder or arson. But it may complicate matters when you apply for citizenship."

Blinking rapidly, he scanned the room as if he expected an immigration officer to suddenly appear.

"The heck with it. I'm worried for nothing," she said breezily. "All they'll do is bring us into a room for questioning, rough us up a little, and next thing you know—"

"Rough up?"

She punched the air with her fists a couple of times.

"No. No. Is no good for Sergei."

"Are you sure?" she said. "Because we can—"

"No good!"

Backing up slowly, his eyes on her as he mumbled in Russian, Sergei made it to the front door. Pulling it open, he sprinted to the Lincoln Continental parked across the street. With a shriek of tires, he sped away.

Athena brushed her hands against each other as if shaking flour from them. "And that, ladies and gentlemen, is how it's done."

She bowed as the room erupted in laughter and applause. Thorne's leading lady. The funniest, smartest, sexiest woman he ever had the pleasure of knowing. And loving.

"Should I be afraid of you, Athena?" one of the bachelor farmers asked.

"I assumed you already were."

"And of every woman's shadow," another farmer said, thumping him on the back.

"What's your specialty?" Phyllis asked with a wink. "Petty theft?"

"Grand larceny. Why not aim high when you're going low?"

"Oooh!" everyone hooted.

"Where'd you hide the loot?"

"In an overseas account, of course."

"Have you given up your life of crime?"

"Hell no. Do I look like an amateur to you?"

They all laughed while Phyllis wagged a playful finger at her.

"Quite a performance," Thorne commented when the commotion died down.

"You too."

"Me?"

"Getting all alpha-male protective. Didn't know you had it in you, Thorne."

"And obviously there are many things I don't know about you."

"Are you referring to my second career as an outlaw?"

"To your close brush with a marriage of convenience." Mentioning the baby would be...indelicate. "How'd you ever get in that situation?"

"Wine and six plain words—*It wouldn't be the worst thing.* And it's taken me six long hours to devise a strategy to get *out* of the situation."

"You succeeded brilliantly. Though you could have told Sergei we were lovers again."

"You might have had to actually demonstrate those knife skills."

"Worse, the entire population of Laurel would never let us live it down."

"And don't forget your very own words, Thorne."

"Which ones?"

"I'm my own woman and don't belong to anyone."

And with a radiant smile to dazzle him long after she'd gone back to San Francisco, the outlaw Athena Murphy stole Thorne's heart all over again.

Thorne rested on a park bench beneath a pin oak while squirrels scurried along the branches, dropping acorns onto the carpet of dried leaves at his feet. Safe within the boughs of the Norway spruce across the path, a barn owl stared as Thorne massaged the sore muscles of his left thigh. A one-mile lap swim or five-mile run usually cured whatever ailed him—provided he wasn't injured in the process. He watched a teenage boy lope gracefully around the perimeter of the park, short bursts of his breath clouding the cold air. The trade-off of the infinite energy of youth for the wisdom of age wasn't fair in the least.

A loud sneeze behind him sent a pair of skittish cardinals into the nearest bush. Turning, he saw Athena walking toward him, a tissue to her nose.

"Mind if I join you?" she said. "Misery needs company."

He made room for her on the bench. "Are you sick or is it your sinuses?"

She sneezed again. "A cold. Went to bed feeling great, woke up feeling like crapola."

In the unsparing light of early morning, her face looked wan, her eyes glassy. Even the freckles dusting her nose were pale. He tugged her woolen hat down over her ears and tightened the scarf around her neck. "You should have waited to come out till later, Thena. It's supposed to get sunny and much warmer."

"I drove from my mom's house, thinking a walk in the park would help, but I feel worse."

"Same here." He pointed to his aching leg. "Came for a run but pulled a muscle."

"Are we a couple of old farts or what?"

"That we are."

"You'll be glad to know Sergei is gone."

"For good?"

"I haven't seen or heard from him since he took off, fleeing imaginary authorities."

At the end of her shift yesterday, Thorne had asked if they could get together later, hoping to maintain the lively spark Sergei's visit had ignited. But wisely, she had wanted to be sure he had really left, not wanting to encourage another confrontation.

"Pretty tricky, Thena, letting me think Sergei was your boyfriend all this time."

"All's fair when your ex-boyfriend is dating a lot of women."

"Not a lot."

"More than zero—*my* dating status—is a lot."

Though it was very early, quite a few people walked or jogged through the park. They watched a couple dismount their bikes and embrace where the bandstand had been erected for Oktoberfest. "The scene of the crime," Athena remarked.

"I won that kiss fair and square."

"If you consider buying all the raffle tickets ethical."

He plucked her pouty lips with his thumb. "I do. And I'd say it entitles me to more kisses."

"You're living dangerously," she warned.

"I'll risk it."

She sneezed twice as he dipped his face to hers. "You might want to rethink this," she said, blowing her nose. "You've got customers to cook for and serve."

He felt her hot forehead. "Don't even think about coming to the café till you're better. Stay home and work on your book." He used to love taking care of her when she was sick. He'd make chicken noodle soup, pile books, medicine, and tissues by her bed, and read her their favorite poems and Shakespeare plays. "Nerd nursing," she'd called it.

"Working on my book isn't any healthier. My latest and greatest Garland quest got me hit on the head with a...a..." She put her face in her hands. "This is too embarrassing for words."

"It makes more sense than your idea *I* was the author of the LitWit series," Thorne said after she related the events of the evening when she tested her theory that Geraldine O'Neal was Garland.

"I haven't told you the worst part. Geraldine had seen me skulking in her front yard and thwacked me on the noggin with...well, all I'll say is it had length and girth, and size *does* matter."

His roar of laughter sent every form of wildlife scattering in various directions.

"I think I lost brain cells," she said.

"I'm definitely minus a few," Thorne said. "Sometimes I can't recall people's names or sandwich ingredients, but I still remember the botanical names for trees and flowers."

Athena pointed to an eastern white pine. "What's that?"

"*Pinus strobus.*"

"White birches are my favorite trees. What are they called?"

"*Betula papyrifera.*"

"Impressive."

"Have you learned any Russian from Sergei?"

"A smattering."

"What did *lyubov moya* mean?"

"*My love.* But I told you, he's not *my* love. He's too...too..."

"Too much of what you wished for?"

"Age and experience have their advantages," she said with

a wry smile. "And just for the record, you're the only one I'd admit I'm an idiot to."

"As your fellow idiot, your secret's safe with me."

"*Safe.* Who'da thunk that would be such a delicious word?"

"*Now* you tell me. Just when I've threatened Sergei with bodily harm."

Athena rested her head against his shoulder. "Alpha meets beta is the best combo."

"So, I can translate Latin *and* be menacing?"

"Sure. Haven't other women told you?"

"You're the only one I ever listened to. Even when we were apart."

"Yikes. Hearing my voice in your head all those years. Poor you."

She was joking but he knew his Thena. Knew he'd reminded her of their near-telepathic connection.

"One more question," she said. "What's the botanical name for the hawthorn tree?"

The tree from whose branches he'd fashioned a garland for her head. Beneath which he'd proposed to her. *Their* tree.

"*Crataegus laevigata.*"

He watched her face for a reaction, but she was gazing dreamily into the sky.

"From literature to law to a successful café. I envy you, Thorne," she said softly. "You had the guts to step out of the box and change the direction of your life."

"Courage didn't have much to do with it. The truth is, I acted out of anger more than anything else."

She regarded him with a mixture of disbelief and curiosity. "Anger? At what?"

The sky had brightened to light blue, filling him with sudden clarity. Despite everything that had happened between them, their bond would never completely break. Their friendship, when all was said and done, was the best thing between them.

"Can I trust you with my family's dark, dirty secret?" he asked.

"To the grave," she said solemnly.

Thorne sat forward, a hand gripping each knee. "When my dad was dying, he confessed he'd been in love with another woman for twenty years. He'd supported her financially, lived with her whenever they got the chance to be together. During his frequent *business trips*, I imagine."

Athena gasped. "Are you kidding me?"

"I wish I were. He lived a life completely separate from us. The other woman knew of our existence, and all the while, my poor mother...so trusting and dedicated to him."

"I'm so sorry. Your poor mom. Oh, Thorne."

He felt light-headed, his body and bones hollow as if sharing his family's sad history had scooped him out. "He died without her finding out. And I've kept his secret. And will until I'm sure she can handle the truth."

"Why tell her at all?"

"She's been lied to enough in this life. I love and respect her too much to..."

Damn. He was choking up. He was over this by now. The love affair of Graham and Jessica was in the past, overshadowed by the urgent reality that was their son, his half brother, Robin. He had come to the realization that it wasn't only appropriate his mother would learn of his existence, it was necessary. She *should* meet this latest member of the Kent family. Kindhearted as she was, she might even come to love him.

"And the other woman," Athena said. "What happened to her?"

"She was killed in a car accident a year after my father died."

"How tragic. And how hard it all must have been for you." She linked her arm in his. "I wish I had been there to help."

"You don't know how many times I almost called you."

They sat listening to the crunch of leaves beneath the feet of people strolling by, the excited barks of a dog chasing a squirrel, and the occasional squawk of a crow. Regret and melancholy swept over him like a dark cloud. This was who Thena and Thorne could have been—a cozy, comfortable couple enjoying the beauty of a fall day, deciding which house project to tackle, and discussing what to buy the kids for Christmas.

No. Don't go there. Don't even pretend.

"Your anger," Athena said in a low voice, "was it just about your father's affair? Or were you also mad at him for relieving his guilty conscience at your expense?"

"Both. But then I realized the anger freed me to do what I wanted. To follow my passion, which wasn't being a lawyer, adhering to the Kent family tradition. Especially since... since you left me for it."

"You always loved cooking, but I thought literature was your passion."

"It was. It is. But getting a doctorate this late in the game wasn't an option."

"Is your father's double life the reason giving us another chance wasn't an option either?"

"His double life. Yes. Because I didn't believe in forever anymore. In marriage vows."

"Telling me this three years ago in Seattle might have softened the blow," she said.

Three years ago, he would have told her he *did* believe in forever. That his father's deathbed confession made another chance with her all the more likely. But he mustn't weaken now. Mustn't admit the darkest secret of all.

"I was ashamed," Thorne mumbled.

"And resentful."

"I admit I was. You did break my heart, Athena."

She looked up at him, her eyes brimming. "I want you to know that I didn't hate your parents for disliking me. Dread was what I mostly felt. The fear that if you followed their choice of career for you, it would go on from there. Our lives would become a constant series of concessions to the Kent way, until I wasn't me and you weren't you anymore."

"But I did propose to you against their wishes. I made no concession there. I was deeply hurt when you refused to compromise, find middle ground."

He might have told Athena about his mother's recent expression of regret for the way she and his father had treated her. But what would be the point?

"If it's any consolation, Thorne, my career hasn't been a barrel of bottomless joy."

As if there could be any consolation for all they had lost.

"No one's career is," he said. "You take the good with the bad." A safe generality instead of the bold suggestion she consider a career in another location. Namely, here.

"Spoken by the man who loves every minute he spends in his café," she said.

The chime on his phone reminded him he had to open As You Like It Café in an hour. "I love my job until it takes me from something better. Like talking to you." He kissed her cheek. "Thank you, Thena, for listening. For understanding."

"We should carve *Thena and Thorne, friends forever* into that pin oak."

"Not a bad idea. Are we still . . . you know?"

"Yeah. But I have to be your friend *without* benefits—" A

succession of sneezes cut her short. "Unless you want to risk disease and pestilence."

"I'm game. You and Kristie can take over again while I convalesce."

"No way can I manage the café again. I've got a deadline breathing down my neck."

And a departure date breathing down his.

"Have any plans for Thanksgiving?" Athena asked. "I'm cooking for Finn, Charles, and Vivienne. You're welcome to join us."

"I'd love to. Thanks."

"Come over any time. If I'm still sick, you and Finn can prepare the feast."

Thorne got up and stretched the stiffness from his body. "Can I walk you back to your car?"

"No thanks. I'm going to take another turn around the park."

"Don't overdo it, Thena. Give your body a chance to recover."

Her face brightened in a grin. "Overdo it? *Moi*?"

With a wave goodbye, Thorne limped away. His thigh muscle hurt like hell. He was another one of the walking wounded. In more ways than one.

CHAPTER FIFTEEN

Your will shall decide your destiny.

—CHARLOTTE BRONTË, *JANE EYRE*

After five days of coughing and sneezing, Athena welcomed her restored health and the challenge of transforming the ingredients Finn had bought into their Thanksgiving meal. Measure, season, cook, taste—as satisfying as writing an elegant essay. Little wonder Thorne had exchanged the courtroom for the café.

She sniffed the celery, thankful her sense of smell had returned. Definitely list-worthy, she thought, looking at the blackboard on the kitchen wall, gray with age. A stub of white chalk was attached to the worn string hanging from it to jot down grocery shopping items. Past Thanksgivings, each member of the Murphy family would write what they were grateful for on the board, adding to the list throughout the day as camaraderie—and wine—kicked in. Athena, true to her literary allegiances, had waxed poetically about morning dew, glorious sunsets, and, the autumn she'd fallen in love with Thorne, the thrill of romance. Loyal to his friends, Charles never failed to mention the Blakes, who, Lydia complained, bored her to tears. The memorable Thanksgiving after her affair with Vic Johnson had come to light, she boldly wrote his name beneath theirs—thus ending the gratitude list tradition. And family holiday meals.

The smell of fresh celery, Athena wrote on the board. *The deep red of cranberries.*

Being Thorne's friend and confidante again, she added to her mental checklist.

Finn entered the kitchen, scratching his stomach beneath his University of Illinois sweatshirt. "We back to writing stuff on the board?"

"If you want. Though that was never your thing, was it?"

"Because Mom was always nagging me to put my girlfriends' names on it."

"Feel free to write *Mario Spinelli* in capital letters."

"Señor Douche? No, thank you."

Mario had rejected his offer to help him repair homes damaged by the earthquake. "You're rehabbing on the side, remember, Fuckleberry Finn? Like you do everything. Including us."

"He's playing hardball," Athena reassured him. "He wants you back. He just won't admit it."

Finn rubbed his puffy morning eyes. "He has to blink first. I've got all the time in the world."

"Lucky you." She emptied the bag of stuffing into the bowl and added the chopped onions and celery. "What's happening with the website for the café?"

"Nearly complete. Business has been slow, so Thorne had time to give me lots of input."

"Kristie told me I didn't miss much Monday and Wednesday. Everybody has family coming in for the holiday." Concerned Eugene would be alone, she'd gotten his phone number from Joe and called, inviting him to join them. She hoped no response to her voicemail meant he was with Tildy.

Finn filled a Star Wars mug with coffee. "Any word from Sir Gay Goodenough?"

"Nope. I spooked him pretty badly about being a felon."

He grinned. "To think I came so close to being an uncle."

"Sorry to disappoint you, kiddo."

"Are you and Thorne a couple again or what?"

"What. As in, *no*." Athena shoved handfuls of stuffing into the turkey's cavity. The feel of raw poultry's clammy, goosebump skin was *not* on the gratitude list.

"Too bad," Finn said, pouring cream into his coffee. "You guys were great together."

"So you keep reminding me."

"Dad said he'll be at Vivienne's most of the day. Need any help cooking?"

"I've got the turkey, biscuits, cranberry sauce, and sweet potatoes covered. Can you handle the green beans?"

"Sure." Finn poured more cream into the mug. "Know what I love about being single? I don't have to listen to any shit about *lethal* dairy products."

"Mario's right. That stuff'll kill ya."

"Give Thorne a lecture about sugar when he brings the pies."

Pie was, without a doubt, something to be grateful for. As was a lover who remembered every one of your sweet spots.

She scrubbed her hands while Finn wrote *Being SINGLE* and *Eating crap if I want to* on the blackboard. "Want to go for a jog before dinner?" he asked.

"Seriously? You've jogged, like, once in your life. For the junior high fitness test."

"So what?" he said sullenly.

She put the turkey in the oven and set the timer. "You're on. Meet you at the front door at three."

He gave her a thumbs-up that looked suspiciously like Mario's signature gesture and left the kitchen.

Athena opened the window and, bracing her arms on the sill, inhaled the fragrance of dried leaves and chimney smoke. The bare tree branches silhouetted against the leaden sky were starkly beautiful. Oddly, the season of death always filled her with optimism, and this autumn was no exception. Hot, no-strings sex was one thing she and Thorne had going for them. But they couldn't deny the deeper attachment between them. He'd come to her for comfort after his trip to Albuquerque. Confessed his father's duplicity. Worried about her when she was sick. And then there were all the times in the café when they slipped back into their old groove, joking, sharing observations about people, and discussing books. As if they'd never been apart.

Retrieving her ringing phone from beneath a towel, she considered not answering, but even Lydia couldn't spoil her good mood. She grabbed the vegetable peeler, ejected the CD of Josh Groban singing "Love Only Knows," and turned on the speakerphone. "Happy Thanksgiving, Mom. Having a nice day?"

"It's okay. I certainly don't miss slaving over a hot stove."

Since the Murphy divorce, Lydia hosted Thanksgiving dinners exclusively for her friends, designating Christmas as the holiday Athena and Finn were to join her. In later years, she included her ex-husband in the invitation. Charles, however, preferred a calm meal with the Blakes to her rack of lamb.

"Where are you and Tony now?" Athena asked.

"Tony took off two days ago to meet up with family in Maryland."

"You're alone? On a holiday?"

"I don't mind. Traveling with a mentor gets exhausting after a while. There's only so much advice a person should have to listen to."

Athena turned her head away from the phone so her mother wouldn't hear her guffaw.

"Dear God in heaven, this traffic!" Lydia exclaimed. "Is *everyone* in the state of Louisiana going to the airport?"

"You're driving in Louisiana?"

"I'm in a taxi. I've got a flight to catch. I'm meeting Ricki in Puerto Vallarta."

"You made up! That's great news."

"We'll see how it goes. Cautious optimism is my philosophy."

"Tell Ricki I said hi and that the café's doing great," Athena said.

"Did Thorne find a house yet? My assistant hasn't been in touch since she told me the O'Neal property was off the market."

"Last I heard, he was still looking."

"Anything going on between you two?"

Mother, I bonked his brains out.

"Like what?"

"Like second chances."

Third. But who was counting?

"That reminds me," Lydia said. "I ran into Margaret Wheeler in New Orleans."

"Who?"

"One of the girls Finn dated in high school. Anyway, she's divorced and moving back to Laurel to start over. I advised her to look into a real estate career, and she's going to study for a license." Lydia mumbled something to the cabdriver. "Is Finn still there or did he go back to San Francisco?"

Athena scraped a sweet potato clean and placed it in the bowl. "Give it up, will you, please? Finn has zero interest in Margaret or any other girl."

"For Pete's sake, I wasn't born yesterday. I was hoping he was home with you and your father so he wouldn't be..." She gulped, as if holding back tears. "I'd hate to think he was alone on Thanksgiving since he and Mario broke up."

Branwell strolled in, sniffing the aroma of roasting turkey.

Athena wanted to hug her mother, but he would have to do. Cradling him in her arms, she tickled his belly until he smiled. "Don't worry, Mom. Finn is safe with us." If not necessarily sound.

"Let him know I think it's okay if he—"

Athena strained to listen, but the connection was filled with static and Lydia's agitated instructions to the cabdriver to "Turn left! Turn left!" The call ended abruptly before Athena could answer her earlier question and admit she was *cautiously optimistic* about another chance with Thorne.

Who the hell was she kidding? She'd already thrown caution to the wind.

Athena couldn't admonish Finn for not jogging with her, not when he appeared in the kitchen with the sulkiest sulk this side of toddlerhood. Post-breakup holidays were bitching hard. The first Christmas after she and Thorne had split, she'd wept whenever she heard Elvis sing "Blue Christmas."

"Thanks for making the green beans, Finn."

"They're pale and limp. Like my dick," he whined, opening a bottle of pinot noir.

"For Pete's sake, I'll throw some onions on them. Nobody will know the difference." She started slicing an onion with guillotine precision. "As for your penis, you're on your own."

"Are you mad at me or something? You sound like Mom all of a sudden."

Crap. She'd opened her mouth, and her mother popped out. But so what? With Lydia more sympathetic to her son, big sister could take a break. Finn wasn't the only one who'd ever had relationship problems.

Athena tossed the knife into the sink. "The heck with onions. The green beans are fine."

"But not me. I'm—"

"Miserable. Yeah. I get it. We all do. Want some advice?"

"Uh... yeah. I guess."

"I can't believe these words are coming out of my mouth, but man up. Quit complaining and feeling sorry for yourself and face up to what you want in your relationship with Mario. And do something about it."

Finn stared at her as if he didn't recognize her. Then he threw back his head and drank directly from the wine bottle. "Okay if I liquor up first?" he asked, wiping his mouth.

"Whatever it takes. Now help me bring all this food to the dining room."

The turkey was roasted to golden, moist deliciousness, the fresh cranberry sauce glistened, and the whipped sweet potatoes formed a perfect mound. As for the biscuits, they'd pass Thorne's baking standards of perfection. Brushing a few crumbs off her burnt-orange tunic and smoothing her brown leggings, Athena reviewed the table settings. The rustic simplicity of the acorns, twigs, and leaves she'd collected to use as decorations lent charm to the mismatched dishes. Candlelight would do the rest.

Just as she started to worry the food was getting cold, Charles burst through the front door, carrying a bottle of champagne. Vivienne came in behind him, her mane of silver hair flowing. Her father didn't wear a coat, nor did Thorne, who entered next, boxed pies stacked against his chest.

"Aren't you two freezing?" Athena asked. "The temperature has dropped about twenty degrees since this morning."

"It's a short walk from the car," Thorne said. "And the pies kept me warm."

"Wintry weather invigorates Charles," Vivienne said, removing her coat. "Where should I put this, Athena?"

At the same time Athena was rebelling against the

condescension in the way Vivienne held the coat at the end of her long fingers, she found herself offering to hang it as if it were an honor. Slipping the black cashmere coat on the hanger, her eye caught the label sewn inside. Phyllis had described Vivienne's wardrobe as "plain-Jane." Understated elegance was more like it. Vivienne Vander-something was rocking Prada. And the ruby bracelet encircling her slender wrist was thousands of dollars from rhinestones.

Rich, literary, a Laurel native—

Athena shut the closet door and pointed to Vivienne. "Could you be...when did you...I wonder, are you..." she sputtered.

"Now, now, Athena. It's rude to point at someone," Charles chided her.

"Did you want to ask me something?" Vivienne asked her kindly.

"I...uh...Are you..."

Damn. She was as tongue-tied as when Beryl Kent would inquire about her plans for the future. Which presumably would not include her son if she had anything to say about it.

With a look of mild disapproval at Athena, Charles put his hand on Vivienne's back and guided her to the dining room. "The day's not getting any younger, and neither are we," he said. "I say we begin the festivities."

Finn waved the bottle of pinot noir. "I got a head start."

Athena grabbed Thorne's arm to stop him from following them. "It's her!" she whispered excitedly. "It's C. L. Garland!"

He arched an eyebrow. "Vivienne?"

"Who else?"

"Hasn't she been living in Boston for about forty years?"

"Uh-huh."

"And returned only recently?"

"Yes," she replied. Less excitedly.

"Mmm. A bestselling author of erotica under your father's nose this whole time. How about that."

Athena frowned. "What's your point?"

"My point is, he'd certainly know by now if she was the object of your pursuit. Ergo, so would you."

Her frustrating, pointless, wearisome pursuit.

"Curses, foiled again," he said, grinning.

She lightly punched his arm. "Not funny, Thorne."

"Uh... yeah... it kinda is."

"*Ergo*, my butt."

"Back to your spunky self, I see. Guess this means you're no longer off-limits."

"Not necessarily."

He leaned over the boxes of pies and kissed her. The long, lingering kiss she'd been waiting for. "Mmm," she murmured. "You taste as good as your pies smell."

"Good enough to return to the royal bed chamber?"

"I haven't decided yet."

"Anything I can do to plead my case?"

"Ditch the lawyer-speak, for starters."

"Will advice about Garland gain me admission?"

She peeked into the top box at one of his expertly latticed cherry pies. "Depends."

"Take a holiday from her. From your book. From anything making you anxious."

"Including you?"

"Me? But I'm all about poetry and pastry."

"I'm glad you got your sense of humor back. As juvenile as it is."

"I have you to thank for awakening my funny bone."

"Along with the other bone I awakened."

"Does that mean what I think it means?"

"I'm all about puns and playacting. You tell me."

Athena led Thorne and his pies and his poetry-in-motion bod to the dining room as Charles released the cork from the champagne bottle with a loud pop.

"Party time," Finn said listlessly, slumped in a chair at the table.

"What's the occasion, Dad?" Athena asked, helping Thorne arrange the pies on the sideboard.

In the background, the song "Something's Coming" from *West Side Story* was playing on the stereo—her father's go-to Broadway soundtrack when he was in high spirits. "Where are the champagne glasses?" he asked.

"Mom took them." She pointed to the miscellaneous goblets on the table. "These will have to do."

"We haven't celebrated anything since she left," Finn said glumly. "That is totally depressing."

Athena leaned down to whisper in his ear, "Cheer up, Finnster. Mom told me today she's cool with you being gay."

His face brightened. "What? Are you serious? True story?"

"Not in so many words. But I read between the lines."

"Since when is there room between Mom's lines?"

"Since she and Ricki made up."

Charles went around the table filling glasses. "Attention, everyone," he said when he was done. "I want to make a toast to the future Mr. and Mrs. Murphy."

The dancing candle flames were all that moved as the meaning of his words sank in. Thorne was the first to recover. "Here's to the happy couple," he said, lifting his glass. "Congratulations!"

"I was already sitting, right?" Finn said. "I didn't fall into this chair from shock?"

"When did you get engaged?" Thorne asked.

"The evening of the San Francisco earthquake," Charles said. "A memorable night indeed."

Athena sank into a chair and gulped six mouthfuls of champagne. Maybe the world would stop spinning if she got drunk. A paradox, like her gun-shy father getting married again. "You could have told us you and Vivienne weren't...platonic. Why all the secrecy, Dad?"

"Since your mother's indiscretion in the Johnson business, privacy is very important to me. Especially in matters of the heart." He gazed lovingly at his fiancée. "We didn't want to announce anything until we were sure."

"And we are very sure." The small diamond in Vivienne's ring sparkled when she tapped her glass to his. " 'Let me not to the marriage of true minds admit impediments.' "

"We fell in love over Shakespeare's sonnets," Charles explained. "A handsome, leather-bound volume."

The candlelight blurred in Athena's suddenly teary eyes. She didn't dare look at Thorne.

"Does Mom know about this?" Finn asked between hiccups.

"I'll leave it to you and Athena to break the news," Charles said magnanimously. As if he were doing them a big favor.

"Are you going to live here or Vivienne's house?" Athena asked.

"We've set up our cozy nest at the Mortenson place," Charles said.

"Soon to be the Murphy place," Vivienne said. "We look forward to restoring it to its former grandeur."

"So, why'd you have Karl repair the greenhouse?" Finn asked.

"Vivienne believes in a healthy diet and encouraged me to grow my own vegetables and herbs. But we decided since our engagement—"

"Your father cannot live without my library," Vivienne said. "And when he adds *his* books to it..."

"Heaven," he said. "Simply heaven."

Athena finished the champagne in her glass and let out an unceremonious burp. "Mom will be glad. She's wanted to sell this house for ages."

Charles's eyes and mouth drooped. "You and Finn don't want it?"

"We live in California, remember?"

"But it's our family home, Athena."

"We can't afford the upkeep. Or to be sentimental."

"I thought you said—"

"We'll talk about it later. Can we eat now, please? I'm starving," Athena said as crankily as a child.

"Yes, my dear. Yes, yes," her father said, sounding as if he were placating one of Lydia's bad moods.

Vivienne arranged herself in the chair at the head of the table while Charles carved the turkey. Thorne sat next to Athena and spread his napkin on his lap. Across from them, Finn jabbered about stepmothers and surprises. The mound of sweet potatoes seemed to have collapsed, and the biscuits looked as appetizing as hockey pucks.

"Well, well, if this isn't an interesting turn of events," Thorne remarked.

"Lady of the manor," Athena grumbled. "Look at her, sitting where my dad should be sitting."

"He pulled the chair out for her."

"And making us sell our family home."

"She's done no such thing."

"Humph."

"Vivienne is very nice, and you know it."

"The princess wears Prada."

"Methinks she reminds you of my mother."

Methinks you are right.

"Let it go, Thena," he said, buttering a biscuit. "Be thankful your father found someone to share his life with."

"I used to have someone!" Finn wailed.

"Shh," Athena whispered. "Don't spoil Dad's day." Though he was too busy being fed a sliver of turkey by Vivienne to have noticed Finn's outburst.

"I shouldn't be here," Finn blubbered. "I should be with Mario."

She leaned across the table. "Admit you made a mistake," she said in a low voice. "Tell him you changed your mind and want to marry him. You do, don't you?"

"Uh-huh. But he's too stubborn. And proud. He won't take me back."

"You won't know unless you try."

"Think I should ask him for another chance?"

It hadn't done a damn thing for her. But Athena realized, looking at her brother staring into the emotional abyss, she'd beg Thorne in Seattle all over again. "You'll regret it if you don't."

Finn wiped his nose on his shirt cuff. "Guess I've got nothing to lose."

"Go for it, Finn," Thorne said.

"You agree with Athena?"

"I do."

Charles and Vivienne were too engrossed in their own conversation to have noticed Finn's distress. But Thorne, apparently, had heard every word. Including *regret.* Athena flashed him a this-is-not-even-remotely-about-us smile. "Big sister to the rescue," she said cheerfully.

Finn quaffed his champagne and, putting the glass on the table with a flourish, staggered from his chair. "Excuse me while I make a very important phone call."

"You think he and Mario will go the distance?" Thorne asked Athena once he'd left the room.

She stabbed a slice of turkey from the platter Charles had

passed to them. "Absolutely. They're perfect for each other. All they have to do is meet each other halfway."

"A tough proposition, if you recall."

"Live and learn. I, for one, am beginning to think anything's possible."

Thorne fixed her with the soulful look in those spring-green eyes that got her right where she lived, reminding her of the next line of the sonnet Vivienne had quoted—"Love is not love which alters when it alteration finds."

Right where she lived.

Until he spoke.

"Anything's possible, Thena. Unless it's too late. Then all bets are off."

Right then and there, at the exact moment Thorne dropped a heaping spoonful of stuffing—and reality—onto her plate, Athena mentally erased *making love with Thorne* off the gratitude blackboard. As Lydia would put it, she wasn't born yesterday. She knew exactly what he was saying—it was too late for *them*. Their love had admitted *impediments*, to quote Shakespeare, and there wasn't a snowball's chance in hell they'd be Thena and Thorne ever again.

Getting plastered on champagne gave Athena a good reason to send Thorne on his way, sans benefits, Thanksgiving night. She'd woken Friday morning to a pounding headache and a snowy landscape that mercifully muffled all sound. Mindful of the treacherous roads, Thorne had called to tell her he'd closed the café until Monday. She used the same road conditions, and the demands of her book, as an excuse not to see him over the weekend.

When she arrived at As You Like It Café on Monday after a two-week absence, she was relieved he'd been called away on an errand. But since the café regulars now knew they had been college sweethearts, thanks to the scene with Sergei, they teased her all afternoon.

"Is love better the second time around, Athena?"

"When will we hear wedding bells?"

"We thought we saw sparks between you two."

It sucks! Never! No sparks! she wanted to scream.

Kristie, too, had weighed in with a text message:

You were sweethearts!! Why didn't you tell me? Too cute!

Athena fired off a text to Thorne.

They're driving me crazy!

It's your turn. I've been dealing with them since Finn blew our cover.

She nearly rapped Eugene with a Kaiser roll, Geraldine-style, when he gave his excuse for not going to her Thanksgiving dinner: "Didn't want to butt in on your romantic evening with Thorne." To add insult to injury, the This Time Around Book Club members confessed they'd been so titillated by the news that they hadn't discussed Garland's books at all during last Tuesday's meeting, the one she'd been too sick to attend.

After closing the café, Athena drove back to Lydia's house, counting the minutes until she removed her shoes—a lot of good they'd done her, Miss Marple–wise—and changed into slippers and sweat clothes. She prayed for another blizzard so she'd have an excuse to remain in schlump mode as long as possible. Unless Dr. Davenport granted the extension she'd requested, she had only thirty days to submit her manuscript.

Thinking about Thorne for even one minute was an indulgence she could not permit herself. Her latest chapter on the use of pseudonyms in literary history was merely filler. Tangential. Grasping at straws.

After scarfing down a Hot Pocket, she booted up her laptop and checked her notes on Mary Ann Evans, aka George Eliot. She tried to ignore the voices in her head, clamoring for answers to the questions that had tortured her since forever.

What are you doing?

Is this activity meaningful?

Is this what your life is about?

"Shut up," she muttered. "Shut the hell up."

After a half hour of staring into space, churning sentences in her mind, typing, deleting, typing, she pounced on her ringing phone. The interruption might propel her beyond the one phrase she'd written, *As late as the nineteenth century, women writers were...*

"You asked me to keep my ear to the ground, and I did, Dr. M," Elise whispered.

Athena shot up from the chair and paced, unnerved by her reflection in the kitchen window. Scared shitless was *not* a good look for her. "Don't tell me. They filled my position."

"Not yet. But I type the department newsletter, and the big news is Professor Perfect got a humongous advance from a publisher."

"Define *humongous*."

"I don't know the exact figure, but sales of her next book are projected to go through the roof."

"It's all fluff. A load of hooey to make the English Department look good."

"Hooey?"

"Dr. Davenport is always kissing up to the trustees. This is more bullshit."

"Yeah, but—"

"Who would buy a book on Emily Dickinson besides academics and English majors?"

She heard a rustling of paper, then Elise's voice loud and clear as she read the title. "*Erotica and Emily Dickinson: Poetry or Porn?* by Corinne Carew."

Corinne Carew, soon to be *Ka-ching Ka-chew* as she rang up cash register sales.

Assistant Professor Carew, soon to be Associate Professor Carew, while Athena had to claw and grovel and beseech her way back into favor. She tried to say something but a lump as big as an orange was lodged in her throat.

"Uh... are you there, Dr. M?"

She rubbed her neck, licked her dry lips. "Thanks for calling, Elise. I appreciate the intel. But I'm not worried. Reviewers will point out that Dickinson's poems about death and snakes and bees have nothing to do with sex. Corinne is... She's grasping at straws."

"How's *your* book going?" Elise asked.

"My book's going great. What kind of mood has Dr. Davenport been in lately?"

"Not bad. For him. The end of the semester is coming up and his wife's out of town."

"I'm waiting to hear if he'll grant me an extension. I shouldn't need much more time."

None, if she followed her heart and scrapped the whole stupid project, got a job at Southern Illinois College, lived in the Murphy home with Thorne, and helped him run As You Like It Café.

"An extension. Oh my," Elise said.

"While I'm on the line, can you put me through to his office?" Before she fell victim to any more batshit-crazy fantasies.

"I sure can. Good luck, Dr. M." Elise's voice was faint, as if she were running in the opposite direction.

"What can I do for you, Athena?" Dr. Davenport's chilly tone implied all he wanted to do was hang up.

"I've made a lot of progress on my book. I think you'll be pleased with its scholarship and fresh approach to erotica." She spoke very calmly and distinctly. With emphasis on *erotica.*

"All well and good, but have you uncovered Garland's identity?"

"I'm at a very delicate juncture. The pieces of the puzzle should fall into place—"

"In other words, you have no idea who she is."

Or the woman staring back at her in the window with Medusa hair and a look of sheer terror on her face.

"I emailed you a request for an extension," she reminded him. "Have you given it any consideration?"

"An extension for a wild-goose chase? I think not."

"But if you read my initial chapters, you'd see—"

"Garland is your money in the bank. *She's* what you should be focusing on. And Corinne has already captured the market interest in literary erotica."

"But it was my idea. I'm the one who—"

"Ideas are one thing. Execution is another. Anything else?"

I'd like to finish a sentence. I'd like to tell you and Ka-ching Ka-chew to execute flying leaps off the Golden Gate Bridge.

Except sharing her thoughts was what had gotten her in hot water in the first place.

"Thank you for your time, Dr. Davenport. I'll do my best to get the book to you by January first."

"December thirty-first and not a day later," he said. And hung up.

Athena snapped the window blinds shut, unable to look

at her reflection a minute longer. She'd recently mailed the December rent check for the apartment she wouldn't be able to afford once she lost her job. Her thirty-third birthday loomed, and she was most definitely *not* in a relationship.

On the bright side...Dammit, there had to be a bright side.

She stared at the laptop, reading the one miserable phrase she'd written. Not even a full sentence. A fricking phrase.

There wasn't any bright side. Only a very dark solution.

CHAPTER SIXTEEN

Make my happiness—I will make yours.

—CHARLOTTE BRONTË, *JANE EYRE*

Late Friday afternoon, while Athena and Kristie decorated As You Like It Café with blue and silver streamers, balloons, and small vases with flowers on each table, Thorne iced the last batch of petits fours. Dessert and drinks were all Charles and Vivienne wanted for their engagement party, so he'd baked up a storm all week and stocked the refrigerator with champagne, wine, and beer. Baking as a stress buster was right up there with swimming and running.

The source of his stress sashayed into the kitchen, looking like she didn't have a care in the world.

"Good thing you closed after breakfast," Athena said. "It looks like Jackson Pollock was painting in here."

Eggshells, measuring cups, mixing spoons, and spattered bowls cluttered the counter. Clumps of hardened batter and drops of food coloring stained the floor. "I'll clear this mess up," he said. "I know you're busy with your book, but will you have time after the party to help me clean the dining room?"

"Definitely. I've made good progress on my manuscript." She walked to the table next to the pantry that held her laptop. All afternoon between preparations, she'd paused to type another paragraph or two. As she leaned over the table, he feasted his eyes on the delectable curves of her figure in its formfitting purple sweater, short black skirt, and teal-blue tights. Picturing himself removing her ankle boots, one by one, he felt a familiar swelling in his groin. She'd awakened his *bone*, all right—only to leave him starving for more.

They hadn't made love since they were Mr. Rochester and Jane Eyre at Halloween. Five weeks of waiting and longing. And swelling. His emergency trip to Albuquerque, her illness and preoccupation with her book, the weather—all these reasons paled against the painful truth that, as he himself had pointed out at Thanksgiving, it was too late for them.

He'd said it to test her—and himself. To see how it felt to face a future where all the emotions she had aroused in him again were locked away.

Living with a wooden heart wasn't a future he looked forward to.

But Athena hadn't protested. Hadn't offered a particle of hope they'd meet each other in the middle, venture another chance. If anything, she was... He searched for the words to best describe her lately.

Jocular. Jaunty. Jovial.

And it depressed the hell out of him.

"Thena?"

"Hmm?" she said, shifting her weight from one shapely leg to the other.

Thorne's heart raced like her fingers on the keyboard. Better to speak up before he talked himself out of it.

I need you in my life.

We complete each other.

Can't you see it isn't too late?

"Anything wrong, Thorne?" she asked, looking up. "You look like you missed a flight. Or your luggage wound up in Bismarck, North Dakota."

Everything would be *right* once they were Thena and Thorne again.

"The thing is, Thena. I want you to stay—"

Kristie swung the door open. "Brace for impact. Everything's arranged, and I put the *Open* sign back up. Come one, come all."

"Finn predicts a good turnout," Athena said. "Nearly everyone responded yes to the Facebook invitation."

"Your dad's adorable, but I think Thorne's pastries are the main attraction," Kristie said. "I've already eaten two kiwi tarts."

"I wonder if Sharon Benson will show up," Athena said. "We had a great chat in the library recently about organic gardening."

"I ran into her and the mayor at the bank the other day," Thorne said. "They told me they had to go to Chicago for a wedding."

"I hope I get a chance to talk with her again."

Before she left. For good.

"Sharon thanked me for my fundraising efforts for a mental health clinic and promised to facilitate it," he said. "When the mayor started to object, she said, 'You're coughing up the dough, Mr. B, and that's all there is to it.' "

Athena laughed. "I can hear the pounding of carpenters' hammers as we speak."

Kristie cocked her head toward the dining room. "And I hear voices. We better get out there."

"I can't thank you guys enough for doing this for my dad," Athena said.

"And for Vivienne," Thorne said.

She smiled. "Yeah. Vivienne too."

"It was a lot of fun," Kristie said.

"And my pleasure," Thorne said.

"About me staying, Thorne," Athena said as they left the kitchen. "Relax. I already promised I'd help clean up."

The moment to ask her to stay in Laurel had come and gone. When they were alone again, no matter how late it was or how tired they were, he'd go for it. Start by encouraging her to consider the position at the college. End by asking her to be with him forever. It might be his last chance.

Charles and Vivienne, accompanied by Finn, were the first to arrive. They were dressed in matching outfits of black blazers, pale-blue shirts, and black trousers.

"Yikes. They've already turned into the Blakes," Athena said.

"I think it's sweet when couples dress alike," Thorne said, having just come to this conclusion.

"As long as they don't fight over whose underwear is whose," she quipped.

"Ian and I are up for a party like you would not believe," Kristie said. "Zoe's been sick, and we haven't had a night out all week."

"She's not coming?" Thorne asked.

"No. Ian's mom is babysitting."

"You realize you killed his party buzz, don't you, Kristie?" Athena said, laughing.

Kristie patted his arm. "Don't worry. I'll bring Zoe by soon to see *Unca Thor*." She walked away to join Ian and the group gathered around Charles and Vivienne.

"I'm surprised Nora Johnson showed up," Thorne said. "She returned a sandwich to the kitchen yesterday, complaining it tasted like sawdust, and then stormed out."

"She's a pistol," Athena said. "I overheard her tell Vivienne to stock up on estrogen pills because Charles has a lot of steam in his engine."

"How would *she* know?" he asked.

"They had revenge sex for getting cheated on by each other's spouses."

"Whoa. How'd you find that out?"

"Nora told me herself. Rather triumphantly, I might add."

He whistled. "It's true what they say. 'Truth *is* stranger than fiction.' "

Joe and Theresa approached, holding hands. "Getting ideas, you two?" Joe teased them. "Engagements and weddings have a way of being contagious."

"Not us. We're immune," Athena said. Without skipping a beat.

Was it too soon to get stinking drunk?

"It's hard to go it alone in this life," Joe said with a wistful look in his kind eyes. "You need someone to share your thoughts with, to cover your back. Don't wait until—"

"Until gravity takes over," Phyllis said, walking up to them with Dan. "Get hitched while you still have some zip."

"For sex?" Dan asked. "Or to zip out of marriage as you've done a couple of times?"

"Numbskull and Dumbbell had it coming to them," she said with a sniff. She pointed to Charles and Vivienne kissing under the *Congratulations!* banner. "And I know what Charles has coming to him if she pushes up daisies first. A mountain of moolah. Wonder if she made him sign a prenup?"

"What are you talking about?" Athena asked.

"I looked her up on the Internet," Phyllis said. "Turns out, the widow has inherited a fortune. The Vanderfelders have been one of the wealthiest families in Boston since they got off the *Mayflower*."

"Oh, *that* Vanderfelder," they all murmured, as if they were well acquainted with New England blue bloods.

"Marrying into old money," Phyllis said, sinking her teeth into a chocolate cupcake. "Way to go, Charles."

"Should I tell her it's all about a heavenly library for my dad?" Athena whispered in Thorne's ear.

He shook his head, reeling slightly at her warm breath, the tickle of her curl on his cheek, her scent, her... Athena-ness. The sum totality of which was returning to the state of California.

The hell she was. Not if he had anything to say about it.

Athena pointed to Ivy, who sat at her usual post by the bay window, playing the mandolin with her woeful Ophelia face. "You should go over there and console the fair maiden."

"For what?"

"For crushing her crush. Or whatever else she's sad about."

"Only if you come with me."

She grinned. "To cover your back, like Joe said?"

"And my front."

"Don't worry. She's too sweet to hit below the belt."

Ivy was as pale and dispirited as Athena was glowing and energized. "Everything all right?" Athena asked her.

She strummed a few sour notes. "I invited Karl but he refused to come. He said engagement parties and weddings gave him... What's the word?"

"*Hives? Conniptions? The heebie-jeebies?*" Athena said.

"Like I was even *thinking* about marriage," Ivy said. "What is wrong with guys?"

"A heap of things," Eugene said, coming up behind them. "But lots of good stuff too, underneath it. Least that's what Tildy says."

"How is your wife?" Athena asked him. "Have you been staying in touch?"

"Daily. And I'll tell you how she is when I get back from Cleveland next week."

She clapped her hands in delight. "I'm so glad, Eugene! Good for you."

"Great news," Thorne said to him.

"Don't want to put the cart before the horse," Eugene said, "but I think we might set things to rights."

If a crusty grump like Eugene Farragut could be granted another chance, it was possible Thorne could be too.

"Maybe I got it wrong. Maybe it's never too late," he said to Athena in a low voice when Ivy resumed playing and Eugene walked away to congratulate Charles and Vivienne.

"For couples like the Farraguts who've been married for forty-three years," she said. "Maybe."

"I don't want to believe the state of love and romance is as hopeless as all that."

"My father would agree with you. When I asked him why he still got teary-eyed about Lydia when he was falling in love with Vivienne, he said, 'One love does not replace another. Our hearts are big enough for as much love as they can hold.' "

"And you? What do you believe?"

Before Athena could answer, the door opened, and the bachelor farmers spilled into the café, one by one, like puppies out of a box. The youngest of them waved shyly to Ivy, and she waved back—not as shyly.

"If Charles Murphy can get engaged at his age, we've got a shot," one of them said.

"Don't want a shot," another one said. "My old man had a saying when someone got married. 'Another one bites the dust.' "

"Oh, so *that's* why you've never dated."

"Hey, I've—"

"Taking your cousin to the prom doesn't count."

"*Second* cousin."

"It's like they're one gigantic married couple," Athena remarked as they moved en masse to the refreshment table. "They even finish each other's sentences."

"The one talking to Ivy might break free," Thorne said. "Think you can work your magic to get them together?"

"There's not enough time to play matchmaker again before I go. Besides, Mandolin Miss does quite well on her own."

"What do *you* think of Karl?"

"Let me put it this way. When Finn showed me pictures of him working on our house, I zoomed in on the roof soffits."

Finn came up to them and handed them glasses filled with champagne. "Get ready. I'm going to toast the happy couple."

"I'd better do it," she said. "You've been a total downer about love lately."

This Thorne had to hear—Athena describing love in positive terms.

"I'm not depressed anymore." Finn's eyes gleamed. "Mario and I have been talking all week, and we're back together. I accepted his proposal."

"Woo-hoo!" Athena yelled, causing a couple of mall walkers to stumble in their oversize sneakers. And eliciting a *humph* from Nora, glowering nearby.

He took his phone from his pocket and scrolled through the photos. "Check out this desk Mario built for me. And do you notice the apartment? It's clean and organized for a change."

"If that doesn't say *Feng Shui Your Way*, nothing does," Athena said.

"What?" Thorne said.

"You don't want to know," she said.

"I promised I'd try doing new things with him," Finn said. "And not nag him about stupid stuff."

"I'd like to meet Mario sometime," Thorne said.

"You're invited to the wedding. Athena's going to be our best man."

"I've always wanted to be a best man," she said. "Can I wear a tux?"

"The ceremony won't be formal. Mario will probably wear a wet suit."

"How'd it happen?" she asked.

"I did what you told me to do," Finn said. "I thought about what I wanted in our relationship and realized Mario was the love of my life. Nothing else mattered but being with him. It's as simple as that."

While Finn praised the joys of love and commitment in his speech, Thorne looked around the room. Couples everywhere, young and old. Even the geeky piano tuner had his arm around Yolanda from the Garden Club. And standing beside him, smelling of lilies, bringing back the sweetest memories of true love he knew, was Athena. The love of his life.

As simple as that.

Kristie and Ian were the last guests to leave the party. As fond as Thorne was of the Prescotts, he was on the verge of asking them to "please leave now" a half dozen times. Alone, finally, with Athena, he appraised the wreckage. Not a drop of alcohol or crumb of pastry remained, and the dining room had all the appearance of a disaster area. "What do you think, Thena? Tornado or cyclone?"

She stood on the stepladder, pulling down streamers and balloons. "Both. And throw in a teenager's bedroom for good measure."

He snapped open a garbage bag and, sweeping his hand across one of the tables, dumped empty plastic cups and paper plates into it. He was exhausted down to the roots of his hair, but he still had the week's menus to plan and sauces to prep. "Ideally, I would have hosted the party *tomorrow* night. Catch my breath on Sunday."

"I agree. But the lovebirds have a flight to Boston tomorrow morning," she said. "They wanted to tell Vivienne's son and daughter-in-law about their engagement in person."

"Have you told Lydia yet?"

"She's in Mexico with Ricki, and there's no phone reception. I might delay the announcement until I'm safely back in San Francisco with half a continent between us. She's bound to find *something* to piss her off."

One of the balloons floated listlessly toward him. Twice today, Athena had referred to her imminent departure. But her mention of "half a continent" took the starch out of his sails. He slumped against the hutch and rubbed his burning eyes. He was so damn tired. Tired of being alone. Of knowing he would always be alone.

"I can finish cleaning if you're bushed, Thorne." Athena climbed off the stepladder, her arms filled with streamers. Quite a few of her curls had come undone, and a thin tear ran the length of the tights on her left leg. She wore the fern earrings he'd given her. When they'd danced tonight, she held him close and let their bodies melt into each other, looking into his eyes like she couldn't get enough of what she saw there. It had to mean something. Something more than a booty call.

"Thena. I have to—"

"Go ahead, take off if you want. I've got this."

"That's not what I mean... I'm trying to... what I want to say..."

She tilted her head. "Well, I'll be darned. Thorne Kent at a loss for words."

He gathered his strength, focusing his mind like he used to before leaping off the starting block at a swim meet. Now or never. Dive into the deep end.

"Don't go back to California, Thena."

Her eyes widened, and her mouth opened, but no words came out.

"Did you hear what I said?" he asked.

"What... what *are* you saying?"

"Stay with me. In Laurel. Don't return to San Francisco."

The streamers fell into a heap at her feet. He walked to her, his body utterly weightless for the first time in years, every muscle and nerve alive. Her warm, pillowy lips were the answer to all their questions. His hands at the small of her back were exactly where they belonged. Her fingers had no business doing anything besides clutching his hair. Her low moans, the helpless flutter of her eyelashes...

"Thorne," she whispered.

Another kiss, and then he nestled his face in her neck, breathing in her essence like he'd emerged from water and was gasping for air.

"What are we doing?" she murmured.

"Unless I've lost my touch, we're about to go upstairs and make love."

She stepped back slowly, shaking her head. "I thought I could do this... this sex without strings thing. But I can't. I just can't."

"Me neither. For what it's worth, there isn't any other woman in my life. Not since we slept together."

He wanted to hold her again. Hold her and never let her go. But she was looking down, poking the streamers with her foot.

Tell her everything. The real reason you rejected her in Seattle. The worry a child of yours may inherit Robin's disease. The consequences if one did.

The fervent wish she'd face the consequences with him.

"If you stay, we might have a chance—what did Eugene

say?—to 'set things to rights.'" Thorne laughed nervously. "As they say, 'third time's the charm.'"

Or three strikes, you're out.

"You're caught up in the romance of the occasion, Thorne," Athena said evenly. "Like Joe said, it's *contagious.*"

"And you're immune."

"No. Not completely. Just realistic." She lifted her flushed face. "That's a switch, huh?"

"Anything's possible. You said so yourself."

"I did. But this isn't the best time for me to... I can't take my eyes off the ball. Since I solved my Garland problem, I'm writing like gangbusters. I'll definitely make the deadline."

"And drive back to San Francisco at the speed of light."

She didn't deny it or make excuses. She didn't have to. Her life was there, the job she loved, her future. Without him.

He scooped up a balloon that had drifted to the floor and squeezed it. It deflated with an unsatisfying *pop.* "If I may ask, how did you solve the Garland mystery?"

"You're not going to get all legal on me, are you?"

"I'll try not to. My role as lawyer wasn't exactly your favorite."

"Except the way you dressed for the part. You're a handsome devil in a three-piece suit."

"I still have a few in my closet. Go on. Tell me about Garland."

"I made her up. I've created an entire history and personality profile of the elusive C. L. Garland. Kind of like cooking. A pinch of eccentricity, a dash of sass, and a heaping tablespoon of wit. Frankly, my version is probably more interesting than the real one."

Thorne sank into the nearest chair, his thoughts as tangled as the pile of streamers on the floor. "You didn't."

"Sure did. I'm using the same title as my first manuscript,

Hiding in Plain Sight, and incorporating my scholarly analyses of her books. But each chapter is framed by an event that happened in her life."

"*Fake* life. *Fake* events."

"No worries. I'm going to pitch it as a fictional biography, like those popular docudramas. I'll write a brief disclaimer in the preface like, *This is a work of fiction*, blah blah blah."

"No rock unturned," she'd promised. And she'd been true to her word. She would go to any lengths for her career. It was evidently more important to her than anything. More important than them. Only a fool would tell her about Robin. Confess his hopes for them to be a couple again. A damn idiot fool.

"You promised your department chair you'd uncover her identity, not make one up. Why would you do this, Thena?"

"Obviously, to deliver the manuscript on time. And if it provokes Garland, gets her out of hiding if only to say I've got her all wrong, all the better."

"And provokes her to sue you."

"My disclaimer should cover me. In any case, the publicity would be good for sales."

"*Negative* publicity."

She shrugged. "The chair won't care as long as it puts Wyatt College on the map."

"What if there *isn't* any reaction? What if she and her agent and publisher ignore you and your book?"

"Then it languishes and sinks into oblivion like a lot of books. At the very least, I'll have filled in the 'publish or perish' box."

He massaged his temples to soothe the pain of a sudden headache. "You don't want to hear this, Thena, but you're taking an awful risk."

"My career is worth it. It's all I have."

"But is it all you want?"

A sleety rain pricked the windows. A chill wind howled. Despondency hung in the air of the disordered room. Athena didn't answer.

There was no question about it. The party was over.

CHAPTER SEVENTEEN

You must forgive me, for I struggled only for you!

—EMILY BRONTË, *WUTHERING HEIGHTS*

Leave it to Thorne to knock her for a loop.

Twenty-four hours ago, before he had held her and kissed her and asked her to stay, intimating it wasn't too late for them—before that, Athena had accepted Thena and Thorne were over and done with. She had mastered the art of appearing blithe and carefree. Had convinced herself she was.

Twenty-four hours ago, she was writing the book she hoped would level the playing field and bring Corinne Carew down a notch or two. Or at least wipe the fake smile off her face. As fake as Athena's C. L. Garland narrative, born out of desperation to save her career. Born out of the necessity to stop imagining a life in Laurel with Thorne once and for all.

Twenty-four hours ago, the ends justified the means. Because she'd do anything to teach again, to inspire a lifelong engagement with literature in her students.

And today?

Today, Athena was plodding through a bleak Saturday afternoon in Lydia's sterile kitchen with a champagne headache and zero inspiration to add to the three paltry paragraphs she'd written in which the word *if* appeared four times.

Today she was coming to terms with the fact that her ambitions for her book were delusional.

And wrestling with the tantalizing possibility that Thena and Thorne were *not* over and done with. Not by a long shot.

"Hair of the dog," she mumbled, filling a glass with Beaujolais from the last bottle in her mother's wine collection. It wasn't as if she could feel any worse. And she had something to celebrate—Sergei was getting married. An impressive turnabout for a guy who'd driven halfway across the country, fueled by caffeine and sugar, to see her.

"Soon I have bride! Soon I have green card!" he'd bragged in a text yesterday with a photo of him and what appeared to be a fifty-something woman in an aluminum foil hat. "Green like your eyes!"

"My eyes are brown, numb-nuts," she'd texted back.

She sipped the wine, staring at the word *if* in the paragraphs she'd written.

If she weren't down in the dumps, she'd be laughing her head off about Sergei.

If the sidewalks weren't slippery with ice, she'd go for a run.

If she had a lick of sense, she'd pack right now, get in the Mini Cooper, and drive away from Laurel, taking her false biography and her real heart with her.

She had no reason to stay any longer. Lydia and Charles were gone, Finn on his way back to Mario. Thorne would find another waitress.

And another woman to love who wouldn't want marriage or kids or ivy-covered cottages.

Athena swirled the wine, fighting back tears. " 'If wishes were horses, beggars would ride,' " she recited.

Her ringing phone pulled her back from the brink of weepy sentimentality.

"Hello, daughter dear. How are you?" Lydia asked.

Daughter dear?

"Maudlin with a hint of insouciance, mother dear."

"Are you drinking my wine?"

"What else is there to do on a winter day in the Midwest?"

"Catch a plane to somewhere else. Puerto Vallarta was fun, but now I'm in Vegas having the time of my life."

With all its diversions, Las Vegas was as good a place as any for Lydia to find out her ex-husband, the father of her children, her rhumba and mambo partner, was getting remarried.

"Listen, Mom, I have something important to tell you."

"If it's about your dad's engagement to a rich widow, I already heard. Good for him."

"Finn, that stinker. We agreed *I* would break the news."

"He didn't tell me. Nora Johnson left a message on my phone. She probably hoped I'd be jealous or fit to be tied."

So did Athena. For a nanosecond.

"I'm surprised they're settling in Laurel instead of Boston," Lydia said.

"Dad said Vivienne doesn't want to socialize with stuffed shirts anymore."

"Good for her."

Yeah. Good for her.

"They're moving into the Mortenson place," Athena said. "Our house—"

"Will go on the market the minute I get back."

There was no reason in the world for Lydia to think Athena might want to live there. No reason whatsoever.

In the background, she heard an exuberant slot machine and boisterous laughter. "Have you won any money at the casinos?"

"I hit the jackpot!" Lydia exclaimed with a giddy laugh.

Her mother never laughed, or did anything, giddily. "What's going on, Mom?"

"Hold on to your hair, Athena. I'm crazy in love."

Charles, Finn, and now Lydia. What was going on with everybody lately? Why this sudden belief in happily ever after? She gulped half a glass of wine, trying to decide which of the many questions careening in her brain she'd ask first. "So, your road trip with Tony turned into a romance?"

"Not even close. Antonia's not my soul mate and never could be."

"*Antonia*? Wait... *she*? What?"

"She's not my type. And besides, she has a girlfriend, a pregnant physical therapist in Bayonne, New Jersey. How they manage an East Coast–Midwest relationship is beyond me."

Athena waded through this barrage of information—fertility, occupation, location—to get to the heart of the matter. "You never mentioned Tony was a woman."

"Or that I worship at the altar of Sappho."

"The Greek poet?" Athena peered into her glass, wondering if there was another ingredient in the wine. Like a hallucinogen.

"From the island of Lesbos. I'm a lesbian, sweetie."

Frankly, there was entirely too much geography in this conversation.

"Since when?" Athena managed to get out.

"Since always. But I was in denial. That's what Ricki and I fought about. She wouldn't speak to me until I faced the truth."

Athena refilled her glass and drank it without stopping.

"Tony's my official career mentor and unofficial lesbian mentor," Lydia went on. "It took talking and listening and arguing through five states to get me in touch with my true self and let go of my fears. Or was it six states?"

Her mother? Afraid?

"Are you listening, Athena?"

"Intently."

"What I'm saying is, it's Ricki I love. Ever since junior high when she let me peek at her answer on a history test. A multiple-choice question about the Smoot-Hawley Tariff Act."

Athena couldn't think of a single thing to say about Smoot *or* Hawley.

"All these years I thought it had been a girl crush," Lydia said.

"And Dad? Did you love him at all?"

"Hard not to. He tried so darn hard. And he gave me you and Finn."

"So, Ricki's your… You and Ricki—"

"Are lovers. Her Leo and my Aries are a match made in the heavens. Though I don't care what she says, I'm wearing lipstick again. I look too washed out without it."

"Are you sure about this, Mom? After what happened with Vic Johnson?"

"I may have done the nasty between the sheets with him, but it was like eating Girl Scout cookies because, well, there they are, in your cupboard. Vic sure could kiss my socks off though."

Athena snorted a half cry, half laugh, filled with happiness and bewilderment and the sensation she'd never felt as close to her mother as she did this very moment.

"I guess I'll get the Mother of the Year award when Finn finds out," Lydia said.

"You want me to tell him and Dad?"

"Goodness, no. I'll do it. Where is Finn anyway?"

"Heading back to Mario with Branwell. Vivienne has three very territorial cats."

Finn had sent Athena a text at dawn during his taxi ride to the airport, quoting their favorite line from *Adventures of Huckleberry Finn*—"I reckon I got to light out for the Territory."

Love was *Territory* all right. A vast, unknown wilderness everyone knew was out there, but some never discovered. Or weren't brave enough to explore.

"All these happy endings in the Murphy family," Lydia said with a blissful sigh. "You'll have yours too, Athena."

"I'm not holding my breath."

"Any news about Thorne?"

"We're good friends again."

"Is that all? Friends?"

Lydia had bared her heart. This could be the start of a new relationship between them. Mother and daughter sharing their most intimate feelings and dreams. But deep inside, Athena knew it was a fantasy, like sitting around the kitchen table with the Brontë sisters. She and Lydia had lost their chance a long time ago. The story of her life.

"It's all good between us," she said. "I'm going back to San Francisco soon."

"But not to the Russian guy, I hope. Remember what I said about rubles."

"He's out of the picture." And she'd be out of town when Lydia got wind of the café scene with Sergei. "Should I get one of the agents at Laurel Realty to take care of your house?"

"Don't have to. Ricki and I will be back soon. She swears by yoga these days and wants to open a studio in town. I know of a vacant building not far from Thorne's café."

"Give her my love. And whatever you do, don't break her heart. You know how hard she takes it."

"Her heart's in good hands. Like the rest of her," she added with a raucous laugh.

"I'm so happy for you, Mom."

"Ricki's 'my heart's delight.' Guess where I first heard that expression?"

"You read it in a Hallmark greeting card?"

"No. From Thorne. I thought it was fluff and nonsense at the time, but not anymore."

"*My* Thorne? When?" *My* came out as a croak.

"Not long after the divorce. I had stopped by the house for something or other. He and I were watching you play in the snow with Branwell. Snot was dripping out of your nose from the cold, and you were in your rather unattractive boho-meets-bum stage."

"I saved a lot of money buying clothes from Suzie's Seconds."

"The point is, you looked like something the cat dragged in, but Thorne was gazing at you like you were a vision of loveliness. 'I love her so much,' he said. 'She's my heart's delight.'"

Athena shivered in the doorway of Thorne's apartment at the back of the café, waiting for him to answer the intercom and buzz her in. Flecks of snow danced in the arc of light from the bulb above her head. The bleak afternoon had drifted into an evening of blurry forms and smudged colors. A time of day, of year, to lull a person into aimlessness.

But not her. No siree. Her mind and senses were as focused as her purpose. She was about to rewrite her future—a future with Thorne. There didn't have to be any brooding or passionate scenes or even a happily ever after with marriage and kids. Just *together* ever after, through thick and thin, covering each other's backs, laughing over a funny book they'd read, bickering over stupid stuff. Being there for each other.

Thorne descended the stairs, shoving his shirt into his jeans, barefoot. As if his broad shoulders and muscular body weren't perfect enough, the man had beautiful feet. She steadied her shaking knees.

No shoes.

A shirt put on in haste.

Coming down instead of buzzing her in.

Stupid, stupid, stupid. What was she thinking, showing up unannounced? A woman was in his bed, waiting for him to start, or finish, what they had been doing. And why wouldn't he? He'd said there wasn't any other woman in his life. But that was before she'd reminded him she was returning to San Francisco. She'd made it clear her book and career were front and center.

But boy oh boy, he sure hadn't wasted any time.

"Sorry, I should have called first," she mumbled when he opened the door.

"I had to come down to let you in. The intercom and buzzer are out of whack."

"I can go if this isn't a good time for...uh...a visit." She calculated the distance to her car and how quickly she could sprint back to it. "Forget about it, Thorne. I'll call you tomorrow." *From the Mini Cooper. On my way to Cal-i-for-niy-ay.*

"Call me about what?"

"Odds and ends. This and that." She fumbled in her coat pocket for the car keys. Or had she put them in her handbag? Or left them in the ignition?

Holding her by the elbows, Thorne pulled her into the vestibule. "No one's here but me, Thena."

"Uh...'cause I thought. You know. If you—"

"No one's been here since we were Mr. Rochester and Jane Eyre. I'm alone."

A spray of lines around his eyes and the creases around

his mouth marked his face in the unforgiving light. The strong bones of his jaw and cheeks, though, would weather the indignities of age. And if getting old meant being more of who he was, a deeper, truer version of himself, she didn't want to miss one hour of it.

She rubbed a dot of blue ink on his stubbled chin. "Working on the café ledgers on a Saturday night? And I thought *my* life was dull."

"Never, in all the time I've known you, has your life been dull."

"Wait till you hear the latest. My mother called from Las Vegas and announced she and Ricki are soul mates and lovers. I'm still in shock."

His face broke into a wide grin. "Aha! So they are."

"You joked once about their argument being a lover's quarrel. How'd you know?"

"I didn't. Which is why I never mentioned my suspicions. But I'd get a feeling sometimes, seeing the way they looked for each other when one of them entered a room. The way they looked *at* each other."

"Because they've been best friends forever."

"This was different. Like they weren't... whole until the other person was there."

"I didn't have one stinking clue," Athena said. "There should be a big *M* stamped on my forehead for *Moron*."

"Don't be so hard on yourself. Besides your career, you have some pretty special talents. In a few short months, you played matchmaker, saved a marriage, and turned waitressing into an art form." He brushed snow off her shoulders. "Everybody will miss you when you go."

"Yeah. About that." Athena pulled off her woolen hat and shook her curls loose. "Can we go upstairs and talk?"

Thorne took her hand wordlessly, and they climbed the

stairs to his apartment. It was as spare and uninviting as she remembered, the only signs of habitation being a table littered with papers, a laptop, and the Montblanc fountain pen she'd given him, and an armchair filled with unfolded laundry.

He neatly stacked the papers, locked them in a file box, and plumped a few of the sofa pillows. The sofa on which Jane Eyre and Mr. Rochester had tossed away corset and cravat, along with their inhibitions. The door to the bedroom where they'd spent their memorable night was closed, tempting her to fling it open, fling off her clothes, fling herself onto Thorne, and...

"Did you mean it, Thorne? Did you mean what you said yesterday?"

"When I asked you to stay?"

"When you asked to give us another chance." In case he had forgotten that essential detail.

"I meant every word." He brushed his thick hair back with both hands, staring blankly at the floor as if into a dark, bottomless well. "But I get it, Thena. I get that you have an independent life and a great career. Dammit, I'm proud of you for it. Go back to San Francisco. But for God's sake, stay in my life. I didn't realize how much I missed you until we were together nearly every day again. Let's find a way to make it work this time."

She removed her coat and sat as carefully on the sofa as if she were a fragile china cup. "Okay, here's the deal, Thorne. My career's in the toilet. I'm writing a bogus book in a last-ditch attempt to save my job. Which, as it turns out, isn't *that* great. Meanwhile, everyone under the sun is stupid in love, Zoe gets cuter by the day while my ovaries get older by the minute, and you've got this whole baker–barista–community advocate–supportive ex-boyfriend thing going on and...and..."

She gulped down a sob. She was *not* going to cry. She'd bawled her eyes out in Seattle, gotten all puffy and out of control, and had vowed never, ever to make a fool of herself again. "Got a handkerchief? Or tissue?"

He took a handkerchief from his pocket and handed it to her. "Let's back up a little. Why are you saying your career isn't fulfilling? I thought you loved teaching."

"I adore it. But academia is another rat race. Only the rats wear bolo ties and knockoff Chanel suits."

"And you called them on it."

She dabbed her eyes with the handkerchief. "I let a few zingers fly."

"Uh-oh," he said, sitting down next to her. "Thena uncensored."

"Thena banished to the academic doghouse. Uncovering C. L. Garland's identity was going to bail me out." She slumped against him with the full weight of her defeat. "But you're right. Who cares about a fake biography? My book will be ignored by all and sundry, including Garland herself, and the chair will tell me to take a hike. I can't sue for tenure because they'll counter that I'm *difficult*. Besides, I won't have the time. I'll be too busy looking for another position. From my car I'll be living in. With awful reference letters."

"And if you *had* discovered who Garland was?"

"*I'd* be calling the shots."

"So much at stake. You should have told me."

"The situation was humiliating. Anyway, there's nothing *you* could have done."

He gently brushed loose curls from her forehead. "I'm wondering... what do you want now?"

"The same as you. A way to make it work between us." She twined her fingers in his. "I love my students. I could never give up teaching. But I don't have to be at Wyatt College.

Southern Illinois College will do just fine. Or I'll teach at another California school. You can open a café anywhere. Though As You Like It Café would be hard to duplicate."

"So would my loyal customers. And the cost of living is more affordable here."

"I thought you made tons of money as a lawyer? And as heir to the Kent estate?"

"I sank a lot into my business. And I've had...other expenses. The café does okay. But it's never been about the money."

"You *have* found your calling this time around."

"All I want is for us to get *each other* right this time around. But that can't happen until you know the truth." He slowly released his hand from hers. "I have something to tell you, Thena. Something I should have told you a long time ago."

Her heartbeat quickened. "You're already married and are hiding a madwoman in the attic like Mr. Rochester," she joked, trying to defuse her anxiety.

And failed miserably. His crumpled face sent a chill to her marrow.

"It's about Robin," he said through pale lips.

He had lied. They *were* a couple. Or they had broken up but couldn't bear to be apart. Or—

"Robin is my half brother, Thena. My father's son by Jessica, the woman he loved."

Giddy with relief, she repeated a silly phrase in her head. *Tony is a she, Robin is a he.*

"Robin is the reason I went to Albuquerque. I'm his legal guardian. And while he's not a *madwoman*, he faces many challenges."

"Like what?"

"He suffers from paranoid schizophrenia and will require medical intervention the rest of his life."

"How sad. Oh, I am sorry, Thorne."

"He had wandered from the group home, and I helped search for him. Luckily, he came through the ordeal safely."

"This is why you've been proactive about a mental health clinic in the community."

"One reason, besides supporting vets and military personnel at the Air Force base. And why I want to buy a house with separate living quarters. I would like him to live with me but have a measure of independence. And hopefully, once my mother knows everything, she will accept him into our family." Thorne raised his head and met her eyes with a somber gaze. "One day. Just one day and everything would have turned out differently."

"I don't understand."

"The day before you were to visit me in Seattle, I received a letter from Jessica's lawyer, informing me she had died, her son, Robin, was my half brother, and that she had designated me his legal guardian."

"The day before," Athena whispered.

"I was stunned, to say the least. She might have introduced us or discussed his guardianship with me. I suppose she was honoring my request to have no contact after my father died. But understood, too, that I could never abandon my troubled brother. And I couldn't. Any more than I could ask you, or any woman, to assume the emotional and financial responsibilities his care entails."

"Why not? Marriage is for better or for worse, remember?"

"And the genetic issue? Could you have handled that too?"

"Schizophrenia is inheritable?"

"The risk percentage rises for first-degree relatives. And the disorder most likely came from the Kent side, not Jessica's. As far as Robin knows, no one in his mother's family had any mental issues. But a few of my father's relatives spent their lives in and out of hospitals and institutions. I never met them. And it wasn't something he liked to talk about."

"Still...you determined our future on a risk percentage? Without sharing it with me and letting *me* decide?"

"At the time, everything had come crashing down. Learning of Robin's condition in the letter, coming to grips with the demands of his guardianship. The chance, however slim, we wouldn't have the children you always imagined."

"I did too much imagining in our relationship. But I was never so shallow or selfish that I wouldn't share your responsibilities," she admonished him.

"But don't you see? I wanted you to fly free, to succeed, to become everything you wanted to be. To live your life to the fullest." He clasped her hands again, his soulful eyes boring into hers. "Leaving you in Seattle, letting you go, was the hardest thing I've ever done."

"I wish you'd told me then, Thorne."

"I was in a bad place. Overwhelmed with medical information and my new obligations. Hurting you then and there felt like my only option at the time. And I think you'll agree we needed to get to this point first. Come full circle and be best friends again."

"Older and wiser friends."

"Wiser, meaning willing to compromise?"

She nodded. "And support each other, figure out this messy, wonderful world together."

"About children, I—"

"We adopt. Or take our chances. Or do neither. The point is, *you're* my family, Thorne."

"I can't tell you how much this means to me, Thena. To hear you say we're in this together. I was going to tell you about Robin after the party yesterday but..." He smiled fondly. "You had to get all *realistic* on me."

"Look at you. Getting all *romantic* on me."

To be wary and weary of imagination and heroes, only to discover they were alive and well, residing in the heart and soul of the one man who saw her as a heroine, who believed in her and had a vision of her life.

Athena held his face in her hands. "You called me your heart's delight once. Am I?"

"My one and only."

They walked to the bedroom, hand in hand. There was no tearing off buttons, no desperate hunger or gasping for air. Thena and Thorne made love slowly, sweetly, and oh so familiarly. They made love like they had all the time in the world.

Because they did.

The first thing Athena did Sunday morning was open the venetian blinds in Thorne's apartment to let the brilliant sunshine flood the rooms with light.

The first thing, not counting sex in the shower.

She giggled as she waited in the kitchen for the coffee to brew. *Thorny* was as *horny in the morny* as ever, and she had the wobbly legs and goofy grin to prove it. Between making love, talking, and more making love, they'd managed only a few hours' sleep—and she never felt more alive to the beauty of an azure sky and a landscape freshened with new snow. Never more thankful her soul had found its mate. She and Thorne were on the same page about everything that mattered.

He whistled an opera tune as he shaved in the bathroom. This time around, she'd try to stay awake while sopranos and tenors bored her to sleep. Or buy a good set of earplugs.

Thorne never added cream to his coffee, so she stirred

an extra teaspoon of sugar in her mug to cut the bitterness. Naturally, getting reacquainted with each other's routines and quirks would take a little time. Like them both preferring to sleep on the left side of the bed. And his habit of clearing his nasal passages the minute he woke up. Which was either annoying or endearing, depending on how she chose to look at it. As endearing, she hoped, as her tendency to hog all the blankets.

His laptop was on the table in the living room where he'd left it last night. As she sipped coffee, she scribbled phrases on a notepad for the resignation letter she was going to email Dr. Davenport. Not having to think any longer about the chair, or Corinne Carew, or C. L. Garland, was as liberating as releasing her body from a whalebone corset. Writing the biography, fake or otherwise, *was* beneath her. And why on earth would she spend another day among people who had been so eager to discard her?

She and Thorne had agreed that a long-distance relationship was out of the question. She would exhaust all job opportunities within an hour's drive of Laurel, including the position at Southern Illinois College. If she came up empty, he would buy another café in whatever city she got a tenure-track post in.

Athena wrote, *Stick this job up your patootie* and quickly crossed it out. However tempted she was to send it to Dr. Davenport, she was determined to be as dignified on the way out as... as she probably should have been all along. As Corinne was to everybody but her. For all her faults, Corinne did have enviable diplomacy skills. She'd negotiated herself right into new computer equipment and an office with a window. A begrudging admission, but there it was. And the next time Athena was on the verge of speaking her mind, she'd remind herself of Emily Dickinson's dictum—"Tell all the truth but tell it slant."

She opened the laptop to compose a rough draft of the resignation letter. The password setup was the same, but maybe Thorne would consider changing the sonnet number to Shakespeare's fifteenth. " 'When I consider everything that grows / Holds in perfection but a little moment,' " she recited softly.

Instead of the Excel spreadsheet she expected, a Word document with track changes appeared on the screen. For a split second, she thought one of her documents had somehow been transferred to his laptop.

Except she never wrote any papers on Emma Bovary.

And Gustave Flaubert never had Emma compare the thrill of ballroom dancing to fellatio.

She read a reviewing pane on the first page more closely. *Commented [TK1]: Haven't thought of a witty title yet. Maybe a play on the word ovary?*

No. Impossible. This was some kind of mistake. Or a joke between Thorne and Quentin.

Closing the document, Athena clicked on the My Documents icon.

Reading the list of titles was like staring at a grisly accident. She didn't want to look, but she couldn't tear her eyes away:

"David Copafeel"

"Prude and Prurience"

"Scarlet Fetters"

"Sins and Sin's Ability"

"The Lust of the Mohicans"

There they were, along with all the other titles in the Lit-Wit series.

And Thorne Kent was the author.

Thorne was C. L. Garland.

The flow of water from the bathroom sink sounded like

rapids. The sunlight splashing the table blinded her. Nausea rose in her stomach as the smells of coffee, rotting bananas, and the ratty carpet assaulted her nose.

All this time, as she had agonized and strategized over the problem of Garland's identity, searching the Murphy home, posing as a television producer, making a pest of herself to the café patrons, getting hit on the head with a sex toy, she—he—was right in front of her.

As he was now, wearing nothing but a towel and an expression both guilty and unapologetic.

Two-faced jerk that he was.

"C. L. Garland, *c'est moi*," Thorne said, paraphrasing Flaubert's announcement that he and his heroine were one and the same—"Madame Bovary, *c'est moi*."

"Don't you dare make any clever jokes. Don't you dare." Athena slammed the laptop shut and pointed with a shaking finger to the file box where he'd locked the papers last night. "Manuscripts?"

"And quarterly royalty statements and contracts with my agent and publisher. Writing is a business like anything else."

"Well, haven't you been the busy bee? No wonder you look like death on toast most of the time."

He folded his arms across his bare chest. Wet, his hair had lost its golden luster. His skin was chalk white in the glaring light. "All right, Thena. Let's have it out, here and now."

"I don't know where to begin." She wanted to get up from the chair, to stand and face him down, but her bones were as heavy as lead weights. "I've spent the last four months of my life stressing out and spinning my wheels. And they're still spinning."

"Maybe not in the direction you intended. But you did write a book."

For one blindingly mad minute, she wanted to hurl something at him, Lydia-style. The coffee in the mug was hot, so she couldn't throw that. And tossing a pillow would be ridiculous. She picked up the Montblanc pen but dropped it as if it burned. *Keep calm and keep your dignity*, she reminded herself.

It's all you've got left.

Thorne took a pair of briefs, T-shirt, and pants from the pile of laundry on the armchair and put them on. "You came close to figuring it out when you suggested Garland was male. That the writer was turning the pseudonym convention on its head by assuming a female identity. From there, you might have connected the dots that Garland wasn't from Laurel either."

Came close. Connected the dots. Like this was a guessing game they'd been playing.

"I *did* make the connection. And when I suggested you were Garland, you were offended. Told me I was out of my mind. Did you even ask the bank manager or...or..."

"The Chamber of Commerce. No. I lied in both instances to deflect suspicion."

His words came back to mock her. *We always were honest with each other.*

And her own. *Thorne was Thorne, through and through.*

Athena rose slowly, gripping the edge of the table. "I apologized to you, you jerk. You deceitful, lying—"

He held out both hands as if to stop the torrent of her wrath. "Let me explain."

"Oh, you've got a lot of explaining to do. Let's start with why you told the press Garland was from my hometown."

"I didn't. I hadn't even considered giving her a background. But Quentin got drunk with a journalist buddy one night and, as a lark, said he had it on good authority that

Garland hailed from here, and the story took off. I was pissed at him at first, but then I realized this town was the perfect cover."

Laurel, Illinois, where gossip about midlife crises, secret babies, and church candlesticks was more thrilling than a bestselling author's secret identity.

"When I started writing, I never imagined the series would be successful," he said. "Or that you, of all people, would be hot on Garland's trail."

"Or that you, of all people, Mr. Highbrow Snob, would write...what did Ian call it? *Mind candy*?" She couldn't stop a hysterical hiccup from escaping. "And you've been laughing all the way to the bank, like he said too, haven't you?"

"The money was a welcome bonus. I won't deny it."

"Because you're a Kent, through and through. As deceptive as your cheating father. And your corrupt namesake. *That's* the hereditary risk percentage you should be worried about."

Thorne clenched his jaw, his eyes fiery with anger. The same eyes she'd looked into all night and found everything she wanted.

"The way I see it," Athena went on, "you sacrificed me again, kept me in the dark, so you could keep making money. 'Garland's mystique generates sales' were Quentin's exact words."

Thorne lifted his chin with a look of defiance. "Every red cent I've earned supports Robin and is put away in a trust in case anything happens to me."

"How noble of you." It was. But still. "How long has Quentin known you were Garland?"

"Since the beginning. And about Robin. I've needed his emotional support. A good friend to count on."

She flinched as if she'd stubbed her toe. It should have been *her* he counted on.

"Boo-hoo. Poor, friendless Thorne." A childish taunt, but hell if she'd give him one more ounce of sympathy in this life. "When I confessed to you last night that my career was at stake, you said nothing. Not one word."

"It wasn't the right time. In any case, we had decided to start over. You were going to end the Garland project and look for another job. The issue was moot."

"Moot!" she said too shrilly. "So glib with the lawyer words, aren't you? For all I know, you used your smooth legal lingo last night to get laid. And get me off Garland's track in the bargain. You had no intention of giving us another chance but, boy, if you didn't put on a damn good show beneath the sheets. Like in Seattle."

"For all *I* know," he said in a laser-sharp voice, "you only want to get back together because your career is a failure and you're getting older. Frankly, I don't want to be anybody's backup plan. Or sperm donor."

She looked wildly around the room, trying to remember what she'd done with her coat. That's right. It was on the sofa. She shoved her arms into it and felt for her hat in the pockets. Where did she put her damn hat? Screw it. It was warmer in California. She didn't need it. She didn't need anything. Once she opened the door and walked down to her car and turned the key in the ignition, she'd be on her way. Her merry, merry way.

"Thena, wait. Please. I didn't mean it. It's just that you make me so mad."

Athena looked over her shoulder, her hand on the door-knob. Thorne stood in the middle of a ray of sunshine, his hands outstretched, a freeze-frame of every tragic figure he'd ever played on stage. "What does *C. L.* stand for anyway? *Cad* and *liar*?"

"I told you the day we met in the park. *Crataegus laevigata*. It's the botanical name for the hawthorn tree."

The tree beneath which he'd proposed to her, whose flowered branches had formed the garland he'd fashioned for her head.

CHAPTER EIGHTEEN

Die without me if you will. Live for me if you dare.

—CHARLOTTE BRONTË, *SHIRLEY, A TALE*

Athena aligned the pair of Miss Marple oxfords next to the row of shoes in her mother's closet—then grabbed them again and tossed them into her suitcase. They might come in handy for the only other jobs left to her—bookseller or librarian. Bookstores flourished in San Francisco, and she felt an almost perverse delight in the idea of pursuing Lydia's original profession. After all, she was her mother's daughter. Short-tempered, hard to please, romantically clueless for a good part of her adult life.

She tidied the stack of the LitWit series books, along with her well-worn copy of *Wuthering Heights*, on the nightstand and zipped the suitcase shut. She'd gotten everything wrong from the beginning. Confident she'd uncover Garland's identity and be on her way before winter. Certain she could work in Thorne's café and maintain the appropriate emotional distance. The only possible chance she had to salvage her career now was if Corinne Carew fell off her broomstick, deleting Emily Dickinson from her brain, and Dr. Davenport fell out of favor with the dean, deleting himself from the chair.

As for the appropriate emotional distance between her and Thorne, half a continent wasn't far enough.

Putting on her coat, she glanced at the clock. Sunday traffic should be light. If she left right away, she'd be across Missouri before dark. Propping her suitcase against the wall near the front door, she went to the kitchen and gave it one final inspection. Dishes, glasses, and neatly folded towels were in the cupboards. The sink and stovetop gleamed. The counters were clear, the floors swept. The satchel with her laptop was on the table, temptingly close to the garbage can. But she was done with dramatic gestures. It would take less than five minutes to delete the files for *Hiding in Plain Sight*, a task she'd save until she was in a motel somewhere on Highway 70.

"The hell with Garland, screw the book, start a new fricking life," Athena muttered.

But she wasn't done with cursing the man who'd been in plain sight all this time. Who'd let her believe he wouldn't help her because his heart was still bruised from her refusal to marry him.

"Damn you, Thorne. Damn you to hell."

Deceptive, money-grubbing, but worst of all, completely wrong about her.

"*Career backup? Sperm donor?* Don't flatter yourself, a-hole," she said, spritzing the cactus on the windowsill with water.

As for her dumb-as-a-rock idea that they were soul mates—she'd stepped into cow flop again, like the day in the pasture when she imagined she was Emily Brontë. She wasn't a Brontë sister or heroine, and furthermore, she didn't want to be. And she didn't want a Brontë hero either.

Taking one last look around to make sure the stainless steel furniture was exactly as Lydia had positioned it in the living room, Athena opened the front door—and slammed it shut again. She dropped the satchel next to the suitcase and closed her eyes as Thorne knocked.

"Come on, Thena. Let me in. We've got to talk."

Tiny sparks jumped behind her eyelids. "The hell we do."

"Then *I'll* talk."

"You've got more cheap shots up your sleeve?"

"I didn't mean what I said. Not a single word."

"A *moot* point. Get it?"

"Yeah. Moot."

"Good. Because you haven't gotten anything else right, dipshit."

"That makes two of us."

She reopened her eyes, blinking back anger. *Keep calm and... and...*

"I'm not leaving until you listen to what I have to say, Thena."

"Stay out there all night. See if I care."

"If I start performing an aria, Lydia's neighbors will have a lot to gossip about."

"Sing away."

And he did. In Italian, no less. Triple forte.

Athena pulled the door open. "You've got exactly three minutes."

"How about ten?"

"Will you be alive that long?"

The man looked like roadkill. Hair sticking up in every direction as if he'd driven with his head out the window, circles under his eyes, and a blotch on his T-shirt that was either coffee or a bodily fluid.

"Where the hell's your coat?" she asked.

"I forgot it," he said through chattering teeth. "Can I come in?"

She pointed to the suitcase and satchel. "I'm on my way out."

"You didn't waste any time."

"I don't have any to spare. Nor do you." She tapped her watch as she stepped aside to let him in. "Clock's ticking."

Thorne followed her to the living room, thick manila envelopes tucked under his arm. They stood across from each other like characters in a Samuel Beckett play, Lydia's stark furniture the perfect props. They'd reached the endgame. Thena and Thorne were out of options. A curious sensation overtook Athena. She felt stripped of emotion, oddly calm, like the aftermath of a storm.

"Me too," he said softly.

Someday, somewhere, she'd decide to paint a wall yellow instead of green or she'd ponder the beauty of iambic pentameter—and somewhere, somehow, Thorne would think, *Yellow, yes.* Or, *"If music be the food of love, play on."*

"Get to the point," she said. "If you have one."

"When you say the worst thing to someone, there's no taking it back. But I would if I could, Thena."

"I won't deny I've had my desperate moments as an *old failure*," she said, throwing his insult back at him. "But I would never arrange your life to suit my purposes or solve my problems."

"I fought dirty. I went for the jugular. The truth is, you're the most honest, independent person I know. Your strength and spirit are what I've always loved about you." A wan smile flickered across his mouth. "You said I was your family, and I repaid you with cruel words. I am sorry."

They were on the same page, Athena-wise. But Thorne-wise?

"The truth?" she said. "You denied you were Garland—twice—and I believed you. How did I miss the signs you were bullshitting me?"

"I used everything I learned in acting to hide the telltale gestures of a liar."

"Congratulations. You should apply for an Actors' Equity card."

His body drooped, his smile vanished. "I had to lie. There was a lot at stake."

"More than my career?"

"To be fair, you didn't tell me the whole story until last night."

"And if I had?"

"We would have been close enough to tell each other the truth, wouldn't we? It works both ways. But we weren't, so it's pointless to speculate what I might have done."

She held on to the frame of a chair, winding her fingers around the cold metal. "I never dreamed you were capable of such deception. Thorne Kent always took a stand for his principles. You're going to tell your mother everything because, as you said, she's been lied to enough. But what about your principles toward me? Respecting me enough to tell me the truth?"

"I already explained why I didn't tell you about Robin."

"So I could fly free, blah, blah, blah. Noted. What about Garland?"

"I didn't tell you I was Garland because... Well, for one thing, you confide in Finn about everything, and I couldn't risk him divulging it. I'd already been burned by Quentin talking to his journalist friend."

"Since when did you get so good at keeping secrets?"

"Since I learned to hide my father's double life."

"And the other reason you didn't tell me?"

"I wanted to spare you having to choose between your career or us. Relive our painful history all over again." Thorne handed the manila envelopes to her. "Here. Everything you need to know about C. L. Garland, on flash drives and hard copy, is inside. Letters to editors, notes, and rough drafts of the novellas. Write your book, Thena. The authentic version. Save your career with my blessing. And if the department chair doesn't cooperate, tell him I won't make any generous contributions to the college's annual fund drive."

"What's the catch?" Because she didn't believe in heroes anymore.

"There isn't any."

"But there isn't anything in it for you. That's not *the Kent way*."

"Rest is what's in it for me. I'm tired of the whole damn enterprise. Getting up at a god-awful hour to write and edit, taking care of publishing business on free afternoons, coming up with yet another way to describe sex. Which is harder than you'd think. If I had known how arduous it would be, I never would have started."

The word *sex* hung in the air between them like his scent that a shower hadn't completely washed away.

"You realize exposing your identity will probably end your best-seller run," she said.

"If sales flatline, I'll sell the café and resume law to support Robin. And while there isn't a *catch*, I do have one caveat."

"Of course you do," she said drily.

His eyes flashed. "Put aside your own feelings for a minute, will you, Thena? There are other people besides yourself involved. People I want to safeguard from public view."

His mother and brother. Thorne was all that stood between them and the pitiless world.

"There is no privacy these days," he said. "None whatsoever. I don't want the press glomming on to 'the betrayed wife,' 'the schizophrenic half brother.' It's been my worst nightmare. Ironically, it would probably send sales through the roof. But I need you to promise you will obstruct any probing into my family. Lie if you have to. Say I don't have one so no one comes poking their nose into my life and theirs."

"I promise. Yes. Anything to protect them."

Heroes in literature appeared on horseback and in drawing rooms, dressed in capes and cravats. Heroes in real life appeared on doorsteps wearing stained T-shirts, beneath which beat noble hearts.

"I'll say you're a garden-variety lawyer, raised in the Midwest, who only wanted filthy lucre and his fifteen minutes of fame," Athena said.

"I'll prepare my mother before your book hits the stores. Finding out I wrote erotica will be another bitter pill for her to swallow."

"Whatever made you do it anyway? I thought baking and running a café fulfilled your creative needs."

"I started writing after my father passed away. It was like something died and was born in me at the same time. I thought I'd be lucky if I could sell the novellas myself as e-books, but my agent found an interested publisher. Within a year, I signed a contract for three volumes. By the next year, C. L. Garland was on best-seller lists. Getting an agent, getting published—it all happened so fast. And I owe it all to you."

"Me? What did I have to do with your success?"

Thorne smiled sheepishly. "You were my muse. Wit and intelligence in one sexy package."

"That explains all the morning sex scenes." If she didn't crack a joke, she'd crack herself open and spill her heart into his hands. "And you had no qualms about writing *schlock*, as you called it?"

"Not at all. Writing about the novels and characters we loved was a way to stay connected to you and our dream of an academic, literary life. And when I'd hear Phyllis and Theresa whispering about the books, I was gratified by their enjoyment."

"Your books brought pleasure to a lot of people, including me," she said with a sly smile.

"I was a little hurt by your criticism of the pace and wit of 'Sins and Sin's Ability,' " he said with an injured expression.

"Don't sweat it. The orgy scene makes up for its technical deficiencies. I am curious though—why didn't you write a version of *Wuthering Heights*?"

"It was too dear to you for me to spoof. And according to you, I've never gotten Heathcliff right."

"For which I am eternally grateful." His pensive face and the sadness in his eyes sent a throb deep into her heart, her very bones. "Don't ever be anyone but Thorne."

"I never have been. Especially not in Seattle. That was no show, Thena. If I'm guilty of anything, it's of indulging one last night of passion because I knew it would be our last. That I would have to settle again for not being with you. But seeing you everywhere."

"For what is not connected with her to me? And what does not recall her?" Heathcliff asked at the end of *Wuthering Heights*. Before he joined Catherine's ghost on the moors, he saw her "in every cloud, in every tree." If Athena needed a rationale for having wanted a Heathcliff, Thorne had just given her one.

He pointed to the manila envelopes she was holding. "I've arranged the letters by date to make it easier to compile your notes for the book. And the flash drives have—"

"Thorne."

"What?"

Athena held out the envelopes. "Take them back. All of them."

"But your book. Not only will it guarantee tenure, it may become the best seller you hoped for."

Everything she'd returned to Laurel for was at her fingertips. Mission complete. Failure averted. Goal accomplished.

Except she'd exchanged her goal for a better, loftier one.

Just like a heroine.

"No worries. I'm ditching the project," she said. "And career-wise, I have other options. When you decide the time is right to tell your mother everything, get in touch. Whatever I'm doing, wherever I am, I'll fly in and offer moral support."

He walked to her with a determined stride, shaking his head, a scowl on his face.

"Hell, Thorne, if you don't want me to see your mother, I won't."

To her amazement, he scooped her up in his arms and held her close to his chest. "What's all this talk about getting in touch and flying in?" he growled. "You're not going anywhere."

"I'm not?"

"Unless it's to my apartment. Or we can make love right here or in one of the bedrooms. Your choice."

"Your place. Your bed."

Without another word, Thorne carried Athena through the living room, out the door, and into the serene beauty of the December dusk to his car.

What the hell had she been thinking? Damn straight she wanted a hero.

And she'd found him.

Athena brushed the snow off her coat and with a hearty laugh hung it on the rack in As You Like It Café. Thorne had named Friday's sandwich special on the chalkboard *All's Well That*

Ends Well, one of his favorite Shakespeare plays. A lofty name for a simple egg salad sandwich with a dash of horseradish and minced red onion. But then, he hadn't had enough time to come up with a more complex recipe, not while he and Thena had been romping and rollicking the night away till all was well indeed.

"Where've you been, Athena?" Joe asked. "You're nearly two hours late."

"Thorne's been running around like a chicken without its head," Theresa said. "All week, in fact."

The week they'd been romping and rollicking.

"Yesterday he brought me coffee instead of iced tea, and today he gave me two pieces of burned toast instead of a scone," Phyllis said. "If he weren't so damn good-looking, I'd give him a what-for."

"You give him *anything*, even a compliment on his looks, I'll give *you* a what-for," Dan said.

"Ooh, listen to the tough guy." Phyllis pinched his cheek. "Don't worry. He doesn't ring my bells the way you do, Dan-o-mite."

"You ready to serve us yet, Athena?" a bachelor farmer called out.

"I could dig one of those egg salad sandwiches," one of the Garden Club members said. "Get it? *Dig*?"

"We thought you'd run off to Cleveland to bring Eugene back, Athena," another bachelor farmer joked.

"Gee whiz, guys. Cut me a break," she said. "I had a bunch of phone calls."

She'd spent an hour talking to the English Department chair about the position at Southern Illinois College. Five minutes into the conversation, *Dr. Marsden* became *Amy*. A half hour later, they were laughing themselves silly over Sergei. Amy had been in the café the day Athena scared

Sergei out of her life. It turned out the beautiful professor had dated her own share of "what was I thinking" men. She also expressed admiration for Athena's improvisational skills, since every day in her job she was "making it up as I go along."

By the time the call was over, Athena had secured an interview with the dean. "Pro forma," Amy assured her. "As far as I'm concerned, we need an outlaw around here." They'd even brainstormed topics for the book she'd write for tenure, a fresh take on the Brontë family and their literary legacy. Athena was particularly excited by the prospect of forming a theater group to write and perform plays based on climactic scenes in classic literature. Kind of like the LitWit series, without the naughty bits.

She had convinced Thorne to continue writing the series, with a promise to help him come up with more ways to describe sex. The mystery of C. L. Garland's identity—and the series's healthy sales—would remain intact. And while he wasn't ready to break the news to his mother about his nom de plume, Thorne planned to take Athena with him to Florida at Christmas, to tell his mother about Graham, Jessica, and Robin.

She paused before going into the kitchen to get her apron and notepad and surveyed the dining room. The café regulars were her new family, as wacky and wonderful as the one she'd been born into, the café her second home. Since Charles was moving in with Vivienne, the Murphy house would be perfect for her, Thorne, and Robin, who'd decided to move to Laurel. Thorne enthusiastically agreed with her idea to rebuild the greenhouse as a small cottage for his brother—and as enthusiastically rejected her suggestion they hire Karl. With Hoglund Construction bidding on the mental health clinic project, he reasoned, Karl might not be available anyway.

Athena swung open the kitchen door. Thorne stood at the counter, his fingers caressing the dough as they'd caressed her all night long. "Hey, you," she said softly.

He looked up at her with a warm smile. "Hey, you too."

"Everyone's complaining you've been distracted and messing up orders all week."

"My head's in the clouds. I haven't come down to earth yet. Where've you been?"

"My phone call with the chair lasted longer than I expected."

"Good news?"

"Awesome news. And then my dad and Finn called, one after the other. Lydia finally told them about her and Ricki. Keeping my mouth shut for six days has been torture."

"It was her, not me!" Charles had rejoiced. His one regret was that Lydia hadn't realized she was a lesbian sooner, sparing him years of feeling inadequate. "After you and Finn were born, of course." Finn's call was cut short by his hysterical laughter and Mario's request that he please stop jumping up and down like a kangaroo.

"Finn and Mario are taking over the lease on my apartment," Athena said. "It's bigger than theirs, plus they want to make a fresh start in a new place."

"One less loose end to worry about. What about your furniture and books?"

"They said they'll put everything in storage. We can drive a U-Haul back with my stuff after their wedding."

"Sounds like a plan," he said. "Ready to break the news about us to the café crowd?"

"Not yet. I want to have us all to ourselves a little longer."

"I got another 'Congrats, man' text from Quentin. Maybe we shouldn't have told him yet either."

She laughed. "And I got one saying he's glad he's not 'stuck in the middle' anymore. And that he was sorry."

"For what?"

"For saying Garland was from Laurel. His excuse was that he thought the series was something *I* would write, not you."

"He did, did he?"

"And he's convinced you decided to buy Ricki's Café on the spot because you had a subconscious desire to be part of my world."

"I did, did I?"

"Methinks you did. Because I've had a desire to be part of *your* world."

Thorne pulled a tray of hot cross buns from the oven "So, no... second thoughts?" he asked in a low voice.

"Not even a first thought. I practically did backflips telling Dr. Davenport I was pursuing *other avenues of employment.*"

Her formal resignation letter bore no resemblance to the one she had wanted to write to him and Corinne:

Because I cannot abide you both—
I'm sending my farewell—
The future holds but joy for me—
For you a taste of hell

If her revenge scheme with Elise worked out. Trusty, surprisingly devious Elise, who'd started leaving brochures from "concerned colleagues" about halitosis, smelly feet, and other hygiene offenses in Corinne's office mailbox. Professor Perfect, she was happy to report, was obsessively sniffing her armpits and brushing her shoulders for imaginary dandruff. As for Dr. Davenport, Elise had texted Athena a photo of his irate wife marching toward his office, with the caption *Nowhere to hide.*

"I'm almost afraid to ask what your mischievous smile means, Thena."

"Just thinking how everything turned out differently than I expected."

"To your satisfaction, I hope, milady."

"And then some, milord."

His face, his handsome, Thorne-est face, beamed. "Come closer, you saucy wench."

Athena cocked her head, one hand on her hip. "Why should I?"

"I have something for you."

"A new apron? Or your secret recipe for the flakiest croissants this side of France?"

He leaned forward, arms outstretched. Flecks of flour dotted his hair. There was nothing, simply nothing, sexier than a man who loved to bake. "Are you going to get over here, or do I have to pick you up and prop you on this counter?"

In one jump, she leaped onto it and put her face close to his. "Okay, Boss Man, whatcha got for me?"

He handed her a hot cross bun. "Eat."

She sank her teeth into the sweet, buttery pastry, moaning with every bite. "I'm already full," she said after she'd eaten half.

"Keep going."

She took another bite and yelped. "Ow! There's something in here."

"Oh, there is, is there?"

Athena split the bun apart and a ring fell into her lap. A two-carat cushion-cut diamond in an antique pavé setting on a white gold band. The engagement ring Thorne had given her beneath the hawthorn tree.

"You told me to stick it where the moon don't shine," he said, putting it on her finger. "I had other ideas."

The diamond glittered through her tears, through the years, to the here and now. To who they were and who they would become, together, always Thena and Thorne.

"I love you, Thena. You are my heart's delight."

"I love you, Thorne."

"I cannot live without my life! I cannot live without my soul!"

Thanks to Emily Brontë, she'd gotten it right the first—and last—time.

ACKNOWLEDGMENTS

The best journeys are the ones we share with kindred spirits. My deepest gratitude to these fellow travelers on the most thrilling adventure of all—imagination.

Erin Niumata and Rachel Ekstrom, my kind and inspiring agents at Folio Literary Management, for *The Call* from Inverness, Scotland, where the journey began, and for believing in me, making me laugh and, on occasion, babble incoherently.

Alex Logan, my wise and discerning editor at Grand Central Publishing/Forever, for asking all the right questions to bring the novel to the next level (and the next), and for exchanging bird stories in the wee hours. Yes, that was a turkey.

Maggie Auffarth, Julia Fink, Sarah Gray, Kelley Kassidy, Kayla Stansbury, and Justine Winans, Folio Literary Management readers, for *getting* the manuscript and helping me get it right. I hope I did.

The Grand Central Publishing/Forever team for their creative vision and dedication: Stacey Reid, production editor; Alayna Johnson, copy editor; Jodi Rosoff, publicist; and Daniela Medina, art director. A special thanks to cover artist Sarah Congdon for capturing the spirit of the story—and for the adorable pug.

Judy Roth, my first reader, for insight, gentle persuasion, and for appreciating jokes about dangling participles.

Friends, readers, and fellow Brontë devotees for support and the warmth of community.

Bob, Bob Jr., and Eddie, my compass, my True North, for, well, everything. Everywhere and forever.

Emily Brontë, fearless wanderer of the moors, my muse. No coward soul is yours.

ABOUT THE AUTHOR

Annie Sereno holds a BA in Anthropology from the University of Pennsylvania as well as master's degrees in Library Science and British and American Literature. She was privileged to serve the libraries of Harvard University and The National Geographic Society, among others. When she's not expressing her imagination with pen and paintbrush, Annie gardens, swims, and haunts art museums. In possession of a well-worn passport and memories of all the places she's called home, she shares her life with her husband and two sons. Mildly (okay, seriously) obsessed with birds, Celtic music, and all things Australian, she believes there is no such thing as a former librarian, no time to read, or too many shoes. She currently lives with her family in New Jersey.

Book your next trip to a charming small town—and fall in love—with one of these swoony Forever contemporary romances!!

THIRD TIME'S THE CHARM
by Annie Sereno

College professor Athena Murphy needs to make a big move to keep her job. Her plan: unveil the identity of an anonymous author living in her hometown. And while everyone at the local café is eager to help, no one has an answer. Including the owner, her exasperating ex-boyfriend whom she'd rather not see ever again. After all, they ended their relationship not just once but twice. There's no denying they still have chemistry. So it's going to be a long, hot summer…unless the third time really is the charm.

SEA GLASS SUMMER
by Miranda Liasson

After Kit Blakemore's husband died, she was in a haze of grief. Now she wants to live again and give their son the kind of unforgettable seaside summer she'd had growing up. When her husband's best friend returns to town, she doesn't expect her numb heart to begin thawing. Kit swore she wouldn't leave herself open to the pain of loss again. But if she's going to teach her son to be brave and move forward, Kit must first face her own fears.

Connect with us at Facebook.com/ReadForeverPub

Discover bonus content and more on read-forever.com

A PERFECT PAIRING
by Sheryl Lister

As a top Realtor in Firefly Lake, Natasha Baldwin can't complain and really has only two regrets: never pursuing her dream…and how she left Antonio Hayes years before. So when an opportunity arises to show off her passion for interior design, Tasha's excited…until she discovers Antonio is her partner on the project. Now is not the time to let her past impact her future, but working with Antonio immediately sparks undeniable chemistry. Just as a second chance at love is within reach, her big break comes around and she must decide what she truly wants…

FOUR WEDDINGS AND A PUPPY
by Lizzie Shane

When her Olympic dreams were crushed, Kendall Walsh retreated to Pine Hollow to help run the ski resort—while her childhood friend went on to dominate winter sports. Years later, Brody James is suddenly retired and back home. But he isn't the same daredevil Kendall once had a crush on. As the resort's events coordinator, she has no time for romance. Yet when Brody begins tailing her as eagerly as her foster puppy, she's reminded of why he's always been her kryptonite. Could this winter make them remember to be a little more daring…even in love?

Meet your next favorite book with @ReadForeverPub on TikTok

Find more great reads on Instagram with @ReadForeverPub

BALANCING ACT
by Emily March

After settling into life in Lake in the Clouds, Colorado, Genevieve Prentice is finally finding her balance. But her newfound steadiness is threatened when her daughter unexpectedly arrives with a mountain of emotional baggage. Willow Eldridge needs a fresh start, but that can't happen until she stops putting off the heart-to-heart with her mom. Yet when Willow grows close to her kind but standoffish neighbor keeping secrets of his own, she realizes there's no moving forward without facing the past…Can they all confront their fears to create the future they deserve?

FALLING FOR ALASKA
by Belle Calhoune

True Everett knows better than to let a handsome man distract her, especially when it's the same guy who stands between her and owning the tavern she manages in picturesque Moose Falls, Alaska. She didn't pour her soul into the restaurant just for former pro-football player Xavier Stone to swoop in and snatch away her dreams. But amid all the barbs—and sparks—flying, True glimpses the man beneath the swagger. That version of Xavier, the real one, might just steal True's heart.

Follow @ReadForeverPub on X and join the conversation using #ReadForeverPub

CHANGE OF PLANS
by Dylan Newton

When chef Bryce Weatherford is given guardianship of her three young nieces, she knows she won't have time for a life outside of managing her family and her new job. It's been years since Ryker Matthews had his below-the-knee amputation, and he's lucky to be alive—but "lucky" feels more like "cursed" to his lonely heart. When Ryker literally sweeps Bryce off her feet in the grocery store, they both feel sparks. But is falling in love one more curveball…or exactly the change of plans they need?

FAKE IT TILL YOU MAKE IT
by Siera London

When Amarie Walker leaves her life behind, she lands in a small town with no plan and no money. An opening at the animal clinic is the only gig for miles, but the vet is a certified grump. At least his adorable dog appreciates her! When Eli Calvary took over the failing practice, he'd decided there was no time for social niceties. But when Eli needs help, it's Amarie's name that comes to his lips. Now Eli and Amarie need to hustle to save the clinic.